Onyalum Retribution

by NB VanYoos

authorHOUSE™

1663 LIBERTY DRIVE, SUITE 200
BLOOMINGTON, INDIANA 47403
(800) 839-8640
WWW.AUTHORHOUSE.COM

First published by AuthorHouse 07/28/05

ISBN: 1-4208-6856-X (sc)

Library of Congress Control Number: 2005905770

Printed in the United States of America
Bloomington, Indiana

This book is printed on acid-free paper.

Book Cover Art:
Credit: NASA and The Hubble Heritage Team (AURA/STScI)
http://hubblesite.org/newscenter/newsdesk/archive/releases/2004/10/

Author Web Sites:
http://www.nbvanyoos.com
http://www.onyalum.com

I dedicate this first book to my lovely wife Heidi whose love and support through the years is singularly responsible for the realization of this dream.

Ret·ri·bu·tion *n*

… dispensing or receiving of reward or punishment esp. in the hereafter.

Webster's Ninth New Collegiate Dictionary, 1986, MERRIAM-WEBSTER INC., Springfield Massachusetts, USA

"Beware, there are beings of this Universe that will do you harm. The Onyalum possess the flesh of the dead, bringing back a distorted form of the life that once lived within. Their motives are evil, and they will bring death and destruction to you and your peoples. Be wary of those whose recovery seems miraculous, for only my interventions are a miracle. You will know when it is my intervention, for all others, it is an Onyalum."

Mishthrap's Dream, Gospels of Thosolan, Modern Edition, 14th Translation

Beyond Death

Tyler Jensen woke slowly to the sound of traffic drifting through an open window. His body felt sore from the hardwood floor he lay upon. His thoughts swam in a thick haze from the night's party. As was so common these days, he wasn't sure where they were. Memories of the night's activities shot through his mind in incoherent flashes of people, music, and consumption.

From his vantage on the floor, he stared across a large room with vaulted ceilings and sparse furniture. Remnants of the night's activities lay scattered throughout the room. Tables, floors, and countertops were cluttered with debris, while bodies lay strewn throughout sleeping off various effects. His girlfriend Linda lay next to him wrapped in a blanket they'd shared. She lay curled in a tight ball on the corner of a large rug against the back wall.

He still didn't recognize anything, but assumed they were in a large loft that had been converted from an old warehouse or manufacturing facility. From the sounds outside, he figured they were somewhere in the industrial parks. He leaned back against the wall and casually lit a cigarette. He was accustomed to mornings like this and wasn't even certain what day it was.

His head throbbed with a dull pain that pounded in the distant recesses. He spotted a partially filled beer bottle and drank from it to help ease the pounding. The beer was warm and flat, but he only cared about the alcohol doing its job. *Hair of the dog*, he thought absently.

Across from Tyler, a large arched entryway led into another room. Industrious sounds emanated through the opening with the

1

occasional clink of bottles. Somebody was cleaning up the party. *One of the hosts?* Who cared, Tyler never offered to help.

He put out his cigarette in the empty beer bottle and nudged Linda. She pulled the blanket tighter and groaned. Despite the hard night, Linda was still beautiful. Only her mussed up hair betrayed the debauchery that was a regular part of their lives. Tyler didn't understand why she had stayed with him for so long. She deserved better, and he was the first to admit it.

Linda Ashton came from an affluent family in Bellaire. Tyler met Linda six years earlier at a beach party thrown by her fellow UCLA students. He'd been one of the 'suppliers' invited to the outing, but after meeting Linda, he'd spent all his time entertaining her.

Tyler came from a dysfunctional, lower middle class family in the valley. After his parents split, he drifted through the rest of high school before moving out after graduation. During his last years at him, he'd become a distant member of the family he no longer felt a part of.

For several years after high school, Tyler drifted in and out of low end jobs while attending a local community college. He was declared for an associate's degree in business, but his heart was never fully into the academics. As the years ticked by, he lost what limited direction he'd had and soon replaced those limited goals with regular substance use.

It was during a brief stint as an assistant manager in a movie theatre, that he'd met Raul Sanchez at a co-worker's party. Like Linda, he and Raul quickly became friends, and within a few short months, Tyler quit his job to sell drugs for Raul fulltime. Tyler stayed at the community college for a while, and it became his most lucrative market in those early years.

It was a great life. He made five times the money he'd earned in those dead-end jobs and he had all his party supplies provided. It didn't take long before became well acquainted with the 'who's who' of the LA party scene. Fortunately for Tyler, Raul wasn't connected with the typical gangs that controlled so much of the drug market. Instead, his clientele leaned heavily towards the upper middle class and wealthy youth of LA. It was a lucrative and safe market for Tyler, and he quickly established himself as a top distributor.

He'd met Linda while she was a junior at UCLA. Like so many in LA, she was studying to become an actress. Although she drank and occasionally smoked weed, she had never experienced the wide range of products Tyler had access to. It wasn't long before Tyler opened her eyes to the wider possibilities, and after six years together, their lives were a whirlwind of parties.

His exotic lifestyle had lured her from the life she'd known before. It wasn't long before she dropped out of school and moved in with Tyler. Shortly thereafter, she became alienated from her family and turned away from the world she'd been raised in.

Tyler felt guilty for corrupting her, but then his own corruption had long since clouded his judgment. He felt important playing a major role in the 'in' scene, and if anything got you down, you had a pharmacopia of substances to lift the spirits or ease the pain. Linda had readily traded her previous life for this merry-go-round of the in crowd.

Although she didn't need to, Linda worked at a second hand clothing shop that specialized in 'classic' clothes from the sixties and seventies. The money wasn't great, but she loved the styles and the socialization with co-workers. Tyler didn't mind, it brought in a great deal of business through shop connections.

As Tyler lit another cigarette, he wondered what future they had together. She often spoke of marriage and children but she never pressed him on the ideas. Tyler could see she barely concealed her desire to start a new life—a more 'normal' life. He wasn't certain he could provide that life, so he conveniently avoided the issue.

He knew she couldn't go on with the life they led but he feared losing her more than anything else. It had become a constant frustration that drove him further down the path of self destruction. He was beginning to believe he wanted change but he wasn't certain how. The thought of a 'regular' job frightened him more than losing her. The power and prestige of his current career could never be replaced with a typical desk job. He felt trapped.

Each year, Tyler felt the increased damage his 'lifestyle' inflicted on his body and his mind. Even Raul suggested he take a break and 'dry out'. Tyler knew it was sound advice. He'd watched many of his best customers burn out or destroy their lives for the next high. Would that be his fate? He'd even lost customers to overdoses—something he recently feared.

He hit his cigarette, exhaling a large cloud of smoke up to the ceiling. No drug could ease the troubled thoughts that plagued his waking hours. He knew he and Linda needed to find solitude and re-discover their relationship. How often did they wake up in a crowded room? They were rarely intimate, and this weighed heavily on their relationship.

Raul had offered Tyler the use of his villa on the pacific coast of Mexico, but Tyler never took advantage. Perhaps now was the time to take Raul up on his offer. Maybe getting out of town would help clear his mind and provide him and Linda the opportunity to discuss the direction they headed. He realized a hard road lay ahead, but losing her would be worse.

Tyler put out his second cigarette and decided he'd talk with Raul that afternoon. He was approaching thirty and he felt time catching up. He had probably put off vacation for too many years, but it was better late than never. What could be better than relaxing in a Mexican villa far from the high life of L.A.?

He nudged Linda once more, this time her eyes blinked briefly. He was amazed that the simple act of touching her could produce such a warm feeling. It was this warmth that convinced him he was making the right decision. He knew she'd be excited, she had always urged him to take a vacation.

Tyler and Linda left the loft in a taxi. The cab dropped them back at their apartment, and after a quick shower, a stiff drink, and a couple of lines, Tyler finally felt good enough to get on with the day. He left Linda asleep on the couch as he headed out to find his car.

Like always, he found it in one of the many places he used when partying. As a rule, Tyler never partied and drove. It wasn't that he was inherently conscientious, he was simply cautious.

Driving while impaired was an easy way to get caught, and so far, Tyler had never been caught.

Clients and friends were only too happy to take them out for the evening. As long as he provided supplies, rides were never hard to find. Once on the town, it was never difficult to move from one party to the next. His position ensured he had a wealth of friends.

There were only a few times when Tyler had problems locating his car. Once it had been stolen, but the police had found it quickly, stripped, but still intact. He'd lost nothing important and was simply happy to have it back. Insurance restored it to its former glory.

The cab pulled over, and Tyler was relieved to see his car still parked at the client's house. He'd owned the car for four years after Raul gave it to him in appreciation for his hard work. It was a clean, black, BMW 325ic convertible with tan leather and only fifty thousand miles. He loved it nearly as much as Linda. The irony was Raul bought it at a police auction after it had been seized from another drug dealer.

The air felt good against Tyler's face as he cruised towards Raul's with the top down. He stopped at several clients' on the way, unloading the last of his supplies. It was a perfect time to see Raul, he could restock and ask about the villa. He wasn't the only employee Raul had, but he was the top seller. His Caucasian background and rugged good looks opened doors that Raul's other employees couldn't.

He smiled at that advantage as he pulled into the underground parking beneath Raul's condominium. Raul lived in a twelfth floor penthouse replete with its own pool. It overlooked a private beach, and was a nice, private place for Raul to conduct business. Tyler thought it was too ostentatious as he preferred his smaller, hillside apartment overlooking the skyline.

Tyler rang the doorbell and waited patiently in the hallway. Raul's bodyguard, some said enforcer, answered the door with a typical dour look. Without a word, he ushered Tyler in and pointed to patio. Tyler opened the sliding door and found Raul sitting at a patio table with an open laptop.

"Welcome, my friend, good to see you again!" Raul closed his laptop and gestured toward one of the open chairs, "Please, sit down and join me...refreshments?"

Tyler took a seat and accepted his offer, "Sure, bourbon on the rocks with a splash of water."

Raul signaled to one of his house staff and called out the order in Spanish. The person disappeared into the house to retrieve the drinks.

Raul pushed the laptop to the side and leaned back in his seat. "So tell me, how is that wonderful woman of yours? I hope you are taking good care of her, she is far too good for one such as you." He joked lightly.

"She's fine, a slight hang-over from last night", Tyler admitted, "however, I think she's tiring of the lifestyle."

Raul shook his head, "It is a hard life you live my friend, perhaps you both need a break?"

"Funny you should mention that", Tyler began, "I was already thinking of taking you up on your offer of the villa. A few weeks in Mexico might help dry us out...you know, spend time together, without the crowds."

Raul remained quiet for a moment before smiling broadly. "Of course my friend," he exclaimed, "don't just take a few weeks, take a few months. Get away and enjoy yourselves! The villa is yours for as long as you want. I'll call down there today and arrange everything."

One of Raul's house staff returned with their drinks. Tyler grabbed his bourbon and thanked her as she retreated into the house, closing the door behind her. Raul's staff knew when business was being conducted. Raul would want privacy.

Raul moved closer to the table and leaned towards Tyler. "Before you go my friend, I need you to take care of a little business."

Tyler shrugged, "Of course, what do you need? I'm currently out of product, so I wanted to place new orders anyway."

"Good, but that can wait, this is something bigger." With a serious expression on his face, Raul sat back in his chair. Tyler could sense Raul was studying him from behind his sun glasses, evaluating his reaction. Tyler felt slightly nervous.

"What is it?" he asked casually before sipping his drink. His unease grew.

Raul nodded slowly before he began telling Tyler about a new shipment that was coming in. Raul wanted Tyler to help coordinate the delivery. Raul's boss had found a different supplier that was dissatisfied with their current distribution methods. The new supplier suggested new procedures and demanded they put their best man in charge.

Raul had picked Tyler because he trusted him more than most in his organization. Although he apologized for putting Tyler in the predicament, he assured him a generous reward when it was completed. After that, Tyler and Linda could head to Mexico for several months of deserved rest.

Tyler hated this aspect of the business. He rarely got involved in the bulk supply chain where large quantities had to be moved. That was where gun fights erupted and drug busts went down. He'd been ignorant of it for years and preferred to keep it that way. Working with end users was far easier and practically risk free. At least for him!

The large quantities presented huge risk and even larger sentences if you were caught. He'd worked for Raul for a long time, so despite his fears, he agreed to take charge. He kept his mind on Mexico and the several months he and Linda would spend there. This helped lift his spirits despite the growing concern.

Adanni didn't know how far he'd come or whether it would be far enough. His unusual vision showed a three-dimensional map of galaxies in that region of the Universe. He chose one at random and transitioned into it quickly. Around him, bright stars and nebula swirled to the silent music of their galactic dance. He needed somewhere remote—somewhere that wasn't jealously guarded by its creator. *But where?*

He feared retribution this time. He didn't know how, but somehow he'd manipulated matter that went against everything he knew as Universal law. It wasn't supposed to be possible, but somehow he'd done it. *If only I knew how!*

When he'd fled from the disaster, the creator had unleashed unholy wrath on all that remained. Adanni could only imagine the anger that must have erupted. *How did I do it?* He didn't know but was certain the Universe would hunt him down. They would all hunt him down, so he kept moving.

Adanni was the name of the first being he'd ever inhabited. It had been a great life as Adanni, so he'd kept the name in memory of that wonderful experience. After so long, he only thought of himself as Adanni. He was an Onyalum. A being of pure ethereal form.

Onyalum were not made of matter or energy and so they existed between the material Universe and outside it. They were free spirits that traveled the Universe in search of adventures. The Universe had created them despite their reckless value. Onyalum lacked purpose and design but their effects on the Universe were profound.

How did I do it? Still nothing came. Because of their makeup, Onyalum could never affect the 'real' substance of the Universe, matter and energy. Likewise, neither matter nor energy could affect the Onyalum. Until now, it had been a fine balance.

Despite this balance, Adanni had unknowingly affected matter and energy. In a brief moment of anger and frustration, he'd 'uncreated' most of galaxy. The scope of the 'mistake' was undeniable. Creator's would fear him, and the Universe would have little choice but to undo his existence. He was no longer an insignificant threat to their creations. He fled with fear for his very existence.

Focus, there must be somewhere to hide! He stared at the galactic core turning timelessly below him. Its spiral arms spun slowly about its center, trying to escape the inevitable pull inward. His special vision focused on an area in one of the arms. Within it, several planetary systems appeared remote yet capable of supporting life.

Perfect! He'd find a dying life form, take over and lie low for a few millennia. Perhaps that would be enough to escape the fate he feared. He didn't know whether these worlds were guarded, but even if they were, he knew ways to get past. One blind transition into the world, bypassing the space in between, and he would be inside, undetected.

It was risky but the only sure way to avoid detection. He focused on the planet most likely to harbor life and made his jump.

Tyler walked cautiously down a sidewalk moving inevitably towards his car. He was relieved to have completed the delivery, and looked forward to their trip to Mexico. The new supplier's man had also been nervous, but like him, had maintained a cool exterior. They had both shown great relief when it was over.

These large transactions were notoriously dangerous. In that line of work, you never knew if the DEA had infiltrated one of the parties to set up a sting operation. Reduced prison time was a strong motivator to break even 'unbreakable' relationships or loyalties. The unknown was what everyone feared.

If the DEA weren't enough of a threat, these large transactions also drew interest from rivals. The rivals employed many methods to gain information about large movements of supplies. If they thought it possible, they would use that information to 'highjack' shipments or raid deliveries. Those exploits typically involved gun play and death.

At least Raul had sent several men experienced in those types of situations. Although the men made Tyler nervous, he knew he had to rely on Raul's trust. They were likely the best Raul employed. Tyler knew that at least one of the men was related to Raul, although he wasn't sure how.

It was a dangerous business, and you even had to be cautious of your own staff. Power plays and hostile takeovers were very common. Any disgruntled member of the organization could easily cause havoc on operations, especially if a rival bought them off. Fortunately, no one in Raul's organization had turned since Tyler had joined. Still, you could never rule out the possibility.

It didn't matter now. Tyler had completed the transaction safely and would soon make his way south. He'd had one of Raul's strong men drop him off blocks from his car. Always cautious, Tyler insisted on safety first. His knowledge of the product's location was a valuable commodity, and he had no illusions that people would kill for that knowledge.

He turned off the sidewalk and down a back alley. The neighborhood he traveled through was reasonably safe at night, but he performed several jigs and backtracks to eliminate the possibility of being followed. As he came out onto another sidewalk, he stared intently at the small park across the street. It was empty, but Tyler used caution nonetheless.

He stared across the park and spotted his car still safe where he'd left it. He made sure the streets were clear before making his way through the park. He walked casually, trying to eliminate any suspicions from the neighbors. More than once, he'd had neighbors call the police because he'd parked on their street.

He walked beneath the large acacia tree dominating the center of the park, and moved slowly up the small hill to his car. The shade of the tree provided moderate cover from prying eyes. Nearing his car, he began to relax. He never let down his guard, but so far everything appeared to have worked. Nonetheless, caution was an ever present fact in his business.

He made his way up the small hill when a flash of bright light surrounded him. Blinded by the light, Tyler felt paralyzed by a searing pain ripping through his body. As quickly as it had come, the light faded, and with it, Tyler's consciousness. The darkness enclosed him as a single word drifted through his mind, *damn!*

Tyler was floating above paramedics as they pulled a body from their ambulance. Like a dream, the paramedics silently pushed the gurney into a hospital emergency room. Tyler had never been to an emergency room, but it looked similar to those he'd seen on TV.

He stared at the body lying motionless on the gurney. Was that his body? He looked closely and clearly saw his own face beneath the oxygen mask. It was an odd and disoriented feeling floating above his body. Like a balloon, his consciousness was somehow still attached to his body. However, other than 'sight', he was disconnected from the normal senses.

Everything was silent as the paramedics pulled him into a room frantic with personnel. To Tyler, the uniformed people moved in seemingly random patterns, but apparently they had a purpose. *To save me,* he thought.

It was a strange thought. His body lay inert while they stripped off his clothes. They poked him and attached equipment to various parts of his body as they yelled to each other. Tyler saw their mouths move, but the scene was completely silent.

It was like a silent ballet or some dream sequence in a movie. He watched as the terrible story unfolded without sound. It was disturbing yet strangely compelling. He silently cheered on the actors, as he felt and heard nothing.

I must be dying, or already dead. The thought drifted through his awareness as disconnected he was. He struggled to remember what had happened, but his thoughts were random and disjointed, like he wasn't exactly himself. He remembered a job, or transaction he'd been doing, or done, but couldn't remember details.

Perhaps that was it, the transaction had gone badly and he'd been killed. Somehow that didn't seem right, especially judging from the lack of blood. *Drugs!* That was much more likely. His lifestyle had finally destroyed him. Was it a heart attack, liver failure, or a stroke? They were all possibilities. He felt sad that he might never know what killed him.

A fresh flurry of activity drew his attention back to the scene below. They continued to work feverishly on him and finally brought out the electric paddles used to resuscitate heart attack victims. *This is it,* he thought, *my end.*

He watched helpless as they sent electricity surging through his body, over and over again. Nothing worked. The doctor rubbed the paddles together one last time and stepped toward Tyler's body. He applied the shock, and this time, something happened.

An arc of electricity shot from Tyler's body, knocking the doctor to the floor. More arcs shot across the room, shocking people and equipment. Tyler watched fascinated as his body arched and convulsed. Everyone in the room froze in horror, gripped by fear until the arcing stopped. This was obviously something new.

Tyler's body writhed on the bed, shifting and separating before pulling together again. It was a powerful sight, and everyone remained motionless. Again and again, his body would disintegrate then pull back together. Each time, the pieces moved farther apart slowly failing to re-integrate. Tyler watched scene below him, amazed. He'd never seen this on TV.

With powerful arcs of energy shooting in all directions, the last remnants of Tyler's body disintegrated into thin air. At the same time, Tyler felt something pulling his awareness out of the hospital. Fear gripped him as he watched the hospital, the city, and finally the planet dwindle to mere dots in his awareness.

The pull increased as he shot through the darkness of space, far from earth and the life he'd known. Stars and planets rush by him at speeds he couldn't even imagine. The effect was surreal, like watching fields pass by your car's window. The blurred passage was completely silent.

Finally, the stars began to recede into a swirling bright clump. To Tyler, they looked like a picture of a galaxy he'd seen on the science channel. It turned slowly below him as he finally came to a stop.

The silence around him was suddenly broken by a deep voice. Tyler caught only bits and pieces and couldn't recognize the words. Confusion and fear gripped him like a vice. He knew nothing but death could explain this. He concentrated on the voice, trying to hear what was said. *If only it would stop fading in and out!*

Did he just hear "okem may juknn"? *What does that mean?* The voice grew louder and he desperately focused to hear something he could understand.

"More radnij QeQulum, awn solfra deidem manyfre..."

He knew something had to be wrong, it wasn't making any sense. What was the voice saying? Panic threatened to overcome him as he struggled to make sense of everything. Maybe this was hell? Was that satan talking to him?

He'd never believed in religion before, but now he seriously considered it. He caught a word. Did he hear "you cannot..."? He tried to calm down and focus. Whatever it was, it appeared to repeat itself.

"...solfra deidem forbidden worlds. You cannot vergi innuay or okem may any life whalk soo nieta. More will tymin jukn being that xid lodem et blasmous."

He listened patiently as it repeated itself over and over, but each time it did, Tyler could make out more words. Finally, the words all fell into place and he understood what was being said:

"I am QeQulum, and these are forbidden worlds. You cannot enter them or interact with any life therein. I will remove any being that does not heed my warnings."

The voice repeated the same statement, over and over. What did it mean? The translation was more confusing than when Tyler couldn't understand it. At least he figured it wasn't satan. If he understood it correctly, the speaker was QeQulum. Tyler had never heard that name before, either for satan or God.

Maybe this was a god from some primitive religion that only a few people knew about. Maybe no one on earth knew about it? *Wouldn't that take the cake*, he thought. He thought about the TV evangelists and wondered where their god was. The thought didn't bring him comfort.

Tyler felt a growing sensation. It felt like drifting on water, as though he were an oil slick spread over a great distance. He followed the feeling, and began to sense individual parts pieces, drifting aimlessly, yet a part of him. He concentrated on each piece, trying to pull them together. Nothing happened.

He didn't give up and focused harder. Still nothing. He welcomed the distraction despite his futile efforts. He tried one last time. *Did I just feel movement?* He wasn't certain, but it felt like something had moved.

He tried again, and again felt some movement. His spirits began to lift with the newfound success. It quickly became his quest—a quest to regain the pieces of his being. To regain what he thought of as Tyler.

His efforts paid off as he felt the pieces begin to coalesce. The magnitude of the number of pieces he felt as himself was daunting. He concentrated harder, desperate to feel the pieces integrating as a whole.

They shifted and moved towards some center. He hoped that center was him. He willed them to coalesce, and suddenly, as if released from some grip, he felt them rush together. The movement was joined by a burning pain tearing through his psyche. Everything blurred into colorful lights as the pain subsided and darkness fell.

Tyler's mind began to gain focus, as if he woke from a deep sleep. *That's it, it was all a nightmare*, he thought, *I'll wake up next to Linda and everything will be fine.*

The problem was he couldn't wake. Through his awareness, he saw nothing but total darkness. His senses detected nothing. He was floating through a dark void, while his thoughts replayed his death over and over again. *I truly am dead.* He was beginning to realize it was not a dream.

I am dead, he thought, *this is the nothingness I must endure for eternity.* The thought deepened his despair. He took stock of the situation and believed he felt his whole self again. He could feel each piece integrated as a single being, though not as before.

He explored this wholeness, feeling the different parts moving as a whole. He couldn't see the movement, but felt it nonetheless. It gave him a perch to cling to, and Tyler held hard. If he could 'feel', then he had to exist. The question was where?

He focused his awareness on his 'feeling' and experimented. After a while, he could release small pieces, spreading them outward before bringing them back. It was a tiny victory that occupied his mind.

In the distance, Tyler sensed a flickering light. It flashed and pulsated wildly as though fighting an unseen force. As the flashing intensified, the light grew larger. As sudden as it had started, the flashing stopped. Tyler stared at this steady light at the end of a long dark tunnel. Something pulled at his awareness, and Tyler felt himself moving towards the light in the distance. His awareness moved faster as though chasing the light before it vanished. Suddenly, he burst through the end and into a bright white, *room?*

It was a sea of unbroken whiteness giving it the appearance of 'white' space. Surely this was heaven. He still felt whole and directed his awareness to 'see' what body remained. He searched through the brightness and made out a shimmering gray cloud must have been his 'body'. It moved with a million particles like dust, never taking shape but staying close together.

It was small comfort and confirmed what Tyler already knew, he was dead, and this was his soul. All that remained was his essence—his spirit. He looked away from the gray cloud and directed his awareness to his surroundings. Whiteness as far as you could see!

Although he 'felt' movement in his awareness, he wasn't sure he was really turning. Without a frame of reference in the blank space, he couldn't tell up from down, right from left. Still, it was better than total darkness.

Maybe this was heaven? Somehow he doubted that. Considering the life he'd led, the pearly gates weren't going to open for him. He'd never even believed in God. Still, he held out hope. Who knew what the Universe held? He was certain most on earth had it wrong.

In the distance, Tyler 'heard' a soothing voice. He couldn't make it all out, but the words seemed familiar. Like before, he had difficulty understanding the words. It all sounded so foreign, but as the voice continued, Tyler could catch small fragments. At least he was certain it wasn't repeating itself.

A different voice broke in, similar to the first, yet very unique. Some of the words surfaced through the unintelligible speech. The two voices were talking to each other. At least Tyler didn't think they were talking to him. If they were, he'd never have known.

Suddenly a third voice joined the other two. This voice sounded less soothing and more fervent. It spoke rapidly, often interrupting the other two. This voice sounded distressed, or was it anger? Tyler wasn't sure. More of their words began to filter through, building as before. Tyler was certain neither of the voices were QeQulum.

As if a veil lifted, Tyler suddenly understood the voices. The angry voice, he had decided it was anger, dominated the discussion.

"I do not see the reason for this decision, clearly he is a serious threat to all creation." The voice was persuasive. "We believed it was not possible, and yet it has. It could easily happen again. Is this what you want?"

"What we intend or what happens are not yours to question", one of the soothing voices began, "we see everything as 'opportunities' and this unique situation is no different."

The other voice picked up, "We do not agree with your assessment and believe the threat you fear is not valid."

The other voice jumped back in, "It has begun a new journey—a journey as something new and wonderful. We wish to see if it thrives or if it doesn't."

The other soothing voice finished the thought, "It will be watched, and your creations protected. Although we won't interfere in its development, we will ensure it won't interfere in yours."

The other soothing voice began again, "We believe your fears are unfounded and look forward to the new creations you will make. Do not fear, this being shall not threaten your domain. We are infinite and his place in us shall be but a tiny mote amongst your stars."

Tyler heard finality in these words. There was a long pause of silence, as if the conversation had ended. At last, the angry voice spoke—this time with less anger.

"I am devastated by my loss and angered at the senseless destruction. I will console myself with the task of rebuilding, re-creating that which was taken from me". The voice paused. "Thank you for your words—I am humbled by your wisdom. I leave you reluctantly."

The angry voice faded away, as Tyler heard one of the soothing voices speak. "What say you Adanni? Or is it Tyler?" The other voice jumped in, "Perhaps it is neither. You must find a new name, something to commemorate this event."

Tyler didn't know how to respond, he didn't understand anything he'd heard. Were they been talking about him? Who was Adanni? They'd definitely said Tyler. He gathered himself, "I do not understand. Where am I? Better yet, where are you?"

He felt fearful asking them anything. What if they were the voice of God, or gods? Did he have a right to question them?

In answer to his question, a shape began forming in front of Tyler. The shape was basically round yet shifted irregularly. Various colors flowed through the shape, especially when it spoke, "We are here, same as you."

Small comfort, Tyler thought. The other voice spoke, "We will not harm you if that is your fear. Are you Tyler then? You must be since you do not know us?"

Tyler thought about that a moment, "Yes, I am Tyler," he answered, "who is Adanni?" Again, he felt nervous asking questions.

One of the voices answered, "Adanni is you."

Ok, that didn't help. Tyler didn't understand their response and remained quiet, puzzled and confused.

"You are something new," a voice said as if sensing Tyler's confusion, "you are something unexpected. We look forward to your journeys with great anticipation."

The other voice took over, "We will let you discover yourself— answer your own questions, and find your place within us. Do not despair, you are not dead."

The voice was warm and soothing, "You are beginning a new stage of your existence—a stage of discovery and exploration. We will watch you grow into something new and distinct."

The other voice intruded, "Indeed, you will become something wonderful!"

Tyler didn't feel wonderful, but held his tongue. He thought they were far more optimistic than he felt. He was about to ask more questions when the white space around him disappeared. He was alone again, drifting in space.

He watched sullenly as galaxies spun slowly around him. Swarms of questions filled his mind. Who were those beings? What had he become? What or who was Adanni? He wished he were dead. Whatever he'd become seemed far worse than any hell he could have imagined.

Where do I go? What do I do?

The questions hung in his awareness, filling him with the realization he was utterly lost. Never before had he been so alone— he truly needed a drink.

A Needle in the Universe

After the strange encounter with the voices, Tyler began shrinking inward, looking back with longing at the life he would never see again. He knew he'd never been a 'good' person. Selfish was the correct word—always thinking of himself and the next party. Was this his punishment? Not really hell, but maybe purgatory. He wasn't sure but realized Linda and his former life were gone—probably forever.

These thoughts only sank him further into self-pity and depression. *Selfish to the end!* He desperately wanted to get high. He needed some of his products to dull the aching pain of his current predicament.

No cigarettes, no alcohol, no drugs! He hadn't lived such an existence since being a kid. Although his dependencies started easily enough in high school, it wasn't until later that they'd become a crutch keeping him from facing his own inadequacies. They prevented him from seeing his 'true' self. Now, all that was left was the 'true' Tyler locked in an insubstantial cloud—a loser wandering the Universe for eternity.

He wondered about Linda and how she would be handling his disappearance. How long had he been gone? What did time mean for something like him? Maybe time no longer mattered? Maybe Linda no longer existed? The thought chilled him.

Looking back at his life with Linda, he wished for another opportunity to make it different—a chance to make it right. He'd done her wrong by bringing her into his world—a world of false happiness and shortsighted dreams—a world without children, a home, or...family.

Perhaps those things were only a dream as well, but he would never know. His one chance to make a change had been cut short. He knew he'd probably never see her again, and already her face was fading from memory. He clung to it desperately, no wanting to lose those memories, but the new Tyler was changing, and other thoughts and memories kept intruding.

His depression grew steadily, as new things popped into his awareness. Visions of people, places, and things swam past his inner eye in a procession that confused and disoriented. They pushed hard on his mind, desperate to replace the memories he thought were his and his alone. Fear crept into his awareness with the alien intrusion.

Something was trying to replace him—overwrite him with 'their' thoughts and memories. He didn't want to lose himself, so he fought against the intrusion, willing himself to remember who he was and where he'd come from. He clung to the memories of happy times, times when he and Linda had been intimate, together and close. He thought about their first meeting, their first time making love, and their first time partying together.

He remembered her initial trepidation about getting high but how she had finally trusted him. They had a wonderful time. They'd went to an amusement park, high, happy, and without a care in the world. He'd known then he wanted to stay with her forever. But with that realization came fear she wouldn't reciprocate. After five years, he had still feared she would leave, realizing her mistake and returning to the normal life he could not provide. He knew she had wanted it.

He was going to punish himself forever. Punish himself for letting her down, denying her what she truly deserved. His loss was really her gain. Now she could move on with her life, reunite with her family and find someone stable to settle down with. He had no illusions her family wouldn't mourn him. He hoped at least Linda would.

If this new Tyler could cry, he would. His grief and loss were so real and so painful. *I love you Linda, I will always love you!* This lone thought had a calming effect, and the alien intrusions subsided into his deep subconscious. They were still there, lurking…waiting. He could sense them waiting for another opportunity to surface and gain control.

Maybe this was what the voices had meant? Maybe this alien presence inside him was something 'new' and 'different'? Maybe they wanted it to grow and change him. It was a chilling thought. *I can't let that happen, I won't give myself up to this thing!* He would have to fight hard to maintain possession of himself. A corner of his mind urged him to let go, to disappear into oblivion and free himself from the pain and grief.

No, I will not succumb, I will not run from this new reality!

The force of this thought struck him hard. He always took the easy way out, avoided conflict, complexities, and pain. His dependent habits were a certain sign of his unwillingness to meet things head on. He had used the drugs to avoid and suppress, to self-medicate the illness he viewed as life. So where did this power of resolve come from? He did not know—it too was alien. Nonetheless, he held onto it as a shield against the 'other' deep inside.

Like one of his drugs kicking in, a new calmness swept through his awareness and he began to take notice of the space he was in. He was fascinated by the spinning galaxies dancing around him. It was a beautiful sight, like a collage or mobile strung out before him—moving slowly, yet rhythmically. How he could see so much, so close? Surely these galaxies were far apart and should look like mere dots against the black canvas of space. How was it he could see them so close, like he could reach out and take one in his hands? It was puzzling.

He thought about his ethereal self and reached out with his awareness to all the parts he thought were a part of him. He could felt them, still there but spread out thin. He pulled them together, feeling them coalesce into a whole. But no matter what he tried, he could see nothing of this 'essence'. They were there, but they were invisible.

How is it I see? It was a strange thought, but a logical one as the Universe moved about him. What he had become and what other abilities did he have? He heard nothing—everything moved like a silent ballet. He'd heard the 'voices'! The silence in space made sense, but what if he were on a planet? Would he hear?

How would I get to a planet? He could move his awareness, spinning his vision to see all around him. But how could he move in a direction? It was a strange sensation—a sensation only paralyzed people might feel. He had never thought of moving as some task you had to think about. When you wanted to move, you simply did. Very little conscious though went into the process. He felt frustrated.

Assuming he could move, where would he go? What would he do? He wanted to go home, return to earth, his life, and Linda. But where was home? He was fairly certain he couldn't recognize his own galaxy amidst the sea around him. Even if he could, where would he look? He didn't know where earth was in the galaxy, and he didn't know where his galaxy was. He knew there were billions, if not trillions of galaxies in the Universe, so how would he search that?

The daunting nature of the task brought back his depression. Despair rose in his awareness, and with it, the alien presence. *Stop it! Stop it!* He challenged the presence, *I will not give up, I will stay calm.* Again, this force within him calmed his awareness, forcing the alien to retreat once again. It would be back, he could sense it.

Think Tyler, think, where can you go? Perhaps he could look for others like himself, assuming they existed. The voices had indicated he was something new, so that probably made him a loner in the Universe. But surely something existed with which he could interact? Why make him alone? Where was the interest and 'beauty' in that? His awareness screamed at the voices, *Damn you, what do you want of me?* He was sure they couldn't hear, but the release felt good. Anger was a powerful force, reinforcing the power within, giving him a reason to continue. *I curse you for eternity. No one deserves this, no one!*

He stared blankly at a galaxy floating nearby. A part of his mind decided it looked like a brain, convoluted on the outside and slightly oblong in shape. As he stared, the galaxy suddenly grew, coming towards him as if to swallow him whole. The effect startled him and as quickly as it had started, the galaxy snapped back to its original size.

Whooooa...

Although he was afraid, curiosity forced him to duplicate the effect again. This time, he deliberately focused on the galaxy, watching it grow bigger, totally filling his awareness. Then he looked away, and it snapped back to its original size. Was this it? Was this how he could move?

He picked another galaxy and focused. Like the one before, the galaxy grew larger, filling his awareness. Then, it snapped back to as he took his attention away. The effect was disorienting, but at least he felt like he had a chance to move through the Universe rather than drifting aimlessly.

He found a new resolve, a resolve to find earth and see Linda again! He knew the odds were against him, but what else did he have to do? It would be better than doing nothing. He would go on a quest—a quest to find home!

He knew he would have to master his ability to move through the Universe before he could go on his quest. Making a galaxy grow larger was one thing, but moving through it was another. He managed to work out how to 'see' through the sea of galaxies. That turned out to be easy. He only had to focus gently on a distant galaxy, and then 'move' his vision beyond it until another distant one came into view. After practicing a while, it became second nature.

Once he had mastered his vision, he moved to the harder part—actually moving to the galaxy itself. He concentrated and concentrated, but every time he thought he was in it, it simply snapped back when he averted his attention. He was missing something crucial, but didn't know what.

He wondered whether the alien inside knew how, but he figured the risk wasn't worth the reward. Still, a part of his awareness, begged him to communicate and speed up the learning process. He ignored these urgings and continued his own experimentation.

There had to be something that would open the galaxies and move him down to the next level. That was how he saw it, as layers that must be penetrated as you moved inward. *But how?* Nothing came and his frustration threatened to stop his search. Once again, his new resolve forced him calm, *I must think hard about and find that missing piece. But how?*

He practiced focusing on a galaxy, then focusing on something within the galaxy. Each time, his awareness easily peered through the layers, but if he averted his focus in any way, he was pulled back through the layers to where he started. The effect was dizzying and very frustrating.

He stopped his efforts and took a moment to reflect. He stared blankly at the galaxies around him and spotted a gently spinning galaxy with a round center and arms swirling out on two sides. A part of him thought it looked like the Milky Way, but he dared not hope. He stared at it, wishing he could be there among its stars.

Suddenly, his awareness felt caught in a vortex, the galaxies blurred, and the one he'd been watching exploded in a gray-white light rushing past at incredible speed. Fear threatened to engulf him, but he held on through the ride. Where was he going, and how?

As quickly as it began, it stopped. He floated alone, a new vision filling his awareness. Instead of the sea of galaxies, stars and solar systems filled his awareness. In one direction, an intense brightness took up most of his vision. Everything swam slowly around this bright center. It was like a glowing sphere, connecting everything around it with invisible strings.

He felt giddy, unable to control his emotions. He was in one of the galaxies! Somehow, he had pierced one of the layers! Now, he only had to figure out how he had done it.

He calmed himself again and thought through what had happened. What had he done? He had stared at it, ok, but what else? No light went off, and frustration threatened. He stared at the multitude of stars and glowing masses of clouds. If he concentrated on them, they would leap into his awareness as before. But like before, he would back out if his concentration wandered. At least he had come back to the same layer within the galaxy. He hadn't solved the puzzle, but he had made progress.

He studied the galactic debris around him and wondered if this were the Milky Way. If so, earth was floating somewhere within the soup of stars. He held back his hopes, not wanting to get ahead of himself. First, he had to understand what had brought him here, and how he could go farther. Better yet, how could he go back? Could he go back? He believed he could, but everything was proving difficult.

Maybe it was a one way ticket? If that were true, his hopes of finding earth were remote. *Don't dwell on that Tyler...get a grip and figure this out.* His new resolve urged him forward, something he appreciated and disliked. The 'old' Tyler would have given up by now, but the new Tyler pressed on, forcing him to focus like he had never before. He resented it, but continued nonetheless.

His mind tired from the effort, yet he didn't 'feel' tired. Perhaps the new Tyler did not need sleep? He felt the same as when he'd met the 'voices'. It felt unusual, but not displeasing. The weariness he felt was boredom or frustration.

He paused and watched the galactic dance, marveling at its immensity. Science had never been Tyler's strongest subject, and although he'd read about the solar system, the planets, and the sun, he'd never paid much attention to it. Like everyone he knew, he'd wondered what was 'out there' and whether they were alone. Now, however, he felt confident they were not. Still, he didn't really know what existed—just voices without bodies. The memory was eerie.

Before now, such thoughts were fleeting, an occasional dalliance when too high to function. Many times he'd found himself drifting in dreamlike states, wondering at the Universe and his place within it. Unfortunately, as time went by, these highs changed—still dreamlike, but fading quickly from memory. With the memory, the feeling of wonder faded as well. Looking back, Tyler felt all his life had been a dream—some high he'd experienced, yet quickly fading.

No! His resolve screamed through his awareness. It was happening again, he was losing himself. He felt the presence of the other trying to insinuate itself into his consciousness. He searched for his resolve and fought the alien presence.

He had to stay alert and keep himself from sinking into past memories. He looked around the galaxy, this time focused. He remembered what he'd been doing before being breaking into this level and tried to reproduce it. He picked out a glowing cloud of blue, red, and purple and stared at it casually. He watched as it moved past other stars, noticing that it too held stars. He wondered what they looked like spinning through the cloud of light. He wanted to see one up close and was about to focus on it when a blur of light rush past as before. When it stopped, he found himself inside the cloud, the red-blue glow surrounding him.

He was amazed and awed by the scene—it was breathtaking! The cloud shimmered and moved like ripples on a pond. Throughout the interior, clusters of stars shone brightly through the haze. It was a spectacular display of light, movement, and color— an abstract painting, yet three dimensional. For the first time in his life, Tyler gained an appreciation for the immense beauty that was the Universe.

He stared at the intense beauty and began to hope he would master his movements and be able to find home. He was unsure what he'd done to 'transition', but he knew it was not because he concentrated on the object. Instead, the change occurred when he was not focused, yet curious, and wanting to see more. Only then did the transition happen, bringing him through the inner layer.

Ok Tyler, you've done it twice, surely you can do it again. The thought prepared him for another attempt. He picked out a cluster of stars and stared gently at them. He thought about how they looked, one small and intense, the others, larger and less bright. He thought about the largest red star and wondered what it would look like up close. He didn't 'focus' on it, he just thought about being there. Like a door opening, he felt the transition and watched the blur of light as he moved down another layer. This time, it had been effortless and less intense.

He hovered directly in front of the red star, its immense bulk filling his awareness completely. He was awestruck by its size, brilliance, and power. He stared quietly into its depths, amazed at the sprays of light shooting from its surface. They reached out towards him before falling back to the surface like waves crashing on a beach. It was mesmerizing, like staring at a fire, something he'd always loved.

The star spun quietly on its invisible axis, putting on a dramatic show brought tears to Tyler's eyes—if he'd had any. He felt alive and yet very insignificant. The size and beauty of this one star filled him with awe, especially when you considered the number that filled this galaxy alone. This one cloud held at least a hundred such stars. The thought humbled him.

He watched the silent dance and noticed a small planet spin by his awareness around the star. It was so small in comparison—it was a mere dot against the bright red background. He watched as it spun around the other side and disappeared. He was amazed something so small could exist so close to the fiery mammoth. Although he felt no heat, the vision of the molten ball made him feel warm inside. He could only imagine the intense heat so close to the star.

He turned his attention from the star and looked behind at the dark spheres he'd seen in the distance. He focused on one and it grew large enough for him to realize that it was a planet circling the star. It too seemed large. It was dark green in color, but swam with other colors across its surface as they raced around like a spinning top. He thought about what it would be like in the swirling colors and felt the transition.

Clouds of gasses rushed past him at speeds that were dizzying. Their colors were shades of green with white and black mixed in. To his awareness, it 'felt' like he was inside a tornado or hurricane, but he still felt nothing. It was a silent display with no sound to measure the intense fury around him. He watched small vortices below, whipping past like signposts on a road. This planet was an inhospitable place. He was certain no life could exist in that maelstrom.

Although he felt nothing, his awareness could almost 'hear' the rush of the wind around him. If he'd been human, he would have been torn apart like tissue. The thrill was fading, replaced with a feeling of vertigo. He wanted to move back out, but hadn't figured that part out.

He thought of the red star, visualizing its rays of fire dancing on the surface. He thought about staring back at this planet from a distance, seeing it as a dark sphere against the glowing cloud. He felt the transition again, and when it finished, he was back at his original position beside the star. In the distance, the green planet he'd been on continued its slow orbit.

That was it, he'd done it! Finally, he'd moved down a layer and back out again. The success filled him with newfound confidence. He was not trapped, but free to search for earth—to find Linda, and return home!

He visualized the picture of the gas cloud from a distance and easily transitioned out into the galactic pool. He stopped at his original starting point, staring at the cloud where he'd been. His excitement grew as he wanted to master this new ability. With newfound confidence, he began practicing, seeking out different galactic objects, submerging into their layer, then another, and another before backing out once more.

He did it over and over again, each object a blur as he jumped from place to place and layer to layer, pausing only long enough to pick his next target.

When he finally felt he'd mastered his new ability, he stopped in the galactic swirl, a kind of happiness sweeping through him. He looked back at his travels and was amazed he could remember every object he'd seen. He could easily call it up from memory, and if he wanted, travel back to it in an instant. It was unlike anything he'd experienced before. Not even his greatest highs matched the thrill of these transitions.

Unfortunately, like all new things, he knew the thrill would fade, but he knew the memories of each trip would last. For now, he relished the moment, a post-coital calm after the intense rush. He quietly gazed at the movement of stars as the sensation began to ebb.

Now he could begin his journey to seek out earth, and truly go where no man had gone before. He chuckled at the thought.

Tyler wasn't certain how to start looking for earth. The task was still daunting despite his new abilities. He knew there were millions and millions of galaxies with millions and millions of planets and stars. That thought alone was daunting, but with no defined boundary in any direction, where would he start and where would he end? Would he even know if he backtracked? With his new memory, he thought he might at least know when he was backtracking.

He randomly chose a direction and began studying each galaxy along its path. He easily dismissed many of them, as he certain the Milky Way was some form of a spiraling galaxy. At least he remembered that much. He'd probably seen it on TV when Linda turned to the science channel. Considering, his usual state of euphoria, he wasn't sure if what he'd seen had been the Milky Way or some galaxy next door. He hated the lack of confidence, but it was the only thing he had to go on.

He looked at a promising galaxy, but noticed that up close the spiral radiated with so many arms it looked liked a picture of a sun drawn on black canvas. He was fairly certain that wasn't the Milky Way, so he continued hunting.

The next spiral looked promising. It appeared smaller than the other galaxies around it, but with only three spiral arms, it appeared closer to his dim recollections than anything else. It would have to do. He focused on the galaxy and made his transition.

Revolving around the inner core, he was dumbfounded by the number of objects he would have to search. Nonetheless, he chose a direction and transitioned to the next level and back again, darting in and out as quickly as he could.

Many objects were quickly discounted if they were in clouds, had stars that were the wrong color, or had too many stars close together. Even with this filtering, he felt he was taking too long to cover too little a distance.

His frustration increased, but he calmed himself with the realization that he was just starting and it would likely take a long time. Still, that daunting feeling filled his awareness. He was ready to leave when he stumbled upon a system that seemed similar to earths. The sun appeared the same, though he was amazed at its size compared with the planets. He wished he could remember how many planets earth's solar system had, but his rudimentary science background failed to produce an answer.

He tried to recount them by name. He could remember Mars, Jupiter and Saturn easily enough, and thought he could even remember what they looked like. But the others were fuzzy, maybe Mercury or Venice, he wasn't sure. In any event, he would never recognize the other ones anyway.

He focused on the largest planets in the solar system. There were three gas giants, two of them with rings. He wasn't sure about Jupiter, but he remembered Saturn had rings, so perhaps one was Saturn. He definitely couldn't remember their order. The other gas giant without rings might have been Jupiter, but he thought it should be brighter with more red. *Damn, why didn't I pay more attention in science!* He knew the answer but was still frustrated.

He figured the system looked close enough, so he began searching for an earth-like planet. Success, he spotted one closer to the sun than the gas giants. It was small and blue with white stripes of clouds. Excitement built but he quickly suppressed it. He kept it in check in case it turned out to be some alien world.

He pictured the planet in his awareness and wished himself there. The transition was quick and smooth, placing him at a spot above the world's equator. He surveyed the space around him, noting nothing that flashed by in orbit. He'd thought he would have been able to see at least one satellite or something, but the space was vacant and silent.

Below him, the planet spun quietly, large cloud banks skirting the surface with breaks in between. Through the gaps, ocean blue and browns of land could be seen. It sure looked like earth, but it seemed too dead. He thought about some of the shuttle missions he'd watched and tried to remember the view from space. He didn't necessarily remember it looking alive then. *It could be home!* His excitement was hard to keep down.

He watched the planet, waiting for a break in the cloud cover to spot land. There, slightly above what he thought was the equator, a piece of land appeared. It was as good a place as any to find people. He transitioned in a blur of light.

As he came out, he found himself hovering some distance above what looked like an African plain. The savannah was dotted with trees, and every now and again he could make out splashes of water.

From his vantage, he saw what looked like large herds of animals moving slowly across the plain. *Perhaps I am in Africa?* Well if he was, he'd know he'd found home.

He scanned the horizon in every direction but didn't see signs of civilization. He spotted a plume of smoke in the distance, and for a brief moment, a thrill ran through him. The thrill was quickly replaced with disappointment as he noticed the smoke billowing from the top of a mountain. It was probably a volcano, smoldering before or after an eruption. *Damn, nothing but animals.* He began to get frustrated, but the prospect of being in Africa kept his spirits from sinking too low.

Africa was a large continent, so finding civilization immediately was perhaps a bit optimistic. He would continue searching the continent until he found some sign of habitation. After a little thought, he decided picking a west direction would probably be best. He figured most people, on any continent, congregated along the shoreline, next to the oceans that provided life. This made him think of California, the beaches, and Linda.

He wasn't sure how he would actually move along at this level, but figured it must be similar to the transitions that brought him here. He spotted a hillside on the distant horizon and made the transition. In an instant he was hovering above the gentle slope, noting it ended in steep cliffs falling off into a deep gorge. The gorge was enormous and stretched as far as he could see from north to south.

Inside the gorge, water ran rapidly through the valley, fed by numerous waterfalls from the surrounding cliffs. It was a spectacular sight, and Tyler took it in. Steam or mist rose from the various parts of the gorge where the waterfalls spilled their thousands of gallons of water into the river below.

Tyler had never seen anything like it before. He'd been to the Grand Canyon and remembered its immense beauty, but this was something entirely different. The cliffs and the hills surrounding the gorge were filled with dense vegetation, and he could see large flocks of birds winging over the trees.

As the sun began to set low on the western horizon, the effect was a glowing gold sky meeting a deep rich green, speckled with bits of white from the mist of the water falls.

It was breathtaking. He floated above it all like some ghost, able to see but not hear or touch. He broke away from the view and concentrated on finding clues that people existed. He scanned the horizon, but came up empty again and again.

He knew he had to move on, especially with the sun sinking low. Night would soon make the search harder. He picked a distant spot and transitioned again.

As before, he saw nothing but dense forest below him. He transitioned again, and again, and one last time until he found himself near an ocean. The water sparkled blue, silver, and orange from the setting sun. He scanned up and down the coast, looking for anything, a boat, a hut, a fire, a city, anything! Nothing.

He felt hope slipping away, and then spotted a large animal walking along the beach. He focused on the animal and 'zoomed' his awareness to the beach below. Holding his concentration steady, the animal came into focus.

It looked very similar to a giraffe, but not quite right. To Tyler, it seemed like it had a smaller neck than a giraffe, and it had stripes instead of the spots Tyler was sure a giraffe had. On its head, two large antlers spread out into the air above. It made the animal appear like a deer whose neck had been stretched out. The animal had no tail, and the color was russet with stripes of black.

Definitely not a giraffe, Tyler decided. Still…Tyler was far from an expert on African animals, or any animals for that matter. He didn't even know much about dogs or cats. This could be something from Africa, or maybe South America. He didn't know.

He continued watching the animal as it stopped and became very alert. Tyler wondered if it had somehow detected him. He watched fascinated as the animal sniffed the air and looked around cautiously. It stood frozen for some time, and Tyler was ready to leave when it started moving up the beach. Apparently, whatever had spooked it must not have posed a threat.

Tyler laughed at himself for thinking it had detected him. He knew that had to be impossible. The animal moved close to the water when a large flash of yellow sprang from the trees and lunged at the animal. Its size was enormous, at least twice the size of the giraffe like animal. Lean muscles rippled across its short broad body, covered in a thick yellow fur. Along its spine, a dark spike of hair ran the length of the animals back, tapering off near its rear. The animal lay atop its prey, mouth around its neck, strangling it to death.

Tyler was shocked and fascinated. He'd never seen a kill like that before. The predator looked like some kind of cat, but it had no tail, and very large ears. The paws were enormous with gigantic claws that sunk deep into the prey, holding it tight while the strangulation continued.

It was hard for Tyler to gauge its true size, but judging from the palm trees nearby, he figured it had to be about twenty feet tall from its feet to the top of its head, and at least the same in length. Tyler knew it was not from earth, at least not from the earth he knew. Maybe it was something from earth's past, or its future? Tyler didn't like that thought.

He let his focus drift off the animals and hovered above the beach, watching the sun set below the distant waves. The realization he wasn't on earth, or at least not the earth he'd left, sank him in a melancholy. The sun finally set below the horizon, leaving Tyler alone in the darkness with no light except the reflection of stars in the water. He stared at the stars, despair threatening to take hold of his awareness. *So many stars, so many planets.* He sobbed with the thought.

He transitioned off the planet to a point in orbit above it. Below him the planet was dark on the night side, no light except volcanic eruptions glowing like worms across the surface. No lights, no cities, no people. This wasn't earth. He looked around and noticed for the first time the planet didn't have a moon. This was a clear sign it wasn't earth, but he hadn't thought to check before going to the surface.

Still, he'd seen interesting things, and it wasn't without some merit. The memory of the gorge and the animal attack was something he would never forget. It had looked so much like earth, he wondered how many of these 'false' earths he would have to search before finding home. He feared the number was large.

Staring at the planet below, he said goodbye and returned to searching the rest of the galaxy. At least now he had more to filter with.

A moon, I should have looked for a moon! The thought stung a little, making him realize how little he knew about the Universe and his own home. It was amazing how you took it all for granted when you lived there. He shrugged in his awareness and continued transitioning from one system to the next.

Tyler had no idea how long he'd been searching. The new part of his awareness that recorded every galaxy, star and planet he'd seen indicated he had been through half a dozen galaxies and millions of planetary systems. The number boggled his mind.

Out of all those millions, he had encountered hundreds of thousands of planets similar to earth, yet not earth. Although many planets supported life, most of the life was primitive and bestial. Civilizations appeared hard to come by.

Once again, he was weary from the search. It all seemed hopeless. That cheerful thought went through his mind as he found himself orbiting a planet that from a distance, looked earth-like. Now that he was up close, he realized the colors he'd seen were not of water, land, and clouds, but were gasses in an atmosphere that obscured the planets surface.

The system had seemed similar to the one he thought earth was part of. It had several gas giants, one with rings, and another with colors similar to Jupiter. The planet below even had a moon. But up close, the moon looked different and the planet was definitely not earth.

Depression swept through him sinking him into a strange melancholy. He knew his search was probably hopeless from the start, but the thought of seeing home, and Linda, had kept him going. For all he knew, he had spent hundreds or thousands of years searching already. He didn't pretend to understand time or how it worked when you were a 'spirit', but searching millions of systems had to take a great deal of time. Perhaps earth didn't even exist anymore.

The 'new' Tyler had no sense of time. That he could move so fast throughout the Universe made him wonder at how much time each transition really took. He thought he could devise a way to measure it, but was too despondent to try. *Perhaps later*, he thought, *perhaps later*.

He stared blankly at the planet below him. He assumed no life could live in the soup of an atmosphere—certainly not life as he recognized it. At this point, any life he could relate to at some intellectual level would be welcome. The loneliness of his quest was taking its toll.

You'll never find it, give up the hunt. The voice came from within, far in the depths, small but persistent. He knew it was the alien presence, but this time, he did not fear it. He began to think it might be the only intelligent being he would ever find. *No, do not give in now!* It was that new resolve, fighting back to prevent him from being taken over. He felt torn and it only deepened his sadness. In his melancholy, he didn't really care who won.

The planet below mesmerized him with the swirling colors of its atmosphere. Without really intending, he transitioned in a blur of light into the thick atmosphere.

From the new vantage, he could see darkness below him, an indication that land might exist. The atmosphere had a blue tinge to it with streaks of browns and whites throughout. He thought the browns were probably storms moving throughout the blue atmosphere.

In his current position, the atmosphere seemed almost calm, the gas moving only slightly past his awareness. Despite his melancholy, he found himself fascinated by the planet. Subconsciously, he transitioned again down to the planets surface.

From the surface, the sky looked dark blue, almost black. He supposed the thickness of the atmosphere blocked most of the suns light from reaching the surface. Oddly, the isolating darkness felt comforting. He hovered just above the ground, sinking deeper into depression, letting go of himself in the process.

He daydreamed to a time before his change, back to his life on earth. He remembered the good times and the bad, missing Linda and wondering where she was and what she was doing. He thought about Raul, who was currently missing his best salesperson. Tyler knew he could be replaced, but he knew Raul would never be able to trust anyone like he had trusted Tyler.

Perhaps Raul would finally quit the business. His investments and financial prowess finally providing him with the comfortable cushion he needed to leave it all behind. Having family relations in the business, it would be easy for Raul to walk away.

A part of Tyler hoped he would. He'd always liked Raul, even loved him like a brother. Considering Tyler's current predicament, he wanted better for everyone he knew.

He hoped Linda would go back to her family, make up for the lost time she'd wasted with him. Maybe she would marry someone who would really take care of her. He'd failed her completely, dragging her into a world of never ending highs—a world where you never dried out long enough to experience the lows. He'd always admired her for being able to say no, something he'd never done.

Having been without for so long, he yearned for dulling effects to take away his pain and loneliness. He knew nothing existed that could do that now. He would be alone forever, wandering the Universe, detached, insubstantial, and insignificant.

You are not alone, the voice inside insisted. It sounded closer than before, apparently winning the battle of control. He didn't care. Perhaps he should let it take over, let it take what was left of him and force him into the exile within.

No, never, the other, stronger self persisted. He wished he could lock that part of himself away, place it back into the catacombs of his subconscious. It was becoming more than annoying. It was the part that was keeping him lonely, keeping him searching for a home he would never see again. *Go away*, he shouted inward, but he knew the pleas had no force.

He wondered if the internal battles weren't really him just going crazy—some kind of schizophrenia caused by his physical change. He'd taken enough drugs to think it possible. *No, the*

35

thought was flat and matter of fact, but he didn't know which part had said it.

That part of his awareness not focused inward noticed movement off in the distance. He brought his full awareness back and scanned the horizon. Over a distant hill, Tyler saw a swarm of glowing balls of light moving as if with a wind. At the surface, he noticed the air moved only slightly. The glowing lights were floating on that slight breeze.

Hundreds, maybe thousands came over the hill, moving like a school of fish in a current. In fact, with the blue tinge of the atmosphere, the illusion of being in the ocean depths seemed more than real. He watched fascinated as they moved closer. What were they? Were they alive?

Surely there weren't alive. He had no way of telling how big they were, but they looked like glowing softballs. He moved into the school and looked closely at each one as it floated past. They emanated a soft pink glow, and inside each one, he could make out small bits of darkness. They were like round jellyfish up close.

He watched as they moved silently, wondering if they could be alive. They were as insubstantial as bubbles, but seemed alive, as though the school was by design and not random.

He watched as two of them collided and became one larger bubble. They stayed together for a short while, the glow shifting in new patterns and colors. Suddenly, as quickly as they had come together, they separated. As they separated, hundreds of tiny glowing sparkles fell to the ground like pixie dust.

What was that? It almost looked like they had mated, coming together to produce eggs or larvae or something. He was more than curious. The alien inside appeared to be confirming his suspicions, but he ignored it as he concentrated on the globes.

He watched as many more came together mated, then dropped their glowing dust to the ground. He watched them float away after the mating and noticed more than a few began to fade before disappearing completely. *Did they die?* He wasn't sure. He remembered hearing about some animals on earth that would die after mating, their entire purpose for living having been served.

He turned "upstream" watching the school as it swarmed over the next hill, moving with the flow of the atmosphere. Two more split from their mating just ahead of him, the glowing dust released as before. One of them kept coming directly at him, its glow fading as it approached. Nearly gone as it came upon him, he felt himself being pulled together and into the dull ball of light.

It was the strangest sensation he'd ever had. He could sense he was the creature. He felt the parts that made it up, felt the thoughts or memories of its life. It was odd, the creature was so primitive that all Tyler felt was a strong desire to mate, to come together with another of its kind.

He float within the school, feeling strange sensations that he'd missed for too long. He felt the gentle breeze that pushed them along. He sensed this creature had only been born a very short while before, its drive to mate ending in death whether successful or not.

He knew his presence inside had brought the creature back to life, if only briefly. The drive to mate was so powerful that Tyler felt the presence of others around him, urging him to merge with them, the yearning consuming all his thoughts. It was strange, a part of him felt disconnected and observant while the rest of him was consumed by the life he'd taken over.

He felt the presence of another creature close to him and grew excited as it approached, he felt it touch, and slowly they began to merge. With a rush of light and feelings so intense he couldn't describe them, he felt the mingling of their souls, their body and their selves. Its pleasurable feelings grew more and more intense, building in waves that he hoped would never stop. The high consumed him like a fire, burning with pleasure beyond measure.

Finally, as the pleasure almost became pain, it crested in an orgasmic release like nothing he had ever experienced with any drug. The intensity shook the creature's bodies until they tore apart and a cool release swept through him. The release he realized must have been the fertilized eggs.

It hadn't been dust he'd seen before, it was their eggs, floating to the ground to spawn a new generation and repeat the cycle. Tyler had never felt so alive, so purposeful, and so complete. *So this is what mating truly felt like.* He knew it was more than just sex, he felt the greater purpose and completeness knowing the species would survive—that a part of him would survive.

He was giddy and dizzy from the intense experience. He felt washed away in the lingering release, floating happily within the breeze, his mission and desires fulfilled. Like falling to sleep he felt the creature beginning to fade, dying after making its contribution to the continuation of the species.

As the last feelings faded, Tyler felt himself pop out of the creature, watching it disappear into the gloom, forever dead, its offspring the only memory of its life. His motion had stopped, and he watched as the enormous school continued to drift by. *I must do that again,* he thought. No drug or experience had ever felt so intense, so fulfilling. As the memory began fading he quickly moved into the midst of the flow, determined to make it happen again.

If I only knew how it had happened. He watched helpless as they flowed through him, many merging and separating, dropping their glowing dust as they moved past. *What was it I did?* Nothing came to mind.

He thought about the previous experience as he noticed two of them separating just ahead. One floated past on the right while the other came straight at him. As it neared, its light began to fade, its life completed. Tyler noticed the fading creature just as it began to flow through him.

At that moment, he felt the familiar rush as his essence was pulled into the creature, restoring life into the fading body. Although he couldn't see in the normal sense, he sensed the community around him—felt them flowing as one within the wind. Individual creatures passed close to his body, producing a sensation that excited him. He desperately wanted to merge with them—the feeling so intense, driving him in desperation.

They all floated by, or stayed a distance away. He felt frustrated, but suddenly sensed another creature moving faster towards him. The excitement made him glow brighter, fighting to get the chance to merge, but at the mercy of the wind that moved them.

As it drew closer, he felt an electric current coursing through the body, preparing for the event that would surely follow. Like before, he felt their two bodies touch, merging into a single creature, their very beings becoming one. They both shared the deep need to procreate, to reproduce their species and bring new life into the world.

The coupled entity began pulsing with pleasure waves, the intercourse following its intense track to conclusion. The feeling growing more and more intense, the pleasure sweeping through him and carrying him away to a place he'd never known. He knew it would end with the final release, but he desperately held onto it while it lasted.

This was the drug he'd needed, this was what he'd craved to take him away from his current predicament. He lost himself completely in the experience, floating away from consciousness on a sea of pleasure. At last, like a wave breaking on a beach, the pleasure crested in the orgasm and release, leaving him in a euphoric dream, satiated, yet craving more.

As happened the first time, the creature faded once again, releasing Tyler from its bonds, happy but wanting the feeling to never end. He still didn't know what he had done to enter the creature, but he was determined to keep doing it, even if it was an accident.

He positioned himself in the middle of the flow, waiting for the transition he prayed would come. *Look for the dying ones.* The thought surfaced from the depths. Was it the alien trying to communicate? Tyler wasn't sure, but the thought seemed to make sense since he was released when the creature died.

He focused on a single creature, united with another but nearing release. He followed as they swept past, merged and pulsing with a light that Tyler knew was pleasure.

Finally they split, releasing their eggs into the wind. Tyler focused on one of the creatures, looking for its light to begin to fade. But it didn't fade, it merely continued floating in the wind, its' light glowing brightly. He quickly scanned for the other one from the pairing, but couldn't quite make it out in the swarm.

Wait, there it is! Tyler quickly transitioned in front of it as it moved in the wind. Too late, as he appeared in front of the creature, the light was gone, the empty shell falling before it reached Tyler. *Damn!*

He was getting frustrated with the whole process. Apparently, the creatures had differences, perhaps a male and a female. He wasn't sure which was which, but he figure it was probably the male's that dropped dead after mating. That always seemed to be the case.

He scanned through the river of creatures, looking for another pair completing their mating. He saw one, just nearing their completion. He didn't know how to tell which was the male or which was the female, so he planned on watching both as they split apart.

Perfect, after they split they moved only a small distance from each other. He watched for the tell tale signs of the creature dying. There it was! The one on the right appeared to be dimming. Tyler positioned himself, desperate to make this one work.

At last, he felt the pulling sensation as he once again became one with the creature, bringing life back from where it had left. It didn't take long before he had merged with another creature, playing out the dance he was now addicted to. Tyler wasn't certain that the females felt the same experience, but since they merged and mingled as one, it was probably a good bet they did.

What joy to be the female, mating as often as you liked, discarding the males when you were done, then seeking out another mate. The males definitely got the worst end of this deal. However, to die after such bliss wasn't necessarily a bad way to go.

Tyler continued satisfying his lust for the pleasure, forgetting his current predicament, forgetting everything except the search for more. He no longer felt like Tyler, caught up in the excitement of the mating, wanting to never leave, never stop feeling the pleasure that brought him more life than he had ever known.

One after another, Tyler kept up the hunt, taking over creature after creature, merging, releasing, merging, releasing, lost in the high that took away the pain, and made life worth living.

Tyler lost count of the creatures he'd gone through, lost track of time, if time had meaning. He had a single purpose now, merge and release. He took another creature, inhabiting its dying body, bringing it back from death.

He was caught up in the tide, seeking another he could merge with. He felt the presence of another coming towards him, and the excitement grew. It came closer and closer and then suddenly veered upwards, flying past Tyler in a blur.

What!? He had been certain it had been coming towards him. Wait a minute, Tyler felt a strange unease as he sensed all the creatures flowing past. He hadn't come out of the creature, so he couldn't have stopped, yet everything he could sense rushed by.

Slowly, the sensation crept into Tyler's awareness. The body of the creature was no longer moving, its progress stopped by something. Desperation surfaced as the fear that he would never get another chance took hold.

The remnants of the creature yearned to free itself and mate—but it was no use. Without appendages, they were stuck unless something broke them free. They were helpless.

Like the intensity of the mating, the intensity of not mating, the frustration, the anger, the fear, overtook Tyler. He was helpless and sensed horror as the last of the creatures flew past—continuing their journey without him.

The pleasure was gone, replaced with the loneliness of a life wasted. Depression hit hard, dragging him downward from the high he'd enjoyed. He now knew what it was like to miss the true opportunity life offered. He thought back to his own life, knowing it too had been wasted.

Terrible grief and loneliness consumed him, everything rushing back, the reality of it staggering his soul with frustration. A deep darkness descended over his awareness, plunging him into a chasm of self-pity, despair and self-loathing.

He wanted to die. *Why hadn't they destroyed me?* The voices that let him loose on Universe came back to haunt him. Why did they want him to live? What was he supposed to do? What was he supposed to become? He didn't care or want anything to do with it.

Even death of the creature he inhabited would not release him from this misery. He would simply 'pop-out', once again becoming an insubstantial creature of the ethereal Universe—having no one, no life, and no hope. Adrift in the Universe, banished to wander aimlessly, seeking a world that probably didn't exist.

Sure, it exists, you'll find it. Even the voice of determination seemed depleted, no longer able to withstand the onslaught of the depression that consumed Tyler. He drifted inward, letting go and falling into the depths. He wondered whether the alien would be able to take away his pain, banish him to non-existence.

Sure I can, the voice drifted into his awareness. At once alien yet familiar. *No, don't let it out!* The newfound determination resisted, urging him to take control. Tyler's awareness listened as the two parts of him argued and fought for control. He didn't care who won, he didn't care what happened to him, he didn't care about anything.

He was as trapped in his own awareness as by the creature he currently possessed. They would both live useless lives, failing to complete the cycle, failing to recreate their own existence.

Linda had wanted it, wanted it for a long time. But Tyler's selfishness and addictions had kept them from fulfilling their destiny. Now, nothing on earth remained of Tyler except the fading memories of those who knew him. Those would soon be gone, and Tyler would be just another soul lost to history.

Perhaps it was a fitting fate, trapped in a creature on some distant world, alone and dying. If only he could really die! Instead, he would continue to exist, wandering in some purgatory in which he only experienced life through others—never having a life of his own.

He knew the pleasure he'd felt during the mating had been only another drug, another escape from that which he had become. His whole life, short as it was, had been nothing more than one giant escape—an escape from everything that made life wonderful.

Now he was trapped, unable to undo the past, and destined to repeat it, over and over again. He was certain he'd never feel more hatred towards himself than he did at that moment. *A life squandered.* Squandered because he was unfit to live, unfit to follow the cycle that had existed for millennia.

Perhaps it was his upbringing, or perhaps it was his genetic makeup? Perhaps those too were escapes, excuses for failures that were surely his. How sweet to think it was some outside influence that had brought him here, that had made him give up his life and waste away the years that he should have spent building something with Linda.

It may have been an alien or some cosmic event that brought him to where he was now, but he was to blame for the life he had wasted. He hoped Linda not only grieved for him, but felt anger towards him for missing their opportunity. He deserved no less than her wrath.

He felt the creature begin to fade, its life finally ending after its failure to procreate. Tyler didn't know how long they actually lived, but he did take comfort in knowing that the creature he inhabited had succeeded—it was he who had failed.

The last of the life faded from the creature and Tyler was released, feeling the insubstantial essence of his new self spreading out around the creature. He looked with pity at the dead body, trapped in a fissure on the side of a cliff. At least it found death, something Tyler would never find.

He embraced his depression as he transitioned off planet. He was trapped in a melancholy he feared would never go away. He would be the greatest depressed ghost the Universe would ever know, forever tormenting himself for eternity. What better hell than this for someone who had squandered the precious gifts life had offered?

He stared at the distant sun, mesmerized by its glowing intensity. He yearned for it to burn him, destroy him in a fiery blaze of molten gas. He transitioned above the sun's surface, entranced by the pulsing of the star's internal fusion.

He transitioned inside the sun, surrounded by enormous waves of molten fire and lightning that danced to their own rhythm. Still he felt nothing. It was like a silent movie, visually intense, but containing no sound or sensations.

A wave pushed through him, blinding him to the surrounding surface in a white hot light. He transitioned deep inside the star, seeking out a place to hide himself, a place to curl into a ball and sink into the depression that consumed him. *Let the alien take over, I do not want to live, I do not want this existence!*

His anger and resolve drove him deeper into the star and deeper into his own subconscious. He was willing himself away, trying to undo what had been done. He felt nothing of the roiling mass around him, saw only blinding light with streaks of colors. It swept through him and around him, as he forced all the pieces of his existence together into a tight ball.

I want to die, the thought ran through his awareness as he began fading away—sinking further from everything. *Let the alien have it, I don't care.* It was the last thought Tyler had before sinking into a deep, deep sleep.

Fate's Teacher

Tyler didn't know what had happened, but he knew he'd been dreaming, dreaming of Linda and him, together in Mexico. He remembered they'd had a son, a beautiful son with light brown hair and green eyes.

In his dream, he'd known it was a dream, but the pleasure of being with Linda and having a son seemed so real. His awareness lingered on the remnants of the dream, watching helpless as it began to fade.

A new awareness grew as Tyler began to wake. He felt himself lying on something soft and could hear quiet sounds. A persistent warmth spread across his body. *How can I feel?* He knew he shouldn't be able to feel anything. All of it came rushing back to him, how he'd been inside a sun, yet everything was dark.

The sounds grew louder, a crackling sound. Was that a fire he heard? Did the sun make a sound like that? It sounded so mild and comforting, he didn't think it was the sun. *How is it I hear and feel, but see only darkness?* He wondered, but was afraid to change it. The darkness was a pleasant relief from his previous circumstance.

Did I dream? He knew he had dreamed, but couldn't figure out how it was possible for him to sleep. He had never needed sleep since changing, why now?

The sound was definitely a fire. The distinctive crackling and occasional pop left no doubt. Tyler wanted to see what was making the noise, to see where he was. Slowly light began to grow, blinding at first, but then warm and yellow.

Tyler opened his eyes, and was stunned that he had eyes! He blinked several times to make sure. A quick look around revealed he was lying on a soft couch in front of a fireplace. From his vantage, he couldn't make out the rest of the room. He sat up, clearing his head of the sleep that clung to him.

How can this be happening? He wondered. It was confusing, but the change in environment was welcome. He looked around the room and noticed it was paneled in dark wood, barely lit by the light of the fire. The fire was the only source of light, but if Tyler looked away, his eyes adjusted to the darker parts of the room.

The room was somewhat large and contained many bookshelves running from floor to ceiling on the left and back walls. Ornate candles, lamps and figures were prominently displayed on beautifully carved tables throughout the room. To the right of the fire, a large, overstuffed red leather chair sat empty, a small end table next to it with an ashtray, pipe and small teacup on top.

Tyler had a strange feeling that he should know this place, but it was far nicer than anything he'd ever known. The room nagged at his memory. *I know this place, but where?*

Somewhere deep in his memory, a thought rose to the surface, *Uncle Sal's*. That was it! This was the set for the Uncle Sal's show he'd watched as a kid. But this wasn't a set, it looked real. It had four walls, and only one door. Tyler knew sets were not usually real rooms, just stages made to look real.

He stood up and marveled at the sensations of being able to feel. How wonderful it was to have a body again, to feel and hear the world around him. He stared at his body, surprised it looked as he remembered it. He was even wearing his favorite pair of jeans and shirt. Everything he could make out, down to his shoes was just as he remembered.

How could this be, was this also a dream? It didn't feel like a dream, but how did he get here? Was he on earth again?

"I found you here", a deep, soft voice spoke from his right.

Tyler turned towards the sound and stared awestruck at Uncle Sal sitting peacefully in the red leather chair loading his pipe. He looked exactly like Tyler remembered. He wore the same brown tweed slacks, a white button down shirt with a blue tie underneath a red vest. Everything was the same, even the wire rimmed glasses and the thick black mustache peppered with gray.

What was left of his thinning gray hair was combed neatly back, a straight part on the left side. Tyler felt like a kid again, felt the excitement that always preceded this part of the show, the part where Uncle Sal read one of his adventure stories. But this couldn't be? They had canceled the Uncle Sal show when he was in junior high, and he distinctly remembered when Uncle Sal, really Sal Horowitz, had died several years later.

This must be a dream, how else could he have a body and be in Uncle Sal's place?

"I created your body", Uncle Sal said calmly, "and this one as well," he gestured at his own with his pipe.

"But", Tyler began, the words struggling to form in his throat, "I thought I was dead, or something worse. Where are we?" Tyler sat back down, the effect of everything taking away his strength.

"We are inside one of my stars," Uncle Sal said calmly, "I found you here," he said easily, as though that explained everything. "I wondered who you were, or more precisely, what you were. I had never seen anything in so much pain. So, I wanted to help ease your pain," he finished.

He stared at Tyler, lighting his pipe and sending billowing clouds of smoke to the ceiling. He had such a serene look, as if this were all normal, and everything was okay. Tyler remembered the sun he'd submerged himself within. Pain? That statement was at least a correct. He remembered he'd wanted to die, had wanted to turn over everything to the alien inside. Was this the alien?

"Uh, h-how can this be inside a sun, this looks so real?" Tyler asked, not sure he really wanted to know.

"It is real," uncle Sal explained, "I made it myself, inside the star." He shifted in his seat and pointed his pipe at Tyler, "You I made as well. You were just a spirit, so I made you a body—a body I believe you once had." He puffed his pipe again, blowing a smoke ring towards the fireplace.

"Yes, this is the body I once had…but I thought it was gone forever." Tyler sat back on the couch, relaxing slightly, happy at least for the experience if being human again. "I didn't think it was possible to feel like this again, to be me, really me." He smiled at Uncle Sal, a genuine smile of gratitude.

"What happened to your old body?" uncle Sal asked. "Are you an Onyalum?"

"A what? Oneelum? What is an Oneelum?" Tyler was confused by the word, although it seemed to cause something to stir deep inside his subconscious. *The alien?* He didn't know, but it wouldn't surprise him.

"Ahh! You are not an Onyalum. That would explain why I can hear your thoughts."

"Is that how you created all this, from my thoughts?" Tyler was more than astounded.

"Yes, this seemed like a setting that would comfort you." He gestured at the room around them. "Does it make you feel uneasy? I could change it."

"No…no it is fine. This is the set from a TV show I watched as a kid. A TV show I really liked." Tyler actually did feel comfortable, perhaps the sleep had helped.

"I see", Uncle Sal seemed to ponder this for a moment, then looking content, set his pipe down. "I see a world in your thoughts, a world not unlike many I have created, yet it is not one of mine."

"Earth?" Tyler offered up.

"Earth, yes that is what it is called. Is it close to here?" Uncle Sal asked mildly, interest on his face.

"I don't know." It hurt Tyler to have to admit that fact.

"Ahhh, I am beginning to see the pattern." Uncle Sal picked up his pipe and lit it once again, blowing huge clouds of smoke around the room.

Tyler noted the smell and it brought back memories from his childhood. His grandfather had smoked a pipe for a while when Tyler had been young. Although he quit a short time later, Tyler still remembered the sweet, woody smell that his mother would complain about when they came to visit. Unfortunately, he died when Tyler was nine and Tyler had always wished he'd known him better.

"What pattern do you see?" Tyler asked, curious for any information that would shed light on his current predicament. "What is an Onyalum?"

"An Onyalum is a creature of the Universe. They are not made of real matter," he gestured with his pipe all around them, "they exist outside the 'real' Universe, but travel through it, observing, yet unable to interact with anything made of real matter". He stared at the floor deep in thought before continuing.

"Everything in the Universe is made up of matter and a little of the ethereal substance of the Universe. It is what gives matter its 'life'. In this way, all things are connected to the Universe by this fabric of the insubstantial life force. From the smallest particle to the largest star, each contains an ethereal component that binds them all together."

"The complexity of the matter dictates the amount of the ethereal substance it contains. Take for instance the life similar to the bodies we currently possess, they possess a large amount of the ethereal life force, thus endowing them with consciousness and a sense of self."

He paused to refill his pipe and relit it in a blaze of flame and smoke. "For an Onyalum, matter cannot affect them as they cannot affect matter. It is only when the two are merged that one may control the other. As matter dies or is destroyed, the ethereal essence of that matter is released back into the Universe to be recycled again in another creation. At this point of release, an Onyalum may replace the missing essence, thus merging with the matter to take control."

Uncle Sal blew another series of smoke rings towards the fireplace, apparently amused at the ability. Tyler waited patiently. "However," Uncle Sal continued, "this ability to control comes at a cost, for the matter also controls the Onyalum." He paused again, briefly watching Tyler try to absorb it all.

Tyler listened closely, and was beginning to make the connection between the Onyalum and what he had become.

"So basically, the Onyalum can 'possess' someone when their own spirit is released into the Universe?" The concept seemed

49

plausible, but it didn't fit any theology Tyler had heard before. "But, does that mean the person is dead, or gone, or what?"

Uncle Sal looked calmly at Tyler, small streams of smoke releasing casually from the sides of his mouth as he sucked gently on his pipe.

"Your choice of words seems to fit the nature of the Onyalum well. They 'possess' the matter and likewise, the matter possesses them. Once an Onyalum possesses a body, they are unable to release themselves from that matter. Only when that matter is once again killed or destroyed is the Onyalum released. They are prisoners within the matter, yet they control it."

"Okay, I believe I understand. I had the same experience with a simple life form on a planet near here. I was pulled into the creature and trapped until the creature died and released me. Maybe I am an Onyalum." He stared at his hands as though some branding might appear to confirm this statement.

Uncle Sal stared at Tyler with a look of disbelief, "I do not believe you are an Onyalum, but something else, something new and different." He blew a smoke ring before continuing, "I see into your thoughts, something I can do with my own creations, but not with an Onyalum. They are private, mysterious creatures, hiding inside my creations, observing and enjoying the benefits of being real." He paused and looked troubled by something he had thought of. "Unfortunately, many Onyalum are malevolent creatures that seek power and use it to bring about pain and destruction."

Tyler absorbed this quietly. If he was not Onyalum, then what was he? He felt the alien presence within stir. The talk of Onyalum seemed to interest the buried entity. He was about to mention this strange presence inside, when Uncle Sal began speaking.

"I see your pattern as an accident of some sort. Your thoughts betray a simple being, something I myself might have created, yet your insubstantial existence belies that and would indicate you are an Onyalum." He blew a thick cloud of smoke as he said this, once again distracted by the novelty. "I do not believe you were created, at least, not by design." He stopped to empty his pipe and set it down in the ashtray.

"I suppose the Universe may have created you, a new type of Onyalum." He looked at Tyler intently, as though waiting to hear confirmation. Tyler didn't know what to say.

"I believe you are a creation of happenstance and accident. Your previous life would not be so narrow and transparent if you were solely an Onyalum." He stopped and waited patiently, looking for Tyler to say something.

"I..." Tyler began, then stopped thinking for a moment. "I suppose what you say may be true. My previous life was narrow and simple. I never knew anything outside my small world, until I was struck by something that ripped me out of that world and threw me into the middle of the Universe. I am a changed being of new and frightening abilities, but forever lost in this vast Universe." He stopped and stared at the fire. "I don't know what I am."

The statement was flat and emotionless. Tyler stared into the fire, memories of his previous life flashing before his awareness.

"Hmmm..." Uncle Sal murmured slowly. He was staring at Tyler as though trying to pierce the exterior and study the guts of this strange new life form he had discovered. They both sat quietly for a while, Tyler staring into the fire, Uncle Sal staring into Tyler.

Finally, Uncle Sal broke the silence, "I see a lot of pain and sorrow in you Tyler, and I believe I understand the causes. I have seen much pain and sorrow throughout my existence in many of the creations I have made." He stood up and walked over to the fire, opening the screen and throwing more wood onto the dwindling flames.

"You have been taken, by accident, from the only world you knew. Now, you cannot find that world and you worry you will never find it. It must be very upsetting."

With the fire once again burning brightly, Uncle Sal closed the screen and returned to his chair. He picked up his pipe and began loading more tobacco into it.

"I remember a time, so long ago that I could not even describe it to you in terms that would make sense to you, I too knew a world that I cherished. It had been the first world I ever created. Looking back at it now, I suppose it was a rather simple, unrealistic world, but it suited me fine. I had created many creatures to inhabit this world, and they all loved me as I also loved them. I would often live among them, relishing in their happiness, taking care of them, watching them grow and evolve into such wonderful beings" he paused to light his pipe.

"I was new at creating and I suppose I was bound to make mistakes. The star that this world revolved around was a young star. Not my first, but I was still new to the process. Before I realized it was happening, the star imploded causing an explosion that destroyed all the worlds that surrounded it. This wonderful world and all its creatures were obliterated in the blink of an eye." He puffed at his pipe, the memory of the incident drawing his face into a sad expression, an expression that didn't fit Uncle Sal.

"At first I was angry, at myself and at my creations. I lashed out at what was left and destroyed it all. It took time, but I eventually calmed down and set myself the task of creating once again, but paying closer attention than before. I worked for millennia, crafting, perfecting, and guiding my creations. I was determined to build the greatest creations in the Universe, and for a while, I did. I don't really know how many worlds I created. It was hundreds of thousands of galaxies. No other creator worked as hard and diligently as I had, and I had filled the Universe with a magnificent array of worlds and creatures." He was gesturing expansively with his arms, the movement threatening to shake the tobacco out of his pipe.

He put his arms down and stuck the pipe in his mouth, drawing in the smoke releasing it in a large cloud followed by smoke rings that looked more like tiny galaxies swirling across the room. Tyler was intrigued by these interesting smoke rings, watching them gather across on the far wall before dissipating.

"Alas, I finally stopped creating. I looked upon all I had done and wanted to enjoy each and every one. I went to the many worlds, and tried to live among the very creatures I had created, but they did not know me. During all those millennia of creating, my own creations were evolving, creating their own worlds and religions, worlds that didn't include me. Many became hostile towards me, damning me as an evil spirit sent to destroy them. I tried to change their minds. I gave them prosperity, health, happiness, but always they would turn against me. I tried punishing them, showing them that nothing could stand against me, but that only bred fear, and through this fear, a false love."

He shifted in his chair and grabbed the lighter to relight his pipe. Tyler was fascinated; he couldn't believe he was listening to a god, a god telling him about creation, worship and love. Tyler felt more than a little awed.

Uncle Sal began again, his pipe now lit and exuding puffs of smoke as he talked. "Oh, there were many who accepted me, loved me for who I was and not because of what I might do. I spent a great deal of time on these worlds, helping them prosper and grow into something I was proud of. But it was not the same as that first world. Try as I might, I was unable to reproduce the innocence and newness of that first world. It wasn't that I loved my new worlds any less, they simply were different. I knew I could never have that first world again, and the loss of it brought me great sorrow."

The sadness on Uncle Sal's face was real, and Tyler knew this god's loss was even greater than his own, small loss.

Uncle Sal looked at Tyler with great intensity, "You see, loss is a very real part of this Universe because change is a very real part of this Universe. You cannot question it and you may not understand it, but you cannot change it." He leaned forward in his chair, staring directly into Tyler's eyes, a look of concern and compassion taking over the sadness on his face. "You have changed Tyler, like everything else. Your loss is very real and very painful, but it is only part of your journey through this Universe. You have been given something special, something that very few creatures in this Universe can ever experience or understand. Relish your new existence and find your new worlds. They will never be the same as your first world, but that does not make them any less special." He leaned back in his chair, apparently satisfied with his speech. He once again started puffing his pipe.

Tyler knew he spoke the truth. Tyler knew he would likely never find his own world again, but that shouldn't stop him from exploring new worlds and gaining new experiences. He looked back fondly on the excitement he'd felt possessing the small globe creatures, the thrill of the mating and the intense pleasure when they were successful. He would never find that experience on earth, at least not in his previous life.

He realized he'd been indulging in the greatest self-pity and that he had to face up to the realization that he could not change his predicament, but could embrace it and use it to discover a Universe he had never imagined.

"I suppose my anguish was simply self-pity. I never really experienced loss before, and with the confusion of my circumstances, I really didn't know what to do. My loss seems insignificant compared to what you lost. I am sorry to have burdened you with it." Tyler folded his hands in his lap and stared at the floor.

"Nonsense," Uncle Sal said jovially, "I was not burdened. It was something I'd not experienced in a long time. You see, a great deal of time has passed since I have interacted with any of my creations. By now, no one knows me or knows that I even exist. They have evolved beyond needing me, and I simply let them continue to grow without my intervention. Perhaps that is for the best. But I enjoyed finding someone who needed my help—I'd forgotten how it felt to be needed."

Uncle Sal put his pipe down and sat up. "Come, let me show you some of my creations. Perhaps you will find something in them that will help you rejoice in your newfound existence."

Tyler got off the couch and followed Uncle Sal to a door concealed behind the paneling on the right wall. Uncle Sal seemed to press gently against the side of the door, releasing it a crack. Light poured into the room from the small crack, a brightness that seemed blinding after the dim firelight.

"Before we enter, I want you to know that we will not be visible to the inhabitants. Their physiology is far different than yours, and they are not aware of any life outside their world. I do not wish to upset them with something that may be disturbing to the belief systems they have created."

Uncle Sal slowly opened the door and walked through. Tyler followed him into the bright light. As the door closed, Tyler found himself standing on what appeared to be a small dirt road through a small village. The sky was as blue as earth's, but the clouds seemed a slight reddish color despite the sun being directly overhead. Like a sunset at noon.

Tyler was taken by the fresh smells of vegetation and the incredible quietness only broken by the sounds of small animals in the fields and woods around them. Small creatures flew amongst the trees and high overhead. Tyler supposed they were birds, although the vibrant colors were very different than anything he remembered on earth.

The tiny village consisted of three small buildings constructed from what Tyler assumed was dirt or other natural materials. It gave each building a light tan color with mottled streaks of brown. The roofs were made of wood or some other material fashioned into tiles layered from the top of the roof to the bottom where it met the exterior walls.

The roofs sat upon the structures like small pyramids with fours sides instead of the two Tyler remembered on earth. Each building was two stories tall and contained ample windows but a single door centered in the front under a small porch.

Surrounding the village, dense woods and open fields spread out toward distant hills. Many of the fields were planted with crops that growing abundantly under the warm sun. The setting was rural and tranquil. The air temperature was pleasantly warm with only a touch of humidity. A light cool breeze blew in from across the fields, bringing the rich smell of tilled soil and growing crops. Uncle Sal let him take it all in before speaking.

"I created this world billions of years ago. I was determined to create a peaceful world rich in diversity and abundant with resources. The weather on this planet is very moderate from pole to pole, a challenge to get right. It rains regularly, but not too much or too often."

He pointed to the village buildings, "These structures were built by one of the many intelligent creatures that have evolved on this world. There are actually five intelligent life forms on this planet, more than I have ever created on any other world. I suppose the pleasant, abundant riches of this world helped spur on this incredible development."

Uncle Sal walked towards a building on the left side of the street, stopping at the top step of the porch.

"This was the last world I ever created, and the one I am most proud of. You see, not only did five different creatures evolve into intelligent life, but they all coexist peacefully. The usual plagues of my creations, war, famine, disease, competition, do not exist here. Come, let us go in and see some of these wonderful people."

Tyler watched as Uncle Sal walked through the closed door. It was very disconcerting to see, especially when one of his arms came back through and gestured for him to follow. Tyler shrugged and walked up the steps and through the door. The transition through the door was smooth with no feeling.

They stood within a small foyer, a stairway straight ahead and two doorways on either side. Small hooks were fastened to the wall by the front door and colorful garments hung there—light coats and jackets, for the evenings no doubt.

Uncle Sal headed through the doorway on the right and walked through the simply furnished room towards the back of the house. Tyler followed, taking in the intricately carved furnishings and knickknacks throughout the room.

They walked through another doorway into a dining area with a large table set with dishware and steaming bowls of food. Uncle Sal took it in before heading through another doorway into a kitchen. Tyler hurried to keep up while taking it all in.

Through the opposite doorway of the kitchen, they turned right and entered a small room where candles burned against the far wall. The candles were lined up on a tiered dais beneath the figure of a creature that vaguely looked like an elephant, but was too thin and human shaped. On the floor of the room, kneeling before the candles and figure were four seemingly human shaped figures bent over in prayer.

"They are worshipping their god before they eat," Uncle Sal walked through them and towards the figurine on the wall. "Undoubtedly an early predecessor of these creatures, now deified and worshipped."

Uncle Sal turned away from the figurine and looked closely at the kneeling figures on the floor.

"They developed this religion thousands of years ago, in an attempt to explain the bounty of their lives. I was never here for them, so they do not know me. Unfortunate I suppose, but I am still happy and proud of what they have become."

The figures on the floor each spoke strange phrases in turn that Tyler did not understand. Suddenly they stopped, rose from the floor and made gestures towards their god before turning to leave the room. Only then did Tyler see them fully. Although their proportions appeared human, their faces were definitely not.

The skin was a pale yellow color and the mouth was very generous containing two fairly large teeth or tusks that protruded from either side. The nose, or more accurately, the trunk, hung down at least four feet from the face and appeared to have small fingers or joints at the end.

The slanted eyes were slightly out on the side of the face, and the color was a deep green that looked intense against the yellow skin. The hands were small and had only four chubby digits, three and what appeared to be a thumb.

Tyler was amazed to see something that was like a human but not like one at all. He was seeing a truly intelligent alien life. He watched fascinated as one of them used their trunk to extinguish the candles and put them away in a box to the right of the figurine. The creature had four small, round breasts concealed by the loose clothing it wore. Tyler assumed it was a female.

"Beautiful aren't they?" Uncle Sal was smiling as he watched his creations go about cleaning up after their worship. Tyler wasn't sure beautiful was the word he would use, but then he couldn't help but think of them as some distorted human being, grossly crossed with an elephant.

Uncle Sal looked at him with a look of deep concern on his face. "Your bias against these creatures does not speak highly of your kind." He walked past Tyler and back out towards the dining room.

Tyler knew he was being superficial, but he had never before seen intelligent life so similar to a human. It was clearly going to take time for him to get accustomed to different life forms. He didn't think of himself as prejudice, but more likely cautious and wary of something that was different.

Tyler followed the female out of the room and through the kitchen into the dining room. They all stood waiting for her to arrive before taking their seats. Uncle Sal stood against the back wall, arms folded, looking thoughtful.

Tyler wasn't sure if he had upset him or not. "Look I didn't mean to think such things, I've just never seen another intelligent life form. It is true though, my species does have a history of judging others by their looks or by their differences. We only have one intelligent life form on my world, and our dominance came at the cost of many other, lower life forms."

Tyler leaned against the doorway from the kitchen and watched as the family began passing and serving the food at the table. He knew his excuse wasn't an excuse, but it was all he had. He simply couldn't help his reaction, but he sincerely hoped that he could one day change it.

Uncle Sal looked up at him, concern replaced with a light smile. "I understand Tyler, your world is not unlike many of the worlds I have created. Competition and dominance play a major role in the lives of its inhabitants, thus creating a wedge between themselves and any others that may threaten their existence or survival. The distrust is inherent in the evolutionary processes that control them. Do not worry, I believe you will overcome these limitations."

Uncle Sal stood up from the wall and walked back towards the front of the house. "Come Tyler, there is much more to see."

Tyler followed him back to the front door and walked through it as before. He had expected to come out to the front porch as before, but instead he found himself on another world, standing next to a deep chasm.

The sky was dark red with black clouds or smoke that obscured the sun. The air smelled acrid, like a forest fire. The ground shook violently, almost knocking Tyler to the ground. When it stopped, Tyler watched a plume of red hot lava spew from a volcanic dome off in the distance. All around, plumes of smoke rose in the distance. Tyler could see no life, plant or otherwise.

Uncle Sal had a somber look on his face as he stared at the lava flowing from the distant volcano.

"This world is being torn apart, reaching the end of its existence. The dominant life form left this world thousands of years ago, settling on another, more stable world. You see, this world is a moon orbiting a gas giant that has been collapsing on itself for millennia. The gravitational pull has become so strong, it is tearing all its moons apart."

He stared across the expanse, watching the plumes of smoke that indicated the last moments of a dying world.

"You see Tyler, this too is part of life in the Universe. As it is created, so too will it be destroyed. There is neither right nor wrong in this pattern, it is only the natural flow of creation. This too would have been your fate, had you remained on your world. Now however, you have been given a gift few will ever know, the gift of eternity. Choose what to do with it, and that will determine right or wrong. I cannot choose your fate, it is only in your hands."

Uncle Sal stood silently, staring at Tyler with a serious look. It made Tyler feel self-conscious about his own inadequacies. He knew that what he'd said was true, that his own destiny was his to choose. It was the inevitable decision that Tyler had been avoiding. He didn't want the responsibility. He wanted something he could blame it on, something or someone that would take on the responsibility for him.

"I feel the presence of something inside me, perhaps it is an Onyalum, I don't know." Tyler felt guilty at hiding this from Uncle Sal the whole time. He knew he'd come close to giving up and turning over his life and essence to the alien. Now, he felt ashamed at such a cowardly act.

Uncle Sal looked at him with something that looked like pity.

"I know about that presence in you. I wasn't sure what it was, but now I am. I do believe it is an Onyalum that has become irreversibly combined with your essence, creating the new Tyler."

"What if it takes over? I almost let it before you found me."

"I do not think you will let it, at least not anymore. I believe it will simply become a part of you, another part of your being."

"But what if it is a malevolent Onyalum? Will it make me do bad things and make wrong choices?" Tyler was concerned that he might change more into the Onyalum and that might lead to bad things, things he couldn't control.

Uncle Sal smiled gently, "I do not think so Tyler, but maybe it will, maybe it won't. That is a journey you must take alone. I wanted you to see that life abounds throughout the Universe. You are not alone. You may be something new and unique, and you may be judged by that, perhaps even unfairly, but you must make the choices that will determine how Tyler fits into this Universe."

"I don't want to hurt or destroy", Tyler began, "I don't really know what I want. I realize I will probably never find my world, but can I really find happiness on another?"

"You won't know until you try."

Tyler thought about this. He knew Uncle Sal was right, that he would have to make his own decisions and try out new worlds. He would have to overcome his own limited background, seek out new life forms and build new relationships. It was he who was different, and he would be the one who would have to adjust to the strange worlds he would encounter.

Tyler began to feel excitement, a chance to see something new and different, something alien. He looked forward to it.

"I am glad you are excited, but remember, loss is a very real part of life," he gestured at the dying world around them, "you must be prepared for the eventuality that you will always go on when those around you will not. You must live for the moment, knowing that the moment will be gone as fast as it came. Enjoy those moments and others around you will also enjoy them. Then you will make the right decisions."

"I understand what you are saying, and I don't know how well I will take the losses, but I am willing to try."

"Good! Come, let us start you on your journey." Uncle Sal turned away from the edge of the cliff and walked towards a door that stood alone amidst the decaying world. The effect was strange, like something out of the twilight zone.

Before opening the door, Uncle Sal turned towards Tyler.

"I want you to know that I am willing to help you whenever you feel you need it. I cannot make your decisions, but I will be willing to discuss them with you or simply talk as a friend. Many creators will not offer you this type of friendship, they will be wary of you, because they will look upon you as an Onyalum. Be prepared for that."

Uncle Sal put his hands on the doorknob, preparing to open it.

"But how will I find you again?" Tyler knew he would need this friendship, it was the only one offered so far.

"My name, the name I was given when I was created, is Thosolan. Simply think my name very hard and very directly, and I will hear you and find you."

Uncle Sal opened the door and through it Tyler could see the intense bright burning of the inside of the sun they had started in.

"My body will not survive going through the door will it?"

"No, you will lose your body once again, but you will be free to begin your journey. There are many worlds in my galaxies, please feel free to explore them and experience the life that is so precious."

"Thank you, Uncle Sa…, I mean Thosolan, your friendship and help means a great deal to me. I will try to experience the worlds you have created, hopefully making myself into something better than I was before."

Tyler headed for the door, but was stopped short by Thosolan's hand. Thosolan extended his hand as though to shake. Tyler was more than a little taken aback by this human gesture, but took Thosolan's hand in a warm embrace.

"It is you that you must make proud Tyler. Only then can others be proud of you. Good luck, and remember, I am always here if you need me."

Tyler nodded, and stepped through the doorway, feeling only a momentary burning before entering the silence of the Universe.

Admiral's Luck

Tyler had understood Thosolan's message and was determined to find a new life. He understood that going back was not the answer. Instead, he had to move forward, discover new worlds and find new relationships. Since Tyler was inside one of Thosolan's galaxies, he figured it was as good a place as any to start.

He left behind the star and began looking for systems that appeared to contain life. This time however, he was determined to find intelligent life, not just glowing orbs of light.

As he had done before, he began searching from a certain point and worked his way counterclockwise through the galaxy, moving inevitably inward towards the central core. His search brought him through many unique systems, many filled with varied life forms, but nothing intelligent. Still, he maintained his patience and continued to search.

As he spiraled in further toward the galactic core, he came upon a system that contained two earth-like planets. Each planet contained the telltale white and blue indicating ocean and cloud, but the planet further from the sun also contained large areas of brown, indicating a drier climate.

It was enough to satisfy Tyler, so he focused his attention and made the transition to the planet closest to the sun. With the larger body of water, Tyler figured he would likely find life.

As he came out above the planet prepared to transition to the surface, sparks of light from one of the two moons orbiting the planet drew his attention. His ability to focus on distant objects made the light appear close, but not enough to determine what was causing them. Perhaps this was an astrological phenomenon related to this moon? He wasn't certain, but decided to check it out before heading down to the planet.

He focused on the moon and made his transition toward the lights, coming out above the moon. He was amazed to see the lights were hundreds of spaceships engaged in a battle above the moon. Ships of all sizes darted amongst each other as the larger ships fired enormous pulses of light. From Tyler's vantage, it reminded him of a swarm of angry bees whose hive had been disturbed.

One very large ship dominated the battle surrounded by smaller ships, similar in design. The smaller ships appeared to be protecting the large ship by firing their pulses of light at the angry bees. Tyler was fascinated. He'd watched science fiction movies on earth, but never in his wildest imagination did he believe he'd actually witness such a battle.

Finally, he had found an intelligent life form, even advanced. He grew excited at the prospects of meeting such highly evolved beings. Despite the ongoing explosions and pulses of light, he was ready to face anyone capable of intelligent conversation. As he watched, he noticed the battle was moving fast.

Already, the larger ship had sustained heavy damage and was beginning to list out of control. The aggressors were also showing signs of extreme damage as many small, lifeless ships littered the battlefield. Tyler was disappointed to see the end of such an epic battle—clearly it had been a major campaign.

He was ready to go back to the planet when an enormous explosion rocked the larger ship. The blast blew away a huge section of the side of the ship near the bottom all the way to its top. The gaping hole that was left behind was littered with twinkling debris spewing from the gaping wound.

The power of the blast pushed the listing ship closer toward the moon, and the ships inability to control its movement put it in peril from the moon's gravitational pull. As Tyler watched fascinated, the power on the large ship flickered intermittently before it plunged entirely into darkness. The dark ship tumbled in slow motion, bleeding profusely as it began its fall towards a certain death.

Tyler was awestruck, the immense size and armaments of this ship made it seem impossible to defeat, but the swarm of bees had done their job well. They had essentially disabled what must have been the flag ship, although their success came at a high cost to their own fleet.

Many of the smaller ships began pulling off from the battle and moved desperately towards their dying leader. Tyler thought the bigger ship had to be the command ship, like an aircraft carrier in the center of a fleet. He watched as it rolled slowly in a death spin that kept taking it closer to the moon below.

The smaller ships already surrounding the flag ship appeared unable to get in close as the large ship spun from the explosion. The ships were searching feverishly, looking for some way to dock and help their dying commanders. Tyler was fascinated—never had he seen a real military battle except on TV, now he was watching a real one in space.

Wanting more of the experience, he transitioned just above the large ship as it spun slowly below him. As it made another turn, Tyler saw the gaping hole come back into view. Nothing in or around that hole was alive, only the debris from the explosion twinkled in the light of the moon below.

Tyler wanted to see inside such a ship, assuming there was anything left to see. He transitioned close to the top of the large hole and kept moving to keep up with the ship as it rotated. Several smaller ships had finally managed to land on top of the large ship and appeared to be engaged in firing their engines to slow the large ship's spin. Tyler hoped they would succeed. His constant need to transition to remain motionless was taking its toll?

Slowly the spin subsided before finally stopping. Tyler took advantage and transitioned to a point outside the hole. At that range, he could make out the shredded metal of the ship's interior. Slowly, picking his path carefully, he made his way through the wreckage looking for some passageway or opening to get inside. He knew that somewhere toward the center of the ship, something had to remain.

He saw a glimmer of dull light to the left and made his way towards it. A small light above a doorway glowed dimly, apparently some sort of emergency lighting. Tyler knew he couldn't open the door, but wasn't sure how to get past it. He couldn't see what was on the other side and assumed his transitions were based on what he saw.

He was puzzled and frustrated. Because he couldn't think of a way to get past the dilemma, he was ready to try anything. He thought hard, picturing himself on the other side of the door. Slowly, he felt the familiar feeling of a transition as everything blurred. It worked! As he came out of the transition, he found himself inside one of the ship's wide passageways. All around the corridor, debris floated, bouncing off the smooth walls.

He made his way through dim light, looking for anything that indicated life. Nothing. He wasn't sure how far he'd come, but it seemed liked he'd been moving around in a clockwise fashion. He backtracked and decided to move through one of the interior doors.

Once again, he made the transition and found himself inside a storage closet, cluttered with the floating contents of the shelves. He didn't recognize any of the debris and quickly moved back into the hallway. He tried door after door, but most led to additional passageways or rooms which contained no life, dead or alive. *Is this some sort of robot ship?* Tyler was beginning to think maybe it was.

He took another passageway that appeared to lead somewhere towards the inner part of the circle he'd been traveling. He came upon a doorway on the right side of corridor and decided to check. Making the transition, he found himself inside a dimly lit room littered with floating debris.

Apparently this room had lost whatever force had been keeping the rest of the ship on its floor. Tyler looked about—distant banks of panels still showed blinking lights. In front of the panel, Tyler saw what looked like a large chair. From his current position, he couldn't make out if anyone or anything were in the chair so he moved closer to check.

If anyone was on the ship, he was curious to see what they looked like. Elephants? Tigers? Monkeys? He could only guess.

He moved just above the chair and looked down on a poor lifeless figure. The creature was floating limp against the straps of the safety harness keeping it in the chair. Tyler was a bit surprised, it appeared very human. Two arms, two legs, one head and a little dark colored hair covering its head, made it appear human. Tyler looked closely at the face. The skin was very white, almost translucent, and there was no facial hair of any kind.

The lack of a defined nose took away the human illusion. Instead, two small flaps centered on the face must have been the equivalent of a nose. The mouth was small, with thin blue lips that Tyler thought might not actually be the normal color. He guessed the poor creature had been suffocated since no physical wounds were obvious.

The creature's hands were small and human looking with four fingers and one thumb. However, the ends of the fingers were far different than a human's. Instead of normal, 'human' fingernails, this creature had three pronged claws on each finger, except the thumb. The claws were not long, but Tyler guessed they could inflict serious damage. This feature gave the creature a decidedly 'animal' look to it.

The eyes were actually opened, but they didn't seem real. They were completely black, large and slightly oval shaped. Again, Tyler thought this could be due to death. Without eyelashes and eyebrows, the face looked more like a caricature a child might draw. Tyler had to remind himself that most of the creatures he would encounter would not be human, although this one had similar characteristics.

He looked up and down the body hoping to find some indication of whether it was male or female. He couldn't tell from the featureless, thin body in a shiny, slick white single piece suit. As Tyler watched the lifeless body, it began to shake violently like a rag doll in an earthquake. It startled Tyler and took him a moment to realize that the ship itself was shaking. He wondered if another explosion had caused the quake or whether the smaller ships were trying something else in a frantic attempt to save it from the surface of the moon.

Tyler left the body and the room behind and continued down the corridor looking for additional signs of habitation. Now that he knew there were life forms aboard, he knew there had to be more than one.

Apparently this corridor also had lost its ability to hold things to the floor as Tyler came upon a lone figure floating lifeless through the passageway. This creature looked similar to one he'd found in the chair, so Tyler kept moving.

The corridor ended at a set of large doors with red lights blinking above them. To the right of one door, Tyler could make out some writing, but he couldn't read any of it. The various symbols appeared alien, but Tyler assumed it indicated what the room was.

Taking the plunge, Tyler transitioned through the doors and into a very large circular room with multiple levels. The ceiling of the room hung overhead at least forty feet. The walls of the room contained multiple walkways and permanent seating in front of banks of lights and screens. The screens, however, were mostly dead.

The center of the room was dominated by a large semicircular console surrounded by many chairs with one large chair behind. This large chair was currently unoccupied, and took up much of the middle part of the console. Tyler thought it might have been the 'captain's' chair.

Although not familiar with ships of any kind, Tyler believed he'd found the ship's bridge. He based this on the large view screen that dominated the far wall in front of the semicircular console. It reminded him of the bridge of a ship on an old science fiction show he's watched as a kid.

All around the room, small fires glowed from various consoles. At least the room must have had an atmosphere. Everywhere Tyler looked, bodies were strewn about. All were lifeless and most remained strapped to their chairs or hovered just above the floor.

The scene disturbed Tyler as many of the bodies had large wounds caused by debris or the violent shaking of the explosion. It would explain why some of the chairs that had been ripped from their flooring, bodies still in them.

As far as Tyler could see, small globes of red blood, at least Tyler thought it was blood, floated about the room like marbles, occasionally staining some of the creature's white uniforms. If Tyler had been in a real body, he was certain he'd been sick.

He'd had enough and was ready to leave when a movement caught his eye. One of the bodies floating about the room had moved. He watched as it began to jerk uncontrollably. He moved closer, curious to see if it was still alive. As he neared it, he could make out its face. The eyes were closed and the mouth gaped open slightly, looking more dead than alive. The body jerked again, this time violently, the movement bringing it closer to Tyler.

He watched it as it finally stopped convulsing and began to glow slightly. Tyler was fascinated by the smoke or cloud of light emanating from the creature. As the light spread, it slowly dissipated across the room.

Tyler wasn't sure what the light was, but he had a suspicion. As though to prove the point, he was pulled towards the body. Like the small glowing orbs he'd possessed earlier, he was being sucked into the body of the dead or dying creature. Tyler realized too late that the glowing cloud hadn't been smoke, but the ethereal spirit of the creature leaving its body in death. Like the glowing orbs before, Tyler was now trapped inside the creature.

As Tyler entered the body, he felt enormous pain and his consciousness faded. The body convulsed without his control, and though he desperately tried to open the eyes, he could only make out a blur of incoherent images. He struggled to stay conscious, and hoped desperately that the body would die again, releasing him from its control.

Sounds of a siren or something like it rang in his ears, but in his haze, he couldn't tell if the sound was outside or inside his head. As the last remnants of consciousness began to fade, he thought he'd heard voices. At that point, all Tyler cared about was the receding pain as he descended into a cool, peaceful blackness.

Tyler slipped in and out of consciousness, not knowing where he was or what was happening. In those rare moments he would drift awake, he felt as if he were lying down on something soft. Try as he did, he was never able to stay conscious enough to open his eyes or sense anything more than the pressure on his back.

In the blackness of unconsciousness, he dreamed of a strange world, filled with human, and yet not human creatures. At times he was himself, human, yet at other times he was one of the 'not-human' creatures. Everyone in this dream world spoke strange and exotic languages, and although Tyler couldn't understand what they were saying, an occasional word would suddenly make sense. It was very disconcerting, and Tyler felt alien and alone.

In this dream world, he was a part of it, yet he knew it was a dream. A whole lifetime of this 'alter-ego' seemed to pass by Tyler, like a movie in his mind—a movie he was part of. He felt lost in this other life and began to desperately cling to what he knew was Tyler—or what he thought was Tyler.

Frustrated, he began to demand that the others in his dreams call him Tyler, not this 'Admiral' they kept referring to. Everyone always looked at him strangely before laughing it off. His frustration would build, but he kept trying anyway.

He wasn't sure what had happened, and he struggled to piece it together. Unfortunately the 'other' life kept intruding, forcing him back into the strange world he did not understand. A world where he knew he didn't belong. He struggled against it, trying to will himself awake, to escape from the alien surroundings, but it was useless, the movie continued to play with Tyler trapped in the role of the 'Admiral' character.

At one point, Tyler found himself on the bridge of a large vessel. On this bridge, he barked commands at everyone scurrying around him. It felt quite odd since he really didn't understand much of what he was saying or for that matter, what was happening. Helpless, he looked upon the scene, a part of it, yet apart from it.

Something serious was happening, Tyler had figured that much out, but he still didn't know what. His 'other' self continued barking orders, an occasional word making sense to Tyler. Words like 'armament', 'condition', and 'prepare', reinforced Tyler's sense that something seriousness was taking place.

As this scene played out, Tyler felt the room begin to shake. Deep rumbling sounds reverberated off the walls forcing everyone to grab onto anything that would hold them steady. Tyler or his 'other' self desperately grabbed for the arm of a nearby chair, but just missed grasping it as he was flung across the room slamming into the side of a console. A bright white light flashed across his eyes as a deep searing pain ripped through his left side.

Stars swam through his vision as he felt himself slip into a dark oblivion of pain. He felt his mouth open to scream in pain, and then awoke upright in a bed, screaming into a quiet and empty room.

His mind searched for an explanation. Was he actually awake or was he still trapped in the dream world? It felt real enough as he began to rub himself. A painful spot on his left side brought back the memory of the bridge and slamming into a console, but he knew that couldn't have been real.

The pain in his body felt real enough. For some reason the body didn't feel like his own. He stared around the room looking for anything familiar. It was a bleak utilitarian room with blank white walls that belied no signs of where he was. He looked down at the bed he lay on. White linen sheets covered by a cream colored blanket all seemed normal enough. At his side, a small table held a lamp and small electronic devices with several lights, one blinking blue. Again, none of it helped.

He searched his mind looking for clues. The 'other' self kept intruding, memories that were not his own swam to the surface, confusing Tyler. Through shear force of will, Tyler brought forth his own memories. He remembered Thosolan, the glowing orbs, his predicament, everything. He remembered the dying ship and being sucked into the dying body.

It all made sense. He was still in the body, trapped in what appeared to be a hospital room. Was he still in space? Was this some sort of floating hospital ship? The one window in the room to his left was covered by a blind, blocking the view. However, light from outside seeped in around the edges. He figured he probably wasn't in space.

He assumed he was on the blue planet he'd originally wanted to visit before being distracted by the battle above the moon. He carefully felt his face, and the lack of nose seemed to confirm what he'd already known. He looked at his hands and stared blankly at the unusual three pronged nails that protruded from each finger. It felt very surreal and very alien.

The dull pain he felt along his side, back, and legs seemed to intensify as he sat quietly. The minor exertions he'd already made seemed to sap him of strength. He fell back onto the pillow, exhausted, but willing himself to stay awake.

At least here he felt more like himself, despite the new body. Flashes of 'other' memories swam in his mind, but he found he could ignore them easily enough.

He lay motionless on his back staring at the ceiling, wondering where he was, and who he was. Wasn't this what he'd wanted, a chance to experience other worlds, other people, and new experiences? It was, but now he wasn't sure he was actually prepared for it. The glowing orbs were one thing, but an intelligent life-form scared him.

Who was this creature, what did he do on the destroyed ship, and what life did he have here on this world? Tyler could sense and see visions of the creature's memories, but like the hidden alien deep inside, he was afraid to let the memories surface.

Go on, take a chance, and experience the life you have taken! The voice of the alien urging him on only made his fear stronger. He feared losing himself to those memories, losing what was left of Tyler and becoming the 'Admiral'.

That was it! The memory had come unbidden, but he knew he was an Admiral. Like a floodgate opening up, the memories of the battle above the moon overran his ability to stop them. Names, faces, places, everything began to intrude. Panic gripped Tyler and he fought to keep the Admiral's memories from overtaking him.

Slowly he pushed them back into his subconscious, leaving only his own thoughts and memories. A few scant thoughts about the battle lingered, and Tyler realized that something had gone terribly wrong to cause the crushing defeat. He knew that the ship he'd been on was the best their fleet had. If they had lost that, they were severely crippled.

Tyler felt weird with these 'other' thoughts. So crisp and militaristic, they simply didn't mesh with what Tyler thought of as himself. He pushed them aside and began falling back into sleep.

He yearned to stay awake, but the deep exhaustion and pain forced him back into the blackness. At least this time he didn't dream.

The sound of movement in the room woke Tyler from his deep sleep. The pain had once again subsided to a more bearable level, and Tyler felt ready to face the strange new world.

He lifted his head enough to view someone over by a bureau he hadn't noticed the previous time. Their back was to Tyler, so he couldn't make out what they were doing. He slowly lifted himself into a seated position, quietly so he wouldn't disturb the person.

He looked them up and down, and decided it was a female, though he couldn't point to any one characteristic to back up his assumption. The small height and wider hips were his only clue from his current position. The woman wore a one piece suit of a white material, not unlike the uniforms from the ship, but in her case, gold trim along the sleeve and waist, gave it a more distinguished look.

The head was covered with dark brown hair, shoulder length and neatly styled. Tyler wondered if this was someone the Admiral had known. If so, he wondered if he would recognize her.

The person finished and closed one of the bureau drawers before turning towards Tyler. She did not notice him sitting up at first, but as she realized it, shock came over her face, quickly replaced by tears and a look of sincere concern.

She spoke rapidly through her tears, but nothing made sense to Tyler. She wiped at her face but was unable to stop the stream flowing down her cheeks. Tyler realized the Admiral must have known her. A daughter? Wife? He wasn't sure.

The woman slowly calmed down and muttered something quietly before she left through the door, lingering slightly in the doorway before disappearing. Nothing she had said made any sense to Tyler. Though the language was fluid and beautiful, Tyler had not picked up one word. He felt concerned.

What if they couldn't understand him? How would they treat him? He was certain it probably wouldn't be well. Injured in battle and unable to speak or understand anyone else, they would certainly think he was brain damaged. Tyler didn't like the thought of that. Spending life in rehabilitation, or worse, an institution for the mentally impaired didn't sound like the experience he had been looking for.

The door burst open, and two official looking men in white smocks carrying strange devices in their pockets strode towards Tyler. At first they said nothing, one of them looking at the electronic device that was on the table next to Tyler.

They spoke to each other before turning their attention to Tyler. Tyler wasn't sure, but he thought they were asking him questions. It didn't make sense to him, so he sat there quietly staring back at them.

After several attempts at questions, they conferred with each other before taking out more devices to examine Tyler. Tyler watched patiently as they examined him from head to toe, some devices chilling to the touch while others seemed to operate without contact.

Satisfied, the two men once again conferred with each other before speaking to Tyler and leaving the room. Tyler was frustrated. He needed to understand them, to communicate, but he didn't know how. *I can communicate with them.* The alien voice offered up gently. It was tempting, but Tyler didn't want to give up control, at least not yet.

He thought about the Admiral's memories, still held back, but pushing for an audience. Maybe they could provide him the missing language. He wanted to try and use them, but once again held back because of fear. Perhaps he should try to say something first? He wasn't sure if he would even be able to speak, regardless of the language.

It was worth a try—maybe he would get lucky and it would come out in the admiral's language. He opened his mouth and spoke.

"I ammb Tyleers." It sounded bad, even to Tyler, but at least he had made a sound. He wondered why it didn't come out right. Maybe the Admiral's body was having difficulty with English. He tried again.

"Weer ammb I?" It sounded the same. He quickly rattled off some more.

"Tee bruun thok chump ober tee feenst."

"Maarwy had a leetol lamm, eet feese waast wheet at thow."

He fell silent. He wasn't sure he could understand what he had said. At least he could talk, if only he had a language to talk with.

The door opened, breaking Tyler from his reverie. It was one of the 'doctors', at least that's what Tyler assumed they were, and the woman who'd been there earlier. They were speaking to him, but again he couldn't respond. The doctor asked again, but this time pointed to the woman next to him. Tyler realized that he was probably asking if he recognized the woman.

Tyler didn't know what to do. He couldn't communicate, but he knew he better try. He had to make them at least suspect that he was close to being normal. He nodded his head in agreement and spoke one word, "Yeees."

The doctor and woman looked puzzled, and stared at each other to confirm the other didn't understand it either. The doctor pointed to himself and asked another question. Tyler responded by shaking his head negatively and saying no. It came out 'Nuh', but was close enough. They didn't understand English, good or bad.

Shaking his head from side to side, the doctor looked even more puzzled. He said something to the woman and once again left the room. The woman looked concerned and pulled up a chair from the corner. She sat down and refused to look directly at Tyler, choosing instead to stare about the room randomly.

Tyler studied her face carefully. She had very delicate features, small ears, mostly hidden by her hair, small hands, and the small nose flaps of this species. In a way, she was attractive to Tyler, and once again he wondered if she might not be his wife. It made logical sense to Tyler, but no recognition came to mind.

He felt like dipping into the Admiral's memories to search her out, but he still couldn't bring himself to do it. She sat at the end of the bed, still looking very concerned and slowly rubbing her hands together. Finally, she got enough courage to look Tyler in the eyes and spoke to him quietly. He thought it was a question, and when he didn't respond, she looked down and began speaking in a steady stream.

A look of sadness came over her face and the tears once again began to fall from her eyes. Tyler felt helpless. He wanted to help, wanted to make her feel better, but he didn't know what to do. She kept talking and crying, grabbing some sort of cloth from her suit to dry her eyes. At times she looked at him but quickly looked away, the pain of seeing he had no recognition of her too much to bear.

Tyler too felt sad, unable to ease her obvious pain. Whoever she was, she certainly had intense feelings for the Admiral. If only he could talk to her, but nothing she said made any sense. Out of nowhere, a single word floated into Tyler's consciousness, 'Eyleeria'. Not knowing why, he opened his mouth and said the word.

The woman immediately stopped talking, a look of shock on her face. Tyler said it again, and this time she began to smile, a fresh set of tears pouring from her eyes. Without warning, she jumped out of the chair and wrapped her arms around Tyler, her head crying into his shoulder.

He didn't know what he had said, but apparently it had worked. Perhaps it was her name. At the very least, it was something she had recognized. Tyler gently put his arms around her, patting her back in a reassuring manner, ignoring the pain this caused his body. She held him tighter, the tears beginning to get his bedclothes wet.

Finally, the pain no longer bearable, he pushed her away gently. Reluctantly, she released him and sat down on the bed at his side. She began speaking again, this time more quickly and excitedly. Tyler didn't understand any of it. She didn't seem to care, a look of glowing relief on her face. She dried her eyes while she spoke and began gesturing with her hands to emphasize her speech.

It was all lost on Tyler, but he was glad he had brightened her up. *Eyleeria*. The word rolled through his mind, and he admired it for its poetic sound. He decided against saying it once more, and simply lay back in his bed to ease the pain that inflamed his side.

She noticed his discomfiture, and got up from the bed. She helped tuck him in and then kissed him gently on the cheek before walking towards the door. He once again felt tired, and looked forward to a nap. She paused at the door and turned towards him. He could see her face had changed. Instead of the usual white color of her skin, her face glowed with a warm rose color. It made Tyler feel an attraction towards her, although he didn't know why. He assumed this was a good sign.

She said something softly to Tyler before leaving the room, closing the door quietly behind her. The silence weighed heavily on Tyler' eyes and he let them fall shut. He could feel sleep coming over, and he let it come, welcoming the rest. This time, Tyler dreamt of the Admiral and Eyleeria.

Tyler awoke to a quiet, dark room. The lights had been turned down, and nothing seeped in from around the blinds on the window. He figured it must be night, and lay there quietly staring into the ceiling. He replayed the encounter with Eyleeria, and realized that it was her name. He had dreamt of her and the Admiral, and in his dreams, he, or the Admiral had called her Eyleeria. He probed the memory of the dreams, but they faded quickly before he could get much from it.

There had been something else about the Admiral and Eyleeria, but he couldn't remember what. He knew there was some bond between them, but what that bond was eluded him. He thought about the Admiral's memories. He had bottled them up in his subconscious and was still reluctant to let them out.

He wanted to find a way to release them slowly, so that he could organize them and keep them from running over his own. *I can help you do that*, the alien suggested. Tyler considered the offer carefully. He feared the alien presence, but had gotten quite good at suppressing it. Did he have enough control to cooperate with it?

He wasn't sure, but he desperately wanted to know more about the Admiral and find a way to communicate with the people around him. He took the bait, *Ok, tell me how to do it.* He could feel the presence begin to swell up from the depths at his response. He tightened his control and held it back.

How can I help you if you hold me back?

You can simply tell me what I need to know, Tyler responded coldly. He tightened his control, letting nothing of the alien to escape the confines of his subconscious.

No response. Tyler didn't know if the alien was contemplating the situation or refusing to cooperate under Tyler's terms. Tyler urged him gently, *very well, I can simply try it myself, without your help.*

No, I will help! Tyler could sense desperation in the inner voice.

Fine, who are you? Tyler asked.

I am called Adanni, I am an...Onyalum.

I see, Tyler contemplated that and thought about what Thosolan had told him, *how is it that you and I are now joined together?*

I was trying to avoid detection and made a blind transition to your world. When I came out of the transition, I came out where you currently existed. Our two spirits tried to share a single body, but that isn't possible, so we somehow merged into a single entity.

Adanni fell silent and Tyler thought about what he had said. It made sense, but he wondered why his essence had ended up being the dominant one.

Because I am from the ethereal plane and you are from the real plane. You dominated the body we collided in, and so you dominate the new creation that we have become.

So, you can read my mind as well? Tyler asked a bit concerned.

Why not, that is where I reside.

That was true enough—still, it worried Tyler.

What is it you want? To dominate and take control? Tyler didn't know what kind of answer he would get, but he wanted to confront the issue now, while he still had control.

No, no, not to dominate, but to share. Is not part of you a part of me? Why should you get all the control and me just a small corner of your subconscious mind? I too want to experience new worlds, new people and new things, it is why I was created. I traveled the Universe long before you were created, and I have valuable experience. Experience that can help you now!

Tyler thought about it. Was he speaking the truth? He had a good point, it wasn't fair that Tyler controlled it all. But how could he trust him, especially after what Thosolan had told him about the Onyalum?

Why should I trust you? The way you talk, I suspect you assume you have more right than me to control this creation. After all, you have more experience.

Tyler waited, realizing he didn't know what to do regardless of the response. This was new territory, and he wasn't sure how things worked. What if he gave up control and could never get it back? How could he be sure he wouldn't be thrown into the subconscious, Adanni gaining all the control? He couldn't be sure.

It sounds as though you have made up your mind, am I to be trapped down here forever? Adanni's voice seemed broken, no longer pleading. Tyler didn't think it was fair, but he couldn't bring himself to let go of the power he currently held.

Alright, before I give up any control, you must do something to help me trust you.

Name it.

You said you could help me with these memories of the Admiral's. What can you do?

When an Onyalum occupies a body whose spirit has left, the memories of that body are still intact and accessible to the Onyalum. It is how we 'fit in' to the world of that body, by using the memories and becoming that person.

Tyler thought about that for a few seconds, *can these memories take over?* He was curious about the effects from integrating them into his own.

Ordinarily, no, but we are no longer ordinary. I do not think so, but there is no guarantee.

Ok, how do you integrate them in?

Right now, you only have access to them. You have suppressed them like you have suppressed me. Give me control of those memories and I can help integrate them in.

Will I then know the language?

Yes.

Tyler waited, trying to think of how he could give him access without relinquishing all control.

How would I give you control of those memories? I don't even know how I control you.

Easy, simply think about what you want and then focus hard to make it happen.

Tyler hesitated, what if he was simply being led into a trap? What would change after it happened? Would he still be Tyler? The fear began to mount again, holding him back. He resisted the urge to force Adanni back into exile and began to think about giving the Admiral's memories to Adanni. He could sense the barriers holding both back, and in his mind he brought them together.

As the two merged, Tyler felt his barrier begin to weaken, he forced it back up, but couldn't control what the two did now. Suddenly, he felt the memories begin to stream into his consciousness and become one with his own. Instead of the flood as before, they came out slowly and organized. He could see each one individually, calling them up as though they were his own.

It was a unique and strange experience, but he relished it. He no longer feared possession by the memories as they each fell into place among his own. Tyler found he was not confused about which were his memories, and which were the Admiral's.

They streamed on and on until at last they were in place. Every experience from when the Admiral was born until he died was now accessible to Tyler. He ran through them all, learning everything he could, his life was now an open book and Tyler read feverishly.

The Admiral had been born Nayllen Osloo on Poolto, one of two inhabited planets in this system. Poolto was the fourth planet from the sun, and did not contain the wealth of water that, Krildon, the third planet from the sun did. This had always been a problem, and was the primary reason for the war between the two worlds today. Although born on Poolto, the Admiral had spent much of his youth on Krildon as the son of the official ambassador to Krildon.

At ten years of age, his father had sent him back to Poolto to attend the prestigious school of warfare. Although his father didn't agree with war, he had wanted his son to have the advantages and benefits of a life in the military ranks. The Admiral had excelled in all his classes, graduating at eighteen the highest in his class.

Everything his father had hoped for came true, the doors opened up for the Admiral and he moved up through the ranks quickly. Midway through his career while still in the Advanced Space Tactics College, war broke with Krildon. Trade negotiations between the two worlds had fallen apart and the prospect of loosing the precious water Poolto needed forced them into action.

The Admiral's father, Nattur Osloo, was still ambassador to Krildon when the war broke out. Although officially protected under treaties during wartime, Krildon denounced the Admiral's father as a spy and sentenced him to life in prison. His mother, Eynia Heerden, had been sent back to Poolto, no longer welcome on the world she had spent most of her life. It had been years since the Admiral had seen his father, and news of his imprisonment hardened him towards Krildon, a world he had once admired.

Early in the war fighting turned brutal, and weapons of mass destruction had rained down on both worlds killing millions. Because of the horror those attacks had inspired, each world built a system that would protect them from such destruction in the future.

The systems, each modeled after the other from stolen blueprints, consisted of a ring of powerful weapons encircling each planet. The weapons were fully automated and contained enough firepower to destroy any incoming weapon or ship.

The codes for these weapons were the most sophisticated ever made and changed constantly. Only the Imperial Palace of Poolto had access to them.

This new protection changed the course of the war, sending it deep into space. Both worlds waged a war for the precious resources each world mined in the asteroid belt. Immense battles between fleets from both worlds raged for control of the asteroids, planets, and moons that contained the resources each needed to build and sustain their military.

It was in these battles that the Admiral made his mark on the history of Poolto. Known by the enemy as the sorcerer, he won battle after battle with tactics never before seen. His name became legendary and he instantly became a hero to the people of Poolto— a hero the people of Poolto could rally behind. The Emperor knew this and never missed an opportunity to be seen with the Admiral.

The Emperor himself had promoted the Admiral to his current rank, Grand Admiral, the highest military rank of all. He controlled every ship, soldier, and weapon that Poolto had. He was the Supreme Military Commander, the most powerful man on Poolto, after the Emperor.

Early in his career, the Admiral had married. His wife, Toosia Slay, daughter of a prestigious Councilor on the Emperors Supreme Council, came from both wealth and political connections. Although love had not been the driving factor for their marriage, Tyler did note the Admiral had deep affection for his wife. Unable to conceive children, their marriage had deteriorated over the last 10 years as her guilt and depression overtook her life. The Admiral, unable to deal with such emotional problems, distanced himself from his wife, burying himself in his work. The Admiral had not seen his wife in almost two years.

Without a family life, the Admiral's work became his entire life. His primary staff assistant, Eyleeria Snillen, had filled the void left behind by his broken marriage. Their affair had persisted for five years in secrecy, and Tyler now realized why she had been so emotional when he had first awakened and said her name.

The Admiral had a strong attachment to Eyleeria, but love was not a feeling Tyler could locate in the memories. The relationship was a mutual friendship and need brought about by close proximity and the ongoing stress of the war. The Admiral had suspected she wanted more, but he was unwilling to give it. His marriage to Toosia was more than political. The Admiral did actually love his wife, and could never bring himself to destroy her even more with the dissolution of their marriage.

Tyler did not feel prepared to deal with these emotional issues himself. He had always avoided his own emotional situations, and the complexity of this one scared him.

He continued scanning the memories looking for the accident that had brought Tyler into this situation. The memories indicated that the battle over the moon of Krildon had been intended to severely weaken their ability to build and sustain their fleet. It has been intended to be a surprise attack on their maintenance facilities and factories close to their home world.

The Admiral had planned this 'unheard of' attack himself and had limited the knowledge of the operation to only those commanders he trusted. The plan had been to create a diversion on one of the asteroid colonies held by Krildon, drawing off much of their fleet to that distant location.

A new technology Poolto had developed would simulate a large fleet on the war-path, presenting a situation the Krildon military couldn't ignore. Having drawn off much of the Krildon fleet, the Admiral would bring the 'real' fleet to within the very outer range of the weapons protecting the Krildon planet.

From there, they could attack most of the moon bases and orbiting maintenance facilities by overwhelming their protection grid with constant bombardment. The trick was surprise and numbers.

They should have had both, but something had gone horribly wrong. They found out too late that the diversion had not worked. Although it drew off some ships from the Krildon home world, the bulk of their fleet was left intact and ready to fight. Somehow, Krildon had been expecting the attack!

That meant a traitor in the Poolto military. No one but trusted commanders and a very select few bureaucrats knew about the attack. The Emperor knew of course, but his staff was small and heavily trusted. That narrowed the list considerably, but the Admiral had deep trust of his own commanders, having fought side by side with many of them. That left the bureaucrats or someone within the Emperor's staff.

Tyler shrugged it off, although the intrigue of it all did spark his curiosity. He knew he had much greater things to deal with than a mysterious traitor he didn't even know how to trace. It began to sink in that the small-time drug dealer from L.A. may have bitten off more than he could chew. Despite having all his memories, Tyler didn't know how he would pretend to be an Admiral.

I can help you with that as well. Did I not hold up my end of the bargain?

Tyler had to admit, Adanni had given him what he had wanted, but he was still unsure how much he could trust him.

Alright, you came through, a first step towards trust. Let's start with letting you speak as an advisor to me, helping me navigate this world and this body. I will not give over any control of this body to you, yet, but I will let you observe and offer advice. Is this acceptable?

What choice do I have? You hold all the power.

Exactly.

Tyler was certain he'd made the right choice, but he realized it didn't come off very fair. He would have to watch the advice Adanni gave him, if he was one of the Onyalum who corrupted and interfered, he might try to control the situation even behind barriers Tyler had in place.

Don't worry my good friend, my intentions will always be noble!

I hope so, otherwise, I will be forced to exile you permanently. Your point is well taken.

Adanni's inner voice didn't seem to contain malice, so Tyler thought he had found a good starting point for building their relationship. It would have to do for now as Tyler knew he needed Adanni's experience to pull this off.

Geez, the Grand Admiral in a war between two planets! Tyler thought, *I couldn't have picked worse if I'd tried?*

Yes you could have. There was no emotion in Adanni's voice, just a simple statement of fact. Adanni didn't elaborate, and Tyler wasn't sure he wanted to know what could be worse, so he didn't respond.

A dim light crept around the edges of the window shade, and Tyler realized he had spent much of the night with Adanni and the Admiral's memories. He knew someone would soon come, and he wanted to be prepared. With the Admiral's memories integrated, he finally knew the language of these people, but could he speak it.

He practiced before anyone came, making statements, and issuing military commands, or commands as he imagined the Admiral might have made. His memories seemed to confirm this, and it was all that Tyler had to go on. He would have to trust the memories.

After practicing his speech for a while, his memories of the Admiral seemed to confirm he sounded like the Admiral. That was a crucial step. He needed to make a good impression if he were to be released from the hospital, and returned to duty. Although he was scared, Tyler was looking forward to the experiences of this new world.

He lay back on the bed, tired from his efforts, but feeling much better than the previous day. At least he believed it had been the previous day. Sleeping as much as he had, he really wasn't sure how much time had passed.

The door opened slowly and an older woman entered carrying a tray laden with bottles and devices. She hadn't noticed Tyler was awake, and moved across the room to the bureau. She put the tray down and began fussing with the contents. Tyler didn't know what she was doing, but thought this would be a good time to practice his speaking. He took a deep breath.

"Good morning." he said quietly.

The woman stopped what she was doing and turned to face him, a look of disbelief on her face. She stood silent for several moments, and Tyler began to wonder if he had said it right. His memories confirmed he had used the correct greeting for the early part of the day, so he tried again.

"Good morning, what is your name?"

"Uh....oh good morning sir, you caught me off guard, forgive me." She bowed her head slightly, waiting for him to respond.

"Nothing to forgive, what is your name?" he asked once more.

"Yes, my name, well I am Weerna Soldan, I mean nurse Soldan, I work at this hospital." She appeared nervous, and Tyler realized that the Admiral really was a major figure on the planet.

"Well nurse Soldan, please relax, I mean you no ill will."

"Oh! It's not that sir...its just that you have been here so long without talking, it seems almost like a miracle. I'mmm, I'm just very happy sir, that's all." She smiled weakly, but did appear more relaxed.

Tyler thought about what she had said—he had been here a long time. How long he wondered?

"How long have I been here?" he asked calmly.

"Well, I am not sure I should be the one to discuss this with you," she hesitated, "I should go and get doctor Falill to discuss these matters with you." She turned towards the door to leave, but stopped just short.

"Sorry sir, I mean, with your permission, I would like to get your doctor." She bowed her head slightly again, showing extreme deference.

Although her request was strange, he released her to get the doctor. "Yes, you have my permission."

She lifted her head and left quietly through the door. He could hear her rapid footsteps down the hallway before the door closed and left him in silence.

He realized it was better to let her go. Her obvious discomfort in his presence inhibited their ability to communicate, and he wanted someone who was less deferential and could provide facts.

He propped his pillow up and sat back against the backboard, silently waiting for 'his' doctor. The Admiral's memories drew a blank on the doctor's name, but that wasn't surprising, as the Admiral had never needed one.

The Admiral knew the armed forces' Chief Medical Officers, of course, but that relationship was purely official and neither of them even practiced medicine. The Admiral had always made it a general rule to familiarize himself with all the officer's on board his ships, including the medical staff. But beyond the Chief Medical Officer, he rarely had exposure to the medical teams, unless something went wrong.

It surprised Tyler that the Admiral didn't have a personal physician. For someone so important to this world and its safety, Tyler thought the Emperor might demand that he have one. But, this wasn't Earth, and maybe good health was a characteristic of these people. It wasn't something the Admiral's memory necessarily provided for Tyler. He could wait to learn more.

One of the doctors Tyler had seen during the previous encounter strode through the door purposefully, nurse Soldan following close in his wake. She stood slightly to his right and back behind the doctor while he looked over the screen of a small device he held in his palm.

Without looking up, the doctor addressed Tyler.

"I see you are better today Admiral. How do you feel?" With that question, he looked up from his device and smiled slightly at Tyler.

"I feel fine," Tyler responded "I still have some pain in my side and back."

The doctor took this in and quickly wrote something on his device.

"Well, of course you do, the injuries you sustained nearly killed you. To be honest, we were surprised you weren't killed." The doctor jotted more notes on his device before continuing. "After our last encounter, I was beginning to think you might also have serious brain injuries. Your inability to speak or understand us was quite a shock, but I kept the faith that you would recover these abilities. You just needed more sleep and recuperation."

"Yes," Tyler agreed, "well imagine my own surprise at not being able to understand you. How long have I slept since that previous encounter?" Tyler was curious.

"Well," the doctor started, apparently distracted by his devices, "about a week, give or take a day."

"A week?" Tyler said incredulous. To him, it felt like yesterday. "How long since I first got here?"

"Well now, that is amazing!" the doctor began, a look of reminiscing overcoming his face, "I guess its going on about eight months since they brought you here. Of course, that's after about a month on the hospital ship bringing you back from the battle. I tell you, we really were surprised you weren't killed!"

The doctor went back to jotting notes on his device. Tyler thought about the time. Nine months since the accident—it was even hard for Tyler to believe. How had his essence kept the body from dying, clearly it had been severely damaged.

As though reading Tyler's thoughts, the doctored answered his question. "We believe your incredible good health is what sustained you all this time. It is truly remarkable you have never been sick a day in your life." The doctor put his device behind his back and smiled at Tyler.

"Yes, well I am grateful it saved my life." Tyler responded.

"Indeed," the doctor offered, "we certainly can't take the credit. We have simply been providing your basic needs and monitoring you. The medical ship did all the repairs to your body, we have simply been in charge of managing your healing process."

"I see." Tyler could now see why nurse Soldan had been so surprised when he had spoke to her. "Thank you, doctor, for your excellent service."

"No need to thank us Admiral, it is our job!" The doctor turned towards the nurse, "Nurse Soldan, please administer his meds, and help clean him up. I suspect there are more than a few people who want to talk with the Admiral...assuming you feel up to it Admiral?" He turned back towards Tyler, a questioning look on his face.

Tyler was certain he didn't want more company, but he knew he couldn't avoid it forever. Better to face it now and prepare for this new world.

Tyler lied, "Yes, I think I could manage a few visitors."

"Good! Nurse Soldan will help get you ready while I go and spread the good news of your recovery. The Emperor himself has kept a constant vigilance on your progress, so he will be very excited to hear the news!"

With that, the doctor nodded to nurse Soldan and left the room, staring down at his device as he walked.

It took some time for nurse Soldan to clean him up, even with Tyler's help. But after some painful rigors, they were able to dress Tyler in clothes befitting his rank. Various staff members came through, helping nurse Soldan, adding pictures, flags and what Tyler assumed were flowers, to the stark room. It seemed rather unnecessary to Tyler, but he dared not argue the point. He sat back and watched as he was transformed into a rather regal and ostentatious representation of the Admiral.

Looking back through the Admiral's memories, Tyler saw he had to present himself as bigger than life, loyal to the Emperor, the planet, and his troops. Tyler realized that all of this was a necessary evil for someone as important to the planet and its population. He was, after all, a hero to this world.

As the last person hung a large portrait Tyler recognized as the Emperor above his bed, Tyler was ready for more sleep. Instead, he sat upright wearing a rather regal, yet basic, white jump suit with gold and blue trim down the shoulders, sleeves, and front. Although he wore nothing on his head, the thin hair had been washed, trimmed and neatly combed back.

His nails had been trimmed and then sharpened to fine points. This scared Tyler, but a quick check of memories made him realize how important they were for both appearance and for use in touch. On this world, a person's nails were a distinctive aspect of the species, and as adults, their ability to use them was honed with fine motor control. Someone like the Admiral could pick up something as small as a grain of sand between any two nails. Still, they looked like claws to Tyler, and that made him nervous.

On the right side of his chest, small insignias were placed with care in neat rows. Tyler searched the memories to find out what they were and discovered they weren't medals or awards as he first thought, but were marks of the Admiral's rank and years of military service. In all, Tyler felt like he looked pretty good considering he'd been in a coma for nine months.

After the last person left, Tyler sat alone accessing the Admiral's memories. With little effort, he could call up bits of the Admiral's life, different snippets of his world, and more of their language. It was beginning to become automatic. Tyler was quickly becoming fluent in the sing-song language, and though it still required effort to read their language, he felt more confident that it would come in time.

He scanned the transformation of the room, and realized how efficient they had been at modifying the stark room into a room with a distinctive decor. He suspected it had been scripted long before today—waiting for their hero's return to consciousness. The fluidness was not an inherent attribute of people suddenly brought to task, so clearly someone had orchestrated it, and Tyler was fairly certain it was not nurse Soldan.

With the room so quiet, Tyler felt himself begin to nod off. The preparations had tired him out and he longed to sleep once again. He was tentatively excited about what would happen next but still nervous about playing the Admiral. The Admiral was so much bigger than life; a character larger than anyone Tyler had known before. Tyler knew he had enormous shoes to fill, but then he also had access to all the Admiral's memories. He hoped it would be enough to fool whoever was coming.

The sound of the door banging open startled Tyler from his dozing. One man walked straight to the side of the bed while two others stood behind him in crisp military fashion.

The first man wore a similar white suit as Tyler's— appropriately trimmed in gold and blue. On his chest, he also wore the requisite insignia. The man appeared older than the Admiral, and his insignia seemed to confirm this. If Tyler was reading it correctly, this man had over twenty-five years of service to the Admiral's eighteen.

The insignia indicated the man was a Grand Marshall, if Tyler understood the rank correctly. Almost automatically, the Admiral's memories served up everything on the man before him. His name was Grand Marshall Goolen Sliss, and he was the Admiral's most trusted aide, confidante, and advisor. He'd served the Admiral for over seven years, having been passed up for promotion early in his career. Grand Marshall was the highest, non-command rank you could attain in the military.

Marshall Sliss and the Admiral had been a perfect match from the very beginning. The Admiral was the thinker and planner, and the Marshall was the organizer and doer. It was the Marshall who made sure all the plans were carried out properly and to the letter— reporting discrepancies back to the Admiral when necessary. His strengths lay in his efficient organizational skills and his ability to analyze battle plan logistics. More than once, his insights had prevented tragedy from a plan that hadn't taken into consideration all the logistical complications.

Behind the Marshall, two underlings, Vice Secretary Beelen and Command Communications Officer Kooren, stood nearly at attention, though entranced by their handheld devices. Like additional appendages, the Admiral had never seen Marshall Sliss without the two subordinate officers. Both wore dark blue suits trimmed in white as befitting their junior ranks. Both were worker bees, carrying out the Marshall's orders and directing the communications for the Admiral's command staff. Their efficiency was legendary.

Officer Kooren constantly wore communication devices on the left side of his head, attached to his ear. Tyler couldn't call up any memory of seeing him without the devices. As always, he listened intently to whatever traffic was carried across the air waves to the device on his head. As needed, Officer Kooren could relay commands and orders to staff and units almost instantaneously. The Admiral had always admired his efficiency, and had relied upon it many times in tight situations.

Like Kooren, Secretary Beelen also carried a small device. Unlike Kooren, Secretary Beelen's device was not attached to his body and was similar to the one Dr. Fallil had used. It was a communication device, but based on the Admiral's memories, it also served as the official recorder for the Admiral's staff. Tyler realized that these three were inherently responsible for all of the organizational aspects of the Admiral's office. Without them, the Admiral could never function to his maximum capacity.

The minor details of his life, including his personal life, were always handled by Eyleeria. It was these four people Tyler would have to deceive if he was to impersonate the Admiral. Knowing their efficiency and intelligence, he was more than a little concerned.

The Marshall, always efficient, didn't waste any time. With a sharp crispness, he executed what Tyler assumed was some sort of salute, "Sir, it is with the greatest relief and joy that we are able to once again be in your presence."

Quickly recalling how, Tyler returned the Marshall's salute. In response, all three bowed before Tyler. Coming up in unison, they stood crisply, waiting for Tyler.

"Marshall Sliss, Secretary Beelen, and Officer Kooren, I too am overjoyed at this reunion—thank you for your concern." Tyler finished by nodding his head slightly as appropriate for someone of higher rank. He was more than glad the memories were providing him with the required rituals and behaviors the military expected.

With the formalities out of the way, all three relaxed slightly and the two junior officers went back to paying attention to their devices.

The Marshall scanned the room briefly before continuing, "I am satisfied with the efforts the hospital went through to make this room presentable. We have a busy schedule for the next several hours, and we need you to look your best sir." The Marshall signaled for his subordinates to sit down on a couple new chairs brought in during the 're-decorating', while he pulled up one beside the bed.

"As I am certain no one has spoken to you about the incident, or about what has happened since, I must fill you in before the news conference." He sat back in his chair, looking as though he didn't know where to start.

Tyler heard 'news conference' and his anxiety shot through the roof. "What news conference?" he asked, trying to sound casual.

"Not my doing sir," the Marshall pleaded, "you can thank the Emperor for that." Tyler noticed more than a little irritation in the Marshall's voice when he mentioned the Emperor. "We were contacted by one of the Emperor's aides, Banteer Niishen about an hour ago. It appears the Emperor wishes to hold a news conference with you before you answer questions from the press. It starts in two hours, and I have to brief you before then."

"I see," Tyler said, "The Emperor and his hero, reunited again?"

The Marshall gave Tyler a strange look but continued, "Well, yes, it will be a Public Relations stunt and nothing more. Your status as Grand Admiral is naturally a critical element of the war effort, so your absence for the last nine months must be explained."

Tyler thought about that for a minute, "You mean no one has known about my coma?"

"Apart from your staff, the Emperor, his staff, and the hospital workers...no." The Marshall didn't appear the least bit astonished by this fact as he delivered it in a very dry tone.

"After the incident, your staff and the Emperor's decided that such a defeat was not in the best interest of the war effort, so your injuries and recuperation were kept a closely guarded secret."

Tyler couldn't even imagine how they had pulled that off for nine months. He began to respect the authority he had and the significance of his role on this planet.

"What did you tell the public of my disappearance?" Tyler asked.

"That is what we must talk about before the conference."

The Marshall began his briefing, explaining the shock and devastation the incident had on the military. Unable to repair the Admiral's flag ship after the damage it sustained, they had evacuated all the live personnel from the ship before it was plunged into the Krildon moon.

The Marshall quickly ran down the total losses to their fleet: one flag ship, three fast attack cruisers, two squadron carriers, and twenty attack squadrons. All told, it comprised forty percent of the Poolto Fleet. In terms of lives, over twenty-five hundred soldiers had died in the incident—three hundred on his flag ship alone. Officially, they were only reporting a twenty percent loss.

The Marshall explained that this large loss couldn't easily be covered up, so they had made the announcement that the enemy had conducted a sneak attack on one of the fleet's supply stations in the asteroid belt. The Poolto fleet, caught 'off-guard' by the sneak attack, had been unable to come to full battle readiness in time to ward off the attackers.

Although they officially released all the attacker's ships were destroyed, the true amount of damage they had inflicted was less. Still, it was quite large. The official count of the actual losses to the Krildon fleet was approximately half of the 'officially' released losses, or about thirty-five percent of their fleet.

To date, the story held, but questions by family members of the fallen troops, and the persistent bombardment by the press were beginning to mount. Although the Emperor's staff had been quick to denounce the press as unpatriotic when they questioned the incident, they were very careful when responding to the families' inquiries. Many of the families had been provided compensation to 'make-up' for their losses, but the buy off was only going so far.

There was a feeling of unrest and fear on Poolto, and the questions kept mounting. As for the Admiral, it had been reported he'd been elsewhere during the sneak attack, and thus, was able to launch his own retaliatory attach in response. It was this 'retaliatory' battle that had kept the Admiral out of the lime light for the last nine months.

The Marshall admitted they had even brought out old recordings of the Admiral addressing Poolto in rallying speeches now played often on the air. After some creative editing, they had changed it enough that just about everyone had bought the ruse. Today's news conference was to be the triumphant return of the Admiral after his highly successful, secret retaliation against Krildon.

The Marshall confirmed that Tyler was to be interviewed in the hospital, after sustaining some 'minor' injuries during his great battle. At the same time, the Emperor was to present him with the Distinguished Medal of Poolto, his fourth, in tribute to his undying patriotism, courage and dedication to the war effort.

After the ceremony, the Admiral was to field questions about the incident and the retaliatory strike from the press. Each press member had been individually picked by the Emperor's staff and briefed with what questions 'were appropriate'. This was all under the guise of planetary security, so suspicions weren't running high, yet.

The Marshall quickly ran down the details the Admiral would need for the Q and A session. The twenty percent loss of the Poolto fleet in the Krildon sneak attack he already knew. This was followed by only minor losses during the retaliatory battle that had supposedly been launched against the Krildon.

The retaliatory attack had inflicted a staggering sixty percent loss of the Krildon fleet and had reclaimed several asteroid outposts taken earlier in the war by the Krildon. The reality was that the real incident had inflicted only thirty percent damage to the Krildon fleet, and the outposts reclaimed had actually been abandoned prior to the battle due to their lack of resources and non-strategic locations.

Tyler listened to it all, staggered by the immensity of the lie that had been fabricated. He thought of earth, and wondered if the governments had ever done the same thing. He vaguely remembered Nixon, but that seemed small compared to this. He had always assumed the government lied, although there was never any real evidence to support it. But seeing this, he began to think he'd always been right.

The Marshall stopped his recitation, waiting for Tyler to react. Tyler remained silent, trying to decide how best to respond. The Marshall waited beside him with infinite patience.

"Very good Marshall, I'll want to review it with you to be certain I have it down." Tyler lied. His memory recalled every word the Marshall had said, but he needed practice speaking to be sure it sounded real and not rehearsed.

The Marshall nodded his head slightly, apparently satisfied with the response.

"I have other business, military business, which we must attend to as well," the Marshall began, "but your current situation and the pending news conference must take priority. We can address the rest of it tomorrow. I can say, however, it concerns Vice Admiral Teesen, and is of utmost importance."

With that, the Marshall finished, leaving Tyler slightly mystified by the remark. His memory served up Vice Admiral Teesen flawlessly. Teesen had been left behind in charge of the remainder of the fleet. He was more than capable, and the Admiral had relied upon him many times during battles.

His record of service was equally impeccable, and he'd been awarded by the Emperor nearly as many times as the Admiral. The Admiral himself had also awarded him for meritorious service during multiple conflicts. What could be so urgent that the Marshall would mention him? Tyler wondered, but didn't come up with anything.

Tyler hated it when people gave him only a taste of something, holding the rest for later. He remembered Raul, who'd also do that. However, with Raul, Tyler suspected it was intentional, to keep Tyler safe.

Searching the Admiral's memories, Tyler confirmed that this was a common attribute of the Marshall, and that surprisingly, the Admiral did not mind. It bothered Tyler, but he dared not change how the Admiral reacted to it. The Marshall and the Admiral were like a hand and a glove, and Tyler needed to be careful he followed the Admiral's memories as much as possible with the Marshall.

Tyler went over the information the Marshall had given him before both were satisfied he could handle the news conference. The practice made Tyler feel more comfortable, so his anxiety level eased slightly. The Marshall suggested Tyler eat a light meal before the conference, and it was only then that Tyler felt the strong pangs of hunger overcome him.

Tyler wondered how they had fed him while he was in a coma, and he was a little concerned about how he would handle food after so long asleep.

The Marshall sent Secretary Beelen to fetch both food and the doctor, and he asked Officer Kooren to track down the Admiral's assistant, Eyleeria, so she could be there for the conference.

Tyler sat back in the bed and watched as Marshall Sliss launched everything into action with his usual efficient manner. He felt the hunger start to overwhelm him, and he wondered what kind of food these people ate.

Tyler felt much better after eating. The Doctor had recommended a bland and light meal, but it had suited Tyler just fine. Afterwards, they made him wash it down with a series of pills and liquid medications that he was to take regularly for some time. They mentioned what each did, but Tyler had ignored it all, wincing at the horrible taste most had.

As the time approached, Tyler felt a great deal of discomfort. It took him a little while to realize he needed to relieve himself. He wasn't sure where or how, and the Admiral's memories weren't providing answers. He tried not to panic, and finally asked nurse Soldan quietly. Thankfully, she didn't appear embarrassed by the request and called for an attendant to help her take Tyler to the facilities.

Tyler felt weak, but when they tried to get him off the bed and walking, he quickly realized how weak the Admiral's body had become during the coma. The nurse told him about the techniques they used on coma patients to prevent atrophy of the muscles and reassured him his strength and ability to walk would come back quickly. However, she confided that he would probably need some extensive rehabilitation therapy before that would happen.

Tyler sighed at the long road ahead. Nothing he could do, but grin and bear it. Whether accident or intentional, he was stuck in the Admiral's body and had to live with it.

Finally relieved, Tyler was helped back to his bed and was quickly fixed up after the ordeal. It had been difficult having an orderly help Tyler go, and Tyler had seen more than a little concern on the orderly's face. Who really wanted to see their planet's hero unable to relieve himself? It was slightly degrading.

Once again re-assured the Admiral 'looked' ready for the news conference, they left him alone with Marshall Sliss and his aides. Kooren had tracked down Eyleeria, but she seemed almost embarrassed to be there, and wouldn't make eye contact with Tyler. He noted that Marshall Sliss also noticed her discomfort, but made no comment. Tyler didn't know how to react to her, so he simply didn't.

The Marshall began filling in Tyler on the details of the conference: who would be there, how long they would have, etc. Tyler heard it all and knew he wouldn't forget. He believed he was ready, so he patiently waited for it to unfold.

There was a sudden sound of commotion outside the door, and they all turned in unison to see what it was. Finally, Tyler could just make out a very firm voice that seemed to quiet the racket. The door opened softly and a very exquisite woman walked through. She had a very angry look on her face and she leveled an evil glare at the Marshall.

"Marshall Sliss, why have you instructed your men to deny me entrance?"

"I am sorry Mrs. Slay, I had not instructed them to specifically deny you—their orders are to deny anyone not on official business." He bowed slightly as he finished, appearing both ingratiating and arrogant at the same time.

Tyler wondered what the orders really were. Mrs. Slay looked at each one briefly before ordering everyone out of the room. Tyler almost thought she had meant him as well, but she moved another chair close to the bed as she herded everyone from the room. The

Marshall protested that the conference was to begin, but he finally acquiesced and took the two aides with him from the room.

The elegant woman turned towards Tyler and stood quietly assessing him. She wore a long black robe inlaid with shining stones along the opening. Her hair was a pale gray color and shined as brilliantly as the stones that adorned her. She slowly took off her wrap and placed it on one of the chairs, her graceful movements made something inside Tyler excited.

She was beautiful, sensual, and regal. Tyler had yet to see anyone on this world as stunning as her. The part of him that was the Admiral, yearned for this woman, bringing up memories of his wife, Toosia Slay.

When she turned back and saw Tyler looking at her, her face turned angry and she started yelling, yet almost crying at the same time.

"How dare you show feelings like that for me! All these years you have avoided me, shunned me, and now because you are injured you think I will have pity on you and forget everything that has happened? Damn you Nayllen!"

Tyler was more than startled by her reaction. "I…I'm sorry Toosia, I don't know what to say."

"Right!" She spat it out like venom, "You have nothing to say. Do you know how long it took the Marshall to contact me about this? And then, he lied to me about where and how it happened! You know I have my sources, I am not your dumb public waiting for you to tell me what is 'truth'—I know a lie when I'm told one!"

"Darling, I am sorry about that, I had no control, I was in a coma."

"Don't call me darling, at least not when we are alone." She pulled a chair over towards him, but stayed back from the edge of the bed. As she sat down, Tyler could again feel the strong desire intruding on his senses. It contrasted sharply to the poor reception he was getting.

"Damn you Nayllen, what did I say, stop showing those feelings for me!" She turned away abruptly to wipe tears away, but as she turned, Tyler thought he saw a brief rainbow of color flash across her face.

She composed herself and turned back towards him—the colors gone. He wondered at the bright color display and quickly dug into the Admiral's memories for an explanation. He found it! The facial colors were a feature of this species, a mating mechanism that was an integral part of their foreplay. Great, he had been flirting with her!

That was what she had meant about showing his feelings—his own face must have been giving away his feelings of desire. But she too had flashed colors, what did that mean? Maybe there were still feelings there? Tyler wasn't sure, perhaps the response was automatic.

"Look Toosia, I have been in a coma for nine months, give me a break." He tried looking as helpless as he felt, but she looked dubious and angry. "If I am showing my feelings," he quickly continued, "then I am sorry, but that does not change them."

"Really?" the venom was back in her voice, "I saw your assistant...what's her name, Eyleen or something? Don't delude yourself into believing I don't know all about you two!"

"It's Eyleeria." He said quietly.

"Whatever, I don't care!" she screamed, "if you have feelings for me, then why aren't you with me instead of her?"

She broke down again, a look of grief replacing the anger that had been there. Tyler watched helpless and saddened. What could he say? He'd always loved Linda and had never strayed from her from the time they first met. This was something entirely foreign to him.

He searched desperately in the Admiral's memories, looking for something he could offer up. It was clear the Admiral still had strong feelings for his wife, but they had drifted apart after their failure to conceive. Tyler imagined it would be a monumental task to repair the damage so many years had wrought.

She wiped tears from her eyes and composed herself.

"They tell me you will be leaving here to recuperate at Tooland, I hope you don't expect me to be there?" Tyler was surprised at how quickly she switched topics, "The truth is, I have been staying with my parents in Baneer for the last six months. Father is very concerned about the events unfolding lately, and he fears that the planet is about to crumble. I have been there trying to support you and your efforts to the council, but many are beginning to harbor ill feelings towards the war."

Tyler didn't like the sound of that. The last thing he wanted to experience was a civil war on an alien planet.

"Do they still support the Emperor?" he asked.

She looked a little startled by the question, "Yes, of course they support the Emperor, and you as well. They simply are beginning to question the cost of this war and whether it can be won. I have even heard rumors of possible peace talks with Krildon. Father does not think it possible, but I suspect even he is thinking about it."

She sat back in her chair, a look of exhaustion on her face. Tyler could feel the desire and love for this woman well up inside of him. He wondered how the Admiral could have ever left this woman, a woman he so obviously had loved. It made Tyler think of Linda again, and a deep sadness descended over him.

"My own father believed there could be peace, even after they imprisoned him." The memory of the Admiral's father filled Tyler with even greater sadness. He knew he needed to snap out of the malaise or he would never survive the news conference. "Peace or not, neither side is in any position to do anything about it. As long as we move forward with this ruse, the people will rally for blood. That, I am sure, is what the Emperor wants."

"Of course he does! Why do you think I am here, out of concern for you?"

Tyler heard the anger creeping in again. The comment hurt, but he figured the Admiral deserved it.

She went on dramatically. "He wants me here in this time of hero worship—the epic hero and his devout wife, concerned for his safety and that of the planet." Tyler didn't think sarcasm suited her. "I'll play his games, but only because I do care about this world and its people!"

She got up from the chair and moved it back against the wall. Grabbing her wrap again, she put it around her shoulders and snapped the intricate clasp holding it in place. Her face looked as beautiful as when he first saw her. She was once again a commanding presence, in control and looking very determined.

"I will not leave you Nayllen, not yet at least. I could not do that to you or my family during this time of crisis; however, if we ever see some resolution to this war, I do not want to be your wife anymore."

She delivered the statement with no emotion, but Tyler could see the strain it caused her. His memories dredged up happier times, after the Admiral had first met Toosia, and after they were first married. He was a young, brash new officer, moving up fast, and she was the beautiful young daughter of a Councilor, intelligent, witty, and oh so beautiful.

Tyler could access all the reasons they had drifted apart, but it still made no sense to him. It was hard for Tyler to imagine why the inability to have children could cause such a deep and saddening loss. But then, isn't that what had been happening to he and Linda? Didn't his career and his fears get in the way of something beautiful? Suddenly, he understood it a little better.

"Toosia...I..." he wasn't sure what to say, "...I cannot stop you from leaving, and I really don't blame you. I am the one to blame in this, I was the one who left you and buried myself in my work."

He wasn't sure how this was affecting her; she stood stolid in her resolve. He continued nonetheless.

"The war made it easy for me to be gone, but that is no excuse for not calling, writing, or contacting you. The great leader, conqueror of worlds, couldn't even deal with his own life!"

He saw a small waver in her resolve and she looked away briefly, avoiding his direct eye contact.

He pressed on. "It was easier for me to ignore your problems, ignore our problems and only focus on the next battle. Somewhere during that time, I became incredibly lonely, missing you, but afraid to come back. Eyleeria was someone near, someone who wanted to help. Like you, I have also hurt her."

She looked back at him, a look of surprise on her face. He imagined she couldn't believe this admission. He didn't know whether the real Admiral would have done this, but Tyler didn't care, he needed an ally, some one to help him be the Admiral during this difficult period in the planet's history. He wanted her, but he was fairly certain the feelings would not be mutual.

Once again, she wiped a small tear from her eyes, looking down to hide her discomfort. He knew everything he said was not what she had expected or even wanted. Rejection would have been easier, and he could see it was probably what she wanted.

"I will not ask you to stay or to forgive me, I am not worthy of your forgiveness. He knew that was true, "All I ask, is that you visit me, just once, while I am recuperating. You don't have to stay, just stop in and let me talk with you for a little while. I don't want this to be the last time we ever speak to each other, I have more I wish to say to you."

The question was obviously unexpected, and he could see her struggling with it.

"Damn you Nayllen! Damn you!"

Tears welled up in her eyes, but she quickly got them under control, still refusing to look at him. He could read indecision in her face, and she was about to speak when the door opened up and several people streamed into the room.

The lead person stood just inside the doorway, eyeing both Tyler and Toosia carefully. On either side of him, small functionaries filed into the room carrying a devices they aimed and scanned across the room and furniture. It was the Emperor's Aide, Regent Anweer Sneerd.

"Ahhh, Admiral and Mrs. Slay, my deepest apologies at this interruption, but the Emperor is on his way and we mustn't delay the conference."

He bowed slightly at each of them, but a smug look hid behind his jovial face. The Admiral's memories provided ample dislike for this person, and by the look on Toosia's face, he assumed she felt the same way.

When the Regent spoke, his voice came out somewhat high pitched and grating. It contrasted sharply with his commanding presence. Like almost everyone else, he wore a black single-suit, trimmed with an intricate design across the chest and down the sleeves.

On his shoulders, garish white lapels fluffed thick, almost obscuring his thin neck. His face was a thin oval shape, with dark penetrating eyes, that Tyler was certain missed nothing. On his head, he wore a round cap that reminded Tyler of something he'd seen Jewish people wear. This cap was also black, and it contrasted with the man's pale gray features. Tyler decided the overall effect was evil.

The Admiral's memories provided Tyler with a complete picture. Regent Sneerd was the second most powerful man in the Imperium, behind the Emperor himself. He was the equivalent to Marshall Sliss, but working for the Emperor. His ruthlessness and efficiencies were legendary, and he was not a man you wanted to cross paths with. The Emperor gave him carte blanche to carry out whatever 'policies' he saw fit to administer the Empire. Tyler could sense from the memories that the Admiral had been cautious around this person.

"Regent Sneerd, we were just finishing up, no need to apologize." Tyler hoped it sounded convincing—he was certain he needed to fool this person.

Toosia gave him a small nod, however a look of disgust was present on her face. "Indeed, how could the Emperor's Regent ever be an interruption?" The sarcasm dripped from her words, and it was not lost on the Regent, who simply smiled, and nodded his head slightly.

Tyler watched as a sudden flurry of activity swirled around them. He wondered what they were up to as they inspected every single item in the room, even the bed.

"Excuse me Regent, but what exactly are these people looking for? My people brought all this in earlier, and I trust it meets with any requirements the Emperor would have?"

"Indeed Admiral, it is adequate," he said adequate like a rich person visiting poor relatives, "we are simply doing a minor security sweep, nothing to worry about."

"Security sweep! Whatever for? I am sure Marshall Sliss has checked everything—twice at least."

"Indeed, Marshall Sliss is notoriously efficient, and yet, one can never be too careful. One wouldn't want anything to happen to the

Emperor, would one?" He leveled a measuring look at Tyler as he said that last part. It made Tyler feel uneasy.

"No indeed, 'one' wouldn't want anything to happen to the Emperor." Tyler tried to keep sarcasm out of his voice. "Is there a threat to his eminence that we should be aware of? I have always believed that he was loved by all his people."

"Oh yes, he is loved! No threat is present that we are aware of, but troubled times call for greater scrutiny. After all, we can never be satisfied when it comes to our Emperor."

Tyler was dubious, he smelled something else behind the action, but he didn't know what.

Like Tyler, Toosia looked dubious, she leveled an unbelieving stare at the Regent before speaking.

"Then the War opposition movement does not have anything to do with this?"

Tyler was a stunned by her statement. Even if her father was a councilor, Tyler didn't think this was an appropriate question to ask the head of the Imperial Staff.

"Ahhhh," the Regent appeared casual considering the brashness of the question, "you mean those few disgruntled families who have lost loved ones in the war? They are of no concern to the Emperor; we have addressed their grievances...adequately."

Tyler wondered what 'adequately' meant. He didn't get the sense this man would give anything to anyone without something in return. Tyler could almost imagine 'adequately' meaning 'deadly', but memories told him that although the Regent was a dangerous man, he wasn't open or predictable. People had been known to disappear from time to time, but no one had ever linked these things to the Imperial Palace.

As though satisfied with their efforts, the various functionaries nodded faintly to the Regent before filing out. The Regent nodded back in approval as they filed past. As the last of the security left, the Regent followed them to the door with one hand held up to his left ear. As he turned slightly, Tyler could see a small communication device attached to his ear. The Regent stood by the door with his back turned towards them while he whispered quietly.

Tyler couldn't make out anything he said but noticed something odd with the hand the Regent held to his ear. Tyler hadn't noticed before, but one finger on his hand had an extraordinarily long set of nails. All three nails were at least four inches long, and looked extremely sharp. While his hand cupped the device, the dangerous nails tapped gently against the side of his head. Even at four inches, the nails looked lethal.

Along the outside nail, Tyler could make out a design or some form of writing. He didn't recognize it from across the room, but the effect enhanced the Regent's evil appearance.

The Regent turned back towards Tyler and dropped his hand away from his ear. As if this were a cue, several functionaries once again filed into the room carrying lighting equipment and what Tyler thought was a camera.

The Regent eyed them closely before directing them to set up the equipment. Within minutes, the room had been transformed into a small TV studio. Considering the small size of the room, Tyler wondered where the reporters would stand now that the equipment had been added.

Tyler felt a deep unease as he realized the conference was about to begin. He suddenly felt inadequate for such an undertaking and felt a pang of fear at being uncovered as a fraud. Toosia moved to the left side of his bed, and Tyler had an overwhelming urge to grab her hand. Unfortunately, after their first encounter, he was certain she would react poorly to that action.

As though reading his mind, she gently reached out towards him, but instead of grabbing his hand, she carefully smoothed out the bed covers across his lap. She gave him a curt smile before returning to her position next to him. Tyler wanted to finish their earlier conversation and hoped they would have time after the conference.

He readied himself for the ordeal, trying to put down the fear he felt. Tyler knew that the Admiral had never been nervous in front of either cameras or the Emperor, so he desperately tried to calm himself. He could feel the presence of the Admiral's memories pressing upon him, and he let them take over while he pulled back watching from a distance.

Tyler was still afraid that the Admiral's personality might overtake his own, but he was willing to risk it to pull off the news conference.

Adanni, the voice from within, whispered quietly in Tyler's mind.

Let me take over? I have a great deal of experience with this sort of thing. Once, I was a King for over eighty years on one world. These are simple beings, I can easily handle them. Let me help you?

Tyler felt a brief temptation by the offer but wasn't ready to share control. The Admiral's memories were one thing, but an alien spirit was something else entirely. He rejected the offer and reinforced it with a small show of force. Adanni backed off, but not before pleading for a chance to watch. Tyler conceded, but kept a tight leash on the menacing presence.

The Regent, once again cupping his ear, suddenly made an announcement. "The Emperor is coming!"

The Regent opened the door and stood looking out into the hallway. Holding the door while bowing, the Regent backed into the room slightly. Without shifting from his uncomfortable position, he heralded the Emperor's arrival.

"All please hail the Emperor Hallen Yooso IV, Ruler of Poolto, and Savior to its people."

Tyler bowed as much as he could while sitting in bed. Several tough looking security men filed into the room wearing black single-suits, earpieces and side arms. Two of the men moved to one side of the room while the others stayed just inside the doorway. They didn't bow, but stared directly forward as though no one else were in the room. Tyler was certain these men were watching everything.

The camera and lighting crew bowed deeply, their eyes looking directly at the floor below them. Even Toosia bowed deeply, her face rather neutral.

The Emperor walked slowly into the room, scanning it quickly with a measured stare. He paused inside the doorway and waited quietly for several moments. No one moved or made a sound.

The Emperor turned his head slightly toward the Regent who still held the door open. "Thank you Regent Sneerd, your introduction was as eloquent as always."

That was the signal everyone had been waiting for. Everyone stood up from their bow and returned to normal. The Regent closed the door behind the Emperor who walked slowly towards Tyler's bed side.

Tyler was amazed, the Emperor was rather small and diminutive than the Admiral's memories seemed to suggest. The Emperor wore a shining gold single-suit, but no insignia, trim, or markings. Other than being gold, it was rather unremarkable. Tyler wasn't sure what he had expected, but something more regal came to mind.

"Admiral Osloo, I cannot tell you how happy I am to have my Supreme Commander back with us again. Regent Sneerd can tell you how concerned I was after your great battle. We were certain we had lost you that time…but alas, you have this remarkable way of surviving these horrible battles…despite the odds." He gave Tyler a tight smile, "For this, we are truly grateful!"

The Emperor's voice was soft, almost soothing. He spoke quietly, and yet was a commanding presence. Tyler began to realize why this man didn't wear any mark of his office—his presence alone commanded the respect.

"Thank you your eminence," Tyler bowed slightly, "I too am happy to have survived."

That had been the truth, and Tyler felt compelled to tell the truth to the Emperor. Although the Emperor's face was almost warm, something deep in his eyes were cold and calculating. Tyler found him menacing but not as openly as the Regent. Nonetheless, Tyler couldn't imagine anyone expressing 'love' for this man—he simply didn't have the look of a benevolent dictator.

The Emperor looked away from Tyler and directly at Toosia. Tyler hoped she wouldn't say anything confrontational like with the Regent.

"Good to see Toosia, how is your father and mother?"

"Very well your eminence, thank you." She stared back as an equal, but didn't appear confrontational, "They long to be invited to one of your palace affairs again—it has been too long without one."

The Emperor gave her a large smile, "Indeed it has!" he easily agreed, "I too long for another affair, but duty keeps me so very busy." He glanced at Tyler, "Nasty affair war, very nasty."

Tyler was fairly certain the Emperor didn't mean what he said, but the way he said it made Tyler almost believe the Emperor hated war. The war had solidified the people behind their Emperor and had forced aside the domestic issues that usually kept the public pre-occupied. Tyler wondered how 'beloved' the Emperor would be if there wasn't a war?

Again, the Emperor gave Toosia a smile, "Thankfully, I have people like your husband to help us through these difficult times. We are eternally indebted to his selfless service."

Toosia gave a curt smile, Tyler could sense tension. He was sure the 'selfless service' didn't sit well with Toosia. Who else, other than her, would know what the Admiral's service had cost? Tyler believed the Emperor knew the true cost to their 'marriage', so he couldn't work out why the Emperor had made the comment. Tyler was pleased to see that Toosia didn't rise to the bait and maintained her neutral expression.

The Emperor turned back to Tyler, "Tell me Admiral, are you ready for this news conference? I realize it is soon after your 'recovery', but your planet needs you…" he paused as though considering, "I need you." He finished almost sounding sincere.

"Yes, I am ready." Even Tyler answered, he felt decidedly 'un-ready'.

"Good!" the Emperor exclaimed, "I assume the good Marshall has filled you in on everything up till now?"

Tyler shook his head in agreement, "Yes, he prepared me well your eminence."

"Unfortunate really…I regret having to proceed in this fashion, but as servants to our world, we must always put Poolto and its people before our own needs."

Tyler didn't think it was Poolto the Emperor was thinking of. "Yes, we must think of Poolto first." he agreed without emotion.

With a measured stare, the Emperor stood quietly. Tyler was certain he hadn't sounded sarcastic, but looking at the Emperor now, he wasn't so certain.

"Well...yes then, we can proceed together." The Emperor said calmly.

Tyler thought the Emperor's statement sounded more like a question than a statement. He wondered if the Emperor were sizing him up, trying to see where the Admiral stood on the issue of the great lie. The Emperor's reaction made Tyler suddenly worried and he quickly followed with a response.

"The Admiral is always with his Emperor, in all matters." He finished with a bow of his head, hoping the deference would calm the Emperors fears.

The Emperor gave Tyler another of his tight smiles, "Indeed you are Admiral, indeed you are!"

Tyler churned inside. He knew that if he couldn't fool the Emperor, he would not survive the experience. As a drug dealer, Tyler had often dealt with dangerous men in power but he didn't really have any experience with men such as the Emperor or the Regent. Leaders of an entire planet wielded great power beyond that of a simple drug dealer, and Tyler felt completely inadequate to the task.

He wondered at what he'd gotten into? When he had left Thosolan, he'd imagined experiencing a simple life; becoming a farmer, or a common laborer. But now, Tyler found himself in the midst of a planetary conflict where he was the national hero.

He'd seen enough movies to know about the threats near the top. Paranoia was common, and he remembered all to well the time when Raul had told him about the constant vigilance he maintained to keep his position. At the time, Tyler hadn't paid much attention to the comment, but now, he was beginning to understand what it meant.

The Emperor scanned the room once more before turning towards the Regent, "Regent, I believe we are ready to proceed!"

Tyler was almost relieved. At least the awkward moments with the Emperor were over. The Regent opened the door and briefly conversed with several people filling the hallway. Quietly and quickly, four people entered the room, bowing deeply to the Emperor as they took up positions at the end of the bed.

The Emperor, quietly on Tyler's right side, watched intensely as the conference got underway. The Regent closed the door and stood in front of it, staring back at the camera behind the reporters. He nodded a signal and the lights and camera were switched on.

The camera pointed directly at Regent Sneerd who stood calmly, apparently waiting a cue to begin. Tyler didn't catch the cue, but suddenly the Regent spoke.

"In cooperation with the Poolto Communication Ministry, his Majesty, and the Supreme Council, I present to you, The Emperor Hallen Yooso IV, Ruler of Poolto, and Savior to its people!"

In unison, everyone in the room bowed except the cameramen who focused in on the Emperor. The Emperor stood passively, a newly uncovered look of concern filling his features. Tyler could just make him out as he bowed slightly.

"Thank you people of Poolto, I appreciate the time you have allowed me to speak with you today." Everyone in the room stood upright. "It is with great concern, but much happiness that I stand before you today in a hospital where our fearless Supreme Commander, Admiral Nayllen Osloo, recuperates from injuries sustained in an epic battle in retaliation for the cowardly act of violence set upon us nine months ago. Our heroic Admiral was successful in his mission, ravaging the enemy fleet, and taking back resources that were stolen from us long ago."

Tyler was amazed at the cool composure and sincere emotion the Emperor poured into his speech. Tyler almost believed it himself.

"...we must stand together in this time of need, steel our resolve, and pay back, in kind, those losses we have suffered due to their evil purpose...Today, we are here to both celebrate this great victory, and to once again mourn our great loss. We have been spared the loss of our Admiral, a warrior unlike any our enemy has ever faced. Indeed, his name spreads fear amongst their kind, and they no doubt rejoiced when they thought him bested...But fear is what they will once again feel after Admiral Osloo destroyed sixty percent of their fleet and survived to tell the tale! Once again, his name invokes nightmares in their dreams, fear in their hearts, and doom in their souls!"

Tyler was overwhelmed by the speech. He wasn't sure he liked putting fear into anyone's heart, let alone doom in their souls. It was a very powerful speech and Tyler did not doubt it would rally the planet once again.

"...pleasure that I award our Admiral, in some small way, for his courageous, untiring, and loyal service to our great cause. Once again, I am honored to present the prestigious Distinguished Medal of Poolto to Admiral Nayllen Osloo for his dedication to the war effort, and his extreme courage under fire against our enemies."

Regent Sneerd brought a small box forward and handed it to the Emperor. The Emperor opened the box and held the contents towards the camera, a large smile upon his face. He almost looked like a proud father, presenting the winning trophy to his son after the 'big' game. He seemed so genuine, Tyler wondered what he truly felt for 'his' Admiral.

The Emperor shook Tyler's hand before handing him the box and its medal. As dictated by protocol, Tyler bowed and accepted the award. Just as quickly, the Emperor continued his passionate presentation.

"Thank you once again Admiral, we hope you will heal soon to once again serve your planet and its great people." He turned back to the camera, an expression of concern once again returned, "We must now move this conference forward so that we do not interfere with the Admiral's recovery. Before we leave, however, we would like to field a few questions from the press we have invited here today. Gentlemen, you may proceed." He gestured magnanimously at the four reporters at the foot of the bed.

Tyler had no doubt this was all scripted for the public. The order of questions had already been decided, and the man stepped forward slightly, holding out some sort of device towards the bed.

"Your Eminence, we have the official report of the revenge Admiral Osloo inflicted upon our enemies, but if you can, share with us what reports you hear from Krildon?"

"That is a wonderful question, and I would love to share this with you all. Although I cannot reveal how we come by this information, I can tell you it is both accurate and from Krildon. The Krildon people, arrogant from their barbarous attack on our fleet nine months ago, are reeling with the news of our counter attack the Admiral led against them. As I said before, our Admiral's name invokes fear in their hearts and wipes away the arrogance from their face. They are a defeated people, and will not be able to move against us for a long time. Next question please."

The first man moved back again, making room for the second reporter. "Admiral, how did you sustain your injuries, and how serious are they?"

Tyler, as rehearsed, ran down the cover story as best he could, "I sustained my injuries after our flag ship was struck by an enemy missile. We had sustained extensive damage prior to that, and our shielding had already failed. Fortunately, the hit was not directly to the bridge…or I might not be here today."

Tyler recited the script perfectly and hoped it sounded sincere. He noted that the dramatic content was having an impact on the people in the room, and recognized the irony in how the real event wasn't far from their fictional one.

"Once we had chased the remnants of their fleet from the battle, I was picked up by a hospital ship and transported back to Poolto. I am happy to report that my injuries are not serious, and the Doctor assures me I will make a full recovery very soon."

The Emperor quickly jumped in, "While our good Admiral is recovering from his injuries, I have been told he has appointed Vice Admiral Teesen to Command our troops in his absence. We both have nothing but the utmost confidence in Admiral Teesen's ability to protect our world. Thank you, next question please."

Of course, Tyler hadn't made been the one to appointment Admiral Teesen, so he wondered who had. His first guess was the Emperor, and this made him uneasy, especially after Marshall Sliss' cryptic comments concerning Teesen.

With only one reporter to go, Tyler felt more relaxed. He wanted it over, and hoped afterwards to get more information about what was 'really' happening. If the Admiral was in a coma for nine months, many things had probably changed. He was beginning to fear the Admiral had lost power during that time. The failure the fleet suffered in their attempt to attack Krildon would undoubtedly blemish what had been an incredibly illustrious career.

Tyler knew he was in over his head, but there was nothing he could do to change that now. He thought back to Thosolan's words and tried his best to focus on making this a successful experience.

He snapped out of his reverie as the last reporter asked his question.

"Considering the damage both fleets suffered, how do you see the war continuing, and do we have an opportunity to take advantage and win it?"

The reporter stood looking at Tyler holding out a recording device for him to respond. Tyler knew the scripted answer and began reciting it word for word. Although he didn't believe they could win the war, he also felt certain their enemy couldn't either. It sounded, at least, like stalemate was the current state of the war. He finished his litany and added a brief wish at the end, "…and with the help of God, we may yet smite our enemies!"

Tyler thought the comment appropriate for someone in power. He had heard it so many times back on earth. He waited patiently for the conference to finish but noted the room fell deathly silent. He looked around at the stunned faces, suddenly realizing he had made a terrible mistake. The reporter stood up with an astonished look on his face and then continued to question Tyler.

"So Admiral, does this mean that you have found faith in God during your ordeal and now seek his assistance in our War?"

Tyler was taken aback, he had mentioned God, but didn't really mean anything by it. Why did the reporter seem so curious about it, it was only a comment. Tyler was ready to respond when Regent Sneerd dashed forward and took control.

"The Admiral doesn't believe in this 'new' religion, he simply made a mistake in his comment. There is nothing to it gentlemen, nothing at all!"

The Emperor gave Tyler a quick glance, a look of concern or maybe anger on his face. As quick as it was there, it was gone.

The Emperor took over, "Poolto, we are greatly rewarded with our Admiral's continued success and survival during this trying period in our history; however, the Admiral must take his leave to complete the recuperation process and once again join our campaign against Krildon aggressions. Thank you for this brief opportunity and continued sacrifices during our time of need. We will keep you up to date on the progress of the Admiral's recovery. Thank you and good day."

The Emperor finished with a slight nod toward the camera, a signal to end the broadcast. The light on the camera went out and both sets of lights in the room went dark, temporarily blinding everyone in the sudden darkness.

Tyler was reeling from what had happened, trying to figure out where he had made a mistake. Perhaps mentioning God hadn't been a good idea after all? Although it seemed reasonable to him, apparently it was taboo on this world. Tyler had actually met the god of this world, so giving some acknowledgement seemed natural.

The room came alive with chatter, mostly from the reporters. The Regent, quickly took control of the situation.

"The Emperor Hallen Yooso IV, Ruler of Poolto, and Savior to its people, thanks you for your gracious participation in this very important communication to our world. His eminence will now take his leave."

The room became deathly silent and everyone bowed in unison. Tyler bowed as much as he could from his position in bed, and noted that the Emperor continued to stand next to him, staring down intensely. Tyler continued to stare at the bed sheets across his lap, beginning to get nervous as the Emperor stood silently beside him. Finally, the Emperor spoke, breaking the tension in the room.

"Admiral," he began, "we look forward to the return of your 'old' self to duty. We will look in on your progress with special interest."

With that, the Emperor's guards filed out of the room followed quickly by the Emperor. Once the door closed behind him, everyone rose and stood staring expectantly at Regent Sneerd.

"Gentlemen, we appreciate your cooperation in this important matter. We ask that you bear with us for a few more minutes while we debrief from this conference downstairs. My attendants will direct you appropriately as you come off the elevator."

He nodded at the reporters who seemed not the least put out with the request. Tyler thought the 'debrief' sounded a bit ominous, and was glad he would not be participating in it. He knew that his rank would keep him from such mundane affairs.

Tyler watched everyone file from the room carrying the many pieces of equipment needed for the conference. The Regent held the door as they passed and then lingered briefly in the doorway as though he wanted to say something. Instead, he merely bowed slightly to both Tyler and Toosia before walking through the door and disappearing into the corridor beyond.

As the door closed, the room grew and silent. It was hard to imagine they had just held a National News Conference broadcast around the Poolto Empire. Tyler was glad it was over, but he knew his performance would be intensely scrutinized. He glanced at Toosia who stood quietly next to him, staring at the floor in thought, a look of concern on her face. Tyler wanted to press her further, get her to come and visit him during his recuperation. He opened his mouth to ask the question, but was rudely interrupted by people moving into the room once again.

He turned to see Marshall Sliss enter the room followed closely by his aides and the Admiral's assistant, Eyleeria. Eyleeria stood behind the other three staring innocuously around the room, avoiding direct eye contact with Tyler or Toosia. Tyler caught her give Toosia one hard glare, but quickly backed off when she saw Tyler watching.

Toosia, however, ignored them all. He wanted to ask her to wait, but the Marshall was irritated and pressed Tyler to discuss the conference.

Tyler acquiesced, and the Marshall began his own 'debriefing'. Without a word, Toosia quietly slid out behind everyone. Tyler watched helplessly as the door closed behind her. He knew he'd have to track her down, and once again pick up their conversation. Strange feelings for her ran through Tyler and he didn't know if they were his or the Admiral's. Either way, he had to talk with her again. Perhaps she would wait until they were done? He thought about asking Eyleeria to go and tell Toosia to wait, but stopped himself as he realized the inappropriateness of that request.

As Tyler listened to the Marshall, he realized his experience on this world had started off poorly. His thoughts drifted back to the crippled ship, and he wondered why he hadn't been more careful. In the future, he would be more vigilant.

Calm before the Storm

Tyler had been fully 'de-briefed' after the conference on his one mistake. Apparently, the Imperial Palace had abolished religion long ago. In its place, the Imperial families had placed themselves as the 'spiritual' head of the planet, claiming no god existed to believe in.

After several millennia of rule, the religion had disappeared, and very few people still held onto the beliefs. Unfortunately, as a result of the war, old religions began making come backs. People were flocking to the religions, calling upon god to help them in their time of need.

The Imperial Palace was careful not to prosecute the heads of these religions for fear of making martyrs out of them. Instead, the palace went out of their way to spread lies and propaganda against the religious movement, making sure to downplay the actual size and rate of growth. These people were labeled as 'disgruntled' citizens, whose unpatriotic beliefs and actions worked against their common cause. However, they stopped short of calling them 'enemies of the state'.

Tyler's comment had rocked the fragile boat. Considering the current crisis and the fabrication of their 'lie', Tyler's comment threatened to release forces currently held at bay. At Marshall Sliss' urging, they had quickly released a press briefing that indicated the Admiral had no link to, or sympathy for those 'few' people espousing a belief in the dead religions. It went on to point out how dangerous these 'old' beliefs could be, and how they threatened the very war effort they needed to win.

To date, most in the press and the general public seemed satisfied with the rebuttal. Since the religious people were a 'fringe' element of the planet, it was easy to convince most people that their national hero could not conceivably be a part of it.

Tyler did believe Thosolan was not involved with this planet's affairs. Thosolan had admitted to letting his creations evolve on their own for millions of years. However, a part of Tyler wondered what god the old religions believed in. Did they believe in Thosolan? Maybe it was some other god? Thosolan by another name? More than one?

He was curious, but knew it was far too dangerous to ask questions. He was already neck deep, so now he tried to smooth out the wrinkles and get a better feeling for this world and his role within it.

Tyler had stayed an additional week in the hospital after the press conference. Doctors ran several additional series of tests before announcing he was fit enough to move. His plan had been to move into his Tooland estate to recuperate and undergo physical therapy. Tyler was pleased to leave the hospital, despite the excellent care nurse Soldan had provided. He wanted to be far from the public eye, somewhere that he could focus on healing and learning.

During his last week in the hospital, Tyler had tried tracking down Toosia. He'd failed on every attempt. He left numerous messages, both verbal and written, but received no replies. These regular attempts to contact her brought frowns from both Marshall Sliss and his assistant, Eyleeria.

He understood Eyleeria's position, but wasn't certain about the Marshall's'. Perhaps the Marshall and Toosia harbored ill will towards each other? Tyler searched, but the Admiral's memories could neither confirm nor deny this. He wasn't yet comfortable to press the Marshall about such person things, but it didn't stop his failed attempts.

At one point, Tyler suggested contacting Toosia's father in the Supreme Council. The Marshall had adamantly opposed the idea. According to the Marshall, there were many members on the council who were not happy about the 'lie' they perpetrated against the public, and the fact that the national hero went along with it, had forced all of them to comply. Admiral Osloo was not very popular with many on the Council, including Toosia's father.

Despite these troubling reports from the capital city, Tyler continued his daily attempts to contact her. He didn't lose hope yet, but began wondering whether she would ever speak with him again. Nonetheless, he refused to give up.

After his release from the hospital, the ride to Tooland had been both interesting and peaceful. Although this world had a lot of technology, they still maintained much of the natural beauty the planet had to offer. Both the technology and the culture were more advanced than earths, and that made it all the stranger that humans and these creatures were so similar.

These comparisons to earth pre-occupied Tyler as the ground car carried him silently to the Admiral's Tooland Estate. The vehicle was a marvel to Tyler. Somehow, it hovered quietly about three feet above the roadway. Tyler didn't understand the physics involved, but memory revealed the force to be created by something called 'Paaymeen'. Unfortunately, the word had no translation in English. Tyler didn't care, as long as it worked. As he replayed his memories of earth, he realized he didn't really know exactly how a car on earth had worked. Regardless, the ride was absolutely smooth and quiet, even at speeds which blurred everything along the roadside.

Tyler estimated the ride at about four hours. Along the way, he had searched the Admiral's memories for information on the estate. The Tooland Estate had been in his family's possession for many generations. His parents had given it to the Admiral and Toosia as a wedding gift, but the Admiral had rarely spent time there. Tyler figured it was partly due to the fact that it was in a very remote, mountainous part of the planet, but primarily because the Admiral's work had always kept him in the capital city or space.

Toosia had never liked the estate because of its remoteness and lack of a husband. Although the estate continued to run and operate as if people lived there, neither he nor Toosia had been there in over five years. The last time the Admiral had visited, it was to overlook paperwork regarding the production of the 'Sloose' berry wine the estate produced to help offset taxes.

As the ground car wound its way up the mountain to the estate, it slowed to a more modest speed allowing Tyler to watch some of the incredible scenery this part of the world offered. This country was very mountainous with enormous peaks soaring thousands of feet above them. Although the mountains were primarily rock, here and there, Tyler saw small patches of green revealed in crevices and spread across valley floors. The rock itself was nearly black with streaks of white and gray to break it up. It appeared both hostile and beautiful at the same time.

He tapped the Admiral's memories for the regional history of the area. The estate was embedded in a long chain of mountains that split the continent into separate pieces. Originally, the region had been home to the Admiral's ancestors for thousands of years. At one point in history, they had been the seat of power for the continent.

The people of this region had been both powerful and warlike. Their positions in the mountains had provided the perfect defense, and those from the flatlands constantly waged war in an attempt to claim the land. The Admiral's ancestors were known as some of the fiercest warriors in the history of Poolto.

Their mountain fortresses were legendary as they had been easy to defend and hard to assail. For thousands of years, their power and position separated them from the rest of the continent. It wasn't until the second Emperor, Goolo Deena II, established peace between the Admiral's people and the Empire.

Now, after thousands of years under imperial rule, the world had become smaller and the history became legend as it was gradually forgotten. The tribes and regional cultures of the past no longer held meaning for the current people, and the regional differences and beliefs had been replaced by a common set of ideals created by the Imperial Palace.

This was especially true when Poolto made first contact with Krildon. Independently, both worlds developed along similar paths and timelines. Although Poolto had been first to enter space and travel to Krildon, earlier communications had been established using wireless technology. Shortly after both worlds invented the radio, they turned their antenna skyward and heard the other's voice from across the ecliptic plane. Even before they had 'seen' each other, they had established a relationship between their two worlds.

It was from this remarkable meeting of the two worlds that the great transformation of Poolto into a single 'world' began. The people of Poolto began to think of themselves as a 'single' people from a 'single' planet. Likewise, similar cultural changes took place on Krildon. Together, both worlds began to think of themselves as citizens of the solar system.

The relationship that developed spurred on a technological race for vehicles capable of traveling to the other planet. The race had ended when an unmanned craft traveled from Poolto to Krildon and back again. From this humble beginning, the two worlds forged a relationship spanning thousands of years. They grew together, traded together, and explored together—partners in the joint exploitation of their solar system.

Tyler thought back to earth and its own regional differences. He was certain most people on earth still believed they were alone in the Universe, so they still thought of themselves in regional terms rather than as a race. However, considering the war that currently tore both Poolto and Krildon apart, Tyler wasn't convinced the transformation had really benefited anyone. It had only moved the inevitable conflicts off-planet and with another species.

Tyler was beginning to understand more of the world he was now an integral part of. They weren't that different from humans. Like man, the people of Poolto had descended from arboreal animals along the equatorial regions of the planet. However, as man had descended from the great apes, these creatures had been nocturnal tree dwellers, preferring the night to daylight. Their position as the top predator of the nighttime canopy developed their claws, their brains, and their opposable thumbs.

Poolto had never had large predators, so their species quickly became the dominant one on the planet. Over time, their dominance afforded them the luxury to live both in the daylight and darkness. Despite this change in active time, the species still retained many of their ancestral traits, such as a remarkable ability to see in darkness.

Instead of low light being reflected off the back of the eyes, their eyes had developed the ability to see thermal radiation or heat. At first, the ability had taken Tyler by surprise. His eyes registered the darkness, but people and objects always seemed brighter, as if glowing. Only after searching the Admiral's memories for an explanation had Tyler adapted to this 'additional' sense.

Despite these obvious differences, the specie was very similar to humans. Their reproductive methods, diet, culture, and governance were all similar to those on earth. It made Tyler wonder how common earthly traits were in the Universe.

Tyler knew from memory that the people of Krildon had descended from a non-arboreal creature very similar to earth's early dinosaurs. Their opposable thumbs and brain size derived from their positions as a fast and furious predator. Their early ancestors had caught most of their prey on the run. Because of that, they still retained much of the strength and agility of their those ancestors. This made them far faster and stronger than the people of Poolto. Until the war, this had never been an issue. Only the characteristic claws of Poolto were a physical advantage over the Krildon who had nails similar to humans.

The Krildons appearance was very different from either humans or the people of Poolto. They stood on long legs that looked more like dog legs than human. Their height could soar up to nine feet unlike the average Poolto height of four. Their arms were small when compared to their legs and their hands held five fingers, each sporting 'nails' that looked very human.

The Krildon had a distinctive brown color to their skin, no hair, but a set of ridges that ran from the front of their narrow heads down to the base of their necks. It gave them the appearance of a lizard although their faces looked mostly human except narrower. Despite the similarities, the length of their nose, and the thin lips once again gave them a slightly reptilian look, especially when viewed from the side.

On either side of their heads, very small and compact ears lay flat against their skulls. The eyes were somewhat large for their narrow heads, but they faced forwards and were predominantly colored bright yellow with dark, black, almond shaped pupils. They were a daytime species, and like man, their nighttime vision was extremely poor. This deficiency was surpassed by their nearly perfect eyesight. No person on Krildon ever needed eye correction and could accurately see intricate details over a mile in distance.

Despite these obvious physical differences between the two people, their worlds were more similar than different. Both societies had been turbulent and warlike during their early history. Both had developed amazing civilizations and cultures, seeking out knowledge and science in an attempt to understand and control their environment.

When they had first made contact, they had reveled in their similarities, and each had sought out a way to combine their worlds in a peaceful and prosperous way. After two thousand years of prosperity, the peace had finally broke, and war threatened both planets. For Tyler, it was both sad and discouraging to see such technologically advanced peoples fighting like primitive tribes. Perhaps a species could never get past the survival of the fittest instinct.

In the early days, before the war, the fighting had been small skirmishes over resources within the asteroid belt. As each world had plenty of business ventures, they were always jockeying for the next big payoff. The great expansion on both worlds led to the development of powerful technological societies, and with that, a growing hunger for more and more resources.

As a natural consequence of Krildon's position within the solar system, it was blessed with a greater abundance of water than Poolto. Early in the history of these two worlds, the difference hadn't been important, but as more and more colonies and mining operations expanded out into the far reaches of the solar system, water had become both precious and expensive. This had turned Krildon into a very powerful trader with Poolto.

This disparate supply of water became a constant source of conflict leading up to the war. It was said that Krildon business interests had been deliberately sabotaging Poolto water production facilities in the asteroid belt, then swooping in with the required water marked up for huge profit. Nothing had ever been proved, but the growing suspicions fed the increasing distrust developing between both worlds.

Thus began the era of skirmishes over resources and water supply. Over time, these skirmishes fed the political climate that increasingly sought to support their own people's interests instead of those of the 'common' solar system.

The increasing division grew into an all out confrontational debate and threat of war. Looking back, no one could pinpoint exactly when it all broke down, but many historians point to an incident on one of the largest mining colonies both worlds had vested interests in.

The colony, called Cisten III, had been one of many joint efforts between two companies, the Liisten Corporation from Poolto, and the Cirran Company from Krildon. For decades, the joint operations had run smoothly, both companies benefiting from the profits the mines produced.

Prior to the incident, discord began between committees that oversaw the operations for both companies. The Cirran committee members had insisted water for the colony continue to be provided by a Krildon supply company that Cirran had a huge stake in. Meanwhile, the Liisten committee members insisted they break from the 'expensive' water supplier and build their own production facility.

Both committees argued for years without resolution. Finally, in frustration, the Liisten Corporation announced a buyout offer for the Cirran Company. They generously offered twice the appraised value for the operations, but Liisten summarily rejected it and made a counter offer to buyout Cirran.

The resources provided by the mine were critical to Liisten interests, and they didn't want to start paying market prices for these riches. The battle raged through the courts on both worlds, but no compromise was reached. The publicity of the battle became a political hot potato, as each world saw the other as trying to 'cheat' them out of their rightful resources. Expensive, negative marketing campaigns reinforced this concept.

The crisis came to a head when a devastating accident rocked the mining colony. Through no fault of either company, an unchecked reactor problem went critical. The plant's crew struggled to get it under control, and nearly succeeded, but their efforts were too late to stop the inevitable reaction. The power plant blew in an explosion that nearly split the asteroid in two.

The colony suffered an incredible loss of forty-five percent of the colony's structures and fifteen percent of its residents. They probably could have survived and rebuilt, but the incredible force of the explosion had sent the asteroid on a collision course with another even larger asteroid where most of the mining operation was located.

Despite an attempt to evacuate before the impact, the two asteroids collided, splitting the smaller into three fragments and the larger into two. The ensuing destruction was catastrophic for the colony. Virtually everything on the colony was lost. Over twenty-four thousand people were killed in the collision—people from both Poolto and Krildon.

Both worlds called for immediate formal investigations and the blame game began. Not surprisingly, both worlds concluded the fault was with the 'other' world's corporation, and therefore, all proceeds and awards should be granted to their own world's company.

Neither planet budged from the stalemate, and both began freezing off-world accounts of both planets. Trade and commerce between the two worlds ground to a halt and hostilities in the off-world colonies became open and violent. The two thousand years of peace had been shattered.

Soon, open hostilities turned into open war, and within a year, both governments formally declared war on the other. It was during this time that the Admiral was finishing school while his parent's still served on Krildon. As ambassador to Krildon, the Admiral's father attempted to divert the war that was coming. Once it had been officially declared, the Admiral's father had been recalled to Poolto. Both worlds ejected the other's people from their planetary surface and from all planetary properties.

The Admiral's father refused the recall, and until his arrest, he had worked hard to prevent the war from happening. His efforts failed, and Krildon eventually arrested him as a spy. He was thrown into prison, and his wife sent back to Poolto.

The Admiral had always believed his father loyal to the Emperor and to Poolto, but his refusal to leave Krildon when recalled, had been viewed on Poolto as a direct disobedience to an Imperial order, and the Emperor branded him a traitor. The Admiral knew that if his father did return, he would have been imprisoned on Poolto. Instead, he was trapped on Krildon, a prisoner of war.

Early in the war, the Krildon government had begrudgingly allowed the Admiral to communicate with his father on a restricted basis, but after the missile attacks that nearly destroyed each world, no further communication had been established with his father. The Admiral wasn't even sure he was still alive.

The missile attacks destroyed hundreds of population centers, killing billions on both planets. Each barely survived the vast destruction. This only solidified the hatred that had grown between the two species. In an awful act of retaliation, the Poolto government had publicly executed all remaining Krildon prisoners. It was rumored Krildon did the same.

For the last twenty-one years, both worlds built enormous military machinery. Both worlds constructed a ring of protection surrounding their planet, protecting from both invasion and missile attacks. The war moved off- world into space where epic battles were waged to gain control of the resources needed to feed their war machines.

It was in these battles that the Admiral made a name for himself. He had won more battles than any other commander in the history of Poolto, and some began to talk about the legends of his ancestors and their prowess as warriors. As these legends were revived, the Imperial government used them as a means to rally public support for the mounting costs of the war.

It placed an incredible burden on Tyler's shoulders. The more he learned, the more he was discouraged. Both worlds would never stop growing, thus both worlds would always need more resources.

The hatred between the two species had evolved into a deep prejudice that both governments fed through propaganda.

Tyler suspected neither world would ever know peace again. Nothing short of mutual destruction or an outside threat from a third party would ever end the conflict that now existed. The loss of billions would never be erased by peace talks and negotiations—only blood and violence would be accepted now.

It was these thoughts that disturbed Tyler as his ground car pulled into the Tooland Estates. He stared out the window coldly, eyeing the place he would spend his next few months.

The palace, at least that's what Tyler thought of it, sat upon a hill at the base of a snow capped mountain. As Tyler surveyed the land stretching out below, he could make out the thousands of acres of Sloose Berry orchards that memory assured him were tended by the hundreds of workers.

Somewhere in those orchards, one of the largest wineries in this region produced the highest quality Sloose Berry wines on the planet. Tyler was curious to taste some of it, but his memory warned him that the Admiral never drank wine, or any other spirit. Apparently, the Admiral saw drinking as a character weakness and refused to partake in it. Ironically, his winery produced the best on the planet.

Tyler didn't care. He wanted a drink, and if he was careful, no one had to be the wiser. After all, what privilege was rank if you couldn't reserve the right to change your ways. He was older now, a national hero and injured, surely that warranted a drink of his family's wine.

The thought cheered him slightly as they pulled through the enormous gates. Tyler noted the gates were open, and appeared as though they were never closed. Considering his position, he could understand why security wasn't much of an issue. After all, the 'enemy' was on Krildon, not Poolto.

The palace was set far back from the front gates, and the drive up to it wound gently past manicured lawns dotted richly with tended gardens, trees, and statuettes. Tyler didn't think the effect fit the Admiral, and he thought he understood why the Admiral never spent time there.

It was late afternoon when they arrived, and the sun descended behind the palace giving it a glowing appearance that was warm and inviting. Although the size was overwhelming, up close, its appearance, though stately, was not as intimidating as from afar. Tyler thought he might enjoy living here.

The car glided to a stop in front of the main entrance, and Tyler stole one more glance out the window back towards the gate. Stretching away from the palace, the grounds sloped gently towards the main road. From there, the ground dropped more sharply to the valley floor and the orchards. All of this was framed by black, rocky peaks, some covered with snow. All of them glowed faintly red with the late day sunlight and the effect was both stark and stunning.

Tyler decided it was far more beautiful than L.A., especially with the crisp clear air of the mountains. Tyler was certain he would like it here, especially the wine!

They settled Tyler in the second floor residence of the east wing. It came complete with nine bedrooms, several offices, a fully staffed kitchen, no less than eight bathrooms, and four common rooms filled with art, furniture, and electronic devices of every kind. It was more than Tyler had experienced in his life, but he quickly grew accustomed to the lifestyle.

Because he was undergoing therapy, Tyler moved around using an electric chair on wheels. It surprised him that they used wheels, but he had been told by one of his nursing staff that they did not have 'floating' chairs, as the energy requirement were too great for such a small item. Although the nurse had giggled a little at the question, Tyler didn't think he had raised suspicions. After all, it was legendary that the Admiral had never been sick a day in his life.

Although the Admiral's memories were complete, small items such as wheelchairs were not always adequately covered. The Admiral had a wealth of knowledge on the history of both worlds, battle strategies, administrative management, and financial planning, but knowledge of the everyday things tended to be... incomplete.

Tyler assumed it was because the Admiral had never needed to do many of them for himself. The Admiral had been born into wealth and power, and this wealth afforded him servants and assistants to take care of the mundane tasks of living. His life had been one of great intellect, epic battles, and military campaigns.

Tyler didn't mind, he was more than happy to enjoy the benefits of wealth. He had never had it on earth, and so he took full advantage of it at every turn.

He learned to use many of the electronic devices, and when not in therapy or staff meetings, he took time to go through the enormous number of channels their version of television had. From watching these channels, he learned more about Poolto's society than he could glean from the Admiral's memories.

Although all the channels were controlled by the Poolto Communication Ministry, they offered a remarkably open forum for varying beliefs, including that of the religious 'few'. Although they did not get their own air time, they always showed up in other shows, either as a news segment or as an individual espousing the beliefs.

Even in sporting events, signs in the crowds would word religious statements like 'God will save those who believe', 'God begs for you to stop the war', and 'Let no more die in vain'. Tyler thought back to earth and how often the same sort of signs appeared at sporting events.

The cameras were typically good at avoiding these 'preachings', but now and again, their message got through—enough that the everyday person was beginning to ask questions about the 'new' religion. Tyler understood why his innocent comment had caused such a commotion. His own curiosity was often piqued by what he saw, but he kept it to himself.

Life in the palace grew routine. Tyler took the abundant free time to increase his knowledge of the planet and to function as an Admiral again. He was grateful for the Marshall, who despite his obvious discomfort at many of Tyler's questions, remained patient and faithful in explaining things.

Tyler was growing accustomed to relying on the Admiral's memories, and as they integrated with his own, he felt comfortable impersonating the great man. He was confident he was successfully fooling everyone, and any minor discretion that slipped out was routinely ignored as a 'side-effect' of his prolonged coma.

Tyler increased his functioning as the Admiral, and as he did so, began to understand the dilemma the Marshall constantly warned him about. In one of the earliest meetings at the palace, Marshall Sliss had finally disclosed his utmost important item concerning Vice Admiral Teesen.

Apparently, while in command during the Admiral's coma, Vice Admiral Teesen had taken it upon himself to plan a counter attack to take advantage of the debilitated state of the enemy fleet. Teesen figured by gambling the rest of their own fleet, Krildon would be caught off-guard before they had time to recover their full defensive capabilities.

Tyler agreed it was a huge gamble, and pointed out that their own ability to mount such an attack or defend themselves if it went badly were only marginally better than the enemies. In response to Tyler's observations, the Marshall detailed what remained of Poolto forces—unfortunately, the numbers were small and the experience young. Many of the Admiral's best commanders were lost in the great battle, and now the Vice Admiral wanted to commit what was left to a suicide mission. They didn't even know why the first attack had failed.

Unfortunately, the Vice Admiral held the ear of the Emperor, and his plan was being given strong consideration in the Imperial Palace. The Emperor and his staff were careful not to leak information, especially to the Supreme Council, but the Marshall had spies within both Teesen's and the Emperor's staff, so he'd uncovered the disturbing information.

The Marshall cautioned Tyler to keep the knowledge secret for now as he suspected there were spies in their own organization. The Emperor had money and wasn't afraid to spread it around for political and military intelligence. Since the Emperor controlled the intelligence arm of the government, he made sure he had current information on all government and civilian organizations.

Although the Marshall employed spies of his own, his network paled when compared to the Emperor's. Up until a few years ago, these measures never seemed necessary, but as the Admiral's popularity as a war hero grew, the Marshall saw changes in the personnel assigned to their staff. It became obvious the Emperor was keeping a close eye on 'his' Supreme Commander.

Eventually, the Marshall's suspicions were confirmed when one spy had approached him offering to work as a double agent. After some preliminary checks, the Marshall had agreed, and thus, the Marshall's intelligence network began. Although small in scope, it encompassed the Emperor's staff, various bureaucratic agencies, and even the Supreme Council. It was enough to ensure the Admiral was not surprised by either branch.

Considering the information obtained through this network, the Marshall and the Admiral wondered how they'd ever operated without one. The war had forced many to participate in activities they once thought absurd or 'dirty'. Now, in addition to the standard costs of war, Tyler suspected they were beginning to pay a high price in terms of their society and its values.

Tyler spoke with the Marshall, in private, about how they could thwart the Vice Admiral's plan without appearing 'not loyal' to the Emperor or the war effort. They both believed the Admiral could use his enormous popularity as national hero to counter the plan. Unfortunately, if the Emperor was determined to strike the final blow, they were unlikely to dissuade him.

The only thing going for Tyler was the fact the Emperor was highly intelligent and probably didn't want to waste his remaining forces in the event the plan failed. Tyler figured he may yet be able to convince the Emperor that the plan was too risky, especially in light of the failure of the first attack. However, Tyler knew it would take more than his own opinion to sway the argument in favor of caution.

For now, they kept their ideas to themselves while studying the details of Admiral Teesen's plan and documenting the flaws they uncovered. It was difficult to find flaws since the plan was actually quite brilliant. The Admiral's memories convinced Tyler that Vice Admiral Teesen was no fool.

The Vice Admiral had won many battles for Admiral Osloo, and he was nearly as decorated. If it hadn't been for Admiral

Osloo, Vice Admiral Teesen would most likely have become the Supreme Commander and national hero. He was a formidable man and Tyler didn't like the prospects of having him on opposite sides. However, Tyler also didn't like the prospects of losing the war.

The plan's most obvious flaw was the enormous gamble that required too many things to go right without adequate backups. In this, Tyler saw Teesen was being careless. Most of the time, Teesen's gambles had paid off, but there were a few times in his past where they had not, and it had cost his men dearly.

He was a brilliant tactician, but his plans simply required too many things to go right. This latest plan was no exception. It required supply routes that didn't exist, asteroid bases that hadn't been captured, and fleet movements that went undetected. These things were unlikely at best and impossible at worst. Krildon suffered severely from the last attack, and Tyler knew they would step up their vigilance in the aftermath.

If they hadn't recently executed the Admiral's failed battle, they might be able to pull it off. But now, all reports indicated Krildon had increased their surveillance of Poolto activities. More than a few scout craft had been shot down or detected near remaining bases and supply points. They were under the microscope, and the Vice Admiral's plan did not take that fully into account.

According to the Marshall's spies, the Emperor's staff noted the same discrepancies, but the Vice Admiral had brushed it aside as a non-issue in light of the great ruse the plan called for.

They didn't know how the Emperor's staff had reacted to Teesen's response, but they knew the plan was still moving forward. The plan called for two more carriers to be completed before they could begin, so that held the launch back for at least another four months. That gave Tyler and the Admiral's staff time to intervene.

Meanwhile, word was leaking out of the intelligence agencies that that they were busily working on their own surveillance of the Krildon fleet. Their goal was to determine Krildon's defensive capabilities and the speed with which they were rebuilding their forces.

To date, Krildon appeared to lag behind the Poolto effort after losing a great deal of their manufacturing capabilities during the Admiral's attack. Although this appeared as good news, the Marshall was suspicious of the accuracy. After such a major attack, the Marshall believed Krildon would be doubling their efforts and simply keeping them secret.

Using the Admiral's memories, Tyler concurred with the Marshall's analysis. It made logical sense. Unfortunately, the military relied almost solely on the Empire's intelligence agencies, and lately, the Admiral and his staff were being excluded from this information.

The official response to inquiries about the missing intelligence was that '...until the Admiral fully recovered, they were instructed to not 'burden' him with ongoing operational details'. As the Marshall put it, "We are systematically being cut out of the position of power we once held."

It was unclear who was behind it, Vice Admiral Teesen or the Emperor. Either way, the national hero was no longer relied upon as the master military strategist. They would have to find a way to change that if they wanted to stop the next attack.

Despite this heavy burden, Tyler was successfully playing the Admiral, but he felt increasingly overwhelmed by the decisions he was being forced to make. He sensed the Admiral's staff waited patiently for him to act—they hoped to regain their power and get back on a track of success.

Unfortunately, Tyler was not yet able to do that. More than a few times, Adanni had intruded into Tyler's thoughts, insinuating he ought to take over some control. He constantly assured Tyler that his own experience would enable him to navigate the political mess and put the Admiral back on top. Tyler was often tempted, but still declined. Until he was fully recovered, he had no intentions of letting Adanni make personal decisions for him.

The stress was beginning to take its toll. Physically, he was recovering quickly, but mentally, he felt inadequate to the task even with the Admiral's memories to guide him.

This added stress provided Tyler the excuse he'd longed for to 'try' the Sloose Berry wine. He began having the wine delivered from the palace's immaculate cellar to his 'viewing' room every day. Tyler had befriended a palace staff member named Feernii Oolaa shortly after arriving in Tooland. Among Feernii's many responsibilities, he was in charge of food and beverage. Because of this, he possessed the only keys to the wine cellar and was well versed in its many contents. Feernii hand selected each bottle regularly sent to Tyler.

Tyler had convinced Feernii to keep the deliveries secret as the doctors and nurses would 'disapprove' of this consumption. Remarkably, Feernii never knew the 'original' Admiral abstained from alcohol, so he was only too pleased to finally be able to demonstrate his knowledge of the wonderful cellar.

Tyler didn't really care if Feernii had known, for him, it was a distinct pleasure to enjoy the calming and uplifting effects of alcohol once again. Since that fateful day that turned Tyler into something 'new' and 'different', he had not experienced the pleasure of drinking. Although it was only wine, Tyler still relished the experience.

During the many monotonous days at Tooland, Tyler sat through boring meetings and physical therapy patiently waiting for both to end so he could retire to his viewing room and enjoy a bottle of wine. Like his previous life, Tyler's daily consumption became routine and nothing to be 'concerned' about.

The wine tasted extraordinarily good, and Tyler chided the Admiral's memories for never indulging. Between the wine and the wonderful meals, Tyler could just bear the daily grind of recovering his health and managing the Admiral's staff.

After two months at Tooland, Tyler truly felt at home. Early on he had imagined the experience would be 'alien', but as the days sped by, he realized life on Poolto wasn't that different than life on earth. He never wanted to leave Tooland, but the Marshall informed him a trip to the capital was imminent.

Tyler sat comfortably in one of the many luxurious, overstuffed chairs that adorned his favorite viewing room. His mind dwelled on the impending trip. Because his recovery had been moving well ahead of schedule, the trip back to the capital had been moved up.

Tyler wondered if his ethereal presence in the body had made the difference in its recovery. He had brought the body back to life, so perhaps his spirit brought enhanced health as well.

Either way, Tyler no longer moved around in the wheelchair, and other than minor pain and stiffness in his back, he felt nearly normal. The doctors were amazed at the speed of his recovery and gave him the thumbs up to leave Tooland in three weeks.

Already, the Admiral's staff began dismantling the temporary headquarters they had set up in Tooland. Tyler knew they were more than ready to move back to their headquarters in Yooso. Tyler didn't hold with their enthusiasm, especially since it meant taking on even greater responsibility.

He topped off his wine glass and stared blankly at the bank of view screens across the room. Each viewer tuned to a different channel, and as usual, Tyler watched all of them at once, combining newscasts and talk shows to further his knowledge of Poolto.

Stories from the capital were common, including speeches by the Emperor about the war effort. Tyler didn't miss the fact that no show mentioned the Admiral, despite the Emperor's assurances to keep the public 'informed' on his progress.

Tyler wasn't surprised. After the news conference in the hospital, the tone from the Emperor's staff had become cold and distant. This was why the Marshall pressed for their return to Yooso. The longer the Admiral was missing from the political scene, the less his presence would mean.

Tyler sipped from his wine and looked up as one of the telecasts mentioned the Admiral's name. A reporter was interviewing one of the surviving commanders from the last battle. Tyler recalled his name as Baaylir Tredeen, squadron leader from one of the lost carriers.

Tyler set his wine glass down and pressed the controls to mute everything but the commander's interview. The reporter had just asked him what he thought about the military's current capabilities to fight after the losses they'd suffered.

"...counter attack, we have been feverishly rebuilding our fleet. Although my own squadron's carrier was destroyed in that last battle, we have been reassigned to one of the new carriers scheduled to come online in a few weeks. While we wait, we've been re-supplied with missing fighters and personnel."

The camera was zoomed close on the commander, so Tyler couldn't make out where they were. Wherever it was, it looked to be nighttime, and that meant either space, or somewhere near Tyler's time zone. They could even have been near the capital city. Tyler listened intently to the rest of the Commander's comments.

"...training everyday. Of course, for security reasons, we cannot discuss either where we are based or where we are currently training. Suffice it to say, my squadron, and those of many of my colleagues are ready to fight again. We look forward to Admiral Osloo's return in several weeks so we can hear more about his brilliant plans to move this effort forward."

Tyler sat back while the reporter asked the Commander about what he had heard from Admiral Osloo's staff. Tyler thought the Marshall had wanted to keep their return a secret, but apparently someone had leaked it—at least to the commanders. Now it was in the news.

Oh well, it was going to come out eventually, and Tyler hadn't been convinced of the value of secrecy anyway. He switched from the channel and picked up his wine once more, relishing the particularly exquisite taste of the current selection for the evening. Feernii had told him this particular vintage had won several prestigious awards within the wine industry and because of its small productions, each bottle was worth a great deal of money. Tyler didn't care, it tasted great.

He noticed he was nearing the end of the first bottle, and eyed the second one sitting across the room on the bar. Although he'd originally started with only a glass or two each night, he had quickly progressed to one or two bottles. Holding his half-full glass, he relaxed in the chair and thought about the trip ahead.

He hoped to find Toosia in Yooso, but wasn't sure if tracking her down would be easy. His failed attempts at contacting her finally convinced him to give up after a month and half. Because they were moving to the political hub of the planet, Tyler feared he needed someone like Toosia to help him navigate the maze of power.

As he relaxed, he pictured her once again as she had stood before him in the hospital room. As he met more and more people from this world, he began to appreciate how beautiful Toosia really was. Her features were delicate, and yet commanding—she was a regal presence in any room.

He felt a familiar stirring inside, and turned his thoughts away to keep from getting excited. No use getting worked up if he couldn't see her.

A knock at the open door startled him. He glanced over to see Marshall Sliss standing with hands behind his back. He looked embarrassed at having interrupted Tyler. The Marshall and the rest of the staff had taken up residence in the West wing, so Tyler rarely saw them after hours. He preferred it that way.

Tyler motioned to the Marshall, "Come Marshall, join me in a glass of my family's most excellent reserve!"

The Marshall hesitated, but walked over to a comfortable couch perpendicular to Tyler's chair. As the Marshall sat down, Tyler held up the bottle of Sloose Berry wine, questioning whether the Marshall wanted any.

"Oh, no thank you sir, I was just heading for bed." He gave Tyler a puzzled look.

"What's wrong Marshall, do you abstain from such things?"

"No sir, I have been known to imbibe now and again, I simply didn't realize you did." He looked slightly embarrassed mentioning it.

Tyler was certain the Marshall knew the old Admiral had always abstained, so Tyler needed to confirm his doubts.

"Yes...yes I did abstain from such things before the accident, but since I survived, I am beginning to take more interest in the things I have sworn to protect." At least Tyler wasn't lying—he really did feel that way. He only hoped the Marshall believed the excuse.

The Marshall paused, absorbing the Admiral's words. Convinced or not, he didn't appear ready to press the matter.

"I see your point Admiral...sometimes it is necessary to re-acquaint ourselves with the world we are fighting for. Perhaps I will join you after all."

The Marshall walked to the bar and brought back an empty glass. The Admiral poured the remnants of the first bottle into the Marshall's glass, and both men leaned back into their seats.

"Tell me Marshall, what brings you here so late at night?"

"I don't know if you saw or not," the Marshall gestured towards the view screens, "but our trip to the capital has been compromised."

"Yes, I saw Commander Tredeen's interview." Tyler let that hang before continuing, "I thought it went very well."

"But sir, he released our return to the capital before we were ready!" The Marshall was clearly agitated by the leak. Tyler could guess why, but it didn't have anything to do with the secrecy of their trip.

"Yes Marshall, I understand that. Now tell me why it is so important?" Tyler was tired of the secrecy.

"Sir," he began, "I realize that it may seem 'cloak and dagger' to keep our return a secret, but you need to realize that a major power play is going on in the capital, and your early return will have a pivotal role in how that plays out."

The Marshall paused. Obviously, he was trying to find the right words to convey his fears. He wrung his hands before reaching for his glass of wine. He drank firmly from the glass before proceeding.

"The Emperor has lost faith in you sir." He said it matter of fact, a look of relief on his face.

Tyler was slightly amused—that was the big secret the Marshall had been holding inside? The signs had been there all along, and after the conference, it wasn't a giant leap to come to that conclusion; yet Tyler sensed something else, something the Marshall held back.

"Fine, I can accept that and even could have predicted it. But again, why does our return need to be a secret?"

"Sir…" again he paused, "Sir, I don't know if you realize just how fast your recovery has been. Many around here are touting it as a miracle, not that they believe in such things."

"So I heal fast, what is the big deal?"

"The big deal is this...the Emperor is trying to move you out of power, replacing you with Vice Admiral Teesen, so he'd hoped to use your 'slow' recovery as a plausible explanation to the military and the public. The Emperor saw this as an opportunity to force you into retirement after your decades of noble service." The Marshall took another large drink, "The retirement, of course, would place you in an advisory position on the military planning council, but your command would be taken away, and thus, your power."

"You know all this for fact?"

"Well, most of it." He admitted, "Your placement on the planning council was a projection on my part."

"And a good one at that!" Tyler agreed.

Tyler thought about what the Marshall was saying. Clearly, his return so early, and in such good health, would serve to make him more popular in the eyes of the public and the military. This would work against the Emperor's plans to retire him for fear of the public backlash.

Tyler used the Admiral's memories as a strategist, and clearly deduced how the surprise return would have had a greater impact politically. If the Emperor had no time to prepare, then the Admiral and his staff could quickly resume power.

"I understand the dilemma—we missed an opportunity to regain most of our power without a nasty fight. Can't we still use this return to our advantage?"

Tyler thought about Toosia once again. Her father's power on the council could give them a leg up, but unfortunately, they'd alienated many on the Council, so that avenue seemed remote.

"Well...we could." The Marshall didn't sound very certain. "There are many elements in the military that would prefer your leadership to that of the Vice Admiral. Their faith in your abilities will be restored with your 'early' return. Of course, I've already been working that angle...scheduling interviews with key personnel who support you."

The Marshall leaned forward, a look of promise replacing his concern, "I suppose that in some ways, Commander Tredeen has already begun that process."

Tyler's mind leapt ahead, "Of course!" He exclaimed, "We marshal our support in the military, and Vice Admiral Teesen will have no other option than to step aside for the triumphant return of his Supreme Commander."

"Yes," the Marshall agreed, "then the Emperor would have no choice but to publicly acknowledge your rightful return. In fact, he would have to issue an official proclamation of your return to duty, and announce his faith in your fitness to take over the war effort. Yes, we may not be out of this game yet!"

The Marshall finished his wine and stood up, "Admiral, I beg your leave that I may tend to some actions on this new approach."

Tyler smiled, so formal, and yet, the Marshall was clearly happy with the turn of events.

Tyler was also happy. For the first time since becoming the Admiral, he felt like he had made some of his own conclusions, and contributed to a new strategy. He had relied upon the Admiral's memories to guide him, but the projections felt like his own.

"Yes, Marshall," he raised his glass, "thank you for your continued support and loyalty, I will see you in the morning."

The Marshall bowed slightly before leaving, a renewed spirit in his step.

Finishing his wine, Tyler watched the Marshall retreat. He glanced across the room at the other bottle, but decided against opening it. He knew tomorrow would be busy.

Tyler slept restlessly, tossing and turning in the enormous bed. Dreams, nightmares and stressful thoughts plagued his sleep, some his own, many the Admirals'. With only a week left before their return to the capital, the activity at the palace had built to a frenzied pitch.

Fortunately for Tyler, as the leader, he was exempt from most of frenetic activity. His key role was to prepare for the big gala the Marshall had scheduled for their return.

It would all kick-off with a large press conference outside the Supreme Military Command headquarters where a parade of experts, military personnel, and medical doctors would prepare the public for the miraculous recovery, and return, of their Admiral.

The Admiral's staff had prepared an exemplary speech that Tyler was to present. Tyler had spent the last couple of days practicing it in front of the PR staff and had memorized it perfectly. Since his newfound abilities enabled him to remember everything, that had been the easy part. Now, however, his delivery still fell short of expectation.

He assured his staff he would have it down before the event, despite lacking the confidence he could deliver.

These inadequacies kept Tyler restless in bed. He was gaining more confidence, but there were still times when the 'Tyler' in him desired an escape into the Universe—to flee somewhere else, somewhere simpler and easier.

The thoughts haunted his sleep and plagued his dreams. Occasionally, memories of Linda drifted through his awareness. Where was she? What was she doing? Had she married? Tyler knew the questions might never be answered, and that drove him further from the sleep he needed.

He drifted in and out, feeling disconnected from everything around him. Like a distant observer, maybe like Adanni, he saw himself as if from above. He watched as he turned restless in his sleep.

Suddenly, the door to his room cracked slightly, a figure slipping into the room and closing the door. The disconnected part of Tyler's awareness saw only a dark shape moving across the floor. The restless Tyler in bed, stirred briefly, seeing a glowing figure moving towards the bed.

Part of him thought it was a dream, part of him thought it was real. Through tired eyes, he watched as the figure moved to the side of the bed, their body's heat a brilliant glowing halo.

Tyler watched fascinated as the figure shed a simple gown and moved gently under the covers beside him. He knew it had to be a dream, as he felt no level of concern at this intrusion. It felt like a dream even though he could feel the soft, warm body next to him.

In the deep recesses of his sleep dulled mind, he worked out that the person must be Eyleeria. Who else in this palace would dare make such a brazen act on their commander? He moved to speak, but delicate fingers reached out, pressing his lips gently.

Through the alien night vision, he could make out the glowing face next to him, but his mind didn't accept what he saw. He watched as she moved across the bed and over top of him. Now he knew he was dreaming! The face above him, angelic and beautiful, was that of Toosia.

He didn't care if it was only a dream—he wanted her like nothing else before. Mesmerized by her beauty, he watched as her naked skin danced with multiple colors flashing in fantastic patterns. He imagined his own skin dancing in response to hers and felt an excitement growing within him.

His hands reached out to caress her sensuous body and delicate breasts, exciting her with his touch. The glowing colors on her skin increased at his touch, pacing the excitement he felt within her and himself.

The people of this world shared a similar anatomy with that of humans—even their genitalia. Tyler had often delved into the Admiral's memories for examples of their love making. The Admiral's affair with Eyleeria had, at its' peak, been very active sexually. The Admiral had used the release as his dominant method to deal with the stress of command.

Like humans, the male of the species possessed a penis. Although thin and long, it was completely contained within the body when flaccid. When excited, it moved out of the body to merge with the female.

As Tyler penetrated the dream Toosia, both arched back with the intense pleasure. Their skin reacted with a brilliant display of colors. Once inside, Tyler felt himself swell, filling her completely as the pleasure overtook his mind and built in intensity.

He watched from below as she closed her eyes and threw her head back rhythmically, moving with the music of their passion. Her skin pulsated with colors that hypnotized Tyler and bonded him with an intense feeling of love. The feeling was so great, Tyler wondered how the Admiral had ever left the woman.

As if in slow motion, Tyler watched as Toosia arched in an intense orgasm that made her skin fluoresce a brilliant red. Her genitalia pulsed with the excitement and wrapped tighter around

Tyler. The pulsing steadily increased, bringing Tyler towards the apex he longed for.

With a burst of blinding light, Tyler exploded into her, the release sending waves of pleasure through his entire body. In response to his release, Toosia continued to pulse in wave after wave of orgasmic pleasure. Tyler felt himself lost in a vertigo.

He had no idea how long the orgasms lasted, or when they had finally separated from each other. The dream was over, and at long last, Tyler fell into a deep and restful sleep. Tyler didn't care if the dream had only been a fantasy constructed from the Admiral's memories of his wife. He had needed the release from anxiety and the deep sleep necessary to regain his strength for the trip ahead.

No dreams or troubled thoughts invaded the peaceful blackness that he willingly surrendered to. At long last, Tyler slept a deep and tranquil sleep.

Tyler woke late in the morning alone in the large bed. Considering the time, he was surprised the staff hadn't woke him earlier. He figured rumors of his sleeplessness had spread throughout the staff, and concern for their boss had let him get the sleep that had eluded him for so long.

Tyler felt more refreshed than any other time since becoming the Admiral. He was filled with a renewed sense of purpose and a greater resolve to be the Admiral everyone would rally behind. For the first time since they had planned it, Tyler looked forward to their return to the capital. He was aware they faced many obstacles, but he also knew the 'Admiral' could handle them.

Sadly, there wasn't a trace of the memorable experience of the night before. It had seemed so real, he could barely believe it had been a dream. The intense love he felt for the Admiral's wife lingered, but the effect was uplifting rather than depressing.

A part of him sensed there was no hope in them reconciling the differences, but he vowed to try and mend the wounds anyway. The Admiral's carelessness had created the chasm over the years, it seemed only fitting that he be the one to bridge the gap.

Tyler finished the morning ablutions and dressed in a semi-formal uniform ready to face the day. He knew his kitchen staff would be waiting for his appearance before starting breakfast. He felt an enormous hunger and headed to the dining room where he often ate alone. He took advantage of being alone to catch-up on the upcoming day's agenda.

Once alerted to the Admiral's presence, the palace staff put in motion the ballet of morning routine that occurred every day. He knew from experience that once breakfast was underway, multiple staff members descended on his bedroom, changing the bed linens and cleaning the bathroom.

Tyler thought it extravagant, but over time, be became accustomed to the lavish lifestyle. As he rounded the corner of hallway, he came to the double doors leading into the dining room. As usual, one of his servants stood with doors open, bowing as Tyler walked in and took his seat at the table.

Early on, Tyler had told the head of his staff that the bowing made him feel uncomfortable. Unfortunately, the person in charge had assured Tyler the staff could not stop even if they wanted. The Admiral was a national hero—the greatest since the emperor who had united their planet. Everyone felt a debt of gratitude for his great deeds and they showed their respect in one of the simplest ways they knew.

Tyler couldn't argue the point, so once again, he became accustomed to it, accepting it as just one more part of the Admiral's world.

He took his usual seat at the end of the great table, closer to the large fireplace that dominated the room. It was more than a dining room—more like a great room created to entertain large numbers of dinner guests. Throughout the room, large sitting areas were filled with plush comfortable seating. Even the fireplace was surrounded by cushioned seating ideal for more intimate moments. In front of the fireplace, a large overstuffed sofa softened the formal atmosphere the room generally had. Tyler guessed it could accommodate at least eight people, and it was flanked by a smaller sofa on the left and a large chair on the right. It set a more comfortable tone in the room, and made Tyler feel more relaxed.

As Tyler sat at the end of the table, the back of the large chair faced Tyler. It gave him a great view of the entrance while being close enough to feel warmth from the fire. The table was always spread with various plates and utensils that Tyler still hadn't figured out. He often wondered why the table remained set when no one but he ate at it. No matter, it took away the feeling of loneliness when only he was there.

Per instructions, Tyler's setting included a small video tablet next to a glass of 'Goonjee' juice that he had taken a liking for. Tyler likened the juice to a combination of bananas and raspberry, although he never would have picked that combination back on earth. Perhaps the Admiral's palate was sufficiently different to admire the unusual combination.

His video tablet would contain notable news stories, the daily agenda, and logistical data his staff wanted him to review. He knew this day would be mostly clear while they completed the packing. One meeting with the senior staff members to review the moving progress, but otherwise, the day was free. He felt like leaving the palace for a tour of the vineyards and winery.

Since arriving at Tooland, he had been cooped up in the palace, tending to his recovery and matters of military import. Soon they would be leaving, and Tyler would miss the opportunity to experience the full value of the working estate. He certainly could review it all from dipping into the Admiral's memories, but he wanted the experience himself. And besides, he convinced himself he needed to get outside in fresh air. As big as the palace was, he felt claustrophobic.

Tyler drank the juice while waiting for the staff to bring his morning tea. The tea was made from the leaves of an ancestral tree that had been a mainstay in their diet since anyone could remember. Even today, the traditional methods of drying the leaves, crushing them before steeping in hot water were maintained. It was an integral part of their culture, and considering their arboreal history, it made perfect sense to Tyler. The tea was quite wonderful and was said to have great healing powers.

Tyler didn't care about the healing, it was the 'Tiin'tiin' that he was after. The chemical was a strong stimulant and overly abundant within the leaves. It had replaced the coffee Tyler still yearned for from earth. Tyler knew this was its true value to the culture, not the healing properties.

The head server, Koolen, placed the steaming tea gently on the small plate to Tyler's right. As usual, he added a syrupy substance made from a root extract that served as the primary sweetener on Poolto. Tyler thought it too sweet, but insisted on a small quantity to cut the bitterness inherent in the tea.

Koolen finished with the tea before running down the morning's menu. Tyler nodded acceptance before turning on one of the video monitors he had installed to watch the morning news.

Too engrossed in tracking down his favorite shows, Tyler ignored Koolen as he walked over to the large chair with its back to Tyler. Tyler thought he heard Koolen speaking to someone, but was too engrossed in his monitors. Finally locating the right channel, he turned his attention to Koolen who was speaking softly to someone in the chair. Tyler was curious—no one ever came into this room while the Admiral was eating. Probably the Marshall, although it was rare for him to remain so quiet.

"Yes, thank you Koolen, I'd love another cup."

"Yes mam, I'll return with it straight away."

Koolen moved away from the chair carrying a cup and saucer, presumably off to retrieve the requested drink. Tyler felt confusion. Had that been a female voice he'd heard? Whose voice was it? Eyleeria? He doubted she would be so bold.

"Good morning," he said gently, "would you care to share breakfast with me?" He waited patiently, unsure of who would respond.

The voice finally answered, sounding more than a little petulant, "Well Nayllen, after so long, you do not even recognize the voice of your own wife? I'm hurt."

He fell silent, tongue-tied in shock. Toosia rose elegantly from the chair and moved towards the table. Once again, he was mesmerized by her beauty as the dream from the night before came rushing back. His mind reeled with the possibilities. Had it been a dream or had it been real? Was it some premonition of her appearance? He was speechless.

Gracefully, she walked around the table and sat down next to Tyler. She wore a shining gold single suit open at the throat and plunging down just enough to show cleavage. Her hair was twirled and bound in a fashion Tyler noted was quite common these days. It was held in place by a gold clasp shaped like a leaf.

Her face, soft and sensuous, still carried a look of concern. She sat back in her chair, folding her hands in her lap and staring directly at Tyler. He was still too shocked to respond. In his mind, a play of strong emotions consumed him. Dare he ask about last night? What if it had been a dream? Why did he still feel this intense love? Would she ever reciprocate?

All those letters he had written and messages he had left, he figured she would never come to see him. Why now? *Had it been a dream?* He wasn't sure and feared that the memories would give him away.

"Glad to see you too Nayllen." She spoke softly continuing her measured and patient stare.

"I...uh, I..." he stuttered desperately, unable to figure out an appropriate response.

"Please, don't let me interrupt your morning ritual," she said without malice. "It was not my intention to...fluster you."

Flustered? He looked at his hands and saw a gentle play of lights fluorescing on his skin. He was excited and she knew it. *Damn!* He struggled to control his emotions but thought he saw a small flash of light move across her calm face. He couldn't be sure he had seen it. Considering she showed not emotions one way or the other, it may simply have been wishful thinking on Tyler's part.

"Why are you here?" he finally managed to ask.

"Don't get too worked up, I am here at the request of Marshall Sliss. He is concerned about your return to 'duty' in the capital. As you know, we all believe the Emperor does not want your return, therefore we expect great resistance." She paused, briefly staring at his fluorescing skin once again. "Fortunately, your popularity will make it difficult for the Emperor to deny you, so we are trying to understand how he will play this."

She stopped, letting Tyler absorb what she had said. He tried to control his thoughts and saw his skin finally returning to normal.

He was embarrassed, but the feelings from the night before were too intense.

"At this critical juncture," she began again, "a division between us would not be prudent as it could provide the necessary fodder to keep you out of power."

Again, she paused. Was she choked up? Tyler couldn't tell, but her voice wavered slightly.

"My presence in your life during this period will be purely political. It is in my own interests, and those of my family, to play your wife until you are once again Supreme Commander. Until that time, I will remain with you and offer my counsel during your time in the capital."

She slumped slightly, the pressure of the emotional speech lifted. He was both excited and saddened at the same time. He wanted nothing more than to have her by his side, but her reluctance to 'play' his wife filled him with sorrow. He realized last night had been a dream.

She stared at the table, currently unable or unwilling to look at him. He was about to respond when Koolen returned with Toosia's tea and Tyler's breakfast. They both sat silently while the servers efficiently laid it out. Neither showed emotion, but Tyler was torn inside. He needed her counsel, but more than that, he needed her love. Dream or not, his feelings for her were real and he fought to hold them to himself.

The servers worked silently, obviously sensing the tension between the heads of the estate. Their marital problems were well known to the palace staff, and it had been years since they had been together at Tooland. The other servers finished and headed back towards the kitchen leaving Koolen standing quietly beside the table.

"Is there anything else I may get you?" He waited patiently, no sign of discomfort. Koolen had been on the staff for many years.

Tyler gave him a reassuring smile, "No thank you Koolen, this looks wonderful."

"Very good sir, please ring if you need anything." As quietly as he had come, Koolen left.

Tyler immediately went on the offensive, "Toosia, I cannot tell you how happy I am to see you! I know this is hard, but I really am a changed man. I understand the pain and isolation I caused you in the past, but I desperately want to make up for it now. All I ask is one chance." He hoped his pleas sounded sincere. "Would you care for some of my breakfast?"

"No, thank you, I ate when I arrived this morning."

Well, Tyler thought, *that answers the question of last night.* He felt disappointed, but still held onto hope. She hadn't immediately rejected him, but then she wasn't warming up either.

"Well good…very good." He said softly.

He backed off, and like her, fell silent while he ate. He tried to sort out the feelings he had for this new twist in the Admiral's affairs. He knew being with her would make it difficult to conceal his feelings, but he feared those would upset her even more. He didn't want to make her feel uncomfortable in a situation she could not escape.

He ate silently, as they both watched the daily newscast. He didn't pay much attention to what was being said—he was still caught up in his own inner turmoil. He figured she was also fighting her own turmoil, but outwardly, she showed no signs of emotion.

He finished eating and turned off the video. He knew they had to address the issue now rather than later. If his career meant she would be miserable and suffer, then he would gladly give it up. He wanted her and he wanted her to be happy.

"Toosia," he started, not certain how to say it, "I have made many mistakes over the years, all of them because of my career. I have no right to expect you to love me anymore, or ever again, but I must let you know that my feelings for you are so strong that it causes me pain. I love you and I want you back in my life. If that means I lose my career…then I don't care."

He studied her for any signs of emotion, but she sat quietly, neither accepting nor rejecting what he had said. He didn't care which way it went, he had needed to say it.

"I know you are making a sacrifice for me that must cause you great pain, and I cannot accept that. If my career is going to cause you pain and suffering, then let my career be over! Let the Emperor blow up the planet for all I care...I want you back in my life. I want to make up for all those years I neglected you, even if it takes the rest of my years."

He paused, again, seeing no emotion on her face. Well, it had been a gamble, but a gamble he had to take.

He continued, "Do not stay with me if you cannot love me, or forgive me...or be a real part of my life. Do not stay because of your family, or my career, or because of your reputation. Stay because you still have feelings for me and want to give me a chance to earn back your heart and your love. I don't care about my career, Toosia, I only care about you."

The speech had a familiar ring to it. It was the emotional speech he had wanted to tell Linda before he was ripped away from that world. Like Toosia, Linda had suffered because of Tyler's career. He had always put his work and himself before her needs. She too had put herself last, sacrificing a family for the love she carried for Tyler. He felt both pain and guilt at the memory, and looked to Toosia as a way to wash that away. How much was residual memories of the Admiral's and how much was Tyler? He didn't know and he didn't care, it was a great relief to have finally said it.

Toosia sat motionless, nothing to show of her feelings. He waited patiently, fearing she would reject him. Emotions he'd never felt swelled in his heart, and an empty hollow feeling grew in the pit of his stomach. He got out of his chair and knelt before her on the ground. He gently grasped one of her hands and bowed his head to her. Her hand trembled slightly in his—the only sign of emotion so far.

"I vow to you right now, right here, on my family's ancestral estate, I will never do anything to hurt you again. I will spend my remaining days doing whatever I can to regain your trust, your love, and your respect. Please, stay with me because you want to Toosia...stay because you want us to be together, as a family."

Well, there it was, in the open. He'd put his heart on his sleeve and could only wait to see what she would do with it.

Slowly, she removed her hand from his and cupped his chin gently, lifting his head up to face her. She had a small, tight smile on her face, and tears welled from both eyes.

"Love was never in doubt Nayllen. I have always loved you, and always will. We grew so far apart over these long years, that the pain from those wounds is still fresh." She wiped her eyes with a napkin before continuing.

"I kidded myself into taking this role because of my family, my pride, and out of fear. But inside, I wanted to believe you'd changed from your coma. When you woke and I saw you for that first time in the hospital, I had not been prepared for the obvious feelings you had for me. I didn't know how to respond, so…so I shut you out."

She wiped her eyes again and took a sip from her tea.

"My resolve to end our marriage was strong, even after that first visit. But something about you had evoked strong memories and feelings that I had buried long ago. When I received all your letters and messages, these feelings only confused me. Again, I couldn't respond."

She wiped more tears from her eyes, and gestured to Tyler's chair, "Please Nayllen, sit down."

He rose from his knees and sat back in the chair, waiting for her to finish, hope building slightly by what she was saying.

"When Marshall Sliss contacted me about three weeks ago, I was initially dubious about what he had suggested. It took me an entire week to respond, much to the Marshall's distress I'm sure. However, the more I thought about it, the more I had to know whether your feelings were sincere and genuine. In the guise of helping your career and my family, I accepted the Marshall's offer to help."

She sipped more tea, obviously gaining resolve from the stimulant.

"Seeing you now, and hearing your words…" she broke down sobbing, finally unable to control her emotions.

Tyler leaned forward and took her hand into his again, trying to comfort her. Her hand trembled at his touch, almost pulling away, but finally firmly grasping his for support.

"I...see and...feel a change in you that I thought could never happen again. I do want to be with you Nayllen, I really do!"

She broke down completely and Tyler got up to comfort her. She grabbed his waist as he wrapped his arms around her gently. He felt his own emotions welling up and barely held back his own tears. It wouldn't do to have the 'Admiral' crying, although that was what Tyler wanted to do.

"I know it will take time Toosia, but we can make this work. We can find each other once again, and be a family we both deserve."

She sobbed gently into Tyler as he held her tight. He didn't know how it would work out, but he had a chance, a chance to right so many wrongs. Perhaps being the Admiral wouldn't be as bad as he first thought. Perhaps the complex life of a powerful man would finally give Tyler something he never had, a family.

It had taken some time for both to compose themselves before Tyler signaled to his staff to cancel all his meetings for the day. Marshall Sliss had protested until Tyler indicated he and Toosia would be inspecting the grounds of estate. At that comment, the Marshall backed down quickly and wished them well. Tyler reassured him that he would be available again tomorrow.

With his meetings canceled, he and Toosia called for ground transport to tour the Estate. They traveled off the mountain and down to the village to see the caretaker and chief operator of the winery.

All throughout the inspection tour, they held hands, embraced warmly and stared into each others eyes. Tyler knew he was on a date he would never forget. He sensed Toosia felt the same way, even though she was apprehensive about showing affection.

They did not talk much with each other, but listened and talked excitedly with the people they met along their tour. The chief operator of the winery was a man named Kiiren Oslaan, tenth generation caretaker of the estate's winery. The Admiral had no memory of Kiiren, but did remember the man's father and grandfather.

Kiiren admitted to taking over the operations after his father had suffered health problems five years earlier. Although Kiiren was the youngest in his line to take over operation, the winery had vastly improved under his short tenure.

Kiiren excitedly showed them the awards and accolades the winery had received over two of their finest years yet. According to Kiiren, this year's harvest was looking to be even better. He assured Tyler that they would receive several hundred cases of this latest batch for the estate cellar.

Kiiren was both affable and talkative, causing both Tyler and Toosia to escape from the emotional state of breakfast and enjoy the tour. Although the 'Admiral' had rarely shown interest in his family's wine production, Tyler was more than interested.

He was fascinated by the process that created the wonderful wines he had been enjoying, and Kiiren's intense passion for the business could get anyone excited about it.

It has been one of the best times Toosia and the Admiral could remember having. They felt like an old couple, familiar and warm, while being excited like a first date. Since Tyler had changed into an Onyalum, he had never felt so happy. He didn't want the day to end.

After the tour and lunch at the winery, they headed back to the palace where the Marshall and the palace staff had prepared an incredible dinner just for two. Both laughed at the Marshall's obvious gesture to foster their newfound relationship, but both accepted it and embraced it nonetheless. They had finally parted, retiring to their separate rooms to bathe and dress for the romantic evening.

Tyler donned the Admiral's finest formal uniform while Toosia dressed in an elegant gown of dark blue. The gown clung to her body, outlining the shape beneath. It was breathtaking, and Tyler showed his approval with pulses of light flickering across his face.

When they both met in the dining room, Tyler helped Toosia into her chair, lightly kissing her cheek before taking his own seat. The kitchen staff had not disappointed, and they were lavished with multiple courses of exquisite foods from all over the planet.

With each course, samples of the estate's best wines were served at the perfect temperature. Tyler felt like a King.

Several hours later, the dinner concluded, and Tyler excused the staff as he and Toosia retired with after dinner drinks to the couch in front of the large fireplace. The fire burned brightly, filling the room with a dancing glow of yellow gold. Toosia was barefoot, her legs stretched out on the couch, settled into Tyler's arms.

The moment was so peaceful, so happy after the day they'd had. He gently caressed the skin of her arm, his hands moving across her body, feeling the familiar curves he longed to explore. He felt hot and excited and noticed a small play of colors across her exposed skin.

He wanted to take her right there, to make love to her like the dream from the night before, but he held back. He didn't want to ruin the road to their recovery by rushing into the physical part of their relationship. Although he sensed she also wanted to make love, she too held back, still tentative in the renewal of their emotions.

They held on to each other well into the night, both finally succumbing to sleep in the warmth of the fire. Tyler woke late in the night, the fire just embers and a soft glow. Tyler noted that one of the staff had placed a blanket over Toosia who currently lay curled up with her head on his lap.

She looked so peaceful, he didn't want to disturb her. They'd both drank a lot of wine throughout the day, and although Tyler was used to it, he wasn't sure she was. Gently, he slipped out from underneath her and stood up. He was stiff, but otherwise felt good for sleeping upright on the couch.

She didn't stir at his movement, so he gently shook her trying to wake her quietly. She rolled over and continued to sleep. He didn't want to leave her on the couch, so he wrapped her in the blanket and carried her back to her room. She was light in his arms and he easily made the journey to her quarters while she slept.

He put her to bed, removing her gown and covering her with sheets. She rolled away from him towards the center of the bed, still asleep. Quietly, he left her room and headed back to his own. He couldn't remember when he had ever felt this good and not been

153

high. The wine had helped, sure, but the feelings of love he now felt for Toosia were more powerful than any drug Tyler had before. It scared him and thrilled him at the same time.

As he lay back to sleep, and could almost feel her against him. He thought of her lying naked beside him, feeling her skin and watching the color of lights dance upon it. As the fantasy grew, the wine took effect sending Tyler into a dreamless sleep.

Yooso

The last week with Toosia had better prepared Tyler for the return to the capital. Not only was their relationship rekindled, but he found her counsel invaluable in preparing him for the rigors of the political arena.

As Supreme Commander of Poolto forces, the Admiral had spent a great deal of time in the capital. However, in that capacity, he rarely felt compelled to enter the political ring. His military record was sufficient to maintain his position within the Poolto hierarchy. Only now, when he appeared on the verge of losing that position did politics become a necessity.

Marshall Sliss' inside spies were confirming their suspicions about the Emperor and Vice Admiral Teesen. Teesen had completely convinced the Emperor that his battle plan would work, so both ignored the obvious perils and quickly embarked down a dangerous path.

Both knew Admiral Osloo's opposition to the plan, so both had much to loose by his return. After the previous defeat, neither wanted an internal power struggle to disrupt the progress of the war. Tyler didn't want the power struggle either, but he couldn't just sit by and watch them lead Poolto to its destruction. He had to play the only power card he had—that of national hero.

They knew neither the Vice Admiral nor the Emperor would move against them openly, so there arrival and the planned press conference was not a surprise. Nonetheless, Marshall Sliss was concerned about other ways they could affect the 'return' to duty.

Ultimately, the Emperor dictated who was in power, so they needed to convince the press and the public that he was still the right man for the job. Otherwise, the Emperor could easily keep him suspended, pending his 'full' recovery.

All these possibilities haunted Tyler as they traveled the last distance to the city by an elegant and large ground vehicle. Tyler thought of it as a limo, but it dwarfed any limo he had seen before. This vehicle was at least a hundred feet long and twenty feet wide. It took up nearly two lanes of the roadway, requiring an elaborate escort to clear the path.

Within the monstrous interior, most of the Admiral's senior staff rode contentedly, still working on the press conference that soon would be launched. The back compartment was reserved for the Admiral, and Tyler rode with Toosia, Marshall Sliss, and the 'twin' aides, Kooren and Beelen. As usual, Kooren and Beelen were lost in their communication devices, coordinating everything for the arrival.

Two other passengers rode in the compartment, and Tyler thought their inclusion unusual. At the Marshall's insistence, two bodyguards rode disguised as additional aides. Both were more than a little imposing, and Toosia kept eyeing them distrustfully. Since Poolto had been united, there had never been an assassination attempt on any person of significant power—especially a national hero.

Tyler thought precaution was overkill, but the Marshall had insisted. In his own words, "We cannot underestimate the threat you pose to the Emperor and his plans!" Tyler still thought it unnecessary, but he had to trust the Admiral's most trusted advisor.

The Marshall had introduced them as Officer Peeren and Diitii, but Tyler didn't really want to make their acquaintance. He figured it probably wasn't their real names anyway. The Marshall had assured Tyler the men had been recruited from top commando units created to infiltrate and sabotage key enemy installations in the asteroid belt.

The Admiral had never liked their methods, but he couldn't deny their effectiveness. More than once he'd relied on their abilities to disable strategic defense systems so that his battle plans could be carried out. They were highly effective but amoral and opaque. Only the Marshall had detailed information on their activities, and he alone commanded them. Not even Vice Admiral Teesen had access to their operations. Secrecy had been a top priority when the units were formed.

Other than being imposing, both men looked the part of a military bureaucrat. They wore simple single suit uniforms with the official 'aide' insignias on each lapel. Neither carried visible weapons, but the Marshall assured Tyler they were lethal if needed and capable of handling nearly every situation.

Unlike Toosia, the two men didn't bother Tyler. The only thing unnerving was the way they looked straight into your eyes when talking. The eyes were penetrating, measuring, and assessing everything and everyone around them. That was slightly disconcerting to Tyler, but then he had never met anyone with that kind of cold, measured intensity. Not even in the tense world of drug trafficking had Tyler met people like them.

Tyler stared across at them, each one staring out a window on either side of the compartment. The windows were tinted so no one could see inside, but Tyler was certain these men missed nothing that was going on outside.

Tyler looked out the right side window and noticed a congregation of people on the side of the road just outside the downtown district of Yooso. The congregation was large but dwarfed by the shear size of the capital city of Poolto. Skyscrapers rose thousands of feet into the sky, blotting out the clouds as the car entered the monumental chasms of Poolto's greatest achievement.

As they sped by the onlookers, Tyler saw signs being held up that welcomed the Admiral back to duty, wishing him and his wife well. Tyler knew the Marshall had organized the congregation and made sure the news networks picked up on it. The Marshall had spent big on their return, and Tyler hoped it would pay off.

Their car sped through the streets toward the center of the city and the seat of power. The streets were shadowed in a false darkness from the tall buildings, but the lights lining the streets filled it with a dim twilight reminiscent of Las Vegas at night. The city didn't look like Vegas with buildings that dwarfed anything Vegas had to offer.

Tyler estimated most buildings were hundreds of floors tall, and as he stared up into the small space between them, he saw that many were interconnected by walkways and transportation systems hundreds of feet above the street. He assumed most never made it down to street level except when leaving the city. Over head, he spotted many vehicles speeding by as their own car crawled along the dark roadway.

From the Admiral's memories, he could pull up a lot of detail about Yooso. Like many large urban centers, this one was not without its problems and vices. Gambling, illicit drugs, and sex were a mainstay in the city. Like most capitals, the criminal element walked side by side with the most powerful people on the planet. It was rumored that the Emperor allowed this, maybe even encouraged it.

Tyler didn't understand why, but the Marshall had confided that the best way to maintain control and power was to make your enemies your allies. The criminal element supported the Emperor because he looked the other way—within reason.

This was where Tyler and the Admiral's political inexperience was a glaring weakness. He knew Raul had several political and law enforcement connections, but the risk of exposure and arrest were a constant threat.

This was why Tyler had needed Toosia, she had spent most of her life in Yooso. Although she never aspired to politics herself, she had moved within the 'political' inner circle because of her father's position on the council. She understood trade-offs, negotiations, and the common wrangling that were at the heart of Poolto politics. She understood many of the vast connections each politician had and where their allegiance lay. Surprisingly, it was not always with the Emperor.

With her assistance, they hoped to forge the relationships that would bring public support to the Admiral's side and ensure his return to command. The Emperor either controlled or swayed many of the Councilors, but it was his spies within the Supreme Council that was the real concern. It was virtually impossible to do anything that the Emperor didn't find out about. Many Councilors had been brought down because of their impropriety and lack of caution.

Everyone knew the Emperor was not above using his criminal connections to discredit or destroy an 'unruly' Councilor. Usually, the Councilor themselves had caused the downfall by succumbing to their own greed and corruption. This was the place that most people of Poolto knew nothing about—the place where decisions were made that affected their lives, although not always open in a public forum.

Tyler knew he had to be careful. He was out of his league and had to rely upon those around him to navigate successfully. Fortunately, once back in command, he could leave the city and command from afar as before. He hoped that would happen. A part of him wanted to quit being the Admiral and just retire to Tooland with Toosia by his side. *Maybe someday.*

Tyler watched blinded by light as they broke through the maze of skyscrapers into a blue sky above the center of the city. The seat of power lay within a five square mile area, surrounded by the artificial jungle of buildings they had passed through. The scene was stunning and Tyler had nothing to compare it with on earth.

The entire area was composed of what Tyler could only call a lawn. He didn't think it was grass that covered it, but the green color looked like grass. According to the Admiral's memories, the 'lawn' was really formed by a plant that maintained a consistent height of six inches. The plant also contained a very sticky substance that was nearly impossible to remove, and was intended as another protection from ground attacks, or intruders not authorized within the grounds.

Beyond the protective lawn, Tyler made out the maze of complexes that held the power of the planet. He knew it had been built like a wheel with the Emperors palace at the hub and spokes extending out towards the other government complexes.

Surrounding the palace at the end of each spoke was the Supreme Council, the Ministry of Justice, the Supreme Military Command, the Ministry of Finance, the Ministry of Information, and the Ministry of Government Affairs. Combined, this was the power of Poolto.

Tyler knew this was the most defended parcel of land on the planet, even though at first glance, it appeared unguarded. The enormous city that surrounded it was the first line of defense against land and air attack. Hidden within the great jungle of skyscrapers lurked particle weapons and troops to protect the capital. The city at its thinnest point was ten miles wide, and the buildings provided an excellent barrier to enemy assault. Tyler didn't think an assault could ever be launched on the city, but nevertheless, it was protected in the event one was.

The enormity of the city boggled Tyler's mind, even coming from L.A. At least in L.A. you could occasionally see the sky when the smog was low. The city was spread out, but now spread up like Yooso. Even pictures of New York didn't compare with the size and scope of this seat of power.

Tyler knew the fleet had ships that could rival the city in size, but to see it in the open like this was simply amazing. Inside a ship, it was difficult to 'see' its true size.

Tyler watched as the cityscape disappeared behind the tunneled entrance that burrowed underneath the government complex. Once inside, each vehicle came under the control of the security forces guarding the complex. The maze of roadways underneath the complex could be dynamically changed or blocked using a sophisticated system that manipulated the walls, roads and ceilings.

Only the security forces knew the layout which changed constantly. That was why all vehicles were remotely driven into the complex. As they drove through the dimly lit maze towards the capital buildings, there was nothing to see. Tyler knew from the Admiral's memories that the majority of the government operated in buildings that were predominantly below ground level. The maze they currently drove through could easily take them further down underneath the complex. Unfortunately, the occupants of the vehicles couldn't tell.

Tyler knew the complex descended nearly a thousand feet below the planet's surface—a fact that wasn't publicized. The entire complex was self-sufficient with its own thermal power sources, underground food production, water treatment, and waste disposal.

After the missile attacks early in the war, the Emperor ordered the massive complex built to withstand such an attack again. Unfortunately, the latest in modern missile technology had been shown capable of destroying most of the complex with a direct hit. Few in the government knew this except the Imperial palace, the intelligence community, and the military. Without the defense grid surrounding the planet, they were still vulnerable. Fortunately, so was Krildon.

After what seemed an interminable time driving through the underground maze, they came to the center of the complex. Nearly three hundred feet underground, the complex opened up to what could only be called an underground paradise.

An enormous cavern had been constructed that housed the government buildings from above. With the assistance of artificial light, a lush landscape with trees, gardens, lawns, and walkways spread out within the cavern. Everywhere Tyler could see, people sat in groups, walked between buildings, or lounged on the lush lawns. It was an incredible sight, and the Admiral's memories had done it little justice.

Tyler carefully shielded his surprise and amazement from the others within the car. To the 'Admiral', this would have been nothing new. But to Tyler, it was captivating, and he had to make some comment on what he saw.

"After my time in the hospital, I have begun to realize how beautiful this world is. Perhaps for the first time in my life I realize what a treasure I have pledged my life to protect. This complex is truly a wonderful creation we have made so far underground."

No one commented on his remark, but Toosia and the Marshall gave him a curious look before staring out at the cavern he seemed so enthralled by. Their reactions did not indicate they saw the same beauty he did, and Tyler thought it was a pity to be so immune to something so grand. Then again, he was seeing it for the first time.

They drove through the underground complex towards the Supreme Military Command building. Out in front, a large group composed of government officials and the press waited patiently for their arrival. Like clockwork, everything they had planned lay in wait. He steeled himself for the press conference and felt confident in his knowledge and ability to handle it. He was, after all, the national hero. That put him above everyone else, and he knew he needed to act that way.

The Marshall, Toosia, and his staff had done a tremendous job coaching him, but now, all that preparation would be put to the test. He watched as their cavalcade pulled directly in front of the building where a large platform had been erected on the front steps.

On the platform, many senior military officials and bureaucrats sat patiently waiting. At the front of the platform, a large array of microphones and small cameras stood prepared to mark this historical event and transmit it around the entire Empire. The scope of the event would only be eclipsed by an Imperial speech by the Emperor himself. Tyler felt butterflies in his stomach.

Although it was underground, the transmission would reach nearly every home and business on Poolto. It was even transmitted to all the colonies currently controlled by Poolto, and some that were not. He knew the Krildon military would jam broadcasts reaching their possessions, but that didn't matter. This event was for Poolto only.

The vehicle came to a stop and the Marshall and his aides quickly departed to ensure everything was ready. While Tyler and Toosia waited in the car, he felt her grab his hand and squeeze it gently.

"I wanted to let you know that it will be very busy for the next few months," she said, "and I want you to know how special this last week has been for me."

She looked so beautiful and yet so fragile. He knew she would provide the strength he needed to succeed here, but he could hardly believe she was capable as she looked so vulnerable at that moment.

She kissed him lightly on the cheek before continuing.

"I will be in and out of your life during this time, but you will not be out of my heart. I will provide you the best counsel I can, and I will comfort you when we are together."

She paused briefly, staring out at the throng waiting for their embarkation.

"You have changed Nayllen, and I suppose I have too. I know we are just beginning to discover one another again, and I don't want all of this to get in the way of that. I promise I will not let it, if you promise me the same."

He looked into her eyes and felt a lump in his throat. This was the one thing he feared about his fight to regain his position. At what cost would this last effort take on his personal life. He knew he must do everything he could to preserve what they had just begun.

"I won't let this ruin what we've regained. I will not make the same mistakes I did in the past." He paused, leaning over and kissing her on the lips. As they separated, he wiped a small tear from her eye, "I love you Toosia and I will not let you go."

"I love you too Nayllen," she wiped her eyes and smoothed her gown, "let's go show them what force a united Osloo family can wield."

Tyler smiled back and signaled they were ready. As the aide opened the door, the crowd erupted in a deafening roar. There were only several hundred spectators at the event, but the sound was like thousands.

Tyler stepped out of the vehicle and turned to assist Toosia. Together, hand in hand, they both walked towards the platform, the crowd urging them on with claps and shouts of encouragement. They stopped amid the noise, and holding hands together, raised their other hands in an acknowledgement of the warm reception they'd been provided.

This only made the crowd louder, and many of the security forces holding them back struggled to contain the excitement. Tyler had never experience anything like it and he was more than a little concerned for their safety. He knew crowds could get out of control, even small ones. Still, this was a crowd of government workers and he doubted they would incite a riot within the confines of the cavern.

He wanted to avoid any problems so he broke with their script and walked with Toosia towards the crowd. He held out his hands and shook as many hands as were offered to him while they walked down the lines. It may have been out of character for the Admiral, but Tyler didn't care. The people wanted their national hero back, and Tyler noted the cameras on the platform turned towards him as he steadily made his way along the crowd.

It took nearly fifteen minutes to complete the trip, and more than once the lines almost broke. However, after the handshaking the crowd began to settle down and Tyler and Toosia made their way to the large platform overlooking the street. As he passed the Marshall and dropped Toosia off, he noticed the Marshall gave him a small look of disapproval at his actions.

It didn't matter to Tyler, it had calmed the crowd and would be viewed all over the planet. Overt connections with the people went a long way politically—even a non-politician like Tyler knew that.

Upon his entrance onto the platform, everyone stood and clapped in unison. He made his way down the line of dignitaries and military leaders, shaking hands and commenting on how good it was to be back and see them.

The Admiral's memory provided a detailed biography of every one of them, so it was easy to make the necessary small talk. Once the greetings were over, he finally made his way to the front of the platform where Vice Admiral Teesen waited. They briefly shook hands, both wearing large smiles for the cameras. Tyler stood back while the Vice Admiral introduced him to the waiting public.

All along the front of the platform cameras lit up as live feeds were sent all over the Poolto Empire. It made Tyler a little giddy when he thought about how many would be watching. He watched the Vice Admiral carefully as he delivered his welcome speech.

"It is with the greatest pleasure and greatest honor that I am able to welcome back to this great city, the planet's most beloved hero, Admiral Nayllen Osloo."

The Vice Admiral clapped and turned back to face Tyler with a big smile. Tyler knew the script, so he bowed and humbly shook off the admiration and accolades inherent in the introduction.

The applause went on for several minutes before the Vice Admiral spoke again.

"Our thoughts and hopes have been with the Admiral during his difficult recovery, and we all longed for the day when he could stand here once again, a symbol of what this world has to offer this universe, a man whose courage and devotion is only equaled by his exemplary service."

Again the crowd erupted into a long applause. *Difficult recovery? Symbol?* Tyler already glimpsed the thrust of their attack—they wanted to show him as someone who barely survived and may not yet be fully recovered. The Vice Admiral knew of his recovery and how little difficulty it had been. He had just drawn the lines in the sand.

The crowd once again died down and the Vice Admiral continued his speech, recounting past battles that the Admiral had won. Always he referred to the past, speaking in past tense as though the Admiral's career were over. Teesen was crafty, Tyler had to give him that. But Tyler also knew that this speech had been prepared with the assistance of the Emperor's staff. He knew they would be working together.

That was fine with Tyler, they too had prepared a marvelous speech, and being that it would be the last one delivered, it would have the greatest impact. He brought his attention back to the Vice Admiral as he heard the key word that signaled he was nearing the end.

"...today, nothing is certain and we are still at war. The Admiral's counsel and experience will yet help us through these difficult times."

Counsel? Tyler could barely contain himself as he waited for Teesen to finish. He trusted the speech he would deliver would shock everyone and would signal his intent to become the Supreme Commander once again.

"Ladies and Gentlemen, may I please introduce to you one of the most honorable and heroic men of our time, Admiral Nayllen Osloo."

The Vice Admiral stepped back from the podium and applauded as Tyler stepped forward. This renewed the crowd's efforts and the applause, whistles, and shouting took a while to settle down. Tyler played the moment brilliantly, letting it go on as long as the crowd would support it. He waved to the crowd, to the cameras, and most importantly, to the people watching at home. *Difficult recovery? Just wait.*

They had worked hard on the speech, and the first thing they had to do was reaffirm their allegiance to the Emperor. This would rally the crowd around both of them, hiding the division they knew existed. They must maintain the illusion of a unified leadership, a common government working together on a common cause. That was how they would win the support.

Tyler stood silently, waiting for the crowd to settle back down. Those on the platform took their seats and the crowd below finally fell quiet.

"Thank you Vice Admiral Teesen, your exceptional leadership has been greatly appreciated during my absence. We are indebted to your service and your support." *Let him chew on that.*

"Please, a round of applause to show our great appreciation to the Vice Admiral." Tyler led the applause as he turned to the Vice Admiral, all smiles and good will. The crowd followed lead.

He turned back to face the cameras, "You have all graciously welcomed me back, and for that I am grateful. But it is not I that you should honor here today. No, the one we should honor is the one who continues to stand for Poolto in this grave time of crisis. It is the man for whom I have pledged my undying allegiance and offer my greatest respect. He alone has led our great peoples forward into the future, a future I have the utmost confidence he will deliver to us with victory and everlasting peace. That man is our great and magnificent Emperor Hallen Yooso IV...a man who is descended from the greatest men our planet has ever known."

With that, Tyler moved back from the podium and faced upward towards the imperial palace at the center of the complex. Raising his hand, he saluted the Emperor's palace, a gesture he was certain the Emperor was watching from within.

Following his lead, everyone on the platform turned towards the palace and saluted gracefully. Tyler finished his salute and returned to the podium.

"Let's hear a great cheer for our Emperor, defender of Poolto, leader to all, and the man for whom we all owe our greatest debt of gratitude."

The crowd responded with a generous cheer and applause as they all turned towards the palace.

"To the Emperor!" he shouted.

Tyler joined the applause and let it last as long as possible. He had thrown down the gauntlet, and now the Emperor would have to tread carefully.

Finally, the crowd subsided and returned their attention to Tyler. He had his pleasantries out of the way and was ready to deliver the speech they had prepared. He had shown the public a united government, and now he would solidify that image even more.

He waited until there was absolute quiet before beginning. All the cameras were pointed at him as he alone addressed every citizen of Poolto.

"People of Poolto, it is with grave concern that we face one of our most pivotal moments in history. Not since the late great Emperor, Yooso I united our planet and brought peace to our warring peoples have we had such a need for a united Poolto. Our enemies are weakened and we stand on the brink of an age where this war may be won!"

He waited for the applause to quiet before continuing. *I have their attention now.*

"As a student of history, and in particular, military history, I see this day as a day not unlike that faced by one of my ancestors during the great campaign that won them the power to govern themselves, free of the tyranny they had endured for so many millennia."

There was no telling how many remembered that history. Fortunately, those that had ruled with tyranny were long out of power. Tyler had chosen the memory just for that reason. *No need to open old wounds.*

"My ancestor had won a great battle against their enemy and stood on the brink of victory. It was at that time that everyone around him called for a final push...a final blow to their enemy when they were at their weakest. But, it was at that very moment that my ancestor chose not to heed the advice, but stepped back and surveyed the situation before leaping into battle." *Let that sink in. Do you hear Emperor?*

"This pause in the campaign nearly caused a rebellion within his own ranks, but his resolve and his leadership held them steady and together. That moment in their history, that moment when he rejected the cry for vengeance from his people, that moment when victory was so close they could almost touch it, that was the moment when his decision turned the tides of war and determined their fate forever. A fate that ultimately brought them victory!"

He surveyed the crowd, watching as his speech held them captivated. He could almost hear their thoughts, "What happened? Why did he wait? How did they win?"

"Unbeknownst to my ancestor or his advisors, the enemy, in a last ditch effort to win, had planned a counter attack that would have caught my ancestors off guard and likely turned the tide of the war. Not only would their forces have been severely incapacitated, but they would have lost much of their land and its people. In the heady aftermath of a great victory lay the seeds of their greatest defeat. In their haste to end the war, they would have committed their troops to an action that would have placed them in peril, a peril they had no way of knowing, or understanding."

Ahh, look at them waiting to hear how it went, I have them now!

"My ancestor knew only one thing. He knew that his enemy could not, and should not be underestimated. Like a cornered beast, he knew the enemy would fight a last, desperate fight, one that would destroy them all, and take hundreds of years to recover. He knew he couldn't move until the enemy showed their hand, until he had solid intelligence on their actions. He knew his duty was to defend his people first, and win the war last. He knew that a victorious war could not be won at the expense of the land and the people for whom it was fought."

See Vice Admiral Teesen, there is precedence in caution.

"My ancestor understood that the enemy needed time to rebuild their forces and recover from the losses they had suffered.

It was from this fact that he knew they had time to wait, to learn and to plan. In the months after their great battle, they waited and watched. It was in this time of patient planning and vigilance that they learned of the enemy's last gasp."

He paused letting the tension build. *Ok, time to let them in on it.*

"It was during this pause that they discovered the enemy had created terrible biological and chemical weapons and placed them in key regions where food production and water supplies were maintained. Large city centers had been booby trapped as well. The network was large, secret, and ready to be unleashed. The enemies plan had been simple. When my ancestor committed the remaining troops to a final battle, a battle the enemy was sure to lose, the network of weapons was to be released, destroying the land and the people. What did the enemy have to lose? They were defeated and nearly destroyed, why not take their enemy down with them?"

He let the horror of the potential losses they would have suffered sink into the crowd. He wondered how the Emperor was reacting from his palace. By now, the Emperor's staff had undoubtedly looked up the historical accuracy of what Tyler was recounting. *Let them look, it all was true.*

"Instead, heeding the advice of those wanting a massive battle to conquer the enemy, my ancestor chose to negotiate peace. The enemy didn't know he had discovered their plot, and that gave him the edge he needed in the negotiations. You see, instead of cornering them, he chose to give them a way out, a way that would not destroy them both. Instead, he gave his people the freedom they deserved while preserving the dignity of those that had ruled them. The peace lasted nearly a thousand years."

Think about that. It was good to remind them of their Admiral's historical past and the ancestors of power. Peace? Is it worth negotiating for? Can we put down the years of fighting and hatred? Probably not, but it was time to sow the seeds anyway. Considering the Admiral's father's position at the outset of the war, Tyler was walking a fine line between leadership and betrayal. The crowd looked uncertain and a little shocked.

"Am I proposing that we negotiate a peace with Krildon? No! I am proposing that we currently stand on the same pinnacle of our destiny that my ancestor did, and like him, we must bide our time and plan the battle that will finally win this war and bring the everlasting peace we all want and deserve!"

That did it, the crowd erupted into a huge applause. That was what they expected from their national hero.

"I realize we have all suffered and we have all lost during this great conflict. I know that we cannot endure this conflict forever, but I also know the strength of Poolto lies in its people and in its wisdom to do the right thing even in the face of uncertainty, vengeance, or fear!"

He watched the faces in the crowd staring at their hero, looking for leadership and certainty.

"We will not let our emotions dictate our actions. We will not let our cry for vengeance rule our wisdom. We will not let our excitement of a battle won blind our mission. No! We will take this time to decide our path, defend our planet, and plot the victory over our enemies!"

This was it, the finale—he had them in the palm of his hands.

"A united Poolto is a strong and wise Poolto. We will not let our actions destroy all that we have fought for. We will not sit idle nor will we rush into an action that is rash and reckless. We will learn our enemy's weaknesses…we will learn how to defeat them…and we will make our actions and our lives count in this war. A united Poolto cannot be defeated. No, I say we cannot be defeated! We will let wisdom guide our actions and chart our destiny, and god willing, we will win this war and vanquish our enemies!"

With that he pounded his fist on the podium to emphasize his resolve. He thought it was a rather great speech, but the crowd stood motionless. Were they shocked? He couldn't tell. The silence seemed to last forever, and Tyler began to get a little concerned.

Finally, the Marshall rose from his seat behind Tyler and began to applaud. That was enough to move them all into action. Everyone rose and began to applaud. The applause and the cheering became almost deafening. That was more like it, Tyler felt in control again. Now they would have to wait for the post speech analyses and polls to come in to see how they had really done.

All that was left was to announce his intentions to return to duty as Supreme Commander. He would allow time for the transition, but he wouldn't allow an opening to be denied. They all knew that much of their campaign was being fought right here and right now.

The crowd grew quiet, once again waiting for their hero. Tyler moved back to the podium.

"A united Poolto," he began, "a Poolto where we all can make a difference in the war. I am but one man among billions, and I cannot win this war alone. I will continue to work hard as your Supreme Commander, and I will work united with the Emperor and our Supreme Council to plot our course. My staff and I will work in concert with Vice Admiral Teesen to make our transition to full duty swift and smooth. During this transition, I will spend a great deal of time working with the Emperor and the Council. Meanwhile, Vice Admiral Teesen will continue in his role as Supreme Commander until the transition is complete. We estimate about two months to complete the transition. Now, I understand we will open this up to questions from the press."

While the press corps moved into position at the base of the platform and set up their equipment, Tyler moved back on the platform and shook hands with the Vice Admiral and many of the senior military personnel. The Marshall assured him that nearly all of the senior military staff were behind him one hundred percent. After all, most had served with the Admiral in one battle or another and owed him their lives.

That was a great weakness in the Vice Admiral's position. He held little power within the military ranks, and therefore had to rely on the Emperor to retain his current position. Fat chance if the public rallied behind the Admiral. He had more than emphasized the need for a united Poolto, so neither the Vice Admiral nor the Emperor could openly deny him. No, Tyler figured they would have to look for other means to keep him down. Tyler hoped they would not find it.

He made his way down towards the Marshall and Toosia. He shook the Marshall's hand, but saw a look of concern on the Marshall's face.

"What is it Goolen, did I miss something in the speech?" he asked.

"Uh, no Admiral, no you said it perfectly as rehearsed."

"Then what is it, you look concerned?"

Toosia stepped into the conversation, "It wasn't what you didn't say Nayllen, it was what you 'added'."

She too had a look of concern on her face.

"Fine what did I add? Don't keep me in suspense!"

Toosia looked at the Marshall who simply shrugged. She turned back to Tyler.

"That piece at the end of the speech, when you said, 'god willing'. That was not in the speech we practiced." She said it calmly and Tyler couldn't figure out where the problem was.

"Damn, it slipped out again!" He grew angry at himself.

"I understand Nayllen, but why did you say it?" She still looked concerned. "Have you recently found religion?"

"What! Me, find religion? You know me better than that. It's just a manner of speech, a phrase, no one believes it."

He couldn't believe they were taking it this way. He knew religion still existed on the planet, but only a small remnant of people believed it—surely his comment would not be taken seriously?

"Well, manner of speech or not, the only people who say such things are zealots, and they scare the rest of us." She didn't look pleased and that bothered Tyler.

The Marshall broke in, "Admiral, we designed this speech specifically to ally yourself with the Emperor and his power, but your slip of the tongue may have destroyed all that. The Emperor has, on many occasions, denounced the religious factions of this world as crackpots and kooks. Now, you may have inadvertently aligned yourself with those same crackpots as well as with the Emperor. It is a very dangerous thing you have done."

Well, there it was. Back in the capital for less than an hour and Tyler already destroyed everything they had come to do.

172

I told you I should've handled this. You don't have the experience to take on this role, but I do!

Tyler ignored Adanni's remark and forced him back into the subconscious depths. He thought about the press conference and dreaded the questions that were sure to be asked. He grabbed Toosia's hand and held it firmly.

"I am truly sorry Toosia, it just came out."

"Don't worry Nayllen, we can still win this fight, it will just be…a little bit harder."

He heard confidence, but he wasn't sure he believed it. They were ready to move to the podium when the Marshall held up his hand for them to wait while he conferred with Officer Kooren. Apparently, he had received news through his communication device.

Tyler couldn't hear what they were saying, but he could imagine what it was about. The Marshall finished with Kooren and walked over to Tyler.

"Well, the preliminary analysis on the news about your speech has already stirred up the controversy of your religious comment. The networks are all buzzing with the story and what it might mean."

The Marshall stared behind the Admiral and held up a finger to signal a wait for the press conference. He leaned in towards both of them and talked very low.

"We may be able to prevent this from becoming anything too large, but we must be careful during the press questions." He looked around before continuing, and stopped when he spotted Vice Admiral Teesen across the platform, staring at them with a grin on his face. He too had heard the early press reports.

"Ok, look, the rest of the speech was fantastic and we probably got most of the planet on our side; however, we must discount this religious thing immediately. Now, Admiral, we can't let anyone think this bothers us, we must play it off as nothing, so don't bring it up until the press does. Then, deny it without a second thought, casual and easygoing. Don't fight, antagonize, or argue the point with the press. Remember, this is still being broadcast to all of Poolto."

"Don't worry Marshall, I won't make another mistake."

"Good, we can downplay this and still win the support we need. After all, you have pledged your support for the Emperor, so no one can question you on that."

Tyler shook his head and moved to the podium with Toosia at his side. This too was prearranged to show the support he had within his own family. Everyone knew her father was a Councilor and that would go a long way in his efforts.

The press was ready, so Tyler moved quickly into the questions. He started with the reporter on the far left and signaled for the first question. The good news was, the reporter was 'on' their side and had a pre-planned set of questions he was ready to ask.

"Admiral, there had been great speculation on your remarkable recovery, can you please tell us how it went?"

"Certainly...it went very well. In fact, the doctors admitted they had never seen someone recover so quickly." That much was true, he made sure he didn't add how the doctors were extremely confused by the speed. "Fortunately, I am fully recovered and ready to resume my duties."

"Excellent sir, we are all very glad to have you back. Can you tell us anything about the extent of your injuries?" That question was also planned.

"This may not be the right forum for that kind of detail; that is why my staff has prepared a release for each of you at the end of this that contains the full report and doctors comments about both my injuries and my recovery."

"Thank you sir."

Nayllen went in order, selecting the next reporter. Toosia squeezed his hand slightly, their signal for a reporter that was known to be under the influence of the Emperor. Tyler was certain he would jump on the religious comments.

"Admiral, sir, over the years we have not seen you and your lovely wife together very often. It is truly wonderful to see her here today. Over those many years, many concerns have been voiced about your marriage. Am I to now assume that there is no problem?"

Good, they had prepared for this question.

"You assume correctly, there is no problem with our marriage."
Here was their opportunity to connect with the rest of the
population. "Like many on Poolto, our lives have been impacted
by the war. My duties have not always afforded me the family life
I would have chosen for myself; however, my wife, so selfless and
sacrificing, has stood by me through these difficult times. It is a
sacrifice we both gladly make if it helps the war effort."

Touché! Let them try and analyze that one. The Emperor would
not believe it, but the public would.

"Excellent sir, we look forward to seeing more of both of you
while you are here." The reporter looked confounded. "My last
question sir,"

This was it, Tyler was certain.

"...will you both be attending the Imperial Ball together?"

That wasn't expected, why is that important? Tyler wasn't
sure what the motivation was, but he was certain the Emperor was
behind it. He saw the earpiece the reporter wore and knew that he
was being coached by someone far away.

"Yes, we will be attending the ball together."

Tyler turned towards Toosia and smiled before giving her a
light kiss for the cameras. It would play well in the broadcast.

The next several reporters went quickly, each asking various
questions about the war, their plans, their schedules and other non-
personal questions. Tyler almost thought they were going to avoid
the issue altogether.

Unfortunately, that wasn't the case. One of the last three
reporters asked the question that everyone else had avoided. Tyler
didn't recognize the man, and Toosia hadn't signaled him either.
Both were unsure who he represented.

"Admiral, you mentioned in your speech that 'god willing, we
will win this war and vanquish our enemies'. Does this mean you
believe in god and think his help is necessary to win this war?"

Tyler watched as all the other reporters stared from the reporter
back to him and back to the reporter again. They all waited to hear
the response. Time to go to work.

"Certainly not," he answered with the full force of the
Admiral's commanding presence, "I have no faith in deities, magic,

or spirits to help us in this campaign. No, a united Poolto is what will win this war!"

There, would it work?

"Then sir, can you tell us why you mentioned it?"

"I can." *Time to lie,* "It was a phrase my ancestors used in times of great trouble, when a rallying cry was needed to bring the people together and give them the hope that they could succeed! It is only a manner of ancient speech, nothing more."

He waved it off and signaled to the next reporter before the last one could respond. He hoped it would diffuse the situation before it ever got started.

"Mrs. Osloo, if I may ask a question of you?"

Toosia didn't flinch, she was born to this.

"Certainly." She said poised.

"Your father, a wonderful member of the Supreme Council, once stated that peace may never come between us and Krildon, at least not in our lifetime. Do you side with him in this view or do you believe your husband who stated today that victory may be at hand?"

She smiled her regal smile and answered calmly, almost as to a child. "First, you take my father's words out of context. I know what speech you refer to, I helped him write it. His comments were in relation to a negotiated peace that someone else in the Council had proposed many years ago. So early in the war, his comment that peace would never exist between us was fair and accurate."

Tyler smiled, she was so good at this stuff, the reporter looked nervous.

"As for my husband, all I can say is that if anyone knows a way to end this conflict, it is my husband. His years growing up on Krildon provide him an insight into our enemy that few on this planet have. He understands their culture, their language, and their motivation. He knows how they think, and if you know how your enemy thinks, then you know how to defeat them."

Tyler could tell the reporter wasn't expecting that kind of response. He stumbled while he tried to recover and ask his last question.

"Uhh, yes, I see..." he looked baffled, "...wasn't the uh, Admiral's father convicted of treason for his actions at the beginning of the war?"

Uh, oh, they hadn't wanted to bring that up, but at least they had prepared for the eventuality. Toosia looked angry and was ready to respond when Tyler took her arm and stopped her.

"Let me answer that one dear, it is a fair question."

He leveled a heavy stare at the reporter who finally looked away under the glare.

"It is true, as everyone knows, that my father was convicted of treason for his actions on Krildon at the outset of the war. My father was a great man who held onto his convictions, no matter what the consequences. In his mind, he believed that war could be averted and that many millions of lives could be saved if we had only negotiated before it got out of hand. Yes, however misguided, my father truly believed that." He paused to let that sink in. *No use denying facts.* "I, however, have never held with his convictions and at the time, I urged him to abandon his beliefs and return home. He did not listen to my advice and sealed his own fate. As you know, he was executed on Krildon as a spy."

He watched as the reporter squirmed. He wasn't sure who he was, but he bet an open attack on the national hero was not going to go over well with either the public or his employers. He knew Marshall Sliss was marking the man and already tracking down his employer even as they spoke.

Tyler didn't feel pity for him, sensationalism was not warranted here. Tyler didn't care if there were other reporters with questions, he'd had enough.

"Thank you folks for your great questions and the time you afforded us. Your welcome and appreciation has not gone unnoticed. However, we have much to do and we mustn't delay any longer. Thank you for coming and good day to you all!"

He and Toosia waved to the crowd and cameras, smiling before they headed off the platform and onto the steps leading to the entrance to the Supreme Military Command. Once inside, Tyler felt a wave of relief, but more than that, he felt victorious.

They had a long road ahead, but Tyler felt confident they had won the battle today. Time and the polls would tell, but he felt confident. Perhaps he really could pull this off? Perhaps he really could be the Admiral?

Similar to all buildings in the capital complex, the Supreme Military Command contained housing for nearly all staff members. When full, the military complex housed over twenty thousand, including the deluxe accommodations afforded the Supreme Commander.

Above ground, the complex soared fifteen stories into the sky with fabulous views of the surrounding city. The top two stories of the central building made up the Supreme Commander's lodgings and offices. These deluxe accommodations came replete with a full staff just slightly smaller than the Admiral's estate. All of this was paid with taxpayer monies, and more than once the Admiral had commented on the excess extravagance, especially during war.

Tyler and Toosia settled into their quarters, each taking a separate bedroom. They were still not yet to the point where they would share a bed, but Tyler was hopeful it would happen soon. In the meantime, he was happy enough just to have her with him.

After the press conference, they spent time debriefing and reviewing the poll results. The numbers proved to be of great relief as they indicated no backlash from his religious slip. His numbers were stronger than they had ever been—obviously rising on his triumphant return.

They knew the Emperor saw the same numbers, thus it had been imperative to show a strong Imperial allegiance and desire for a united Poolto. This took a lot of the threat the Admiral's popularity posed away from the Emperor, and made the public feel confident their government spoke with a single voice. This would be important moving forward as they made some very hard decisions.

Although the buzz in the press concerning the religious comment had died down, the Marshall's 'networks' indicated it had not gone away completely. Many religious factions around the planet were using it as a propaganda tool to spread their message.

It was expected, and the Admiral's staff felt it too would soon die down. Despite this optimistic assessment, the Marshall assigned resources to key places in the 'fringe' to keep an eye on things.

Everything about the capital complex seemed very foreign to Tyler. Even the Admiral's memories provided little insight into the vast complex. Tyler knew the Admiral had never liked Yooso and he suspected that was why the Admiral spent most of his time in space. The immense size and abundant population made it cramped like a spaceship, but the culture and environment did not match. Tyler received all the respect his position demanded, but he sensed an over abundance of impatience throughout the complex.

Considering the Vice Admiral's new plan, Tyler wasn't surprised everyone felt pressured. The Vice Admiral had done plenty to build momentum behind his battle plan while Tyler had been recuperating at Tooland. This fact wasn't lost on the Marshall who expressed concern that the progress had not been adequately relayed to him while absent. Although they did not meet open opposition, the undercurrent appeared to run parallel to that of the Vice Admiral.

The Admiral's staff all knew they needed a fast, clear path to re-establish their power base. The military wouldn't wait forever, even if their greatest leader urged caution. Tyler knew when push came to shove, they would side with the Emperor who ultimately held all power. The only way to prevent this was to give them a better alternative.

The problem was they didn't have one. So far, intelligence had been spotty at best, and non-existent at worst. The military still couldn't figure out why the Admiral's attack hadn't worked. By all calculations, they should have defeated Krildon and taken their home world. Something went wrong, but they didn't know what.

It was as though Krildon knew of the attack, even though it had been the most well guarded secret. This was why Tyler and the Marshall felt so uncomfortable with the Vice Admiral's plan. What if it became compromised? Could it spell certain defeat for Poolto? If so, why did the Emperor side with the plan? Tyler knew the Emperor was a shrewd man and not prone to rash decisions. Still, something didn't feel right, but Tyler couldn't figure out what.

There was nothing in Poolto history or the Admiral's memories with which to compare the current situation. The government had created the enormous lie and now needed a way to justify it. Tyler didn't believe Krildon felt cornered, especially if they had inside intelligence on Poolto. Unfortunately, they didn't have the same intelligence on Krildon.

Most within the Admiral's staff felt it was impossible to believe a citizen of Poolto could betray their planet, but Tyler knew no Krildon lived within parsecs of Poolto, let alone inside the military. Because the two species were physiologically so different, it would be impossible for someone from Krildon to disguise themselves as a Poolto citizen. Assuming it was a security leak, that left only one conclusion, they had traitor in their midst.

What would be the motivation for someone to betray their home world? Money? Power? Tyler assumed the list was vast. Betrayal was a common theme in the drug underworld on earth, but luckily for Raul, no one had ever betrayed the organization or its network. If they had, Tyler assumed they would have done it for money and power.

On Poolto however, it was more of a puzzle that Tyler thought might never be solved. It was hard to imagine that such a bitter hatred of the enemy could be put aside for personal gain. Nearly everyone had lost during the missile attack so early in the war. The scars from that devastation still ran deep, and Tyler guessed most would never even consider profiting from the ongoing conflict.

Tyler decided it was better to focus on the immediate concern—getting his power back. He thought about that very problem as he made his way to a conference with the senior military staff. Since returning to Yooso, the Admiral had so far avoided meeting with the Supreme Military Command staff. The Admiral's staff had 'held' them off until they could settle in.

The Vice Admiral was running the conference, and that alone was reason for concern. The Marshall confided he didn't see any advantage or benefit to the conference and had already approached the Vice Admiral with those sentiments. As expected, the Vice Admiral had dismissed them with a wave of his hand.

Rumor had it that many in the senior staff were not happy about the lie they had helped propagate, and many were anxious to move past it as quickly as possible. A great victory would help that effort, so the Vice Admiral used this as a tool to promote his own plan.

The fear was real and even the Admiral's staff had admitted to Tyler that it was becoming increasingly difficult to keep the 'lie' concealed. Too many people had been involved and too many had suffered losses. The situation was taking its toll on military morale, and the senior staff believed a new mission was needed to move beyond the problem.

Unfortunately, that played directly into the Vice Admiral's hands. Support for his plan had steadily grown despite the early efforts of the Admiral's staff. Tyler knew they had their work cut out, especially since the Vice Admiral was using the conference to degrade support for the Admiral since they had no counter-plan. Tyler feared it might work.

A leader without focus, vision, and certainty would breed discontentment within the ranks. At that moment, Tyler could offer none of those things. The all knew loyalty went only so far

Tyler walked through the large double doors and into a conference room that held fifty people around a large oval table. Each seat around the table contained a separate viewer to watch presentations and data. In the center of the table, a holo-projector was used to display three dimensional battle plans and reconnaissance intel.

Tyler accessed the Admiral's memories and noted the Vice Admiral sat at the seat reserved for the Supreme Commander. Tyler moved to the seat at the opposite end of the table, thankful for an end seat. Marshall Sliss had already sat to the right of the empty chair, apparently signaling to everyone else that the end seat was Admiral Osloo's. As he took his seat, everyone stood at attention except the Vice Admiral.

"At ease gentlemen, no need for formalities here." Tyler said.

Everyone re-took their seats, and Tyler acknowledged many of the members with a nod of his head. The table still held a few empty spots, but Tyler knew it was still early.

As they waited, Tyler scanned the room. Around the interior walls, chairs and small tables were laid out for the various aides of the senior staff. Tyler noted the Marshall's aides, Kooren and Beelen, were both sitting together focused on their devices. The Marshall sat quietly staring at his own view screen which scrolled streams of rapid information.

Tyler had been informed that, per protocol, a senior official from the Emperor's staff would be attending. As a civilian, he was seated at one of the many tables against the wall. His position was to the back left of the Vice Admiral, and he too was accompanied by several aides. Tyler didn't recognize the man, although the Marshall said his name was Heeller. He was one of Regent Sneerd's right hand men sent to 'observe' and 'report'. To Tyler, he was just a spy.

The conference was scheduled to run for three days, and the first day was filled with keynote speeches, agenda review, and updates on current military readiness. The Admiral was not among the keynote speakers, but the Marshall warned Tyler he would likely be asked at the last minute. Again, that sort of 'impromptu' action would play well for the Vice Admiral.

The clock indicated ten minutes past start time, and the last of the table seats were finally filled. The Vice Admiral rose from his seat and signaled for everyone's attention.

"Welcome everyone," the Vice Admiral began, "I hope these next three days will help bring our war efforts into clearer focus."

Tyler surveyed the table occupants, but most appeared pre-occupied. Many flipped through papers or stared intently at their view screens. This didn't deter the Vice Admiral.

"We are fortunate to have Admiral Osloo joining us for the entirety of this event, an event he would normally chair." Somehow, Tyler didn't think the Vice Admiral looked all that ready to give up the chair. "We also hope he will take this opportunity to share his thoughts on these subjects before we adjourn two days from now."

Well, there it was, the Vice Admiral wanted to put the Admiral on the spot as predicted. The Marshall was right—better to address it now.

Tyler decided to stall the inevitable, "Thank you Vice Admiral, I am more than willing to share my thoughts in these proceedings; however, my staff and I are just settling in, so I am depending on all of you to share your thoughts that I may share my thoughts based on your collective knowledge."

That put the onus back on them, but didn't excuse Tyler completely. He knew the Admiral had a history of delivering momentous speeches at any military gathering. Tyler would need the Admiral's staff to prepare something before the conference ended. For now, he held the Vice Admiral at bay.

The Vice Admiral stared directly at Tyler, "Very well Admiral, we look forward to that sharing. Meanwhile, let's get this conference underway with our first keynote speaker. Marshall Siitoo, I believe you are the first speaker?"

The Admiral knew Marshall Siitoo quite well. He was a fabulous administrator who currently ran military supply. Marshall Siitoo and his staff were meticulous and made sure everything was accounted for. The Marshall had worked miracles over the years with supply logistics and keeping civilian contractors honest and on time. He was well known as the man responsible for trimming fat while keeping morale high. Tyler was assured he was on the Admiral's side.

"Thank you Vice Admiral Teesen. Fellow colleagues, and honored guests." he nodded toward Heeler who sat patiently watching. "We are faced with a crisis from which we have many possible paths."

Tyler listened as the Marshall ran down an overview of the losses they had suffered from the great battle over Krildon's moon. The numbers had risen since Tyler had last seen them. Apparently, many of the surviving ships were being scrapped due to the heavy damage they had sustained. They were barely operational, and fixing them would cost more than replacing them.

Tyler watched his view screen as the statistics scrolled past, painting a picture of the current count of operational resources. It was enough for a good defense, but not a large offensive. He watched the Vice Admiral as these pathetic numbers were displayed. Teesen showed no signs of concern.

Next to Tyler, Marshall Sliss was busy with his communication device, sharing data with others on the staff. Tyler knew they would be preparing something for him based on what they saw here today.

Finally, Marshall Siitoo delivered some good news. Most of the contractors had new shipments of equipment that they'd been working on for the last year. The timing was perfect and would raise force strength to sixty percent of original.

Unfortunately, most of the equipment still required the final stages of testing and certification before being put into service. The current estimate placed completion between four and six months. With dedicated military resources applied to the process, it could potentially be sped up a month.

So, this was how the Vice Admiral justified his hasty battle plan. Tyler could see how they would proceed. The Vice Admiral's plan would require the new equipment, and Teesen, with Imperial backing, would skip most of the space trials and certification testing to ensure delivery. *Dangerous Teesen, very dangerous.*

Tyler recounted many of the Admiral's memories of past battles where entire units were lost because of malfunctioning equipment. This was the reasoning for such rigorous testing cycles they currently had in place. Admiral Osloo himself had set testing as top priority after several bad incidents early in the war. Teesen was now willing to cast all that aside on the slim hope they could overwhelm the enemy's forces without a major battle.

Tyler watched the screen and saw the replacement for his flag ship lost in the last battle. It was the latest and greatest Poolto technology could offer. Unfortunately, like all large ships, it needed at least four months of space trials before it was battle ready. According to the screen, it was already undergoing some of those trials.

When Tyler looked at the new ship, a small part of him felt a thrill of excitement. He quickly realized that the 'Admiral' inside was the source of this giddiness. The Admiral had always felt more comfortable in space. On the great flag ship, he was in command and he controlled the smaller fleet of ships around him. Tyler highlighted the flag ship on his monitor and quickly ran through the specs.

The Admiral's memories confirmed the specs, but Tyler was amazed at the various weapons and capabilities the ships had. It would be a formidable weapon indeed, but not if the Vice Admiral put it into battle before it was ready. Nearly half the weaponry was new designs. To Tyler, that meant bugs and flaws that had to be worked out.

Tyler looked up from his viewer as Marshall Siitoo delivered the last of the supply news. Production on the mining colonies was at a hundred percent, but that actually caused backlogs since the depleted forces weren't able to consume the supply chain fast enough. The Marshall indicated it was a problem they needed to solve immediately as available storage facilities would soon exceed their capacity.

Marshall Siitoo shot Tyler a look after that comment. Tyler knew it was because Marshall Siitoo and Admiral Osloo had designed the supply chain together. The Marshall was assuming they would be the logical people to solve the crisis. Tyler agreed and happily noticed Marshall Sliss taking serious notes. Tyler felt confident they would soon solve this problem.

Tyler nodded to Marshall Siitoo, indicating 'Don't worry, we will work it out with you'.

Satisfied, the Marshall finished his keynote and sat back down. The Vice Admiral hadn't liked the exchange between Tyler and the Marshall and quickly stepped in to take command of the situation.

"Thank you Marshall, please contact my staff immediately so that we can resolve this production problem before we hit crisis. Admiral Osloo, I hope we can count on your counsel to resolve this?"

So, Teesen wanted to be involved? Fine, let him, then he will see who really had the power.

Tyler smiled magnanimously, "Of course Vice Admiral, my staff and my counsel are always available."

They both knew it to be false, but played it out for everyone in the room. Tyler noted that the Emperor's man had watched the various exchanges intently before taking notes.

Don't worry Emperor, all is civil—for now.

The next two speakers took the remainder of the morning describing training and troop readiness, as well as the current defensive plans put into place. Tyler's knowledge of the Admiral's memories confirmed that the defenses were adequate, as long as nothing else changed. At least the Vice Admiral could do something right. Defense had always been his strongest suit, so Tyler wondered at his new aspirations to launch an offensive.

As the last speaker finally finished his summary, they broke for lunch. Tyler was looking forward to the first speaker after lunch. The schedule indicated Marshall Triin, military intelligence, was going to present the latest and greatest intel on the enemy forces. Triin was definitely one of the Emperor's men, and had always worked closely with the Imperial intelligence community. That had traditionally served Admiral Osloo just fine, since Triin had access to a lot of the same intelligence the Emperor did.

Marshall Sliss had many of his own people within military intelligence, and that back-channel had typically provided more intel than was reported in forums such as this. They knew the Emperor loved control of all intelligence, so they constantly watched for misinformation. Power and control went hand in hand with intelligence, but their network had been in place for years, and so far, had never been compromised.

Regardless of its timeliness or efficacy, Tyler was interested in seeing the latest intelligence. According to Marshall Sliss, the intelligence community had been keeping the latest news tight to their chest. That meant it was valuable.

As pre-arranged, Tyler and the Admiral's staff met for lunch to debrief the morning information. The meeting was held in the private conference room that was part of the Supreme Commander's suites. As usual, the kitchen staff provided a wonderful meal, served hot and quickly.

Lunch was two hours long, and they had much to cover in that short timeframe. Marshall Sliss led the debriefing, assigning responsibility to lower staff members for many of the agenda items. There were two major priorities they needed to move on:

the readiness and schedule of new equipment certification, and the supply chain problem.

One of the staff members reported they'd already been contacted by Vice Admiral Teesen's staff to 'resolve' the supply chain problems. Tyler listened intently as the person reported the conversation. Officer Slaas was a very reliable and able member of Admiral Osloo's staff, and she dutifully reported the incident without any embellishments. When finished with the report, she waited patiently for questions and instructions.

Marshall Sliss jumped in, "Ok, we have to work with them on this one, but here is how it will go. I will talk with Marshall Siitoo to bring him in on our plan. At no time should anyone in the Vice Admiral's staff be in charge of any aspect of this issue. However, we will involve them as we dictate, creating an illusion they are involved. Between us and Marshall Siitoo, we can force Teesen's staff out by illuminating their ignorance."

"But sir," Officer Slaas rebutted, "Vice Admiral Teesen has a staff member who will surely be put on this, and he knows as much about our supply chain as anyone in this room." Realizing her mistake, she quickly added, "My apologies Admiral, as much as any of 'us'."

Tyler gave her a reassuring smile and an affirming nod, "Apology accepted Officer Slaas." He scanned the room quickly, "She is right of course, I know the person she speaks of, and his knowledge is nearly as great as my own."

He stood up and walked over to the buffet, selecting a wonderful fruit desert he was partial to. Everyone in the room waited patiently, looking for leadership in solving this problem.

Tyler re-took his seat and placed his desert on the table.

"Ok, here is what we are going to do. The man on the Vice Admiral's staff is Officer Tooloo Kiir, and he was once the best supply officer I had in my seventh fleet. We cannot show him up, therefore, we must recruit him to our side. Officer Kiir will know he cannot usurp responsibility for this operation from Marshall Siitoo, but he will insist on a major piece of it."

Officer Slaas looked worried, "But sir, how can we recruit him?"

"You're not going to recruit him, I am." He let them think about that before continuing, "Officer Slaas, I would like you to set up a meeting with him immediately. Tell him we are looking forward to working with him on this, and that we want to discuss some details with him before we proceed with Marshall Siitoo."

The Marshall chimed in, "Ok, make it happen Officer Slaas!"

Tyler looked at the staff confidently, "He will be suspicious, but he will come. The Vice Admiral will insist upon it. However, they will not suspect that I will be the one meeting him. Let's keep this confidential folks, it is a small battle, but they all add up over time."

Tyler was extremely satisfied with how he handled that crisis—if only he knew how he would recruit the officer. Vice Admiral Teesen had recruited Officer Kiir with a promotion long ago. At the time, the seventh fleet commander had not seen fit to promote the ambitious officer despite his obvious brilliance in supply chain logistics. Admiral Osloo had regretted the loss, but at the time, he'd been heavily occupied in multiple battle campaigns, so he rarely involved himself in such 'trivial' matters. It wasn't trivial anymore.

Funny how things came back to haunt you. Well maybe he could still salvage the situation. At the very least, he had to try. He made a mental note to discuss it with Marshall Sliss and Marshall Siitoo. Their advice would be invaluable in dealing with the young officer.

The rest of the debriefing ran smoothly, and Tyler left feeling satisfied they were making progress towards regaining their power. Although they didn't really discuss the transition, rumor had it many on the staff were meeting resistance from Vice Admiral Teesen's staff. It was never anything too overt, but stalls and delay seemed to be the general tactic used. Unfortunately, Tyler knew time was not on their side.

Once everyone had returned from lunch, Marshall Triin wasted no time delivering his current intelligence report. According to the latest intelligence, their failed attack had caused considerable damage to Krildon forces and had created great concern among the population.

According to the latest estimates, the Krildon forces were currently fifty percent of pre-battle strength. Unfortunately, intelligence on their weapons' production was sketchy at best, so they didn't really know how or when Krildon could rebuild their fleet.

Tyler noted this last bit fed perfectly into the Vice Admiral's hands. They could easily justify an offensive action while the enemy rebuilt. Although their own forces were depleted, Krildon knew this and that gave Poolto an edge for another attack.

The problem was, the enemy would already have adjusted their defenses, and the intelligence they had was still too damned sketchy. What if Krildon's supply chain had been full before the attack? No one knew, therefore, Tyler sided with the cautious approach.

Marshall Triin continued to report on various known assets, their locations, and defensive status. Watching with the Admiral's perspective, Tyler saw an enemy that was ready for another assault, even though he agreed they would not expect it.

As he finished, Marshall Triin shared a small bit of information that he confided the intelligence community was not concerned about, although it was puzzling. Based on the information, they suspected another base was being constructed somewhere around their planet.

This assumption was based on intelligence indicating an increase in shipments of a benign Krildon mineral called 'Scrilt'. The mineral was commonly an additive to certain plastics and ceramics used in space construction. Before the war, several Poolto companies had used the substance to build mining colonies, although the cost proved greater than comparable materials found on Poolto.

Those wasteful companies had been fronts for the intelligence community in a rare insight into the possibility of war with Krildon. At the time, the companies tried to find military applications for the mineral, but never succeeded in creating anything other than pre-fab construction for space applications.

According to Poolto's scientists, the best application was in creating materials for 'non-atmospheric' environments. The substance, when combined with other materials, just didn't have sufficient strength for most military applications. At that time, rumors had circulated that Krildon was experimenting with the mineral as a catalyst in new reactors, but Poolto chemists had discounted that application since the substance had such low reactive properties.

To this day, Poolto intelligence had tracked the mineral's use, but only as an indicator of military base and depot construction. Marshall Triin ended his report with that extra tidbit and turned the proceedings back over to Vice Admiral Teesen.

For some reason he couldn't put his finger on, Tyler was concerned about the Scrilt. The Admiral's memories didn't support direct his anxiety, but something about the mineral shipments had raised a red flag.

He needed more information, but wasn't sure how to get it. He had to talk with Marshall Sliss to see if his resources could track down additional information on Scrilt shipments. Marshall Triin had reported Krildon had shipped an enormous quantity of the material over the last year, so the natural assumption was new base construction.

Perhaps that was all it would amount to, but Tyler still wanted to make sure. If Krildon had found a way to use the mineral in reactors, then it might also have been adapted to military ship propulsion. Tyler could envision a fleet twice as fast and needing half as much fuel. That alone could turn the tide of war in favor of Krildon.

The Vice Admiral finished questioning Marshall Triin before announcing a thirty minute break. Tyler was relieved for the break, the issue still nagged at him and he wanted to consult with Marshall Sliss'.

Tyler leaned over to Marshall Sliss as everyone began filing out.

"Let's chat about this intel report during the break—bring Beelen and Kooren."

Marshall Sliss nodded his agreement and signaled the two officers to follow. They made their way down the corridor and found an empty conference room. Everyone took seats around the small table and turned towards Tyler waiting.

"Ok, Marshall, I need your quick response to the report and what you intend to do with the information." Tyler watched as Marshall Sliss took a minute to scroll back his portable tablet.

"Using our best guess estimation, I would assume their numbers were off by nearly ten to fifteen percent. That's about normal for the intelligence branch; however, I do believe their assessment of the defensive capabilities were right on. I know how they gather that data, and it has remained reliable up till now." He paused waiting for Tyler to respond.

"That was my basic assessment as well," Tyler agreed, "why doesn't the Vice Admiral come to the same conclusions? He has the same experience we do, especially when it comes to defensive capabilities?"

The Marshall considered the question carefully, "Well…he may be blinded by the thought of becoming Supreme Commander, and may move forward regardless of the data." The Marshall looked puzzled for a moment before conceding, "Or, maybe the Vice Admiral has better intelligence than we do. Considering his ties with the Emperor, he may receive 'all' the information from the intelligence community rather than the spoonfuls we're usually fed."

Tyler thought about the Marshall's summation, but something didn't quite add up. He had also considered the possibility that the Vice Admiral was now getting more than usual due to his newfound devotion to the Emperor, but the Vice Admiral could also be fed misinformation to ensure his support of the Emperor's objectives. Or, they really could be sitting on information that clearly indicated an offensive was warranted.

Assuming they had this 'additional' intelligence, it would give them the fuel to discredit the Admiral and gain support for another offensive that might just succeed. *Damn!* Tyler knew accurate intelligence was an extreme edge Vice Admiral Teesen could have over Admiral Osloo's staff. They needed more information, and they had to find a way to get it.

"Alright Marshall, I'll admit that is a possibility. It could be how they plan to win this conflict and discredit me at the same time. I always wondered why they would move down such a risky path after our last defeat. It seems reckless, but I don't credit the Emperor with recklessness, regardless of my personal feelings about him."

"True," the Marshall responded, "he has never acted reckless in the past. Perhaps they have seen a way to win this conflict, and they want you out of the way in the aftermath. Then he would be a truly victorious Emperor, with no one to threaten Imperial power or popularity."

"Ok, assume for a moment this was true, then why should we resist?" Tyler asked, wondering himself. "If he has seriously found a way to attack our enemy and inflict heavy damage, why should we stop it? I am, after all, a true professional, and a victory is a victory even if I didn't design it. I am not a politician and the loss of power does not mean that much to me. The safety and success of Poolto—that is what I care about."

The Marshall absorbed it with a look of deep concern. Tyler was more than happy with the idea of retiring with Toosia to their estates, spending the rest of their lives enjoying each other. The Marshall, however, was military through and through and wouldn't know what to do with himself if he were forced to retire. Tyler was certain the Marshall had never even entertained the notion before now.

Without the Admiral, the Marshall was out. He could vie for another position, but the Vice Admiral, if he became Supreme Commander, would hardly be generous to the man who had worked against him. That was the way military politics went, and the Marshall knew it.

"I don't know," the Marshall said, "at the surface, it seemed reckless. Now however, I am not as certain as I had been. Perhaps we need to reconsider our position and re-analyze their plan?"

Tyler didn't like the uncertainty he had created in his top advisor, time to lead him back.

"Not yet, it is only a theory at this point...one to consider, but not one to base our strategy on. Put a few people on analyzing the intelligence and the Vice Admiral's plan to cover ourselves, but let's not detract from the mission we already started." Tyler watched as the Marshall's demeanor changed back to strict military duty.

"Now," Tyler wanted to change the subject, "I noted the Scrilt shipments were included in the report, but they were downplayed pretty heavily. What do think Marshall, is it something we shouldn't worry about?"

"I agree with Marshall Triin, I think Krildon is building more bases or supply depots."

Tyler had hoped the Marshall could have provided greater insight, but then they could be correct in their assessment. "I can't put my finger on it, but something about this has me concerned. I realize our best resources have discounted the mineral as not having military applications, but with so much being produced and shipped, something large is underway."

"Well, we did do a lot of damage to many of their bases and installations—perhaps this is for repairs or replacements?"

Tyler saw that the Marshall was not overly concerned, but something kept nagging at Tyler.

"Perhaps, but why were the shipments started more than a year ago, before our last battle?"

That puzzled the Marshall who was clearly thinking about it. Tyler kept pushing, he needed this explored and the Marshall was the only one who could get more information.

"Krildon has had a long time to work with the material…longer than our experts. Perhaps they finally found a military application for it. After the war started, we lost our supply of it, so we never continued to pursue research. What if they found way to use it in new weaponry that we know nothing about? Would you want to make an offensive move considering that possibility?"

"No, I wouldn't, but our experts have all discounted this possibility."

"Yes, but that does not make it so, it simply makes it less probable." Tyler looked at Beelen and Kooren, both stared back intently. Apparently this exchange was more exciting than usual to pull them from their devices.

"Officer Kooren, what do you think of this information?" Tyler asked.

Officer Kooren was caught off guard. He obviously wasn't expecting the Admiral to ask for his opinion. Tyler knew it was out of character for the Admiral, but he felt compelled to seek out other's thoughts on the subject.

"Well, sir, I must admit the quantities expressed in the report were considerable. As a communications officer, we get familiar with the size of supplies that move around the military, and those appeared much larger than I would expect for a base or depot." He paused to gather his thoughts.

"I am no expert on material chemistry, so I cannot give any advice on whether they have found a military application for the material; however, I can tell you that about a year ago, I read our own scientists found a military use for a substance that was a common by-product of a certain food production. The details escape me, but the premise was that the discovery was significant to the war effort. Perhaps Krildon has made a similar breakthrough?"

They all sat quiet, contemplating what officer Kooren had said. Tyler knew fresh eyes could often help define a problem. Answers may not be given, but another way of looking at it could be invaluable in finding the answers.

Tyler saw Kooren's comments had an effect on the Marshall. He stared at his tablet in deep thought before he began writing something forcefully.

"Admiral," the Marshall started, "I think that perhaps your instincts may be on to something. I know we have often relied on our 'experts' too heavily, and since they have not looked at this problem for many years, we should assume Krildon has found something valuable."

"I agree Marshall. Is there any way we can get more intelligence on this? How much pull do you have?"

"Enough Admiral, I can put more than a few resources on it if we determine it deserves that priority."

"No," Tyler cautioned him, "don't put too many on it, I don't want to raise suspicions. If they knew we were highly interested, they may simply pull the data we need away from your people. Keep it low key, but make sure your people know it is a high priority." Tyler felt that was how the Admiral would have handled it.

"Very well sir, I'll get my people on it immediately." The Marshall began writing furiously again.

Tyler thought about his own resources, perhaps Toosia might have some idea on how to track down more information. Intelligence was not her strong suit, but she had a lot of insight into the scientific community from her years helping her father. He chaired the committee on science and industry and had many connections they could possibly use.

"Very good Marshall, let's get back to the conference and see what else the Vice Admiral has to share."

Neither looked forward to the last speaker, Marshall Goori. He was notorious as a boring speaker who took his passion for analyzing enemy strategy far too seriously. You would think he was from Krildon, although Tyler knew the man had never been there.

He was a book worm who had specialized in Krildon military history. Tyler knew the Marshall had some inherent value, but he also knew Admiral Osloo had far more insight into the enemy than this man ever would. He prepared himself for a long afternoon.

After the lengthy first day of the conference, Tyler longed for a quiet evening with Toosia. Unfortunately, the Emperor's Ball was a must attend for the National hero. The Emperor often held such events, especially to coincide with events like the Admiral's return.

Tyler was glad it wasn't designed just for him. Toosia told him this particular event was created to provide the Supreme Council a forum to socialize with the Imperial court. Everyone knew it was a political event, regardless of the harmless designation as a ball.

Tyler knew Toosia's father and mother would be there, and he was nervous about meeting them. The Admiral's memories indicated he had a great relationship with both until the many years of his separation from Toosia soured them on his company.

Toosia had admitted that her mother was not happy at their 're-kindled' relationship, and cautioned Toosia against going to Tooland to see him. In her mind, the Admiral losing his power was just desert. She wanted the Admiral to suffer for mistreating her daughter.

Tyler understood her attitude and dreaded meeting her. Toosia's father however, had always supported the Admiral, regardless of how his daughter had been treated. Always the politician, he probably wouldn't let his family's concerns interfere with the business of the state—at least not publicly.

Privately however, Tyler had no illusions. Toosia had always been his favorite child. Everyone knew it, even her brothers and sisters. Tyler felt great deal of anxiety at meeting him, so he was happy it would be part of a more 'public' event.

Tyler thought about the meetings as their ground car emerged from one of the many underground tunnels linking the military complex to the Emperors. The gala was held in one of several large Imperial facilities designed specifically for these affairs. This particular facility was located ten stories underground and would host virtually all the political power on Poolto. Tyler wondered what Krildon would have done if they knew of the event and had access. The thought sent chills through him.

The car pulled up in line behind four others waiting to offload passengers. Tyler watched Toosia fidget, pulling out a mirror to check her appearance one last time. It was odd, she normally was at home with these affairs, having been raised on them since childhood.

Tyler imagined she too was nervous at meeting her parents now that she was back together with her husband again. Memories of Linda flooded Tyler as he recounted the one time he had met her parents. Tyler sensed her parents had disliked him from the outset. His background and questionable direction for the future had conflicted with their view of the proper 'man' for their daughter.

Linda had downplayed the meeting at first, but later, her family admitted their true feelings. Shortly after that, she had severed all contact with them. At the time, Tyler had been happy with her disillusionment with her family, but now, he simply felt guilty about it. He hoped that after his 'death', she had reunited with her family. The memory left Tyler feeling melancholy.

The car finally pulled up to the carpeted entrance and one of the assistants opened their door. Thankfully, no press was permitted to this affair, and they made their way up the sweeping staircase peacefully. The Emperor rarely allowed the press to 'his' affairs, and the need for a security clearance to access underground palace levels ensured they didn't show up uninvited.

Tyler ran through the Admiral's memories, preparing himself for the night's activities. He knew they would be announced, the Emperor would come last, and they would be required to mingle throughout the affair with political 'allies'.

The Marshall had assured him the event would be an opportunity to strengthen existing ties, and even create new ones. Because of this ability to forge new relationships, many speculated as to why the Emperor sponsored these affairs. After all, not everyone sided with the Emperor, especially those on the Supreme Council.

Tyler knew why the Emperor did it. It was the perfect opportunity to keep track of the allegiances being created. The place would swarm with palace spies, listening devices, and recording instruments. Keep your friends close and your enemies even closer.

Nearly everyone suspected this, so very little gossip was heard at these events, but deciphering relationships and strengths, that was enough to be valuable. After several hours of drinking, even slight slips of the tongue could be analyzed for valuable information. The Emperor never missed an opportunity to spy on his subjects.

Toosia squeezed Tyler's arm gently as they moved forward to be announced. They walked to the entrance of the ballroom and Tyler was stunned at the enormous vista spread below him. The ornate stairs that spread wide as you descended looked to be made of pure crystal. The light refracted off the stairs in a dazzling display of rainbow colors, displaying all who entered in the best possible light.

On the floor below, tables lined the dance floor that stretched off in the distance to the other end of the room. At that far end, an orchestra played beautiful music as a soft backdrop to the many conversations ongoing throughout the space.

No one yet sat at any of the tables, and most were clustered in small groups deep in conversation throughout the room. It was difficult for Tyler to make out faces from his vantage, but he hoped recognition would come as they mingled through the night. By his own rough estimate, he figured several thousand people were in attendance.

He wondered how they could announce them all, but a quick glimpse into the Admiral's memories confirmed only senior officials and military personnel were announced.

On cue, the band stopped playing and a flare of horns rang out across the ballroom. Everyone stopped and turned to look at Tyler and Toosia waiting at the top of the stairs.

It was an amazing spectacle, and even the Admiral's memories couldn't take the awe out of the experience. Tyler had never seen anything like it. For the first time, he began to sense the enormous power that was the Admiral. He watched the entire room turn silent, and no one moved as they waited for the announcement.

To their right, one of the many palace staff lifted a device to his mouth, "Ladies and gentlemen, it is with great honor and gratitude that I may present to you the Lady and Admiral Nayllen Osloo."

With this, the room erupted into a roar of applause that felt powerful enough to knock them down. Tyler suddenly felt self-conscious, but noticed Toosia was cool as a cucumber, her earlier nervousness gone. She looked and probably felt at home in this setting.

Per protocol, they both waited for the crowd to subside before descending the stairs. Tyler didn't want to start off the affair with a social blunder, so he waited for Toosia to start before he moving along with her.

After several minutes, the applause subsided and Toosia squeezed his arm gently to signal they could finally descend. Toosia waved casually to several people below as they made their way down the brilliant stairs.

Once on the floor, Toosia began the political introductions and re-acquaintance in earnest. She had whispered to Tyler that they could expect this to go on for at least another hour before the Emperor arrived. Since they were traditionally the second to last to be announced, only the Emperor remained.

Tyler struggled to keep up with the names of everyone they spoke to and the intricate details of the political influence they possessed. He marveled that Toosia could keep up with it all, he knew the Admiral hadn't. Fortunately for Tyler, his new memory kept everything, so he catalogued each face, name, and political affiliation. He doubted he would need all of it, but something might prove useful later on. He was certain the Marshall would debrief him.

Tyler was relieved they hadn't made it to Toosia's parents yet. One particularly nosy woman who seemed to thrive on these affairs had assured Toosia her parents were around. After she had left, Toosia informed Tyler that she worked for the Emperor's personal press office, and was certain she knew everything about anything. She warned Tyler never to say anything around the woman. Considering how offensive the woman had been, he was certain that would never happen.

They mingled for over an hour and had only made it about a quarter of the way around the room. Tyler was tired and ready to sit down, but Toosia reminded him they had to wait until the Emperor arrived. She also indicated that 'their' table was across the room near the Imperial table on a raised platform.

Finally, after they moved away from speaking with a Supreme Council Member, the music stopped and the brass signaled another announcement. To Tyler's relief, it was the Emperor.

As typical of the Emperor, he didn't appear very regal. His attire was no better than Tyler's, except for the elaborate gold trim around the neck and down the sides. On the left side of his chest, he wore a simple insignia pin of the Imperial Palace. Even the palace staff working the ball wore the same pin.

Tyler had to give him credit, he was not ostentatious. The only thing that seemed Imperial was his focused and commanding stare. You could see power in his eyes when he looked at you.

He watched everything with a penetrating stare that indicated he constantly analyzed, weighed, and judged.

To his left, a beautiful woman held tightly onto his arm. She was not the Empress, and according to reports, the Empress now lived on the other side of the planet on an Imperial estate on an isolated island. Although not as immense as the Imperial Palace, Toosia had once stayed there at the request of the Empress. Her only comment was that it was decadent. This piqued Tyler's curiosity, but he didn't press for more details.

The woman hanging on the Emperor's arm was part of his 'personal' staff who regularly appeared with the Emperor during such affairs. Her name was Leeruli Yoonii, and she was rumored to be a distant cousin of the Emperor, although her exact history was being kept from public knowledge.

According to Marshall Sliss, the two had been lovers for many years, and had probably been the reason for the royal parting. Over the years, several attempts had been made on her life, and at the time, everyone suspected the Empress was behind it. Surprisingly, Marshall Sliss had assured the Admiral that such attempts had actually been made by moral extremists who did not like the breaking of the royal family.

After several moral leaders disappeared without a trace, the attacks on Leeruli ceased. She was now a regular fixture in the Imperial Palace. Tyler wondered how much she knew of the politics surrounding the Emperor. Did the Emperor confide in her? Either way, the Marshall had confirmed to the Admiral that she couldn't be turned, and that it was extremely dangerous to try.

The room was completely silent and the announcer once again held his device to his mouth, "Honored guests, the Imperial Palace is pleased you could come to this grand affair. In times of war, this may seem frivolous and excessive, but the Palace believes that continuity in the functions of the government is what keeps us going and defines us as a sovereign entity. The Palace thanks you for helping us carry on this rich tradition established over a thousand years ago."

He paused, but everyone remained quiet. Once again he raised his device, "Honored guests, it is with great pleasure that I present to you, your leader, and the savior of Poolto, Emperor Hallen Yooso the fourth."

The entire room filled with applause that nearly deafened Tyler. The closest comparison he had on earth was the time Raul had invited he and Linda to the Super Bowl in San Diego. Unlike the Super Bowl which contained horns, whistles, and yelling, in the ballroom, it was pure applause.

As Tyler clapped, he watched the Emperor remain cool and aloof. He noticed that Leeruli was not mentioned in the introduction, but she didn't appear to mind. Her face was as stolid as the Emperors, and although she held on to his arm, she stood just behind him as protocol suggested.

The applause continued for over five minutes before finally dying down. At that point, the Emperor and his consort began to descend the stairs. Everyone used this as the signal to begin seating.

Toosia guided them across the dance floor towards the table set aside for their rank. As befitting the National hero, they were seated at a small table containing the Chancellor of the Supreme Council, and Regent Sneerd of the Imperial Palace. The Chancellor had his wife and young daughter with him while Regent Sneerd was accompanied by his lovely niece.

Cordial introductions were made before they all sat down. Tyler noticed that the Regent looked uncomfortable, and although he couldn't be certain, he thought the Regent's niece was flirting with him. It got a little disturbed by it until he remembered he and Toosia's separation had not been lost on the public. Within the circle of power, the separation was known fact, and Tyler supposed many might believe their current relationship was purely political.

Always diplomatic, Toosia ignored the girls' obvious advances on her husband. According to the Admiral's memories, these were common occurrences at such events. Tyler didn't relish the idea of fending off would be suitors while trying to build political fences. He realized it would be a long night.

As the Emperor passed various tables on his way to the raised platform, he stopped to say hello and welcome guests to the ball. Tyler noted that even the Emperor did not introduce his consort.

She stood slightly behind as usual, not saying a word and looking more than a little bored.

Surrounding the Imperial table, other tables formed a semi-circle around the raised platform. Tyler's table sat at the center of this semi-circle, flanked on either side by tables containing the regional Governors of Poolto and their cabinet heads.

The Imperial platform and its surrounding tables contained the bulk of Poolto's leaders. The Emperor took the middle seat at his table overlooking the entire ballroom. His table was flanked by smaller tables containing the various heads of the Imperial cabinet.

Tyler himself could have invited someone from his staff, but the Marshall had refused and urged him to let them work instead. Tyler agreed these functions were best left to the Admiral.

The Regent looked longingly at the Imperial table, no doubt thinking he should be sitting there. Unfortunately, tradition dictated that the heads of each branch sat together. Tyler imagined this was designed to help bridge the chasm that often existed between them. Of course, according to the Admiral's knowledge of history, the design never worked. Nonetheless, they lived on protocol.

Everyone finally settled in, and an army of palace staff began serving a generous and lengthy meal. Per tradition, every table except those in the Imperial semi-circle, was served first. Tyler wasn't necessarily hungry, but he wanted the food to help divert Regent Sneerd's niece.

She sat next to Tyler and wouldn't stop talking. Her name was Greelen Sneerd, and she pointed out that she was the oldest of all of uncle Aanweer's nieces, and therefore was the first one asked to these affairs. Tyler also noted that the Regent cringed slightly when she called him uncle Aanweer.

According to Greelen, this was her tenth Imperial ball and she never tired of coming. By the time the servers had reached their table, Tyler had learned where Greelen lived, what schools she attended, where she worked, what type of men she liked (older men of power), her musical preferences, and what the best clubs in Yooso were.

Tyler was polite, but thankful when a server interrupted a stunning tale of how a friend of a friend of Greelen's had been lost in the war. Tyler supposed she must have thought an Admiral never saw combat, and therefore didn't appreciate the gruesome reality.

Thankfully, before she could finish, Toosia came to the rescue.

"The Admiral is well aware of the casualties inflicted in war my dear. Perhaps you heard of his last battle and the injuries he incurred during the incident?" She said it very coolly, and ended with a curt smile. Tyler smiled inside.

"Oh yeah, I guess I forgot," the girl responded, "anyway, if you have time while in Yooso, I would be more than happy to escort you for a night on the town. I have many connections and we could get into all of the very elite and exclusive clubs."

Apparently, nothing would deter her from her mission. Again, it never occurred to her that the Poolto national hero might not have problems getting into anything he wanted. Tyler gave Toosia a small roll of his eyes, and she just smiled and returned to talking with the Chancellor.

Tyler turned his attention to his food and tuned out Greelen. This still didn't stop her from continuing. Tyler noticed that Regent Sneerd was not paying attention to anything at their table and instead, was scanning the crowd, no doubt analyzing everything he saw.

Across the table, the Chancellor's daughter was staring intently at everyone else. No doubt she was learning all she could about life in the Imperium. Tyler guessed she was about ten, but he was certain she knew more than any ten year old he'd ever known. She hung onto every word Greelen said. *Too bad*, Tyler thought, he knew Greelen was not a good role model.

Tyler was beginning to see why the Admiral spent little time in Yooso. It had been years since he had attended one of these events, and his memories held nothing but contempt for the politics conducted here.

At last, the formal dinner ended and people began mingling about the room. Toosia grabbed Tyler and said a curt goodbye to Greelen. Greelen returned the curt goodbye, and then boldly grabbed Tyler's hand placing a slip of paper in it.

She smiled longingly at Tyler, still holding his hand, "My number in Yooso, in case you want to go out on the town. My uncle says you've spent little time here, so perhaps you would like to see more of this incredible city?"

She let go of Tyler's hand, but continued to smile at him with a little mischief in her eyes. Tyler pocketed the paper politely before saying goodbye.

Toosia was practically pulling him away from the table. It made Tyler feel good that she was jealous.

They moved off through the crowd before Toosia finally spoke, "Do you believe that girl? The nerve, as though I weren't even there. It is totally indicative of everyone in the Palace, arrogant and self-serving."

Tyler was surprised at her outburst, but noted she kept it quiet so only he could hear. His feelings for Toosia welled up once again, and he desperately wished they could leave and be alone. He almost mentioned it to her until they stopped to talk with Tiiten Beerii a Supreme Council member Toosia's father had been friends with for a long time. Tyler sighed, back to business.

The Councilor was very forthcoming, and Tyler was able to discern that the council was split on their support of the Emperor. Although Tyler was still a favorite among many of the council members, the sting of the failed offensive was still hard to get past.

Many on the council, fed by imperial propaganda, were questioning whether the failure was due to the Admiral or due to faulty military intelligence. In either case, the Admiral was ultimately responsible.

Tyler thanked him for his support and lied to him that they would do everything within their power to find out what went wrong. It was a lie because the Vice Admiral would ensure the military placed the blame only on the Admiral. Nonetheless, Tyler knew it was be a big mistake to appear other than completely in control.

As the councilor explained his feelings about Vice Admiral Teesen, an older gentlemen came up to their party and interrupted them.

Tyler didn't recognize him, and judging from Toosia's expression, neither did she. He wore a very simple, yet stylish suit that reeked of money. He was medium height, medium build, and not very distinguishable from most at the party.

Tyler noted one distinguishing characteristic that may him stand out loud and clear. His eyes had that same penetrating and measuring stare that the Emperor's did. Tyler wondered if they were related.

"Ahh," the Councilor exclaimed, "here he is!" He turned towards the stranger as though they had all been waiting for him.

Tiiten shook hands with the stranger before turning towards Tyler, "Nayllen and Toosia may I introduce you both to a good friend of mine, Nayllen Hooss."

Toosia extended her hand, and Nayllen Hooss kissed it gently in response.

"It is my pleasure Lady Osloo." He bowed slightly after releasing her hand.

There was something Tyler didn't like about him, but he extended his hand anyway.

"Nayllen is it?" Tyler asked, "A fine name if ever was one."

Nayllen Hooss grabbed Tyler's hand and shook it firmly, "I agree—it is an honor to share a name with our world's most famous hero."

He sounded genuine, but the way he measured Tyler with his eyes made Tyler more wary. Tyler turned his attention to the Councilor who was explaining who Nayllen Hooss was.

"...he was in the employ of the government himself at one time, diplomatic corps wasn't it? Anyway, now he sits on the board of several manufacturing consortiums that supply our military."

Tyler was surprised that he had never heard of someone who was so prominently involved in supplying the military. The Admiral's memories were complete with many such people, but not Nayllen Hooss.

"...yes I was in the Diplomatic corps in my younger days, but I was never really cut out to be a bureaucrat, so I left for greener pastures."

Tyler took the offensive, "I thought I was familiar with all our military suppliers, how is it we have never met Nayllen?"

For a moment, their eyes locked in an intense stare. As quickly as it had come, it was gone, replaced with a soft, and disarming smile.

"Well Admiral, I have often wondered the same thing. I spend a great deal of my time in Yooso, so perhaps that is why we have never met. I usually leave the military dealings with my underlings, while I attend to the political side of the business." His response was smooth and convincing, "Without proper funding, the military couldn't buy any of our products. Let's just say I work closely with Councilor Beerii and the arms procurement committee."

Well, no arguing that, Tyler knew the Admiral avoided Yooso as much as possible. It was also true that Councilor Beerii was the head of the military procurement committee. It was one reason he made a wonderful ally.

Tyler responded, "Yes, I suppose that must be it. I am too often indisposed to spend time in Yooso, and I fear I may be the worst for it."

"Nonsense," Nayllen quipped, "what greater duty could there be than saving our world. Your time has been well spent my friend."

Once again he smiled a disarming smile at Tyler, and once again, something in his eyes flickered briefly.

"Indeed Admiral," Councilor Beerii chimed in, "no one faults your absence when your missions have been so noble. I'll tell you though, you are more than a welcome addition to this city when you are here."

"Yes, Nayllen dear," Toosia added, "the capital city loves their hero."

"Well," Nayllen began, "I must run, so many more to meet tonight." He put his smile back on and shook both their hands. "It was a true pleasure to meet you, I hope you enjoy your stay in our city."

Tyler thanked him and watched as he disappeared into the crowd.

"A most wonderful man to have on your side," the councilor was saying, "he was instrumental in the on time delivery of the Kiltz Cannon when it was delayed due to technical problems."

"I remember that," Tyler said, "its delivery was instrumental in our victory at the battle of Peendor. He was responsible for that?"

"Yes, he is remarkable, yet very low key. He may sit on the boards of those companies, but if you ask me, I suspect he runs them all. Close ties with the Palace as well."

The Palace, Tyler thought, *maybe that's why I feel so wary.* Perhaps that is where Nayllen Hooss picked up his measuring stare. Tyler made a mental note to have the Marshall dig up information on Nayllen Hooss. If he had dealings with the military, it shouldn't be hard to track down information from his contacts.

After hours of mingling and dancing, which Tyler enjoyed most, they finally tracked down Toosia's parents deep in conversation with a Palace official. Tyler didn't recognize the couple from the Admiral's memories, but Toosia did.

"Hello mother, father, Vice Secretary Giin," she nodded to the man, "and who is this lovely woman with you Vice Secretary? Your wife?"

The man gave Toosia a big, open smile, "Yes, it is my wife, Heelsa, finally come to visit the city."

The man stood up and kissed Toosia on both cheeks.

"So good to see you again Toosia, and I see you brought your husband with you as well." He turned to Tyler, "So good to finally meet you Admiral, your family has spoken fondly of you over the years, I feel like I know you."

Tyler took his hand, "Well thank you Vice Secretary, I am pleased to see my family is in such fine company."

Tyler smiled and reached out to kiss Heelsa's hand. She appeared a little timid but let Tyler take her hand nonetheless.

"You'll have to excuse my dear Heelsa, she is a wonderful woman, but she comes from the country. This city scares her with its size and population." Heelsa blushed, but remained silent.

"Well now," Toosia started, "with so many politicians around, who can blame her." She shook Heelsa's hand and gave her a warm and welcome smile.

"Thank you Toosia, your point is well taken." The Vice Secretary signaled for them to sit down.

"Hello Nayllen, I hope all is well?" Councilor Slay sat calmly, his wife Tooriin quietly beside him.

"All is well Councilor, and yourself?"

"Fine."

Tyler turned towards Tooriin's cold stare, "Hello Tooriin, so wonderful to see you again."

Tooriin merely shook her head at Tyler in acknowledgement. She turned quickly to Toosia, "Are you having a good time tonight dear?"

"Yes mother, thank you."

Tyler noticed that Tooriin looked dubious, but let it go.

Councilor Slay jumped in to get past the awkwardness, "Well you look simply radiant tonight dear, glad you could come. The Vice Secretary was just filling us in on the latest crop reports from around the globe, would you care to listen in?"

"No, no," the Vice Secretary replied, "no more boring crop reports, let's talk about something less serious."

With that, the Vice Secretary began asking Tyler about their winery and Estates. He claimed to be fascinated by the wine making process, and indicated that Heelsa's family often considered going into the business. Although she came from the country, she came from one of the largest farming cooperatives on the planet.

The rest of the evening was uneventful, but both Tyler and Toosia felt they had made some gains in re-establishing the networks loyal and supportive to the Admiral. Tyler reported as much to Marshall Sliss before retiring for the evening.

As an aside, he asked the Marshall to dig up what he could on Nayllen Hooss. At the mention of the name Nayllen, the Marshall had given Tyler a raised eyebrow, but dutifully jotted down the name on his pad before heading off to get his sources working on it.

Tyler prepared for bed, but wanted desperately to join Toosia in hers. They had a wonderful evening despite the nature of the event, and Tyler felt certain she had enjoyed dancing with him. Nonetheless, he held himself back. He didn't want to spoil it now.

He began to undress and noticed the slip of paper in his pocket from Greelen. He pulled it out to toss it away, but as he removed it, he noticed another slip of paper tucked inside it. He opened both to see what else she had given him. The outer paper contained her name, address, and contact number, but the inner paper was type written in small letters.

He opened it up all the way and read from the beginning:

My apologies for the subterfuge, but one cannot be too careful these days, especially at an event within the Palace. I was glad to finally meet you in person as I have followed your career with great interest over the years. Unfortunately, your place in history is about to take a turn for the worse unless you take immediate action. I know what you are trying to do in Yooso, and I have important information that will help you, or hurt you, depending on how you use it. Please meet me at the Grand Anoor Casino tomorrow night, but don't make it obvious. Ask Greelen to take you there, she would be more than delighted I'm sure. However, bring your wife with you to eliminate any impropriety. Your future depends on this - please do not miss this opportunity to rejoin the game. I will contact you when you are in the casino, tell no one, especially the Marshall!
NH

Tyler wasn't sure what to make of it. He recognized NH as having to be Nayllen Hooss, but they had just met at the ball. Tyler couldn't figure out how Nayllen had got the note into Tyler's pocket, they had only shook hands briefly. Perhaps it had been handed to him by Greelen, she could be in with Nayllen.

All of it was suspicious, and the fact Nayllen worked closely with the Palace made it even more so. If the Regent's niece was involved, that made it worse. Tyler had no illusions where her loyalties lay. Tyler didn't trust him, and felt vulnerable that the man knew more about the Admiral than Tyler knew about him. He hoped Marshall Sliss would change that tomorrow.

He slipped the papers into his brief and put his nightclothes on. He finished his ablutions, and headed to bed, worried about what new things tomorrow would bring. He once again felt like a fish out of water. Even the Admiral's memories weren't helping since he'd always avoided Poolto politics. It would cost him now—or rather it would cost Tyler.

He slid into bed and turned the lights off, lying awake thinking about Nayllen. Suddenly, there was movement at his door, and a slender silhouette entered his room. She wore nothing but a light, silky gown, and Tyler could just make out her curves beneath it in the pale light.

"Nayllen?" she asked, "Are you asleep yet?"

Tyler's heart jumped into his throat, "No, I'm just thinking about the evening. What's wrong?"

She stood holding the door, apparently unsure of what she intended. Tyler waited patiently.

"Nothing is wrong," she started, "I just wanted to tell you that I had a wonderful evening, and that I am glad we are together again."

She paused but still held tightly to the door.

"I want this to work Nayllen, I want us to be a family again."

Tyler could hear the strain in her voice. Like before, he sensed her strong feelings for the Admiral, but she still hurt from the betrayals of the past. He felt guilty that he was only a reflection of the Admiral, an impostor. But he couldn't help it, whether from his own loss or from the strength of the Admiral's memories, he loved Toosia and wanted it to work as well.

"I know," he said gently, "I also want us to be a family."

Watching her silhouette, he wanted to pull her into bed with him, hold her in his arms, and make soft and gentle love to her. Unfortunately, he knew he would have to wait for her to make the move.

"I'm glad Nayllen...I really am."

He watched as she fidgeted in the doorway, obviously confused. Finally, she stood straighter and began backing out the door.

"Goodnight Nayllen, I love you." She said as she turned to walk back to her quarters.

Tyler watched her go with deep regrets, "Goodnight Toosia, I love you too."

He lay awake for most of the night, while his thoughts turned from Nayllen to Toosia over and over again. Toosia clearly loved the Admiral, but would she ever share that love physically? Tyler wasn't sure, but he was willing to wait.

The next day, the Admiral sat patiently through various conference speakers. The agenda for the day included additional readiness reports, funding, troop strength, and deployments. Tyler watched as the Marshall made note of everything before sending it off to their staff for analysis and evaluation.

At lunch, he and the Admiral's staff reconvened once again for briefings and order changes. Officer Slaas dutifully reported that Officer Kiir agreed to meet with them. The meeting was set for the day after tomorrow in the Admiral's quarters.

Tyler still didn't know how he would recruit the man, but at least he had agreed to meet with him. Tyler knew he would be surprised when only the Admiral attended the meeting, or then again, he may suspect it and hopes to learn more information. Either way, they had to risk it. Tyler assumed that whatever was said in the meeting it would likely make it back to the Vice Admiral. Therefore, he had to play it cool.

Already, his staff had prepared several scenarios for handling the supply crisis. A contact in the Office of Regional Affairs had provided information on empty, portable, storage systems that could be launched immediately to handle the overload in production.

Apparently, the storage systems had been commissioned for a new mining facility that had been slated for construction the previous year. The bad news was the target asteroid had been overrun by Krildon forces and the construction of the facility had been cancelled.

The Admiral's memories called up the incident and Tyler recalled the vicious battle for that single rock. At the time, the loss had been substantial due to the rich ore that particular asteroid field contained. Now however, it was a stroke of good luck. Based on recent intelligence, Krildon never exploited the field after they captured it, so neither side benefited from the battle.

A young officer finished reporting by saying that the launch date had been preliminarily set for the following week, assuming nothing jammed up the works. Everything would be done through private contracting, so the military bureaucrats couldn't stop the process if the Vice Admiral felt threatened.

Tyler and the Marshall were delighted, although neither showed such emotion. *Let them see what we can still do!* Tyler thought. He knew the Vice Admiral would fume over their quick solution to a serious problem. The rest of the Supreme Military Command Staff wouldn't be as surprised, the Admiral was known for his expert supply chain management.

According to their sources, the Vice Admiral was approaching the problem through the existing military resources and was running into the typically slow processing of such a big problem. Tyler was happy they were delayed. Ironically, it was probably the first time the Admiral was happy about bureaucratic red tape.

The Marshall concluded the news by indicating funding could be provided through the Admiral's discretionary account. The funds had originally been earmarked for flagship weapon systems upgrades, but since that had been destroyed, the money was available for other uses.

Everything was falling into place, and Tyler was impressed with the efficiency and speed of the Admiral's staff. It was no wonder the Admiral had been a hero. Tyler noted that the Admiral's memories indicated every staff member on the team had been approved by the Admiral. Tyler thought his selections were superb.

Tyler made sure the Marshall set aside some of the funds for a night on the town for his staff. The Marshall shook his head in confirmation and jotted down additional notes on his pad.

The last of the news from the previous day's work was the current analysis of the readiness and scheduling of the new equipment. According to their best estimates, the Vice Admiral's plan required shaving all corners skewing their timeline by at least thirty to forty percent.

The Admiral's staff developed a more accurate projection of seven to eight months before most of the equipment could be properly fielded. This mirrored the estimate Tyler had derived based on the Admiral's past experiences. According to the staff, they suspected the Vice Admiral was proposing to bypass systems testing in favor of pure field trials.

While that appeared feasible on the surface, everyone knew system's testing was a critical aspect of the overall testing cycle. Most electronic and computer systems were new designs and required proper testing before release into space.

Tyler called up an incident many years back where skimping on systems testing resulted in an attack cruiser incorrectly setting a course for the sun. The testers couldn't fix the problem and had to eventually abandon the ship, watching in horror as it flew into the sun. Since that incident, the military enforced a rigorous system's testing cycle, primarily due to the Admiral. The Vice Admiral was taking an enormous gamble.

Finally, the discussions turned to the new information released in the morning session. Everyone agreed troop strength and deployments were not an issue in any proposed attack plan. They had plenty of supplies and carriers to transport troops where they were needed. The problem was they had no ships to transport them to. Until the new ships were deployed, the troops remained in training.

This news was to their advantage. Tyler felt confident they could recruit many of the Supreme Military Command Staff with this information. It would be a hard sell, but wielding the Admiral's status, past experience, and knowledge of history, could make it happen.

Already, many admitted they were still loyal to the Admiral but feared repercussions from the Palace and the Vice Admiral. Some even confided they felt 'threatened'.

Let them use strong arm tactics, Tyler thought, *they'll never get loyalty that way.* He sensed Regent Sneerd's hand in play.

They ended the meeting with orders to begin compiling all their information into a comprehensive report that Tyler would deliver at the end of the conference. He knew they needed more time, but he felt pressured to sow the seeds of dissent sooner rather than later.

As Tyler and Marshall Sliss walked back to the conference, the Marshall added additional information withheld in the meeting. Although nothing had yet been confirmed about the Scrilt, he noted that his informants released a report commissioned by the Palace Intelligence Office warning of the possible use of Scrilt in weapons manufacturing. The report, never published to the military, outlined several theoretical uses of the substances.

The report was so highly classified, its unauthorized release would result in treason charges followed by execution. The Marshall was emphatic about that fact as he shared the information with Tyler. Apparently, the report was squashed by Regent Sneerd, and although it was rumored some resources were allocated to dig up more information, the priority had been significantly lowered.

The Marshall said they were trying to track down some of the scientists who had created the report, but it appeared their names had been faked on the report. He finished by admitting that although they probably wouldn't get more information, the reaction at the Palace was, by itself, rather interesting.

Tyler agreed. If the Palace reacted to the Scrilt the same way they had, why would they squash the report? It didn't make any sense, unless they had additional intelligence not indicated in the report. Maybe they already made their own discoveries concerning Scrilt, and want to keep it covert. Maybe that was another edge the Vice Admiral had in his back pocket?

Tyler thought briefly about the note from Nayllen. Maybe that was the information Nayllen wanted to share? Perhaps he had access to the missing intelligence and was willing to share it with the Admiral. Why would he do that? Was he a big supporter of the Admiral's? Tyler couldn't figure out the motivations, but suddenly, the meeting at the casino seemed much more important than suspicious.

The rest of the short walk back to the conference was used to deliver a short synopsis of Nayllen Hooss. According to the Marshall's sources, Nayllen sat on the board of various military equipment manufacturers, chairing several. As most of the companies were privately owned, it was nearly impossible to uncover how much Nayllen owned. His connections ran the entire gamut of Poolto government from the military, the Supreme Council, and right into the Imperial Palace.

His previous government service was a bit of a mystery. Although he had served in the Diplomatic corps, his records of stations and duties were sealed and inaccessible. Most required an imperial order to release the documents, something they would not get.

Like Councilor Beerii, the Marshall surmised that Nayllen ran nearly all the companies for which he was on the board. It was also rumored that he had an 'intelligence' background from his days in the Diplomatic Corps. The Marshall admitted he was unnerved by the fact that someone so influential had never crossed his path. He concluded that he believed the man was both dangerous and powerful.

Tyler thought about his meeting again. An intelligence background made him dangerous, but he could prove to be a possible asset. With Nayllen's connections, Tyler envisioned him having access to greater information than the Marshall could ever obtain. Marshall Sliss almost admitted as much. If he truly wanted to help the Admiral, then he could be a very valuable ally.

Tyler made up his mind, he would meet with Nayllen and see how it played out. If they truly were out of the game as Nayllen insinuated, then they had to use whatever options became available to get back in.

Tyler and the Marshall entered the conference room ready for more rounds of speakers. At this point, the only thing that interested Tyler was further details on the Vice Admiral's plan. Unfortunately, that wasn't scheduled until tomorrow.

During the afternoon break, Tyler contacted Greelen to set up their date for that night. He'd arranged to pick her up early in the evening. She had been extremely excited at the prospects until Tyler mentioned Toosia was joining them.

Despite this obvious fly in the ointment, Greelen had agreed. Tyler was certain she was still plotting how to get her claws into him even with Toosia around.

Toosia was a harder sell than Greelen, and Tyler winced at the look of despair that came over her when he mentioned Greelen. He hastily assured her that he had no interests in Greelen, and finally confided that Greelen was only a cover for some 'business' he had to attend to. He didn't mention the meeting with Nayllen, but confided the evening wasn't only for pleasure. He quickly added that he would explain everything later on that night.

He had consoled her, at least temporarily. She finally agreed to come, but Tyler suspected it was more out of curiosity than to help him. He didn't care, at least she would be there to 'deflect' Greelen's advances.

Toosia currently sat quiet in the ground car as it sped across the city to pick up Greelen. They requested no escort despite the Marshall's protestations. Tyler had finally calmed him down by ordering him to desist. He assured the Marshall that it seemed inconceivable that anyone would injure the planets' greatest hero. The Marshall responded flatly that he could count at least three off the top of his head.

Tyler had dismissed his concerns and was adamant that no escort follow them. The Marshall had finally conceded, but Tyler suspected covert escorts would be placed on them anyway. At least it wouldn't be as public.

Tyler glanced at Toosia and noticed she wore her usual calm. She was dressed in a semi-formal outfit that fit her perfectly. Once again, Tyler was taken aback by her beauty. He knew the Admiral's memories were responsible for changing his own attitude towards Poolto, but he didn't care. He wanted Toosia and he convinced himself the feelings were his own.

He gently grabbed her hand, "I am sorry I have to be so elusive, but this is an important 'thing' I must do."

"I know," she said matter of fact, "I could sense the urgency when you persuaded me to come along."

He didn't think she sounded completely 'persuaded'.

"I promise I will tell you everything later." Tyler admitted to himself that it sounded empty. He knew he would have to wait and see what Nayllen had to say before he could confidently share it with Toosia. He didn't even want to share it with the Marshall.

"Fine," she said, "I hope you don't mind me inviting a friend along. If you are going to be preoccupied this evening, the last thing I want is to spend it conversing with Greelen."

He noted that when she said Greelen's name it came out guttural and offensive.

"Fine, who is it?" he asked.

"Trooden Hiir." She said flatly.

The name triggered a response in the Admiral's memories. Tyler quickly recalled the man as someone who had always wanted to marry Toosia. They had dated briefly in college before becoming 'friends'. According to the Marshall's sources, Toosia had been the one who broke it off.

Tyler felt a twinge of jealousy, but quickly realized that the Admiral had carried on an affair for many years, even while Toosia knew about it. What right did he have to be jealous even if he wasn't the Admiral?

He smiled back calmly, "Good...then you won't be bored."

He didn't pursue it further, and both remained silent the rest of the way to Greelen's. Tyler wasn't certain whether she had invited Trooden to make the Admiral jealous or whether she genuinely wanted to see a 'friend'. The Marshall could never confirm whether she had an affair with Trooden, but it didn't matter now anyway. If she truly wanted a family again, then she could just as likely be breaking it off with Trooden.

Tyler didn't dwell on it. He was nervous enough about his meeting with Nayllen, and the evening with Greelen.

Their car finally pulled up in front of a very tall and very extravagant apartment building. Tyler noted the building contained both apartments and entertainment venues. On the lower floors, the building held several theaters, restaurants, and shopping while the upper floors were reserved for the personal residences. *Plush no doubt.*

Tyler had seen plenty of wealth as a dealer, but nothing had ever been as extravagant as this. Everyone he saw wore expensive clothing and jewelry. Although Tyler wore an expensive suit, he still felt underdressed. So this was the world they were fighting to save. It made him wonder how everyone outside the city lived.

Greelen was waiting as they pulled up and she waved an enthusiastic goodbye to a few people she'd been talking with as she ran towards their car. The driver held the door open as she happily entered, smiling broadly at Tyler and giving a curt hello to Toosia. She quickly took the seat directly across from them, an enormous smile on her face.

Tyler broke the awkward silence, "Good evening Greelen, it is very generous of you to show us around town."

Greelen ignored Toosia completely and poured her charm all over the Admiral.

"My pleasure Admiral, I hope you will enjoy the evening. I have taken the privilege to book us at one of the best restaurants in town. I am good friends with the head chef, and it is useful to be part of the Imperial Family."

Tyler could see the immense pleasure she took in recounting her prestigious associations. Again, he wondered why she thought that would impress the national hero. He supposed it was simply habit at this point.

"Great, I look forward to it!" he said a bit too enthusiastically, "I would also like to stop at the Grand Anoor Casino later."

"That old place!" she exclaimed, a look of disgust on her face, "whatever for?"

Tyler remained calm, "I may meet a friend there for a drink, and he told me it was the best casino in town."

"Well, it certainly is the oldest," her face softened slightly, "who is this friend?"

"School chum," he lied, "in town for a convention or something…thought I would see him again while he was here. It has been years since we saw each other."

She looked hurt by this but quickly recovered with a mischievous sparkle in her eyes. Tyler thought she was already scheming for his imaginary friend. He had to admit, she was attractive, although in an aggressive sort of way.

"Very well, we can swing by there after dinner, but only if you promise we'll hit some clubs afterwards."

"Yes, that would be fine."

He doubted Toosia and he would like her clubs, but he wanted to appease her and keep up the charade. He could see Toosia practically cringing at the prospects. He knew he owed her a great deal after this evening.

They drove to the restaurant listening to Greelen recounting many tales of previous evenings on the town. As he barely listened, Tyler caught glimpses of the city out the window. He was amazed at the immensity. It was like Las Vegas and Tokyo all rolled into one—except many times bigger. It took all his will power to act as though it were a normal scene. He felt a thrill at being part of a great 'sci-fi' epic, but the mood was lost in the sound of Greelen's voice.

Although they traveled in a ground car, Tyler once again noticed the additional vehicles traveling through the skies above them. He cringed when he thought of one of the vehicles falling to the ground below. Based on the crowd density in this part of town, a falling vehicle could easily kill a hundred people. He stared up once gain and suddenly felt claustrophobic.

The car pulled up to the restaurant and Greelen finally fell silent. Tyler felt Toosia squeeze his hand slightly and she pointed out the window to a small gathering of press that was mysteriously waiting. Tyler supposed that if the place were really famous, then is was quite likely the press showed up every night. Still, Tyler couldn't help feeling someone had tipped them off. He glanced at Greelen and decided that he couldn't put it past her to inform the press. After all, what good was it going out on the town with the planet's most famous hero if no one saw it on TV?

"Oh no," Greelen exclaimed, "I was hoping the press would be covering somewhere else tonight. I hope you don't mind?"

She didn't sound very sincere and Tyler thought he could hear a little excitement in her voice. It didn't matter, he was prepared to handle them.

As the press noticed the car, they began moving towards them. The driver held them back before opening the door. Tyler moved into the bright flashes and smiled widely. He turned to help Toosia, and she graciously accepted his right arm. He turned to assist Greelen with his left arm, but she had already climbed out and quickly grabbed his left arm. A girlish smile spread wide across her face.

Toosia remained calm, so Tyler took her cue and escorted them both towards the restaurant. As they moved towards the entrance, they were quickly engulfed by reporters and cameramen. From everywhere within the crowd, microphones were thrust forward to capture every word.

They made slow progress toward entrance until finally receiving help from the doormen. The doormen quickly cleared the press, and Tyler took the opportunity to give them their news.

"Members of the press, we are so glad you are here this evening." The press fell silent with only the sounds of their cameras and equipment a dull background buzz. "My wife and I are out to enjoy the great hospitality this great city has to offer."

Toosia nodded slightly in agreement.

"On my left," he nodded toward Greelen, "is Greelen Sneerd who has graciously offered to show us around town this evening."

At the introduction, Greelen bowed slightly, never letting go of Tyler's arm. He could see she was nearly giddy with delight.

"We look forward to a wonderful dinner and entertainment afterwards."

With that, they turned around and headed into the restaurant, the cries of questions falling deaf on their backs. Once inside, the sounds of the reporters ceased as they stood inside an enormous foyer trimmed in intricate gold around the ceiling and walls. The floor was solid black, and reflected everything like a dark pool of liquid.

As if in contrast, a small table sat at the far wall with a single person behind it. To the right side of the table, a small door stood closed on the wall. Tyler figured it had to be the entrance to the rest of the restaurant, but wasn't certain since its appearance made it look more like a coat room.

They walked toward the table and the person scribbling on something hidden from their view. A small light sat on the table, barely illuminating the person behind it. Tyler could make out a young woman, very pretty, elegantly dressed in a flowing dark blue robe.

They waited quietly in front of the table as the young woman gave them a calm and reassuring smile. The effect of her smile was breathtaking and Tyler realized it hadn't been lost on Toosia or Greelen. Both smiled back curtly a smug look on their faces.

"We are so honored to have the Great Admiral Osloo dinning with us," Tyler thought her voice sounded nearly angelic, "we hope you will enjoy the fine selections our chef has prepared." She bowed slightly as she said this, but it didn't affect her beauty. Tyler realized he was staring mesmerized and quickly tried to look at something else.

"My name is Liiseer, and I will be your host this evening. Think of me as your concierge. If there is anything you require, please let me know." Tyler let his mind think of several things she could provide, and again, he quickly pulled his attention away. Her smile was so warm and inviting, she could easily pull away the attention of a man with two beautiful women on his arms. *Wow!*

Liiseer handed them a small device which Greelen quickly grabbed before Tyler could reach out. Liiseer ignored the obvious discomfort of Greelen and leveled Tyler a gorgeous smile. Tyler could feel Toosia and Greelen's grip tighten as he smiled back.

"Before we seat you Admiral, would you prefer the common room or something...more private?"

For a moment he thought she was going to say intimate. With two women at his side, that would have been embarrassing. Apparently she meant private, as her demeanor didn't change.

"Oh...the common room would be fine," he replied, "thank you."

She gently nodded her head and scribbled once again. As if by a silent cue, the door behind the table opened, and another young woman appeared to usher them in. Her name was Zeeren, and she too promised to provide 'anything' they needed.

So far, this beat any restaurant Tyler could remember in L.A. In L.A., all the workers were studying or trying to become actors or playwrights, so service was usually poor. Here however, it was downright decadent. He had to admit, he was getting accustomed to the lifestyle of the Admiral.

The small door led to a lift that gently whisked them up to the upper floors of the building. Tyler guessed they went at least thirty floors, but as the lift stopped, Zeeren announced the three-hundredth floor. Tyler tried not to look surprised. The speed they must have traveled was mind boggling.

The 'common' room was not so common by Tyler's standards. The tables were spaced very far apart and as they passed from one to another, he could sense the hum of a field around each one. The field blocked the sounds of people in conversation, and the silence was kind of eerie. They marched across the room towards a small alcove set against the window.

Zeeren sat them at the table before fiddling with several switches and heading off. The field was activated and in response, the window became transparent. She had assured them that no one could see them from the outside and that no one would be able to overhear their conversations. Tyler was thinking that if this was the common room, then what did 'more private' mean?

The three of them sat on a plush semi-circular couch that surrounded the table. It sat at an angle to the window giving them a view of the city as well as most of the dining room. Tyler was impressed—the view was spectacular.

Toosia and Greelen sat on either side of Tyler. Greelen much too close and Toosia not close enough. Still, it was nice to have Toosia there in such a wonderful setting. She looked so beautiful, Tyler quickly forgot the angel from below.

"Isn't this fabulous?" Greelen exclaimed. "My friend is the best chef on Poolto."

Tyler had to admit, it was incredible. "Yes, these are incredible accommodations, the view is especially beautiful. I have often seen it from space, but this vantage is truly remarkable."

Toosia smiled, but said nothing.

Tyler noticed that Greelen looked more than proud of herself to be eating here with two of the more prominent people on the planet. He saw her glancing around the dining room, searching for others—no doubt to mark the occasion.

Tyler didn't care, he was waiting patiently and nervously for his meeting at the casino. He thought about Nayllen and his motives again. Why would an arms dealer want to give up the lucrative environment of war? Surely he had a lot to gain from a new offensive. But then again, if it worked, then he was out of work. That wouldn't be a shrewd business move.

However, Tyler had to admit that the general feeling of the planet was for ending the war, but they simply couldn't get past the bitterness and hostility they felt for the enemy. To Tyler, peace seemed very far off. Tyler accessed the Admiral's memories and estimated the same situation was likely occurring on Krildon. He didn't believe anyone could live so long with war and not tire of the ceaseless sacrifices. Still, what motivated Nayllen? Tyler hoped the meeting would help answer that question.

Greelen's voice cut through Tyler's reverie.

"...Admiral, did you hear me?" she said.

"Y-yes," he stumbled, "I mean no, I was lost in thought. Sorry."

"Nayllen dear, Greelen was just telling us about the history of this restaurant, a truly fascinating story. Apparently her 'uncle' is one of the co-founders."

Toosia squeezed Tyler's hand slightly as she delivered this news. Tyler understood the gesture—it explained why they were here. Tyler looked around with even more interest. He recognized a few faces in the dimly lit room and decided most were prominent people of power in Yooso, if not Poolto. He recognized one councilman dining across the room with several guests. Business interests not doubt, here to advocate their causes in the Supreme Council.

Tyler realized this was where the real politics were carried out. It was no wonder Regent Sneerd was a co-founder. His ties to the Emperor would not doubt make the place popular, and although the entire place was built to provide privacy, Tyler had no doubts that Sneerd had found ways to spy on the 'private' conversations.

There appeared no end to the Emperor's reach, and Tyler made a mental note to tell Marshall Sliss about this place. However, he figured the Marshall already knew.

"Well, that is fascinating," Tyler agreed, "perhaps we'll run into your uncle while we are here?"

"Maybe," she responded non-committal, "but he doesn't spend much time here."

As if he had heard their conversation, Tyler saw Regent Sneerd enter the dining room and make his way towards their table. *What timing?*

"Ahh, we are in luck, I see your uncle now!" Tyler said.

He noticed Greelen brighten slightly, and assumed she was ready to play up to her uncle yet again. He assumed Sneerd had probably recommended that Greelen bring them here.

"Yes, we are in luck, I almost never see him here!" Greelen said.

I'll bet, Tyler thought. He looked at Toosia who remained cool and passive. He knew she had no love for Sneerd and was probably thinking the same thing as him. *We are being monitored on our night out.*

The regent entered their privacy ring and bowed slightly.

"Lady and Admiral Osloo, you grace us with your presence."

Toosia bowed her head slightly in response, "Regent."

"Good evening Regent, quite a wonderful place you have here," Tyler said, "your niece was just telling us about your interest in founding this establishment."

"She did?" he asked, "Then she will have told you how wonderful the food is here."

Tyler had to hand it to him, the Regent was cool...very cool.

"Perhaps she also informed you that we have the finest cellar in Yooso...perhaps Poolto." He looked directly at Tyler, "We even stock a great deal of your own label Admiral."

A server suddenly appeared with a tray containing a bottle of wine and several fragile looking glasses.

"I hope you don't mind, I took the privilege of ordering one, compliments of the house. In fact, everything is complimentary this evening, it is only fitting for our planet's most revered hero."

Tyler thought he heard the last bit come out slightly scathing, but realized he may simply be projecting his own thoughts onto the Regent.

Toosia jumped in quickly saving Tyler from having to respond to the compliment, "Why that is wonderful Regent, we thank you so much!"

She was so smooth. Tyler even thought she was serious at first, but then he remembered her true feelings.

Regent Sneerd shook off the thanks and moved out of the way of the server.

"Please enjoy your dinner. I look forward to seeing you again... soon."

With that, the Regent slipped away as quietly as he had come. Tyler looked at Greelen who appeared hurt by the fact that her uncle didn't even acknowledge her presence. For a brief moment, Tyler almost felt sorry for her. The moment quickly passed as she recognized someone across the room.

She waved wildly, and excused herself from the table. Tyler was glad for the break.

"I'm sorry Toosia, I realize this is not exactly the ideal date." It sounded lame even to him. Still, she remained calm and had a slight smile on her face that made her look confident and beautiful.

In fact, Tyler thought the dim lighting and elegant surroundings made her even more radiant than usual. He felt a pull on his heart and suddenly wished they were both back at the Estate, alone, and in each other's arms. She quickly broke the moment.

"Oh please, Nayllen, our host is being wonderful. I am enjoying this...immensely. In fact I am sure we will remember this night for a long time."

Tyler saw through her act. He knew she still wanted to know what he was up to, but she patiently waited and gave him the time he needed. He owed her a lot, and intended to pay it back.

"Well good," he lied, "so am I." He knew he sounded less convincing than her, but then he wasn't well versed in the subterfuge and lying that was common in Yooso. He truly understood why the Admiral never spent time there.

Greelen returned and broke up their awkward silence. Picking up where she left off, Greelen spent the rest of the meal recounting everything she knew about Yooso. Tyler had to admit, the food and drink were exceptional, even if the conversation wasn't.

The ride to the Grand Anoor Casino was filled with more of Greelen's adventures, and Tyler was nearing his breaking point. He gritted his teeth and tried to remain calm and friendly despite the inane ramblings. It didn't help that Greelen nearly molested him. Toosia remained placid and her slight smile made it look as though she were enjoying the whole scene.

Tyler was relieved when their car finally stopped in front of the casino. The place was enormous, twenty stories and three city blocks if Greelen was to be believed. As Tyler looked out the window, he believed it. He noticed the usual gauntlet of reporters once again waited outside the entrance. Greelen noticed them too.

"Oh dear," she exclaimed, "those pesky reporters have found us here as well."

Tyler saw that her face registered giddiness even as her voice sounded displeased.

"Don't worry," Tyler said, "we'll simply ignore them."

They all exited the car, and Toosia and Greelen once again grabbed each of Tyler's arms. The grip Greelen had on Tyler nearly caused pain. She walked erratically smiling and posing for every camera, and Tyler had difficulty keeping them on course. She was getting real mileage out of the evening, and Tyler had no doubt she would recount the whole affair often for years to come.

Tyler put on his best face as they pushed through the throng ignoring the questions being thrown at them. It was a whole new batch of reporters, and they seemed even more aggressive. Apparently it was acceptable to be aggressive outside the casino. Tyler thought back to L.A. and the movie star's complaints about the 'paparazzi'. He now understood their complaints.

Once inside, the press backed off as the security guards eyed them intensely. Tyler was blown away by how elegant and decadent the casino was. It may have been old, but it sparkled like a brand new diamond.

Tyler finally released Toosia and Greelen, although Greelen resisted at first. He wasn't sure what to expect and wondered how Nayllen would contact him. Well, he showed, so now it was Nayllen's move.

They descended the sweeping staircase that put them on the first floor of the casino. Tyler was amazed at how similar it was to casinos in Las Vegas. Gaming tables overflowed with players and onlookers. What looked like slot machines to Tyler lit up the grand room in long, numerous aisles. Even the sounds were reminiscent of Vegas.

He felt the usual twinge of excitement and made a mental note to try some of the games before they left. He was curious to see how many were similar to those of earth. It felt weird to think of earth, but it quickly passed.

They were nearly to the floor when a voice from behind called out to them.

"Admiral…Admiral Osloo!"

Tyler turned back and saw a smartly dressed man descending toward them. He wore a single suit of spectacular material in the colors of the casino, and on the right side of his chest a small pin labeled him as Tiineer Diinn of 'Customer Services'.

Tyler waited for the man to catch up, "Yes, what is it?"

The man caught his breath and regained his composure.

"I am sorry to bother you Admiral, but you have an urgent call from Marshall Sliss." He stopped once again regaining his composure.

"If you would follow me, I would be happy to show you a private place to take the call." He bowed to the Admiral and gestured back up the stairs.

"Ok," Tyler replied, "Toosia and Greelen, will you excuse me while I take the Marshall's call?"

"Please do dear, I too have someone to catch up with. I will meet you all later." The thought irked Tyler slightly as he knew who she was going to meet.

Greelen looked put out, but perked up quickly as if a light went off in her head.

"Well, yes, no problem," she began, "I have some friends who said they would meet us here, so I'll track them down and meet up with you later. Let's meet for drinks on the 12th floor in a couple hours?"

"Splendid," Tyler said, "I'll meet you both there. Perhaps I'll get some gaming in beforehand, assuming the call isn't too critical."

Tyler followed Tiineer up the stairs and through a door marked 'Casino Staff Only'. It led to a small hallway ending in a single door Tyler assumed was a lift.

He was right, but instead of going up as Tyler had assumed, the elevator went down, deep down. There was no indication of where they were, and Tyler lost count on what he thought had been at least 15 floors underground. They finally stopped and the door opened onto a dimly lit room with one table in the middle.

Tiineer signaled Tyler into the room, but stayed in the elevator. Tyler walked into the room and the lift doors closed, leaving Tyler alone.

Tyler wondered where the communication console was as he scanned the sparse room. The walls were a slight red color and the light of the room seemed to be emanating somewhere near the baseboards. It was more a glow than light.

He felt confused when a door suddenly opened to his right flooding the room in a bright white light. Two figures entered the room, and the glow of the walls increased to a normal light level.

Tyler saw Nayllen standing next to someone who appeared to be an assistant. At least the man reminded Tyler of his own staff, smartly dressed, walking behind in deference, and carrying a small electronic pad that glowed dimly in the newly brightened room.

"Admiral, so glad you could make it, I apologize for the subterfuge, but it was the best way to bring you here without raising suspicions."

"So, there is no call from Marshall Sliss?" Tyler asked.

"No, no," Nayllen responded shaking his head, "however, we are aware of his misgivings about me."

Tyler didn't like the sound of that. Did they know everything he did?

"You must be well informed." Tyler said flatly.

"Indeed I am Admiral, more than you can imagine. For instance, right now, the Emperor is entertaining a young woman, a staff aide I believe, in his private quarters. They just finished two bottles of wine and are lazily lounging on a heavily cushioned sofa, talking about the love making they will engage in shortly. Foreplay." He finished.

Tyler was dubious, spying inside the Emperor's private quarters?

"Maybe he is, maybe he isn't, either way, it is treason." Tyler said.

"Indeed it is Admiral, indeed it is. However, I assure you he is there as I have described."

Tyler remained quiet, a look of doubt on his face.

"Very well Admiral, let me demonstrate."

Nayllen signaled to his assistant who did something on his pad. On the far wall, a large screen lit up, partitioned into several smaller screens. Each screen showed a different scene, and it reminded Tyler of his TV room back at Tooland. However, instead of commercials and news shows, the pictures never changed as though stationary. In some, people moved about or sat quietly while others depicted empty rooms. Tyler was impressed.

"What is it?" he asked.

"That is a small sample of the Imperial Palace." Nayllen responded, "I can call up nearly every room if I desire."

He gestured to the assistant again, and after some fiddling, the screen changed to a single view of a plush room, warmly lit and filled with soft pillows and furnishings.

On one sofa, two people were intimately embraced, touching each other heavily, and talking quietly. Tyler noticed that one of them looked a lot like the Emperor. Tyler was stunned, and speechless.

Nayllen signaled to his assistant again, and the clear voice of the Emperor and his consort filled the room. It was as if they sat across from the sofa with them.

Nayllen shook his head again, and this time, the view changed entirely to a new room. Tyler watched stunned as he saw Marshall Sliss and Officer Kooren talking quietly at a small table. Kooren, as usual, was engaged with his devices while listening intently to the Marshall. The Marshall was going through much of the data presented at the conference and had Kooren double check the accuracy of figures. Tyler was doubly impressed and disturbed.

Nayllen signaled one last time, and the screen disappeared.

"You see Admiral, I am a very well informed person. It is my primary mission to be well informed."

Nayllen gestured to a chair and they both sat down across from each other.

"Ok Nayllen, I am surprised, concerned, and impressed…so why did you bring me here? To demonstrate your treason?"

"That?" Nayllen swept his hand towards the now empty wall, "That was just a toy, one of many I possess to conduct my business…to my advantage."

"Of course," Tyler agreed. He was more than nervous now and realized he was sitting with a dangerous man. He should have heeded the Marshall's warning.

"Hmmm." Nayllen sat back and looked at Tyler with deeply assessing eyes.

Nayllen signaled to his assistant and almost an instant later, the door opened and a young woman entered with a tray holding two glasses and a bottle of liquid Tyler didn't recognize.

She set it down in front of Nayllen and poured two glasses from the bottle, bringing one glass to Tyler. She quietly set it down before disappearing through the door as silently as she had came.

Nayllen picked up his glass and signaled Tyler to do the same. Tyler picked it up hesitantly, and watched carefully as Nayllen took a small sip of his before putting it down.

"Don't worry Admiral, I have no intentions of harming you. Go on, taste it, I think you will agree it is quite remarkable, and… exotic."

Tyler lifted his glass and sniffed lightly before putting it to his lips. The smell was like vanilla, but the flavor was slightly more bitter, with a fruity aftertaste. Tyler had to admit, it was very good and exotic.

"That my friend is Krildon Sarrs-Berry wine, a true delicacy and very rare." Nayllen said proudly.

Tyler searched the Admiral's memories for a reference and found that the Admiral's parents drank it on a regular basis while living on Krildon. Although the Admiral had never tried it, he remembered his father had once remarked it was the nectar of the gods, and nothing in the family wine production came close.

Tyler had to admit, he saw the attraction. The aftertaste kept changing slightly, as though several different fruits were part of the drink. At the moment, he thought he tasted banana.

As though reading Tyler's mind, Nayllen spoke, "Like me, your father and mother used to love this drink."

"You knew my parents?" Tyler asked a bit surprised.

"Oh yes…quite well actually."

Tyler was surprised. He could find no memory of this person and it seemed out of character for the Admiral's parents to be affiliated with someone so dangerous.

Again, as though reading his mind, "Of course I knew them a long time ago when I was a very different person. As we all were before the war." He finished and took another sip of his drink staring at Tyler with disturbingly penetrating eyes.

"When did you know my parents?" Tyler asked.

"On Krildon." Nayllen replied flatly.

That truly surprised Tyler. He had expected him to say something else—something closer to Poolto.

"Really," Tyler asked, "and what were you doing on Krildon."

"I worked for your father of course, as part of the Imperial Intelligence Agency, or IIA as we called it."

"I don't think so, my father was not in intelligence, he worked for the Diplomatic Corps as Ambassador to Krildon. My father respected Krildon and would have never betrayed them that way."

Tyler had said it, but wasn't convinced himself. Had the Admiral been so naive? Tyler remembered seeing many reports growing up about foreign Ambassadors expelled from the U.S. for spying. Maybe the Admiral's father had spied as well. That may be why he had been arrested. Nayllen read his mind again, and it was beginning to irk Tyler.

"The Emperor used your father for years, and when your father stood up for what he believed, the Emperor betrayed him to Krildon which caused his immediate arrest. Surely you are not so naive to believe your father was only there as a diplomat?" He took another sip, "Your father 'ran' the IIA on Krildon. All those years, and he never told you?"

Tyler saw the logic, and it explained a lot of strange things the Admiral remembered about growing up on Krildon. But still, he could find no memory of this man.

"No, he never mentioned it."

"No matter, I am sure he had his reasons. As you no doubt have realized, I never met you since I was a very deep agent at that time. It was policy not to openly associate ourselves outside of work. I was a business man at that time as well, although a full agent for the Emperor. I made a lot of acquaintances, and developed a rather extensive network. Of course, after the war started, my network was difficult to maintain, but I've managed." He signaled to Tyler with his glass, as if to say, 'how do you think I got this into Poolto?'

"So you have agents on Krildon?" Tyler asked with deep concern. Despite his ties to the Admiral's parents, this man was not trustworthy.

"Of course, as I said, I am well informed."

"Does the Emperor know?" Tyler waited, assuming this man was really working for the Imperial Palace. He smelled a trap.

"Does he know?" Nayllen smiled widely, "My dear friend he encourages it."

So this was a trap, he was working for the Imperial Palace, a spy for the Emperor. He was going to discredit the Admiral in some way, removing him from prominence, and thereby allowing the Emperor and Vice Admiral Teesen to go forward with their reckless plan. Well, if Tyler could help it, he wasn't going to let that happen.

"So you work for the Emperor?" He asked.

"For him…as well as others."

"Others," Tyler asked, "what others?"

"For now, let's just say they are people who share the same goals as I do."

"Are these the same goals as the Emperor and Teesen?" Tyler quickly retorted.

Nayllen smiled slightly and looked more closely at Tyler. Tyler held his gaze, refusing to back down to him, no matter how dangerous he was.

"You are not as…shrewd as I thought Admiral. A brilliant commander no doubt, but not shrewd at politics or intelligence." He took another sip before continuing, "That explains your constant avoidance of Yooso and your extended stays off-planet. It is no wonder you rely so heavily on the Marshall."

Tyler stayed quiet, absorbing his condescending words. This man knew everything about the Admiral, and Tyler was unnerved by it. He knew he was out of his league, even more so than when they first arrived. What had he gotten himself into, and how could he get himself out?

I can help.

Tyler froze as the voice inside found its way into his consciousness. His growing fear had lowered the mental barriers and he could sense the alien presence trying to exploit it. He forced it back once again with a stern warning.

I don't need your help!

The inner voice fell silent, and Tyler hoped the 'internal' exchange had not been visible to Nayllen. He went on the attack.

"Why am I here Nayllen," he demanded, "what is it you want with me?"

"I want you to join me and help bring an end to this senseless war."

Tyler was caught off-guard by the war comment. Wasn't this man an arms dealer? Why would he want to end the war? "And why would I join you?"

"Not me personally, but my cause and the others I mentioned. I think they could convince you…if given the opportunity."

Tyler couldn't read the man. *What was his motive?* He couldn't see it, at least not right now. He didn't think Nayllen was so 'giving' that he wanted to end the war that had clearly profited him so richly.

"An opportunity to speak with me? Isn't that why I am here?"

"No, you are here so that I could assess whether you would be worth recruiting…or whether we would have to use you in some other way. Ways that would not include your blessings or knowledge."

Tyler was taken a little aback. He could feel the remnants of the Admiral's spirit bridling at that obvious show of force and power. Who was this man and who was he working for?

"I will not meet with anymore strangers," Tyler replied, "either tell me who you are working for, or with, or let me leave now."

He was resolute, even as he was scared.

Nayllen sat back in his chair and leveled his piercing stare at Tyler from across the table. He sipped more of his wine before finally coming to some conclusion.

"Admiral, did you think it strange that we had the same name when we met?" Nayllen asked quietly.

"Yes, I suppose a little, it isn't a very common name, although I hear that lately it has become one."

"Indeed..." Nayllen folded his hands neatly in his lap, "it is not common among your generation or mine for that matter. In fact, I would guess that when you were born, there were only half a dozen or so on the whole planet, myself and my father included."

"So? What are you trying to say, that I was named after you?"

"Yes."

"Please, you have no proof and I have heard no such tale from my parents. It is coincidence."

"Really? A coincidence that I worked with your father on Krildon and that we have the same rare name?"

Tyler had to admit, it appeared more than a coincidence.

"I have no proof that you worked for my father, you could tell me anything." Tyler watched as that made him pause.

Nayllen simply stared at Tyler before standing up. He made a slight signal with his hand and the view screen on the wall displayed a picture of the Admiral's parents and what must have been a much younger Nayllen. All three were standing together, arms around each other smiling. The scene didn't give enough details to make out where it was, but the photo did appear genuine. Of course, Tyler assumed it could easily be faked.

Nayllen turned towards Tyler, "We will contact you within the next day or two, at that time, we must have an answer as to your intent to meet the others or to simply sever all ties and go it on your own. Thank you for your time Admiral, my associate will show you out."

Before Tyler could respond, Nayllen quickly turned and left the room. Tyler was stunned. Had he been too cautious, maybe not cautious enough? Clearly, Nayllen and whoever he worked with had power. Tyler could access the Admiral's memories, but he could find nothing so insidious. Of course, the Admiral had avoided politics, and now at least, it appeared it would be his downfall—or rather Tyler's downfall.

Tyler followed the assistant back into the lift and couldn't help wondering whether this were simply a ruse by the Palace. It fell into character with Regent Sneerd's typical record of dealing with people who opposed the Emperor and stood in the way of their agenda. In more than a few instances, councilmen had found themselves in 'unusual' predicaments that forced them to resign their seats on the Supreme Council.

Not surprisingly, they differed with the Palace on some crucial issue that was held up during a vote. In general, the Imperial Palace got most of what they wanted within the council. Despite its design and intentions, the Supreme Council was still a figure head that rarely made major changes that weren't designed or supported by the Imperial Palace. The Emperor and his staff were the true power of Poolto, and as Tyler reviewed all these memories, he began to understand how thin his odds of coming out ahead would be.

He could read the headlines now: **Poolto's Greatest Hero— Traitor to Home world!** It smelled like a trap, it felt like a trap, yet something about Nayllen confused Tyler. Why would Nayllen want to trap the Admiral? Did he really support the Emperor? Had he really worked with the Admiral's father on Krildon? How could he benefit from an attack plan that would surely fail? *Re-supplying the fleet, that's how.*

Was that it, Tyler thought, *do you intend on rebuilding the destroyed fleet after the Vice Admiral's plan fails?*

Was greed the real motive here? Tyler didn't think that was it. Something about Nayllen gave Tyler the feeling that he wanted more than money—he wanted power. But what kind of power? To hear Nayllen himself, he already had a great deal of power, it was simply behind the scenes. Did he want to be in front? Did he want to be the new Emperor?

Not since the Emperor's ancestors united Poolto had there been a coup—or even a plot, at least not in the open. Tyler wondered if coups happened frequently and were simply kept quiet after being uncovered? If that was it, then why did they need the Admiral? Of course! They needed to seal their authority after the failure of the Vice Admiral and Emperor's plan. The Admiral would be a prominent figure to 'legitimatize' their claim to power.

Still…something didn't feel right and Tyler quickly realized he was in over his head. Plots within plots within plots. Tyler wondered how a politician ever survived? He understood why Yooso had been so distasteful to the Admiral. He remembered Raul once talking about politics within their organization, but at the time, Tyler had ignored what he'd said. Now he understood the precarious position power held, and why the Emperor did so much to maintain it.

Using the fictitious call as an excuse, Tyler begged Greelen's forgiveness at having to leave so early. Although she was obviously disappointed, she took the news stoically since her friends had at least 'seen' her with the Admiral. Since the evening was early, Greelen said she would stay behind with her friends. Tyler, thankful for that arrangement, agreed. He thanked her for the wonderful evening and left with promises to 'do it again sometime'.

Before leaving, Tyler had an awkward introduction to Toosia's 'friend' before leaving the casino. The man appeared friendly enough, and did not appear upset at having to be stood up after so short a time. Tyler offered Toosia the opportunity to stay for a while longer, but she turned it down, undoubtedly wanting to hear more about why they were leaving so quickly. She had appeared calm, but Tyler imagined what crazy thoughts were going through her mind. Unfortunately, he wanted to tell her everything, but was afraid of what that might do to their relationship—especially since it bordered on treason.

After arriving at their quarters, each separated to their respective rooms to prepare for bed. They had spent a quiet, somewhat tense ride back, with Tyler keeping quiet while Toosia maintained her patient demeanor. He knew that would change.

Tyler slipped into bed confused and overwhelmed with fear. Even the Admiral's great courage did not help the situation. The Admiral had faced death many times over, but this new menace was far worse. At least in battle, the Admiral knew every possible threat. In politics, he knew little to nothing. He understood that everything he thought he'd known could all be wrong. The complexity, the suspense, and the fear of being branded a traitor hung heavy on Tyler. It was a true test of his ability to be more than the drug dealer from L.A. He was beginning to feel certain it wouldn't end well.

He heard sounds in the hallway and a silhouette of Toosia once again appeared in his doorway. The light from behind gave Tyler hints of what lay underneath her gown. She stood silently in the doorway as though considering what to say.

Tyler helped, "Do you need something?" he asked.

"I need you to be honest with me, to tell me what is bothering you, and what your secret is." She remained in the doorway, arms crossed and adamant. "Nayllen, you have kept me out of your life for too long, and I am not going to let you do it again, not now!"

Tyler could hear both resolve and pain in her voice. He cringed inside as her plea to be involved pained Tyler because of his predicament. He didn't want her hurt or disgraced. What would she do if he told her? She could be culpable if she knew and it all went bad. He froze in indecision.

"Damn it Nayllen, tell me what is going on or I will leave this time and never come back!"

He could see she was about to cry, and another stab of pain shot through him. He had to tell her. Without her, he was nothing and didn't want to continue the charade.

"Ok, Toosia, ok, please come inside and shut the door behind you."

As he said it, he imagined Nayllen watching the scene from somewhere far away and secret. He had no illusions that Nayllen could eavesdrop on anywhere within the Capital complex. Nonetheless, he had no other option than to tell her here.

Toosia quietly closed the door and moved towards the light switch on the wall.

"Toosia, please keep the lights off..." he didn't know how to finish. If she knew how insecure they were, she would probably get scared.

She accepted and moved through the darkness towards the bed. The dim light coming in through the windows allowed him to see her ghostly figure stop at the side of the bed, arms still crossed, waiting for him to tell all. A halo of light surrounded her as Tyler watched her with his 'second' vision.

He slid over to the other side of the bed, flipped back the covers and signaled her to get in. She hesitated and then slipped under the covers keeping a respectable distance from Tyler. He expected that, but just having her near was comforting.

"Alright Nayllen, what is going on?" she asked quietly.

He wasn't sure how to start, so he simply began from when he received the note from Nayllen. She listened silently as he recounted his encounter, properly editing out the views from within the Imperial chamber and their own quarters. He impressed upon her his belief that Nayllen held a great deal of power...behind the scenes. He laid out everything, including his various theories about the motive behind Nayllen's desire to recruit the Admiral.

Tyler finished with an apology for keeping it from her earlier. He explained how he thought he had now endangered her by involving her in the plot. She lay on her side facing Tyler, her non-emotional face glowing dimly in the sparse light. He could see her thinking about all he'd said, but he couldn't read her.

She looked directly at him, no emotion to betray her thoughts. "I need to sleep on this."

With that, she turned over and backed up next to Tyler. He was too stunned for words, so he simply wrapped himself around her. His thoughts were a jumble of emotions, fear, and confusion, but having her next to him finally pushed those thoughts aside, and both fell into a deep sleep.

Although the sleep came easily for Tyler, it was not restful. In his dreams, he stood within a big ring, darkness all around him except for some overhead spotlights that fell down around him. Overhead, he caught a glimpse of what appeared to be a trapeze, and all around him, other circus equipment lay dormant. The lights kept moving around, but within the darkness, Tyler could hear nothing.

He realized he was in a circus, and it did not feel like a dream. He looked down at himself, and noticed he was dressed in a red tuxedo with knee high black leather boots finishing off the ensemble. In his left hand, he held a large megaphone which he quickly threw to the ground. He recognized the body was that of the 'old' Tyler from earth.

"Hello, is anyone there? Thosoland?" He imagined the friendly god suddenly appearing to help Tyler through the mess he found himself in.

Only quiet echoed back. He thought this was definitely something Thosoland would do since Tyler had plenty of memories of the circus when he was a child. Now however, he was the ringmaster. So where was Thosoland?

He began to think it was a dream, but it felt so real, and he felt so awake. He remembered everything about the night before, the casino, Nayllen, and confiding everything to Toosia.

A voice from all around him spoke, "It was a mistake telling her."

The voice sounded familiar, and yet strange.

"Thosoland, is that you?" Tyler asked the darkness.

The voice responded, "Thosoland is not here...only you and I."

Tyler was a little spooked, but he quickly found his courage.

"I know who I am, but who are you?" He demanded.

One of the spotlights swung around from behind Tyler to stop across the ring from Tyler. The light shone on the opening of a dark portal, waiting. Loud, annoying circus music began to play and Tyler covered his ears to block the sound. It didn't work, the music was just as loud.

Suddenly, a small car emerged from the dark portal driven by a clown. The music played louder as the car rambled through the ring making its way towards Tyler. The clown appeared to be performing for some unknown crowd, waving, gesticulating and clowning around.

The car stopped about ten feet in front of Tyler, and the clown stepped out of it, falling to the ground in character, a look of surprise on its face. It got up in an exaggerated display of surprise, pulled up its oversized pants, and waddled over to Tyler.

Tyler watched the charade patiently and waited for the clown to reveal himself. When it finally spoke, it was the voice from the darkness.

"Howdy Tyler, guess who I am?"

Tyler looked at the caricature in front of him and could see something familiar. He looked through the thick make-up on the face and tried to piece together who was underneath it. It came slowly, but startled him nonetheless. Underneath the make-up and red hair, he could clearly see the Admiral's face.

"What is this," Tyler demanded, "who are you?"

"At the moment, I am you. Or at least I am the person you have created on this world."

"What are you talking about, what world, where is this?"

"Poolto."

"Then I am to believe you are the Admiral on Poolto? Last time I checked, there isn't a circus on Poolto. So where am I?" He was getting more than a little upset with the charade.

"Oh, you are on Poolto, but this is a fabrication I created just so we could...talk. Just me and you, or is it, you and you?" The clown laughed at his own pun and something in the laugh chilled Tyler.

"Adanni!" Tyler was certain.

"Ahhh, the ring master speaks, listen all who shall obey!"

Tyler could clearly hear the sarcasm in Adanni's voice.

"What do you want?" Tyler asked, desperately seeking a way out of the place. He pushed mentally, trying to force Adanni back into his subconscious, but nothing worked.

"Wondering why it is not working?" Adanni asked. "Perhaps because I am in control here...here where you have exiled me!"

No mistaking the anger in that comment. Tyler was shaken by the revelation. Did Adanni control his unconscious dreams while he was asleep? Tyler didn't think it possible.

"You better believe it is possible!" The clown looked directly at Tyler, an angry gaze that held a great deal of menace despite the clown makeup. "I have worked quietly in this place, building my own empire while you tried to destroy the one you control! I can keep you here as long as I want...as long as it takes to kill that body you currently reside in."

Tyler felt a pang of fear, "What? No, you can't do that, I am making progress."

"Progress?" The clown laughed, "Is that what you call it? You are on the brink of disaster and don't even know it. I sense your fear—you're totally out of your league."

Tyler admitted Adanni was right, he was out of his league. But that wasn't what Tyler had meant.

"Ahh," the clown sighed, "you mean progress with that woman you are pretending to love. The Admiral's wife."

Tyler didn't like the way Adanni made it sound like adultery. Then again, he wasn't the Admiral and maybe it really was adultery. Tyler didn't think he was pretending to love her, but did he really love her?

"Right!" the clown jeered, "and I suppose you want to settle down and start a family or something ridiculous?"

"She can't have children, but yes, I would like to settle down with her." Tyler was angry now. He didn't like that Adanni could see every thought he had.

"Fat chance of that," the clown mocked, "you are about to destroy yourself and her, if not the world. I have seen it all before my friend, fallen hero, tragic endings, it is a classic tale played out throughout the Universe since time began."

"And I suppose you could prevent it, given the opportunity?" Tyler saw where this was heading, blackmail.

"Clever lad, but you spoil my offer."

"What offer, to take over and exile me to this place?" Tyler knew that he couldn't trust this alien, even if he could help.

"Of course you don't trust me, as I don't trust you. But look at it this way, I control you here, and you control me there. As long as you need to sleep, I will be a regular part of your world whether you like it or not."

"But, if the Admiral dies while you imprison me here, I will be released, and once again have control?" Tyler concluded.

"Yes...something like that." The clown conceded.

"Then by all means, hold me here until I die, then we'll see what happens."

The clown looked at Tyler with a sour look on his face, "I don't want that same as you. Nonetheless, I am prepared to wage battle with you every night. It will take its toll. Is that what you want?"

Tyler thought about it, but didn't like the alternatives.

"How come I can't hear your thoughts, even up there?" Tyler was curious why Adanni had the upper hand.

"I have more experience at this than you do. Besides, it was I who gave you the Admiral's memories. Where would you be without those?"

"Fine, I accept you were helpful, so what do we do now?" Tyler wanted to get this over with, to see how he could end it without giving too much away.

"Now we negotiate for your life...as the Admiral."

"I said fine," Tyler replied, "what are your terms?"

"A truce, nothing more," the clown replied.

Tyler looked at the Admiral's face buried beneath the grotesque mask but could read nothing. Well, he had to do something to get out of this.

"Ok, what does that mean?" Tyler asked.

"It means I am no longer exiled to this place. Instead, I am allowed to be a part of your life out there. I can observe, comment, and assist. I don't want control, I only want a piece of the action."

Tyler knew he couldn't trust him, and the thought of having someone watching, commenting, and participating was more than disturbing.

"It's too much to ask, I cannot live with another being within me."

"Hogwash," the clown responded, "you live like that now. The Admiral's memories are not yours, and yet you let them live side by side with you, even affecting your decisions and behaviors. What is the difference?"

Tyler went on the defensive, "It is a big difference, the Admiral is dead and you are not!"

"No matter, the end result is the same. Those are my terms, take them or leave them." The clown stood stolidly, knowing he had Tyler on the ropes.

Tyler thought about it but couldn't see anyway out. He would either have to share his life with Adanni or be persecuted every night in his dreams. Tyler remembered life as the drifting spirit, and he didn't relish going back.

"Fine, I see I have no choice, so I agree. However, if I sense even a little exertion of your control on me, I will exile you here permanently and remain a wandering spirit for eternity." Tyler hoped he sounded threatening.

"Sure you would," the clown sounded unconvinced, "whatever you say. Remember, I can hear all of your thoughts; you are transparent to me here and there. But I get your drift."

"Good, as long as we are clear." Tyler replied.

"Clear as your thoughts," the clown said, "now if I am to have a part of this life of yours, I need to help you make it right."

"Now that wasn't part of the bargain," Tyler began, "you said observe, not make decisions!"

"Cool down 'Admiral', I am here to help you out of the mess you seem genuinely destined to get yourself into. I can be of great assistance, as my wealth of experience is enormous."

"Ok, I'm listening, what is your advice?" Tyler waited impatiently.

"Not now my friend, up there when you are awake."

"Fine, will you release me now, or must I wait for more concessions?" Tyler was exasperated and wanted out of the three-ring circus he was currently trapped in.

"Don't look at me, just wake up!" the clown said.

Tyler thought about it and watched as the clown, the circus and the spotlights disappeared.

Tyler woke from the restless night. The room was still dark, but he could make out the curves of Toosia beside him, curled up fast asleep. He thought about the circus dream and Adanni. Was it real, or was it just a dream?

You bet it was real, and don't force me back down there!

Fine, fine, you can stay, but remember what I said, Tyler thought.

All Tyler heard was a *'fine'* in response.

Tyler checked the clock and saw he didn't need to get up for another two hours. After wrangling with Adanni all night, he no longer felt like sleep.

He slipped out of bed donning a robe and quietly walked out to the living area. He was happy to have Toosia close to him, but still feared what he had told her. She was not a delicate woman, and was better versed in politics than Tyler, but this was something entirely different than 'ordinary' politics. He wanted to wake her and ask her advice, but he decided to let her sleep.

He sat down on one of the overstuffed chairs and turned on several screens to watch the latest news around Poolto. In his current mood, he truly felt like an alien in an alien world.

He watched several shows that normally were his favorites, but somehow he wasn't getting the same thing out of it. He knew why. For all the celebrity that the Admiral enjoyed, he really was nothing more than a puppet of forces he didn't even know.

Before he had come to Yooso, Tyler had thought of himself and the Admiral as a real force, but now, that illusion was gone. Only days before, he had watched these programs with a mind towards helping his fellow people of Poolto—now however, he realized he didn't even know them. How could he, he was just an alien pretending to be a hero.

Stop being so melodramatic, there are worst things in this Universe—trust me.

Adanni's voice didn't help, it only made him feel more like an alien—a 'schizophrenic' alien.

Please...I'm going to cry. It's no wonder you've screwed this up.

I've screwed it up? Like I had a choice! Tyler was angry at the accusation. He wasn't the one who wanted to be an Onyalum. He hadn't caused the accident.

Of course you had a choice! You chose to be the Admiral...you chose to live on his world... and you chose to take on the powers of that world! What did you think it would be like? You picked this world's 'National hero', and now you say it wasn't your fault?

Tyler listened patiently his anger simmering silently. Of course he was to blame for getting caught in the Admiral's body. Sure, he could have avoided this world, skipped past the floundering ship and found another—another world that was peaceful, and simple. But was that what he had wanted?

Adanni interrupted his thoughts.

You never wanted simple, you wanted excitement! As I want excitement. I see your past memories, I know what you did, and I know how you felt when you did it. You felt alive, spirited, and in control, even when you were not. Isn't that what you want?

Tyler had to admit, he missed many aspects of his previous life. Was it the partying he missed, or was it Linda? He wasn't sure, but as he thought about the past, he began to yearn for something to 'ease' his mind. *Perhaps a small glass of one of the Admiral's finest vintages.*

Sure, escape, now that you've messed everything up. What do you think Toosia would say, you drinking so early in the morning?

I do my best thinking after I have had a few drinks! Tyler tried to sound convincing, but even he saw the problem with drinking so early. Still…

Shape up, we have work to do! You can have a drink later, when it is more appropriate. Remember, I feel the effects too!

Tyler thought about that, was that how he could suppress Adanni?

Don't bet on it.

Adanni's voice was steely cold, so Tyler put the thought out of his mind.

Damn you Adanni.

Listen up... you've put the Admiral in a very precarious position.

Gee, like I didn't know that! How was the obvious going to help?

You've got to meet with Nayllen and his party immediately.

So you're saying that since I am already in it deep enough, why not go all the way?

No, what I am saying is that you need to know— must know— who is behind Nayllen. If it is a plot by the Imperial Palace, you need to know right away to appropriately plan a defense. Remember, the Admiral has a great deal of political clout, so he can always find a way out. However, without knowing, you are steering blind.

And what if it is not a Palace plot? Tyler had the feeling something or someone else was driving Nayllen.

Then you must know that as well. Nayllen has a huge advantage over you, but you must find a way to overcome it. The Admiral's 'intelligence' is clearly insufficient though not for trying. At this point, nothing Marshall Sliss can do will help you—he is too far out of the loop and could make things only worse. You are the only one who can get the intelligence you need!

Tyler thought about what Adanni was saying. The logic appeared true on the surface, but Tyler still didn't trust him.

You seem to have put a lot of thought into this?

When you have nothing to do but observe from a distance, what else are you going to do?

Point taken...still, I am a little apprehensive about taking this further with Nayllen. He gave the Admiral more than a small threat, and based on his apparent resources, I believe him capable of anything. He definitely has resolve, but what motivates him is still a mystery. I have to consider Toosia and her safety as well.

She is a big girl and can take care of herself. Still, you could always send her to the Estate in Tooland until things settle out.

Tyler thought about her leaving and felt a pang of pain at the prospect. Things were just beginning to change with her and he didn't want to jeopardize that based on his own fears. After all, without her, what was the point?

She can stay for now, but I may have to send her off if things heat up.

Tyler hoped they would not.

"Nayllen?"

The voice from behind startled Tyler, "Whaa..oh Toosia, sorry, you startled me."

"What are you doing out here so early?" she asked.

"Oh, just catching up on some news and thinking about... things." He tried to sound convincing. He really wanted that drink, regardless of what Toosia might think.

She looked at him through beautiful eyes, and the figure underneath her nightdress aroused his desire.

Stop it Tyler, keep control.

I say go for it, Adanni responded.

"May I join you?" she inquired quietly.

"Uh, oh...sure, have a seat."

She moved around the room and settled into a soft couch next to Tyler's. She sat down gently and pulled her legs up onto the couch while leaning against the arm rest. She held her head in her hands and leveled a concerned look at Tyler. He felt slightly embarrassed.

Tyler fumbled with the remote but finally turned off the viewers. He wasn't sure why he was so nervous, they had just slept in the same bed. Still, he hadn't been in a relationship since Linda, and he felt like a teenager on his first date.

"Something is different about you Nayllen, something I can't put my finger on." She stared at him emotionless.

"Really," he tried to sound surprised, "I don't know, I feel the same."

"Do you?" She smiled gently and looked down at Tyler's waist. Apparently the Admiral's body was responding to her regardless of Tyler's nervousness. He didn't know how to respond to this obvious interest in her.

"Don't worry dear, I won't tell if you don't." Her smile turned mischievous, and Tyler could feel the Admiral's body responding even more.

"Tell...oh yes, tell." He was not handling it well and felt the fool for it. Thankfully, she took the lead and got off the couch, heading back to the bedroom.

As her nightdress gently brushed up against her body, Tyler felt an intense desire overwhelming him. He had to have her, and he hoped desperately that this was what she also wanted.

She stopped at the doorway to the bedroom and turned her head over her shoulder towards Tyler, "Are you coming?"

Tyler's heart leapt in his chest pounding like a marathon runner. He got out of his seat and watched as she slipped her nightdress off and went into the darkness of the room beyond.

Tyler followed quickly, his arousal now prominent. He closed the door quietly behind him and slipped under the covers, nervous, excited, and feeling like he was nineteen again. As he reached out to touch her, he could see the colored lights dance across her skin. They matched the rhythmic dancing of his own.

Tyler was enjoying breakfast while scanning the notes his staff created in preparation for the final day at the conference. Today was the day the Vice Admiral was going to 'unveil' his plan to the Supreme Military Command. Supposedly, it would be presented as the next plan of attack, blessed by the Imperial Palace, and therefore, not intended to have objections.

The Admiral's staff had been diligently 'recruiting' Military Command members to their side, but it still looked in favor of the Vice Admiral. Consensus was that the Admiral had lost face with the bitter defeat of the last battle. The losses had been high and the strategic advantage it bought was too low. Apparently, many held doubts about the Admiral's abilities to lead. They revered and respected him, but many now felt new blood and new ideas were warranted.

There was little Tyler could do to prevent the vote of approval from the Supreme Military Command, so his only hope was to have his supporters change the tide with debates after the presentation. He had big guns on his side, and they could sway others who were still uncertain. However, the Vice Admiral also had big guns...the biggest being the Imperial Palace.

Supreme Military Command posts were allocated through the Imperial Palace, and Marshall Sliss had mentioned more than once that many inside the command were going to use this as an opportunity to 'move up' in rank.

At what cost? Tyler thought.

Fools, all of them, Adanni interjected, *they'd sell their mothers for a buck. A phrase from your world I believe. Very apt.*

Must I hear you so early in the morning? Tyler pleaded.

So early? Why it is late! Fortunate for you the conference starts late today. After last night, I am surprised you woke up at all.

Tyler could almost hear a grin in Adanni's words. He had to admit, last night had been wonderful. He had left Toosia sleeping soundly when he got up to get ready. He felt more alive than he ever had. He, or the Admiral, or both truly loved her.

He finished his briefings and rose to leave. The Marshall had requested a short meeting before they entered the conference and had hand selected a private room for the occasion. Tyler figured he wanted to know about the meeting with Nayllen. After what Nayllen had shown Tyler, he doubted the room the Marshall had selected was as 'private' as they wanted.

Nonetheless, he felt refreshed and ready to do battle. As he passed the hallway leading to his quarters, he heard Toosia call to him.

He stopped and waited for her to meet him. He smiled gently as her beauty brought back fresh memories of the night before.

"Yes dear, what is it, I must be going." He wanted to stay with her, but knew this day was too important.

"I just wanted to say goodbye, and thank you." She said.

"Oh, yes, goodbye Toosia, I'll be home late tonight, we have the big presentation today." He knew she understood.

"Yes, I know, I hope all goes well," she said, "I wanted to tell you something else, but if you must leave, it can wait."

"No, no, please tell me." He wondered what she had to say. Perhaps something from her father?

"Oh well, I…" she stopped as if in concentration, or confusion, and the look didn't suit her. Tyler wasn't used to seeing emotion on Toosia's face and it concerned him a little.

"Go on dear, what did you want to tell me?" He tried not to sound impatient.

"I just wanted to say how happy I am that we are back together." She said it with a strange finality, but Tyler accepted it at face value.

"Me too...me too."

He kissed her gently on the cheek and said goodbye. He left her standing in the entryway, a gentle smile on her face, but a look of concern in her eyes.

When Tyler arrived at the designated room for his meeting with the Marshall, he saw two soldiers, crisply dressed, standing on either side of the door. As he approached, they quickly snapped to attention and saluted in unison. He returned their salute before entering the room.

The room was filled with a large table in the center like many of the conference rooms in this facility. This one however, had multiple viewers lined around the rooms inner walls, much like the room Tyler had met Nayllen in.

Tyler knew the viewers were designed to allow those inside to see outside, but he wondered who was outside looking in. He casually scanned the room, but couldn't tell if anything was a spy device or not. The Admiral had limited memories of spying or spy equipment. Apparently he'd left that work for others.

Even alone, the Marshall sat at a seat on the side of the table rather than at the head. Clearly the head of the table was for someone in command, like the Admiral. Tyler nodded to the Marshall and walked to the other end of the table, taking the seat of command.

"Good morning Goolen," Tyler started, "what news brings me here?"

"Good morning sir, I have some disturbing news I must share with you before the conference."

Tyler watched as the Marshall fiddled with his view device, obviously deciding which news to give him first.

"Yes, what is it Marshall?" Tyler switched to the formal title, hoping to get the Marshall out of what looked like an embarrassing conundrum.

"Uh, yes sir, well I'll start with news about the conference first." Tyler was glad to see the Marshal stopped wavering in indecision and returned to his usual, authoritative military demeanor.

"We have heard this morning, from a reliable source, that Secretary Geern is switching his support to Vice Admiral Teesen."

The Marshall stopped to let that sink in. Tyler reviewed the Admiral's memories of Secretary Geern and was impressed by the man's obvious skills. He had held many posts in the Supreme Military Command and was currently in charge of military installations.

It was not a powerful position, but a position that required quality skills as an administrator. It was often a position given to those who would never achieve true 'command' status, but were still an invaluable asset. His advice and guidance over the years had served the command well.

What was the motivation here? He was nearing retirement age and had never shown interest in power or position before now. He had always been a strong supporter of the Admiral's. He was even a close friend of the Admiral's father before the war. It didn't make sense, and Tyler said as much to the Marshall.

"I agree, but the source is very reliable." The Marshal said.

"Ok, so what does the staff think?"

Tyler knew that the Marshall would have run it past most of the staff before meeting with the Admiral. The Marshall may be out of the loop, but he was still a powerful asset.

"After postulating many theories, we settled on blackmail."

The Marshall delivered it with a cold, blank face.

"Vice Admiral Teesen blackmailing a Secretary of the Supreme Military Command? I hardly think that is probable."

It didn't sound possible to Tyler, how desperate was Teesen?

Very desperate. Adanni's voice had slight chill in it.

"We do not believe the Vice Admiral is the one perpetrating this, sir."

"You don't, then who?" Tyler knew who before he had finished the question.

"We believe Regent Sneerd is behind it. We recently discovered that Secretary Geern has battled a gambling problem for most of his life. Apparently, he got into trouble with a local thug named Siir Noos, and this in turn compromised his position on the facilities funding committee for lucrative contracts. Siir Noos has a front company that currently is the sole provider of 'chairs' for all military facilities."

"Chairs?" Tyler was incredulous.

"Yes sir, chairs."

"What a tangled web we weave." Tyler could just imagine Geern quietly trying to push for Siir's company in the meetings. He would never have been suspected. Tyler thought back to his previous life, and the many drug users who got themselves into trouble. Fortunately for Tyler, he had never been involved in the enforcement end of the business, but he knew it could be bad. Blackmail was quite common.

But someone had suspected Geern, and used his weakness against him. It had to be Sneerd.

"Weave a 'what' sir?" the Marshal asked.

Tyler saw the confusion on the Marshall's face and quickly remembered that spiders were not part of the Poolto ecosystem. They had a similar creature on this world, but they used forest materials to build traps, not webs.

"Oh sorry, just an old saying my grandmother once used. Not sure what web means." Tyler lied.

The Marshall let it pass and moved on.

"Apparently, the misuse was mysteriously overlooked by the accounting office audits, and that is why we believe Sneerd is behind it. No one but the Palace could wield that much control of accounting office."

Except maybe Nayllen. Tyler let the thought pass and focused on what it meant to their efforts.

"Damage?" He asked it simply, knowing the Marshal would give it too him simply.

"I believe this will spell our defeat. He was a staunch supporter and his betrayal will pull many over to Teesen's side. At best, we can expect only twenty percent of the command to side with you."

"Defeat, is that all?" Tyler said it with more sarcasm than he intended.

"Well sir, no. The current buzz is indicates that those who side with you may no longer even open debate in the conference. Instead, they may simply remain quiet and let the clear majority take over."

Tyler thought the Marshall appeared awfully calm considering his career was nearing its end. Perhaps he was resigned to his fate? Perhaps the Admiral should be too.

Nonsense, you can stop this, you must stop this!

How? What can I do to stop this? Tyler threw his frustration at Adanni.

Good, you'll need that anger. You must open the debate yourself by actively denouncing the plan. You must throw down the 'gauntlet' and force them to openly choose sides. How many do you think will have the courage to choose against you to your face?

Eighty percent by current estimates. Tyler responded.

Funny, and I thought you were trying to save this world?

Fine, what do you think will happen? Tyler asked.

I think that many of the weak ones will fold under your pressure. If the Palace doesn't have a strong hold on them, they can still choose you without major ramifications. Loyalty is a strong bargaining chip, and you better start playing them if you don't want to be out of it today!

Why are you using so many of my world's sayings? Tyler was more than a little curious about Adanni's choice of words.

When in Rome, was all he got in response.

Tyler noticed a look of concern on the Marshall's face.

"Ok Marshall," he began, "I have some ideas for what we can do, but first tell me the other news you have."

"Well sir, I took the liberty of pursuing additional information about Nayllen Hoos."

The Marshall stopped as if trying to read the Admiral's reaction. Tyler was certain he showed no reaction but was interested nonetheless.

"Go on," Tyler urged, "what did you find?"

"I contacted a source within the Palace," he started, "a source that I usually never contact. However, I felt this was a particularly important issue that warranted a 'deeper' investigation."

The Marshall took a breath and once again searched for reactions but came up short. Tyler remained calm.

"Well, my source reported that Nayllen is a 'necessary' evil to the Imperial Palace. Although he is welcomed and used by Regent Sneerd and the Emperor, the reality is no one trusts him."

He took another breath before continuing.

"They even say he has contacts on Krildon that make him both valuable, for intelligence, but dangerous as a potential traitor."

The Marshall finished with a look of great relief at sharing the dirty details. Unfortunately, it only confirmed what Nayllen had already told Tyler. However, it was interesting the Palace did not trust him, especially Regent Sneerd.

Perhaps this isn't an Imperial trap after all, Adanni interjected.

Perhaps not an 'Imperial' trap, Tyler corrected.

Adanni fell silent and Tyler noticed the Marshall fidgeted looking concerned. Obviously, the Marshall didn't want the Admiral to have anything to do with Nayllen, but he deferred to the Admiral's position before offering this opinion. The Marshall finally broke the silence.

"Sir," he said with hesitation, "do you intend on seeing Nayllen again?"

The look of concern on his face was genuine. Tyler could only imagine how desperate the Marshall was to know what had happened the night before.

"Marshall, I realize your concern is real and I know that you have been waiting patiently for me to share details of my meeting."

Tyler watched his words take effect.

"However, I feel that it may be dangerous for me to share details of the meeting with you." He concluded.

"But sir," the Marshall blurted sounding less than commanding, "I..I fear for your safety, especially if you sense danger."

"I sense danger," Tyler said in a calm and soothing voice, "but the danger I fear is for your safety." He lied, but needed time to sort this out himself. He had a strong feeling that Nayllen was listening to the conversation.

"I have never feared anything or anyone, especially a potential traitor."

The Marshall put on his strongest military demeanor as he said this, and Tyler truly believed him. The Marshall had been in many campaigns with no signs of fear. His loyalty and dedication to his job were remarkable.

Before the Admiral had met Marshall Sliss, it was rumored the Marshall, just a communications officer at the time, had left a fortified compound to adjust a faulty communication dish during a Krildon raid on a mining asteroid. His fearlessness had been noted by his commander at the time, but no commendation had been given to the young officer since the raid had been caused by a military blunder.

At the time, the Imperial Palace and the Supreme Military Command had hushed up the incident to hide serious flaws in the military so early in the war.

Not unlike today, Tyler thought, *have they learned nothing since this started?*

Of course not, they are as stubborn as they are stupid, Adanni finished Tyler's thoughts.

"Your courage is not in question. It is a thin line I walk with Nayllen and I must walk it alone. If things were to go bad, I too could be marked as a traitor. My 'position' would likely save me from such a fate, but I fear you would not be spared."

Tyler thought it sounded convincing, but the look on the Marshall's face didn't match his conclusion.

"Sir, I would face any jury if it meant standing with you."

"I know," Tyler said, "that is why I must ask you to step back from this."

Tyler could see the pain and frustration it was causing the Marshall. The Admiral and the Marshall had been together a long time, and seeing the Admiral push him away was probably very hard to accept. Tyler felt a pang of guilt.

"As you wish sir," the Marshall finally accepted.

"Please Goolen, I know what I am doing, and I know that I must do it alone." Tyler said it warmly, using the familiar first name of the Marshall. "I need you here, working with my staff to help us in our battle with Teesen."

The Marshall perked up slightly.

"You have an idea sir?" the Marshall asked.

"Yes, if you are finished sharing 'great' news?"

The Marshall smiled lightly at the remark, "Yes sir, I am finished. What are you thinking?"

"Marshall, I believe it is time for us to mount an all out offensive. It is a do or die situation, and I do not intend on dying just yet."

Tyler put all of the Admiral's essence into the statement and watched the effect it had on the Marshall. Tyler couldn't quite tell what emotion clearly showed on the Marshall's face but he was willing to call it pride.

"Yes sir, we are ready and willing."

Tyler outlined Adanni's plan to the Marshall who soaked it in quietly while jotting notes. He shook his head throughout Tyler's narration of what was to surely be a historical moment in the Supreme Military Command, if not Poolto. When they were finished, Tyler headed off to the conference while the Marshall headed back to brief the staff. The Marshall assured Tyler he would be at the conference in time for the showdown.

As Tyler made his way through the corridors, he thought about Nayllen and wondered when he would contact the Admiral. If the Palace wasn't backing Nayllen, then who was? He thought about what Nayllen had said about the Admiral's father. Was it all true, had the Admiral been named after this man?

Tyler had to concede the Admiral's memories of Krildon were during childhood and did not contain much intrigue. It was easy to imagine the Admiral's parents as more than 'ambassadors' to Krildon. But spies?

What a tangled web we weave, Adanni said.

Indeed, Tyler agreed.

The Admiral's Soliloquy

Tyler sat through the conference's administrative stuff with what he hoped was a look of genuine interest. He knew his staff was all over the stuff, sorting, prioritizing, making contacts, and ensuring that the Admiral had a part to play in the internal operations.

One of the Vice Admiral's young officers was finishing his report delivered with professional crispness. Tyler couldn't help but think the man would have made a great addition to the Admiral's staff. Too bad he chose the wrong side. Like many who now stood beneath the Vice Admiral's banner, Tyler imagined the man had been bought with promises of power and promotion.

Was the Military really this superficial? Could loyalty simply be bought with promises of promotions?

Don't be stupid, they are no different than any other bureaucracy.

Adanni's admonition stung, but Tyler held his temper in check. He had to admit, his only experience with the military had been selling drugs to GI's from Camp Pendleton. It had been lucrative, but it didn't really teach him about the military. At the time, he'd sort of thought of them as a joke. Who would want to live their life within such an orderly and controlling system?

He looked back through the Admiral's memories and realized the Admiral had likely been one of the few great leaders who had acquired his rank and position by his deeds rather than his connections and political affiliations. It was nothing short of a miracle that he'd survived the brandishing of his father as a traitor.

Considering his lack of connections, his accomplishments must have been great to come away from the incident unscathed.

Tyler was beginning to see how little the Admiral really knew about how the world worked. He had been a brilliant tactician, leader, and administrator, but he had lacked the knowledge necessary to compete in the political arena. Tyler could see why he spent so much time off-world, and why he was quickly losing support in the upcoming battle. No one believed him capable of winning a political fight.

I'm not sure I can! Tyler complained inwardly.

Nonsense, just let out the Admiral in his full military glory, Adanni responded coldly, *just focus your anger and fear at those who would betray you.*

Sure, sounds good on paper, Tyler replied.

Want me to do it? Adanni asked slyly.

No. Tyler was adamant about not giving up control.

Then find a backbone and use it!

Adanni was right, Tyler needed to focus his energies on the task at hand and put aside any doubts he had. He brought his attention back to the conference as the young officer finished to a round of mild applause. Apparently everyone else had been impressed.

At the other end of the table, Vice Admiral Teesen rose during the applause, a smug look upon his face, "Thank you officer Troos, a brilliantly presented report."

The game is afoot, Tyler thought.

"Now," the Vice Admiral said, "we will adjourn for a short break before I present the current thinking on our next move in the war."

Well, Tyler thought, that was it, they were down to the wire. He looked around for the Marshall, but noticed he had not returned. Tyler figured he would make it back shortly as he would want to hear 'in-person' the unveiling of the Vice Admiral's plan.

Tyler got up to get a drink, and noticed how intimate Regent Sneerd and the Vice Admiral were while talking across the room. Without the Marshall at his side, Tyler felt out of his league.

Regent Sneerd lifted his eyes towards the Admiral and showed a little surprise at the cold stare Tyler was giving him. He barely stopped talking to give the Admiral a slight nod of his head. Tyler simply turned around and left the room.

"Admiral Osloo," a voice called from behind a crowd of people waiting for refreshments, "Admiral Osloo?"

Tyler spotted the young soldier waving a piece of paper as he made his way through the throng, apologizing and saluting the impressive ranks he passed.

"Yes, what is it?" Tyler asked.

"An urgent call for you sir," the soldier blurted, "you can take it in another room."

"Is it Grand Marshall Sliss?" Tyler was surprised to get a call from the Marshall.

"No sir," the soldier replied, "the gentleman said you would know who it was."

The soldier had a look of confusion on his face. Tyler imagined some of it was awe at standing next to and talking with Poolto's National hero.

Who could it be? Tyler wondered. Suddenly, it dawned on him, *Nayllen!*

"Oh, yes, I was expecting a call—please lead me somewhere private to take it."

"Yes sir," the soldier responded crisply, the look of concern gone from his face.

The poor soldier must have been terrified to have an unknown caller asking for the Admiral. Tyler was surprised he had taken the call at all. What had Nayllen said to the young soldier to convince him?

The soldier led Tyler to a small room down the corridor. He showed Tyler how to access the call and left quietly, closing the door behind him.

Tyler sat down behind the small desk and turned the console towards him and away from the door. No need to share this call in case someone walked in. He pushed the blinking button and watched as Nayllen's face appeared on the screen.

"Nayllen," Tyler lied, "how nice to see you so soon."

"Save it," Nayllen responded critically, "I know you are not happy to see me again."

"Fine," Tyler said, "what do you want?"

"I want your answer," Nayllen said, "will you meet with my associates?"

"Then I will meet more than one?" Tyler queried.

"Perhaps," Nayllen responded nonchalantly, "perhaps not."

Tyler thought Nayllen looked bored. He could imagine someone in his position was likely not accustomed to making such a routine call. Better to have others pass notes.

Tyler steeled himself and thought about what Adanni had said, "Ok, where and when?"

"When is in two days," Nayllen said simply, "and where is on the mining colony of the Siirneen asteroid."

Tyler was stunned! A casino was one thing, but a mining colony was too much. He said as much to Nayllen.

"Look 'Admiral'," Nayllen responded with a cold calculating look in his eyes, "my associates and I 'know' you will lose your position today, so what have you got to lose? The Vice Admiral's plan is as good as done, and you no longer have clout to demand anything from anyone."

"I am a National hero—that carries come clout!" Tyler blurted before he could stop himself.

It took Nayllen a little by surprise, but he recovered quickly, "Yes, I know, that is why you interest us."

That took Tyler by surprise. *What could they want with his celebrity?*

Careful Tyler, this one is very devious, Adanni warned.

I know, Tyler replied, *let me handle it!*

"Tell me why you want to meet with me and tell me why it must be off-world!" Tyler demanded.

He could see a look of indecision on Nayllen's face. Tyler thought he had pushed him too far, but he had to know more before he was willing to leave the planet—especially if he was to continue the fight with Teesen. Leaving now could spell disaster for any impetus they might gain after today's showdown.

"Very well Admiral, I'll tell you something."

Tyler watched Nayllen's face turn even colder. He had a brief image of him as an intelligence interrogator, grilling people for information, a look of glee on his face. Tyler felt a chill.

"We have need of your position to help us stop the war. My associates believe it is possible to obtain a truce and we need your support to ensure it has a chance."

Nayllen finished the admission and waited patiently for the Admiral to respond.

"And why off-world?" Tyler asked again.

"Security," Nayllen responded simply.

Tyler didn't believe it, but he was willing to let it slide for now. They needed him to help further their cause for the end of the war. Why? He could at least understand why they would want the National hero to back them, but why did they want an end to the war? It still wasn't adding up.

"Considering your current position," Tyler began, "I do not see the motivation for ending the war. You profit nicely already."

Tyler let that counter take affect, knowing he was gambling by pushing so hard. Still, he had to know what he was committing to. Once he was off-world, he would be powerless against them, not that he held much power on Poolto.

"My motivation is not your concern, but suffice it to say that even an old war monger such as myself does not see the value in destroying both worlds. There is always more 'profit' in peace than in war, and I currently hold the upper hand for peacetime profits."

Tyler thought about it and realized he was right. With his connections on Krildon, he would have an instant network of trading between the two worlds before anyone else. In fact, he could even sell his network contacts to potential buyers, making money in multiple ways.

It appeared to be a real motive, but something still nagged at Tyler. After all, he was already rich, was money really a motivator for someone with his wealth? Tyler didn't think so. The rich usually sought power, either through political office or by wielding economic strength. Perhaps that was the true motivation, an economic position that would wield enough power to influence both worlds.

"Fair enough Nayllen, but you can imagine my concern for my family. I would be doing them no justice to take your word at face value."

"I agree," Nayllen replied, "in your shoes, I would do the same. However, I am not in your shoes. No more stalling Admiral, take action."

Tyler didn't like the veiled threat, "And you can help me take that action?"

"We will take action whether you participate or not. However, as I said before, if you do not participate, you may not like the 'actions' we take."

"I get the picture and believe that much of your story."

"Very well," Nayllen said, "will you meet with us or not?"

Tyler could see Nayllen was getting impatient so he decided to stop pushing his luck.

"Yes, I will meet with you and your associates. How will I get there?"

"That is up to you Admiral, but I would create some military pretense. Your position is crumbling and your actions will be scrutinized."

"Fine, where do I go when I get there?" Tyler was certain Nayllen would say something to the effect that he would be contacted when he arrived. Nayllen surprised him.

"We will put you up at the Regional Governor's quarters, at his request, and you should enjoy moderate comfort while you are there. The Governor will meet you at the space port, honor guard in tow of course, and escort you back to his quarters. After that, we will organize a meeting."

Nayllen finished with a greater look of boredom. He looked off to the side at something Tyler couldn't see. Apparently someone had spoken with him and he turned back to Tyler.

"That is all Admiral, I'll see you on Siirneen in two days!"

Before Tyler could respond, the viewer went blank.

Great, now he was going to an Asteroid. He could only imagine the look of shock on the Marshall's face. They would need a pretense for going there, something that wouldn't take away from

their efforts in Yooso. Even better, something that would bolster
their efforts in Yooso.

Fat chance of that! Adanni scowled in Tyler's head.

*Excuse me if I am wrong, but wasn't it you who said to pursue
this?* Tyler spat back in contempt.

Yes, I do believe it was, Adanni replied coldly, *but don't think
I have everything planned out. Remember, I can only read your
mind.*

Yes, I remember it all too well.

Tyler left the room and headed back to the conference areas. He
helped himself to food and drink—choosing some of the wine they
provided. As he walked through the procession he noticed everyone
was ignoring him. They were polite as he walked past, but no one
tried to engage him or look him in the eyes.

Dead man walking, Tyler thought.

They are only scared for their own positions, Adanni
countered, *that is why you may yet pull this off. Are you sure you
don't want me to handle this? I have a great deal of experience at
this type of situation, in fact I once was a King on a world where...*

Please, Tyler stopped him, *spare me your credentials, I'll
handle it!*

*Suit yourself, you can't die, so no great matter, Toosia
however...*

Tyler didn't like what Adanni implied, and he thought about
Toosia and what she would think about his going back off-world.
It had been a major reason for their marital strife, although not the
only one. Tyler thought about Eyleeria and cringed. The Admiral
had an affair with her for years, and since Tyler broke it off, she
had remained eerily quiet and restrained. It scared Tyler a little, but
he figured the Marshall had dealt with it behind the scenes.

As Tyler moved towards the conference table, he spotted
Marshall Sliss in the corridor. He made his way towards the door
as the Marshall signaled him into the corridor.

"Yes, what is it?" Tyler asked, "They are about to begin."

"I know, but I need to tell you what our staff came up with."

Tyler noted the Marshall had a note of confidence in his voice
and Tyler imagined they had a plan that might work. Tyler didn't

want to spoil the moment, so he held off telling the Marshall about Nayllen and the future off-world trip.

"Go on," Tyler urged.

"Well sir, it will require you to denigrate yourself and the entire Supreme Military Command for the battle that nearly cost you your life."

Tyler thought about that but decided his reputation was already in question.

"A gamble, but continue."

"We believe that if you were to condemn the last attempt at a major offensive, then you could adequately argue caution for the next one."

Tyler was following the train of logic but let the Marshall completely outline the plan of attack.

The Marshall caught his breath, clearly excited about the prospects, "If we urge caution, we can bog down the plan in committee meetings that must review the overall plan of attack. During those reviews, we can use the time to develop an alternative strategy while punching holes in theirs. We believe this line of attack may provide your supporters the opportunity to take action without directly rejecting the Vice Admiral's plan."

The Marshall finished, waiting eagerly for the Admiral to respond. Tyler was amused and satisfied to see the fight back in the Marshall's eyes. He had to admit, it just might be what they needed to stall the offensive. In fact, it might even buy them the pretense to go off-world.

"My congratulations Marshall, your plan may just work!"

"Don't congratulate me sir, the staff came up with it on their own, I only acted as a sounding board. Officer Slaas deserves a lot of the credit."

I think officer Slaas deserves a promotion, Tyler thought.

"Plan a party for them Marshall, they deserve it!" Tyler was truly impressed with the Admiral's staff. They were clearly up to the challenges they faced.

"Yes sir!"

Both headed into the conference room just as the Vice Admiral was about to begin. They took their seats calmly and nodded to the Vice Admiral to start.

"Before I begin to lay out our future plans, I would like to inform you that we have a very special visitor who would like to sit in on these proceedings. Without undue delay, I would like to call you all to attention as I present our great leader of Poolto, Emperor Hallen Yooso IV."

Everyone stood at attention including Tyler as a small entourage of attendants entered the room and made way for the Emperor. The Emperor moved to the back of the room towards a table that had been cleared for his arrival. Tyler noted the Emperor was not going to sit at the main table, clearly a political move intended to reinforce the Vice Admiral's new, albeit temporary, position.

"Revered Supreme Military Command," the Emperor formally opened, "I thank you for this opportunity to observe your plans for the future of our great planet. Our lives are in your capable hands and we look forward to hearing how you will defeat our enemies."

With his usual, quiet demeanor, the Emperor sat down and waited for the Vice Admiral. Everyone in the conference took their seats. As Tyler sat down, he cast a glance at the Marshall who was clearly concerned with the Emperors presence. Tyler could imagine what went through the Marshall's mind. 'Who would stand up for the Admiral with the Emperor next to the Vice Admiral'?

Tyler didn't care. It was their only plan of attack, and Emperor or no Emperor, he had no choice but to execute it. As the Vice Admiral gathered himself to begin, Tyler caught a glimpse of Regent Sneerd sitting next to the Emperor. Tyler thought he saw a slight grin on the Regent's face. Clearly, it was the Regent's idea to invite the Emperor.

"Distinguished guests," the Vice Admiral started, nodding towards the Emperor, "and distinguished colleagues, now is the time for our immediate action to end this war in victory."

Tyler was impressed, the Vice Admiral had been well coached.

The Vice Admiral spent nearly four hours outlining his plan. Tyler analyzed the plan using the Admiral's considerable experience and skills, and had to admit it was a pretty good one.

However, it depended on too many 'positive' assumptions that were based on questionable intelligence.

Overall, the plan had been basically what Tyler and the Admiral's staff had expected with only a few new surprises. Again, these new surprises were based on 'best-case' scenarios. Tyler watched the other members of the Command and hoped many were seeing the same flaws he was.

Several on the Command that were purportedly on the Admiral's side were taking furious notes during the presentation, some even used their communication devices to confer with their staff. They were either preparing an offensive of their own or simply preparing to execute the Vice Admiral's.

Those who sat listening intently were already on board with the plan. Tyler groaned inwardly at how many of 'those' he saw.

Don't lose hope, your plan is still a good one, even with the Emperor here.

Tyler wasn't sure he agreed with Adanni's assessment, but he began reviewing what he would say when the time presented itself. He knew he would have to turn over control to the Admiral's memories, allowing that lingering essence of the great leader to dictate the speech and provide the forceful presence that was so commanding.

I am still willing to do it, Adanni said meekly.

Sounds like you already know my answer, Tyler countered.

Adanni fell silent, and Tyler hoped he would stay that way.

Tyler watched as the Vice Admiral began summarizing the plan. Tyler wondered if the Vice Admiral would be so bold as to deny questions and comments as protocol dictated.

The conference applauded loudly as the Vice Admiral finished. Tyler and the Marshall joined in, although neither put forth much effort.

"Thank you," the Vice Admiral almost blushed at the attention, clearly he was pleased with himself, "thank you all!"

Tyler noted that both the Regent and the Emperor were smiling, clearly they felt confident that they backed the right horse. Tyler hoped they were wrong. He waited patiently for the applause to subside.

As everyone stopped clapping and began to talk amongst themselves, the Vice Admiral interrupted the chatter, "Honored colleagues, I beg your indulgence of a few minutes to refresh ourselves before we open the proceedings to questions and comments."

Tyler noted that the Vice Admiral looked directly at him when he said it. Tyler didn't flinch or acknowledge the Vice Admiral at all. At least he was going to follow protocol. Tyler wondered if the Emperor would stay. He suspected his presence had been intended for the last part anyway.

Everyone got up from the table and milled around talking with each other, congratulating the Vice Admiral, or holding conferences with their assistants. Tyler looked at the Marshall who clearly wanted to use the break time to talk.

Instead, Tyler got up and walked towards the other end of the table. The Vice Admiral was shaking hands with several members of the Command who clearly were in his pocket. The Vice Admiral smiled broadly and soaked in the attention being poured on him. Tyler assumed the Vice Admiral already figured the post of Supreme Military Commander was his.

"Vice Admiral," Tyler started using his rank as a signal of his 'real' position, "you and your staff are to be commended for such a wonderful presentation." Tyler saw how his lack of enthusiasm for the plan affected those standing around. Even the Emperor was suddenly interested in the conversation.

Don't worry gentlemen, I am not going to start the battle just yet.

"Thank you Admiral," the Vice Admiral responded, the smile fading from his face, "coming from you, it is a great compliment."

So the Vice Admiral will play it coolly.

"Yes," Tyler began again, "your attention to detail and strategic insights are truly to be commended." That much was true, but the overall plan, well that was yet to be seen.

"Thank you again Admiral, you are most generous with your praise." The Vice Admiral bowed slightly as he said this.

"Yes Admiral," the Emperor interjected, "great praise indeed. Is this to mean that you approve of...the plan?"

267

Tyler thought the Emperor almost said 'our plan', but caught himself before he did.

Tyler bowed as the Emperor moved towards them, everyone followed suit. Tyler noted several younger officers began moving away from what they saw as a pivotal battle.

"Well sir, I believe it has the making of a great offensive, but it may still be too premature to endorse it fully."

Tyler watched as that sunk in. The effect on the Emperor was zero. Tyler hated how closed and unreadable the man was. Instead of instantly reacting, he merely stared at Tyler as though measuring him up.

"I see, then you intend on sharing your thoughts with us after the break?" the Emperor asked.

The gauntlet had been thrown down, and Tyler was committed now.

"I certainly will your Eminence," Tyler agreed, "along with many other opinions I imagine. Something this big will surely draw a variety of thoughts from many on the Command."

Tyler said it loud enough that even those outside the conversation could hear him. He hoped that it would spur them to action, or at least an open backing of his plan to stall.

Tyler couldn't help notice how quiet the room had gotten. Clearly a conversation between the two greatest men on Poolto was both unprecedented and unique.

Good, Tyler thought, *let them see how I am not afraid to stand up for my convictions.*

Easy lad, don't push too hard yet, you don't want to steal your own thunder, Adanni urged.

"Very good Admiral, that is what I am here, to see our Supreme Military Command at work. We all look forward to your thoughts."

The Emperor finished and turned to walk out of the room. Everyone bowed as he and his entourage swept silently out into the corridor. Tyler knew the proceedings wouldn't begin until they returned. He hoped the Emperor wouldn't make him wait too long.

"Excuse me Vice Admiral," Tyler said, "I need to attend to a few items before we begin again."

Tyler didn't wait for a response and headed back towards the Marshall. Tyler thought he heard the Vice Admiral stutter something in response. Tyler's quick dismissal of the Vice Admiral had not been lost on the others.

The Vice Admiral does not carry the power in this room, Tyler grinned inwardly, *the Emperor and his hero are the real power*.

Don't get cocky, Adanni chastised, *the battle has not even begun*.

Tyler ignored the rebuff and walked out of the room with the Marshall in tow.

Before returning to the conference, Tyler and the Marshall walked through the plan of action. Tyler tried out some of the things he would say on the Marshall who gave good feedback. Tyler thought he would modify some of the things, but keep others as he had originally planned. All in all, they felt fairly confident as they headed back to the meeting room.

On the way, Tyler was stopped by another soldier who held a message from Toosia. Tyler read it carefully before rejoining the Marshall. The note was simple:

> Good luck dear, the Marshall has made me aware of your plans. For what it is worth, I agree with your actions as does my father. I know you'll be late, but I am planning on an intimate dinner for the two of us whenever you get home.
> Love, Toosia

Tyler erased the message after he had read it and handed the device back to the soldier. He joined the Marshall, and they made their way back to the conference. He thought about what Toosia had said and a warm feeling grew within him. At least he had a date with Toosia to look forward to.

They entered the conference room late as the proceedings were already underway. Even the Emperor was sitting quietly watching the Vice Admiral.

"...Ahh Admiral, sorry we couldn't wait for you," the Vice Admiral pleaded, "however we just got started."

"Don't worry," Tyler said, "I apologize for my tardiness, I received a note from my wife."

Tyler saw the Vice Admiral didn't know how to respond to that reference to his wife. It was common knowledge around the Supreme Military Command that the Admiral and his wife had been apart for some time. Their appearance together now was confusing to many around the room.

"Oh good," the Vice Admiral said clumsily, "well then we will continue. Secretary Doorn was just sharing with us his opinion of the offensive. Please continue Secretary." The Vice Admiral nodded to the secretary who started once again.

Tyler ignored Doorn's comments as he already knew the Secretary was backing the Vice Admiral. In fact, it was rumored he had helped craft much of the plan.

The Admiral's memories held admiration for Secretary Doorn. Apparently he had been a strong tactician when he had been a younger officer. Somewhere down the line, he had moved away from the Admiral's viewpoints and had sided with the Vice Admiral. Tyler couldn't understand why, the Admiral had been responsible for most of the Secretary's promotions throughout his career.

You stayed off-world too long Admiral, Tyler thought.

Was the Secretary being blackmailed too? Tyler wondered how many were directly beholden to the Imperial Palace for some reason or another.

The Secretary finished with applause, a look of satisfaction on the Vice Admiral's face.

"Thank you Secretary," the Vice Admiral said with a smile, "who else would care to weigh in on this issue?"

Tyler noted that a couple of his supporters had raised their hands. *Good*, Tyler thought, *they are ready to fight*.

As the Vice Admiral was ready to acknowledge one of the Secretaries, Tyler interrupted by standing up.

"Excuse me gentlemen," he started, "if you would defer your questions, I would greatly appreciate the opportunity to express my views."

Everyone nodded their heads as their eyes darted between the Vice Admiral, Tyler and the Emperor. Tyler didn't wait for the Vice Admiral to recognize him before beginning.

"As you all know, my previous experience has no equal in this room. I have won more battles than many of you have ever fought. However, many of you have fought along side me in those victories, and you know all too well how easily victory can turn to defeat."

Tyler nodded to several who had played pivotal roles in many victories.

"The Vice Admiral has presented us with nothing less than a brilliant plan for an offensive." Tyler moved his arm towards the Vice Admiral in a show of acceptance. The Vice Admiral smiled and nodded, clearly troubled by the compliment bestowed upon him by his challenger.

Just wait Vice Admiral, I'm getting to my objections.

"If it weren't for our current circumstances, I wouldn't hesitate in backing this plan."

He paused to let that take effect.

Yes gentlemen, I am openly not backing this plan.

"Instead, I must urge extreme caution before we proceed down this path. Like our previous offensive, we are excited by the prospects of catching our enemy off-guard. However, like our previous offensive, we could easily find defeat if we are not careful. I have always said that an aggressive approach is the one that will win a battle, but I am also a realist and must concede that we lack adequate information about our enemy."

He stopped and watched as that clear slap in the face of everyone involved in the last offensive had its affect. They knew too well that a lack of intelligence was partly to blame for the failure in the last battle. Some still suspected sabotage, but no one had anyone to point the finger at.

Nayllen, were you involved? The thought suddenly hit Tyler.

"We are the best and brightest of Poolto and we will not repeat our mistakes," he gave them some relief from his stinging words, "instead, we will learn from them and work hard to ensure this plan works! We will not let down our troops, our families, our planet, or our Emperor!"

Tyler put the full commanding presence of the Admiral into the last statement. Put them down then rally them up, that was how you led. Now for the big surprise, Tyler thought, not even the Marshall knew about this. It was a huge gamble, but one that might actually succeed.

You attract more bees with honey than vinegar, eh Tyler?

More pearls of wisdom from my world Adanni? Tyler asked, *this time you hit the nail on the head.*

Tyler waited for the group to calm down from his last statement. The Vice Admiral looked concerned as did the Regent. Only the Emperor wore his usual calm demeanor.

As the members of the Command quieted, Tyler walked down towards the end of the table where the Vice Admiral sat. The Vice Admiral had a look of confusion on his face. In fact, everyone in the room looked confused.

All the better, Tyler thought, *just wait till you hear the next bit of news!*

He stopped next to the Vice Admiral and turned to face the entire conference. The silence was eerie and everyone held their breath. Tyler could imagine what was going through their minds. Was the Admiral going to kick the Vice Admiral out and resume his position as Supreme Military Commander? Was he going to unveil his own plan?

Tyler waited, letting the tension build.

"Gentlemen," he began slowly and calmly, "I am no longer a young man, and I have seen far too many battles in my lifetime."

No one breathed.

"Like you, I too want to see victory and an end to this war. It has become our life, our burden, and our pain."

He paused again to see the effect his words had on the group. Even the Emperor appeared confused.

Here goes nothing!

"That is why I propose the following."

He placed his right arm around the Vice Admiral's shoulder and spelled it out.

"I am going to officially relinquish my position as Supreme Military Commander effective this moment. I am also firmly backing Vice Admiral Teesen as my replacement, and hope the Imperial Palace will see fit to make that recommendation permanent."

The shock on their faces was immediate. He continued before they could respond.

"I further propose that my new role within the Supreme Military Command will be to head up a commission to study, refine, and help execute the Vice Admiral's offensive plan."

The crowd was stunned. Even the Marshall had his mouth open in dismay.

"With the help of my distinguished colleagues, we will make every effort possible to quickly put this plan into action. We will use everything we have learned from our last offensive."

He had them now! Who could stand up and say no to this proposal. Even the Emperor looked abashed. Sure, I'll give you the carrot, but I'll still hold the whip!

As if on cue, one of the Admiral's staunch supporters stood up, "I'll second that motion and request to participate on that committee!"

Another Secretary joined the first, "I'll third that motion and also request to sit on the committee!"

The room erupted into a mix of applause, discussion, and clear confusion. He had taken away their power by giving it to them. He watched the Regent and the Emperor closely while people stood behind him congratulating the Vice Admiral. The Vice Admiral looked like a deer in the headlights. Clearly he had not expected anything like this.

As if reading Tyler's mind, the Emperor stood up. The room fell silent quickly as everyone retook their seats and waited for him to speak. He glanced at the Admiral with what Tyler thought was a look of admiration. It passed quickly as he turned to address the Command.

"Admiral," the Emperor turned back towards Tyler, "it is as though we share the same thoughts." He smiled, but it didn't look warm.

"I too believe that the Vice Admiral is the perfect replacement for your hard to fill position. I accept your resignation with deep regrets, but fully embrace your nomination for a successor to take effect immediately. My staff will sort out the details later."

He smiled at the Vice Admiral who still looked confused. Tyler supposed he couldn't believe it was actually happening. No fight, no battle, just a quick nomination.

"As for your heading up the commission," the Emperor paused to let the crowd catch up, like the Admiral, he also knew how to work it, "I whole hardily support the action and praise you for your foresight in ensuring we don't make the same mistakes as before."

Tyler wondered how much that hurt the Emperor to concede. Still, they had their puppet. Tyler guessed they would accept one victory even if it cost them another.

"Thank you Emperor," Tyler responded, "I will serve on the commission with the honor, loyalty, and integrity that I served with as your Supreme Military Commander." Tyler bowed in deference.

"I know you will." The Emperor said flatly before signaling to his entourage to follow him out.

Everyone stood and bowed as he left the conference. Apparently everything the Emperor had wanted to see was complete. The Vice Admiral stood up and tried to take charge of the ensuing chaos. Tyler smiled inside and walked back to his seat. The Marshall shot him a look of both concern and of pride. They would have much to do in the coming days.

You surprise me earth boy, Adanni praised Tyler, *had I not been reading your thoughts, I would not have seen this coming.*

Tyler accepted the praise without comment. Poolto would be buzzing tonight!

The next day brought an onslaught of press conferences, media interviews, and meetings with Supreme Military Command staff. Tyler felt he'd handled them well, especially playing up his new role as a 'Consultant' to the Supreme Military Commander, Admiral Teesen. Of course, nothing was mentioned about the commission he was heading to analyze and help execute the next offensive. That was highly classified information.

When Tyler had told Toosia about his resignation and new position, she had accepted it gracefully. She had worn her usual placid face, but Tyler believed he'd seen a look of surprise and pleasure come over her. He assured her that his role in the military would slowly diminish after their next campaign. At that time, he promised, they would build a more 'normal' life together in Tooland. As always, she accepted it with grace and her unnerving calm.

After the surviving the many press events, Tyler began building the new commission. Because he headed the commission, he had the final word on who would join. Despite this obvious power, he split the board in half with supporters of Admiral Osloo and supporters of Admiral Teesen. He maintained the power to break any gridlock that might occur.

All nominees accepted graciously and had sworn to uphold the virtues of the military code of ethics. Tyler sensed they all wanted an end to the war, but now that he had taking over the administrative aspects of the offensive, most were willing to take a more cautious stance.

Marshall Sliss and Admiral Osloo's staff had accepted the change immediately and once again demonstrated their unwavering ability to organize, plan, and execute. Their efforts essentially led the commission with Tyler providing input and command.

They had embraced their Admiral's resignation, although the Marshall reported a few disquieting rumors about careers and futures. Tyler nipped it in the bud by instructing Marshall Sliss to assure all the staff that their military progression would not be hindered by the change in their leader's status. In fact, Tyler promised them future positions of their choice, assuming they succeeded with the commission.

It had staved off their fears, and most returned their focus to the task at hand. Good thing for Tyler, the task was large and required administrative skills that even surpassed that of Admiral Osloo. Tyler was again relieved to have Marshall Sliss and a wonderful staff.

By the end of the day after the conference, they were well on their way to completing a fully functioning commission with a charter, agenda, and a schedule almost fully fleshed out. It was nothing short of a miracle, and had required a great deal of cooperation between all the staff in the Military Command. They even acquired special offices for the commission located on the seventh floor below the military complex. It had happened so rapidly, even Tyler had yet to see the new quarters.

Everything was falling into place and Tyler felt they were on track to preventing a 'would-be' disaster. He had several last minute issues to resolve before retiring to his quarters. The largest problem was getting field trials underway on several ships near completion. They would try to shorten the length of the trials, but he was certain it couldn't be completed sooner than six months. He knew the Imperial Palace and the Supreme Military Commander would be less than overjoyed with the news, but if they convinced the commission to agree with the assessment, Teesen would have no choice but to go along with it.

On top of everything else, Tyler still needed an excuse to organize a trip to Siirneen. He dreaded meeting Nayllen and his associates, but he recognized the danger if he didn't. So far, a viable solution that wouldn't raise suspicions eluded him. He sat quietly in an empty conference room, racking his brain. Unfortunately, he couldn't ask the Marshall for help since he wanted to remove the Marshall far from the threat Nayllen posed.

I have an idea, Adanni's voice offered quietly.

Tyler wasn't in the mood for Adanni yet he needed to resolve the issue. *Fine! Please share.*

Tyler could feel Adanni bristling at his clipped response, but he didn't care.

I see from the Admiral's memories there are many military installations throughout the asteroid belt. In the past, the Admiral has hosted many 'meetings' to discuss strategies with his commanders. Although they never met on Siirneen before, it is as likely a place as any.

Tyler thought about that for minute. It made sense, but it was a meeting that was usually reserved for the Supreme Military Commander, not a commissioner. How could he pull it off without looking like he was taking back power from Admiral Teesen? The last thing he needed was for Admiral Teesen to get involved.

I've got it! A revelation came to Tyler, although it was really the Admiral's memories. *We can hold an administrative meeting with the second in command rather than the commanders!*

Tyler knew the second in command always directed the supplies and administrative matters for their units. This freed commanders to deal with strategic operations, troop movements, and battle field tactics. *Perfect!*

Ok, Adanni agreed, *what is your pretense?*

My pretense? Tyler knew it was a good question, but he didn't have one prepared.

Adanni interrupted, *how about we plan the meetings around a logistics theme to validate the supply chain required for the offensive? It seems like a logical thing for the commission to do.*

Tyler hated to admit it, but Adanni was on target. They had to validate the supply chain anyway, why not do it with the officers in the field? It would bypass the higher ranking officers that were in charge of the units and regions, but it made sense to work it from the bottom up rather than the top down. After all, who had more to gain or lose than those on the front lines?

Perfect Adanni, you may be useful yet!

Interesting, Adanni replied flatly, *I was thinking the same thing about you.*

Tyler left the conference room to locate the Marshall and get the new plans underway. He needed the meeting three days from now, but he had to be there in one. It was tight, but if anyone could do it, the Marshall could.

As he walked down the corridor, he thought about having to tell Toosia he was going off-world. He didn't relish the prospects but had to face up to it. His mind was filled with many ways to break the news to her, but everything seemed likely to undermine the progress they had made together. As he turned into the staff offices, he decided to be direct and truthful with her.

Telling Toosia turned out to be easy, getting her to stay behind turned out to be impossible. It didn't help that Eyleeria had to go as well. Tyler finally succumbed and agreed to take Toosia. Deep down, he was glad she was coming, however, the danger Nayllen presented made the decision difficult. Toosia hadn't cared about Nayllen or the reasons why Tyler had to go to—she only cared that she joined him.

The Marshall had been just as difficult to convince to stay behind. In the end, Tyler had to plead with him to take charge of the commission and keep it moving forward. Tyler convinced him he was the only one capable of making it happen. Finally, this plea to the Marshall's professionalism made him agree. However, he insisted sending Officer Slaas and Eyleeria in his place. Tyler agreed, although he wasn't in favor of Eyleeria. At least Officer Slaas was nearly as capable as the Marshall.

Tyler had been surprised at the speed of their trip. Apparently, upper officers in the military had access to the best transports possible. In their case, the transport was actually a high speed reconnaissance ship outfitted as a VIP personnel carrier. Tyler recognized the ship through the Admiral's memories. The Admiral had used these carriers to travel off-world or between the flagship and other locations.

Even with the Admiral's memories, the speed had surprised Tyler. Nonetheless, he was happy to get there quickly. Staring into the blackness of space had reminded him of the loneliness he'd felt before becoming the Admiral. At least now he had Toosia by his side.

Tyler was amazed at the size and appearance of the spaceport. It was incredibly clean and modern for being on an asteroid. Of course, it was the regional headquarters for nearly all the asteroid colonies, so appearances made sense.

The Admiral had never visited Siirneen, so Tyler wasn't sure what to expect. Many said the asteroid colonies controlled the war because they controlled much of the raw resources it required. The Admiral's memories underscored this fact as nearly every battle had been fought to protect a colony and the rich resources they provided. Although some asteroids were strategic, most were an intricate link in the supply chain that fed the war effort.

Regional Governor Haal Niis, gave them a welcome that befitted the Emperor. Although Tyler could have passed on the press conference, he donned his best face and gave a commanding speech to rally the spirits of those whose hard work in the mining operations were so crucial. The applause was deafening but Tyler took it with the cool, calm demeanor that was proper for a National hero.

The Governor even arranged a ceremony to present 'keys to the colony' to the Admiral and Toosia. They accepted them humbly, although Tyler was certain neither would ever return to Siirneen. It made the Governor happy and seemed to please both the press and the crowd that had gathered to see such a prestige's celebrity. Tyler wasn't sure why, but he had imagined the people would look more like 'miners', but they dressed and looked like everyone he'd seen in Yooso.

The Governor later told Tyler that over seventy five percent of the inhabitants of Siirneen were actually corporate or government employees involved in the commercial and legal aspects of mining commerce. The mining operations had actually shrunk on Siirneen since the war had begun. The asteroid didn't contain the 'proper' concentrations of the resources needed for the war effort so much of the operations had been moved to neighboring asteroids that fit the profile better. In fact, much of the Siirneen mining was now devoted to supplying the asteroid colonies themselves. Construction supplies and natural minerals used in food supplements were generally all that was produced on Siirneen.

Tyler was impressed as they drove through Siirneen in a small ground car with virtually no security to escort them. It had surprised Tyler at first, but then he realized how tight the comings and goings of an asteroid colony were controlled. He was certain no elements on the asteroid would want to harm the Poolto National hero. *Except maybe Nayllen.*

The thought dampened Tyler's mood, but it lifted again as he watched the city of Siirneen pass by out the window. If he hadn't known he was on an asteroid, he wouldn't be able to tell Siirneen from any other city on Poolto. It was magnificent with towering buildings beneath a false sunny sky projected on the protective dome overhead. It was a truly monumental accomplishment and Tyler said as much to the Governor. The Governor accepted the compliment and began reciting the many outdoor activities the city boasted.

Tyler could sense the excitement in the Governor's voice and could see why this man had been Governor for so many years. Most in a powerful position such as his would covet positions back on Poolto, but apparently this man had refused such positions in the past. He claimed to like the freedom of space and the challenges presented within an asteroid belt. Tyler guessed the man was an adventurer, a person who liked the great 'frontier'. Like most Governors, the Marshall had told Tyler the man was a relative of the Emperor's. It was one reason for his position despite the fact the relationship was distant.

Tyler thought that 'distance' might be why the governor was willing to associate with Nayllen. He could definitely see the advantages to the colonies if the war ended. Although they would lose a substantial amount of business directed to the war effort, they would also stop suffering the tremendous losses that often accompanied a raid or a battle. Tyler looked at the Governor with renewed interest as the man recounted the hundred or so 'cafes' that catered to the varied tastes of the city's inhabitants.

Toosia was as gracious as ever and clearly had the man enamored. She kept the conversation going while Tyler watched the sights and thought about his upcoming meeting. He still hadn't told the Marshall about it, although he now suspected the Marshall had figured something was going on besides the 'Logistics Conference'. Tyler hated deceiving the Marshall, but he wanted to protect him from whatever harm might result from this meeting. A slight chill ran down Tyler's spine as he thought about it.

He looked at Toosia and smiled. She returned his smile and turned back to the Governor's commentary. He hoped her safety was also not in jeopardy.

With help from the governor's staff, they quickly settled into their extravagant quarters within the governor's palace. Tyler could only call it a palace. The Admiral's memories confirmed the Regional Governor's lived posh lifestyles. Being an extension of the Imperial Palace, it made perfect sense. However, it was in stark contrast with the functional military style the Admiral was accustomed to.

The elegance and decadence practically took Tyler's breath away. On earth, Tyler had never known anyone who had lived this well. Even the posh estate at Tooland paled in comparison to the richly adorned walls and ceilings that surrounded them.

Tyler noticed Toosia was not impressed by the extravagance, but then her life in Yooso had been rubbing elbows with the rich and powerful. He supposed this was nothing more than she had seen before, either at the palace or through council functions. Her father regularly attended great balls, and Tyler was certain Toosia had too.

He watched as she changed out of her traveling clothes and slipped on an elegant, but simple gown for the dinner. She was beautiful, and Tyler felt a blush come over him. At that moment, Toosia noticed his attention and blushed herself.

"Nayllen please, we must get ready for dinner," she pleaded.

"I know, I know, its just seeing you looking so peaceful and beautiful...well I don't know, I guess it turns me on."

She smiled back and continued blushing.

"Sorry Toosia, I guess the stress has affected me."

She didn't respond but stood up and moved towards Tyler. He felt himself get excited by her closeness, and he could see her skin reacting with a swirl of colors in response. He wasn't sure why, but she looked even more radiant than usual. This only made him more excited.

"Toosia, I..." She stopped him with a finger to his mouth.

She stepped back and gently removed her gown, letting it fall to the floor around her ankles. She was truly radiant. Her naked body, filled with the colorful lights of their shared excitement gracefully moved towards the bed, slipping under the covers. She beckoned Tyler to join her.

Tyler was mesmerized at first but then quickly removed his clothing and slipped under the covers to join her. Between the heat of their bodies pressing together, and the dance of colors on their skin, Tyler was certain the bedding would catch fire. He wouldn't have cared if it had—he was completely swept away in the flames of passion.

Both lay quiet, exhausted from their love making. He could not remember ever feeling this way with Linda, but he couldn't tell how much was his desire and how much was that of the Admiral. He didn't care whose passion it was, he was simply happy to be a part of it.

Toosia rolled towards him and placed her arm across his chest, snuggling into the crook of his arm. It felt good to hold her.

"Nayllen?" Toosia broke the silence.

"Yes?" He said.

"I have to tell you something, but I don't know if this is a good time or not."

She stopped and Nayllen could see confusion wrinkle her face. He brushed her hair aside and pulled her closer to his body.

"I'm sure it is a fine time to tell me...we are alone after all."

"I know, I know," she agreed, "its just...well its just that it is something I should have told you a long time ago."

Suddenly, Tyler's curiosity was piqued and he felt a little twinge of concern.

"Ok," he replied, "I am sure whatever it is, you had your reasons for waiting."

He let that hang patiently even though he was beginning to churn inside. What could it be? An affair? Health problems? Too many 'bad' things ran through his mind, and he tried desperately to shut them out.

Her concern deepened, and she appeared locked in indecision. Tyler stroked her shoulders gently and moved another lock of her hair away from her eyes. As he did so, he noticed a small tear fall down along her cheek. She tried to hide it, but was unsuccessful still wrapped in his arms.

"What is it honey?" he asked, not hiding his concern very well, "Please tell me."

She finally found inner resolve and broke away from him, wiping away the tears that ran down her cheeks. She sat up against the headboard and folded her hands together in her lap. Tyler knew it was going to be bad. He pushed himself up onto his right elbow and tried to look casual.

"Nayllen, I don't know how or why, but...but I am pregnant."

As if relieved to rid herself of the burden, a new stream of tears poured from her eyes. It took Tyler several minutes to fathom what she had said. *Did she say pregnant?*

I believe she did, Adanni answered.

You keep out of this Adanni—just stay quiet!

Adanni must have taken Tyler's threat serious as he never said another word.

"Pregnant?" Tyler exclaimed, a race of emotions running through him, "Did you say pregnant?"

She continued to wipe her eyes, but turned to look directly at Tyler, "Yes, I am pregnant with your child!"

She almost sounded angry, but Tyler thought that her emotions were probably affecting her speech.

"How?" It was all he could think of.

"I don't know," she sobbed, "the doctors are just as mystified by it. They had told me it was not possible."

The Admiral's memories confirmed this. Years ago, she had been diagnosed as unable to bear children, not even through artificial means. It had been the wedge that had driven her and the Admiral apart for so long. Her pain at not being able to conceive and the Admiral's inability to deal with it had made them strangers to each other. Tyler understood why she was so emotional.

"That is wonderful," Tyler admitted, more than a little surprised at his own reaction, "who cares what the doctors said—they were obviously wrong."

His approval of the situation was all she needed to renew her crying. She leaned over and grabbed him so tight he could hardly breathe. He held her quietly and let her sobbing run its course. Finally, she sat up and with a grim expression, looked him in the eyes.

"You are happy Nayllen, aren't you?"

"Of course I am," he said, "is there anything that might prevent this from...", he didn't know how to say it, "...happening?" He thought about their trip through space and felt concern.

"No," she confirmed, "nothing." She looked down at him, her eyes dry, "They say it is the healthiest pregnancy they've ever seen."

"Was it safe to come here," he asked, "I mean in space?"

"Yes Nayllen, I wouldn't have done anything to jeopardize our child. I checked with the doctors first, and they said it was fine."

"Oh," he sighed in relief, "how long have you been pregnant?"

"Going on two months now." She said it flatly.

What? Tyler's mind was reeling. Two months, but they had just made love the other day? But she had said it was his child. Suddenly, Tyler realized it couldn't be his child.

"Wait a minute," he accused, "we just made love two days ago for the first time in…I don't know how many years. How can it be mine?"

"Oh fine!" she screamed, "and I love you too!"

That caught Tyler off-guard. "Wha…?"

"I suppose you don't remember Tooland?" She chided.

"Tooland? But we never…" suddenly he remembered the first time she had shown up at Tooland. He also remembered the night before when he had dreamt…"That was real?"

"Oh, thank you very much." She was angry now.

"Wait a minute, wait a minute," the picture was starting to become clear, "you came to me that night…in my bed, right?"

"Yes."

She sounded hurt, "I am sorry Toosia, I drank a lot of wine that night, and I really thought it had been a dream."

She softened a little, "Oh, I see." A look of confusion came over her, "I suppose I didn't exactly make it seem more real after that night—you know, being standoffish and all."

"Well…" he wasn't sure how to respond to that.

"I know, I know," she agreed, "I can understand why you might have thought it was a dream. I'm sorry."

"Don't be sorry," he corrected, "it was my fault, I guess I just couldn't let myself believe you had wanted to come back."

"After I found out I was pregnant," she said, "I had a hard time telling you. I wasn't sure where we were going and I didn't want to ruin what we had started."

Tyler could see the admission was hard for her, she obviously had felt very vulnerable.

"Its ok Toosia, really, I am happy." He grabbed her and held her tightly, bringing forth a fresh stream of tears. He continued to hold her and thought about his meeting with Nayllen. How was this news going to affect him? Now he had an unborn child to worry about.

Considering the Admiral's celebrity, the dinner at the governor's palace had been intimate. The guest list included several prominent business leaders, the mayor of Siirneen, some governmental bureaucrats, and the military commander of the Siirneen command post.

Tyler could find no memory of the commander in the Admiral's past, but he did note that the Siirneen command post was predominantly ceremonial rather than strategic. Based on that, he figured this commander was directly connected to the Imperial Palace. The Governor all but confirmed it when he introduced the commander as a distant cousin.

Tyler was impressed with the food and entertainment provided for the occasion. A small orchestra had played for them after dinner and had put on a unique and strangely hypnotic performance of an ancient opera said to be twenty-five hundred years old. Tyler sensed a more primitive sound that added to the emotion and drama. Unfortunately, the language was an ancient dialect, and even the Admiral's vast knowledge of history didn't provide the necessary translation. Nonetheless, Tyler thought it was a wonderful performance. Toosia agreed.

Throughout dinner, Tyler had trouble focusing on the conversations around him. More than once he had to kindly request the speaker ask the question again, or repeat some fact that Tyler had missed. He knew it made him appear rude, but thankfully, Toosia came to his rescue by talking about the day-to-day stress of the war, especially after his injuries months before. Everyone shook their heads in understanding, and Tyler made sure he squeezed Toosia's hands in appreciation.

After the last of the opera had been played, the party enjoyed a marvelous desert and cordial. Tyler was impressed that an asteroid colony was capable of putting on such an affair, especially during war. He found it remarkable how much of the Poolto culture was alive and well out here in the 'frontier'.

Five hours had ticked away, and the dinner party began to wind down. He and Toosia made the rounds saying their goodbyes and they headed back towards their quarters. They were stopped at the entrance to the large dining room by the Governor.

"Admiral Osloo and Toosia," he said warmly, "I am so thankful I had the opportunity to show you my hospitality and gratitude that you chose Siirneen for your conference."

He held out his hands and gently shook both of theirs.

"Please Governor," Toosia responded graciously, "it is we who are to thank you for such a wonderful reception."

"Yes Governor," Tyler added, "we are truly in your debt for such an elegant evening."

"Yes, well I am pleased you both enjoyed it. Umm…Admiral, I was hoping that I might have a private word with you before you retire for the evening?" Tyler noted a little discomfort in the governor's request. "That is if it is alright with you Lady Toosia?"

Lady Toosia? Tyler had to admit, he was a politician. He watched her face for a reaction, but she merely smiled softly and nodded her head towards the governor.

"Of course Governor, he is at your disposal." She replied.

"Oh good, I'll try not keep him long." the governor signaled to an attendant across the room, "One of my staff will escort you back to your quarters my Lady."

The governor whispered instructions into the attendant's ear, and he bowed slightly before offering his arm to Toosia. She took it gracefully, and with a slight smile and nod to Tyler, she headed out of the dining room and back to their quarters.

"Excuse me Admiral, I must see the last of my guests out before we can go somewhere…more private."

Tyler nodded and took a seat in one of the many overstuffed chairs surrounding the interior walls of the dining room. As Tyler waited, he looked around the room admiring the intricate details of its elegant design. It was a rectangular room with two large entrances at either end. One led to the front entrance of the palace while the other led to the interior corridors and quarters. Tyler sat nearest the interior entrance staring across at the few remaining guests the governor was speaking with.

In the middle of the room was an enormous table that could seat as many as a hundred people comfortably, but had been sized down for the more intimate dinner that night. Tyler had figured about 40-50 people had attended the party including the guests each 'official' member had brought.

A set of double doors blended into the wall on the left-hand side of the room. These doors led to the kitchen and were used by the wait staff. Currently, the doors were closed as the staff waited for everyone to leave before clearing.

On the right-hand side of the room, the floor and walls had been cleared to make room for the small orchestra. The chairs for the musicians had been arranged in a semi-circular pattern facing the main table. In the front, a small podium had been centered for the conductor while others were placed on either side of the musicians for the opera singers.

Tyler could only remember one other formal orchestra he'd seen. Linda had taken him to it early in their relationship. Her family had season tickets and she had insisted they go to one of the fall debuts. Although Tyler hadn't liked it at the time, he saw a great deal of similarities between tonight's performance and the one they had seen. The one in L.A. had not been an opera, but the orchestral arrangement had been very similar—hypnotic and ethereal.

Tyler thought about how much of this world was so similar to earth. Different creators and different species, and yet, there seemed little more variety. Love, pain, greed, and war were familiar themes on both planets. Tyler wondered if everything evolved in similar ways, regardless of their origins.

He watched the governor as he tried to bid goodnight to the last of his guests. A party of four seemed bent on discussing some matters before leaving. Tyler noted the governor, always the gracious politician, listened patiently to each in turn. He smiled and looked unperturbed, although Tyler knew he wanted them out.

Tyler smiled inwardly thinking of all the media events he'd been in since becoming the Admiral. He looked back on it all and was still amazed he'd pulled it off...so far.

Adanni broke his reverie, *The hard part is yet to come my friend.*

I know, Tyler responded, *please don't interrupt too much.*

Fine, but I will let you know when something doesn't sound right!

Fine.

Tyler looked back across the room and saw that the governor had finally got his guests to leave. He was walking back across the room, signaling to staff members as he went. He was obviously giving directions for the cleanup.

"Sorry for the delay," the governor apologized, "sometimes my guests are a little ambitious when they see an opportunity to have my ear, one-on-one."

"I understand Governor." Tyler assured him.

"Good, well then let's retire to somewhere more intimate and have that talk."

The Governor led him out through the entrance to the interior part of the palace and down several corridors before stopping in front of what looked like a lift. The governor did something and the door opened with a whish.

"Just a short lift to get there." The governor assured Tyler.

As the doors closed, Tyler felt the elevator begin its descent. He noted that even the interior of the elevator was ornately trimmed. The back of the elevator even held a large painting that Tyler guessed was quite old. He could see why it was called the 'Governor's Palace'.

The elevator came to a stop at what Tyler figured must have been at least five stories beneath the palace. Clearly the palace was larger than it appeared. Tyler wondered how much of the real palace was beneath the upper building. Their quarters, he knew, were on the main floor. The governor's quarters however, probably were not.

The governor extended his arm to usher Tyler out.

"Welcome to where I really work Admiral."

Tyler noticed the corridor looked no different than the ones on the main floor. It stretched off into the distance before ending at a left turn. Tyler could see no breaks in the walls to indicate doorways.

The governor continued his commentary as they walked down the long corridor, "We are currently seven floors beneath the main Palace in what I call my 'office'. However, it is really a bunker of sorts. You see, this area was built after the start of the war when raids on the colonies had been quite common. This bunker had been carved underneath the existing Palace through what is nearly solid iron. I've been told this area can withstand everything except atomic blasts. Thankfully, I have only used it once, and that was a false alarm."

They turned the corner at the end of the corridor and began walking through another long stretch. This one, thankfully, had a door at the end of it.

"Very impressive Governor," Tyler admitted, "do you work here everyday?"

"Well, yes, assuming I'm not out on official business. I had most of my business equipment and communications put down here so I could continue my duties, even under an attack."

Tyler couldn't imagine working underground everyday. He supposed it was no different than the Supreme Military Command complex, but somehow it seemed more cramped. Ironically, the feeling was probably due to the lack of people. The lighting was nearly the same.

They reached the door and entered an enormous circular room. On the opposite side of the room, Tyler saw another doorway that led into what must of have been the rest of the facility. He guessed the room measured at least a hundred feet across and the walls rose up nearly thirty feet before meeting the domed roof that once again rose higher by at least another twenty. Tyler doubted anyone would feel claustrophobic in this room.

On their left, a large table dominated the room, curved to match the contour of the wall behind it. Tyler assumed that was the Governor's desk. It was large enough to sleep four or five people on top.

From the outside edge of the room, the floor sank several feet lower to an area filled with couches, chairs, desks, and small tables. It was rather luxurious and obviously meant for entertaining or meeting people.

Adorning the right-hand wall, if you could call it that, a series of about ten viewers in various sizes filled the space from floor to ceiling. It reminded Tyler of his own room back at Tooland, but the size difference was quite noticeable.

The light in the room was soft and seemed to emanate from various places on the wall and the ceiling. Tyler stared up at the dome above and noticed a series of pie shaped murals covering most of the dome. They were intricately painted murals, and each pie shaped wedge held an entirely different scene. As far as Tyler could tell, the scenes were of the asteroid colony in what appeared to be various stages of development.

"Wonderful isn't it?" the governor asked, looking up with Tyler.

"Yes," Tyler agreed, "is it a depiction of Siirneen's history?"

"No, although one of the panels is," the governor said, "it is a depiction of each of the regional asteroid colonies when they were founded."

Tyler counted seventeen pictures, but the governor pointed out two of them on the right side of the dome, "Those two were captured many years ago and are still under the control of Krildon."

Tyler didn't recognize them, but then the Admiral had cared little for the particulars of asteroids and instead focused more on regions of the asteroid belt.

The governor continued, "You'll notice that each panel ends in the center at the bright round orb that represents our sun."

Tyler looked at the sun and thought it looked made of gold.

"The panels are laid out in their proper positions within the asteroid belt as you would see it from a distant perspective."

Tyler was impressed, and he had no doubt that was the idea.

The governor finally finished, "It was created for me by an artist I had known on Poolto. He is no longer alive, but his work will live on for eternity. It took him over five months to complete it…by himself."

"Truly remarkable." Tyler said.

The governor ushered Tyler to one of the many chairs and sofas in the center of the room. Tyler chose a particularly comfortable chair and sat down. There was no need to be uncomfortable. The governor moved across the room to what Tyler thought was a bar.

"Would you care for a nightcap Admiral?" the Governor asked, "I have an exquisite brandy that was actually made from fruit on your Tooland Estate."

Although Tyler had plenty of wine to drink with dinner, the soothing effects of the alcohol made him desire more. "Please." He replied.

The governor poured two large glasses of brandy and carried them back to the center of the room. The governor gave one to Tyler and took the other one with him as he sat down on an overstuffed couch. Tyler lifted his glass to the governor and took a large drink. He could feel the warming of the drink in his mouth, and picked out tremendous flavors as he swished it around. Tooland came through once again.

"Well, Governor, what did you want to see me about?" Tyler asked.

"Well, it is not just me of course who wants to speak with you," the Governor began before being interrupted by someone entering through the door. It was Nayllen.

"Ahh, Governor, you and the Admiral are here and ready to begin, wonderful!" Nayllen sounded genuinely happy. Tyler didn't think it suited him.

The governor rose from his seat and walked back to the bar to fetch Nayllen a drink, "The usual Nayllen?" he asked.

Nayllen merely nodded and sat down on the left-hand side of Tyler.

"Admiral, so glad to see you made it," he stated it matter of fact as if Tyler had a choice, "and such a wonderful reason you employed to be here. I doubt anyone was suspicious, except the Marshall of course." He concluded.

"Of course." Tyler agreed, remaining as calm as possible. At this point, he just wanted it over.

Patience my friend, patience, Adanni cautioned.

Considering how much Tyler had drank, he was ready to be patient and even felt emboldened. He took another sip to steel himself.

The governor set a glass of some other liquid down on a table next to Nayllen and resumed his seat on the couch.

"Well now," Nayllen began, "I must start by saying that you surprised us all with your resignation Admiral. It was not the action we were hoping for, but considering the corner you had been backed into, it was a truly brilliant move."

Action you hoped for? Tyler thought, it made him a nervous.

"And what action did you hope for Nayllen?" He asked boldly.

"Well, there were many possibilities of course, but let's just say that yours was…well, unexpected."

Tyler was once again unnerved by his lack of answers. A burning anger began simmering below the surface.

Easy killer, easy, Adanni spoke quietly, *remember, he is a very dangerous man.*

Tyler agreed and let his anger simmer silently.

"Anyway," Nayllen started again, "that is not exactly why we are here. We are here to discuss our need for your assistance in ending this war."

Tyler saw that the governor was shaking his head in agreement but remained quiet. Tyler wondered how he fit into this scheme.

"Fine," Tyler said coldly, "I am here, so what is it you want from me?"

Nayllen took a moment to survey Tyler, and then simply stated, "Why nothing less than the Supreme Military Command codes for disabling all fleet ships."

Tyler was amazed at how Nayllen said it so casual, as though it were no small matter, like borrowing some money.

Tyler responded, "I am surprised with your connections you don't already have them."

"I too am surprised," Nayllen admitted, "but they are the one thing I have been unable to get my hands on. Not even the Emperor has access to them."

Tyler knew from the Admiral's memories that only the Supreme Military Commander had the codes. They were originally established to prevent two possible things from happening. First, they were designed to prevent a mutiny from inside the military or a take over by the Imperial Palace. Second, they were designed to prevent the use of their own ships in the event they were captured by the enemy. From the Admiral's recollections, they had never been used before.

"Didn't you hear?" Tyler asked sarcastically, "I am no longer the Supreme Military Commander."

"Indeed, that is why your actions were not what we were hoping for. However, all is not lost, it will be some time before the official turn over takes place, and we still have time." Nayllen looked directly at Tyler, a smug look on his face.

"Assuming I ignore the fact that this is the most traitorous action I could ever take, why should I turn them over to you and how will that help you win the war?" Tyler was more than curious.

"Fine questions," Nayllen agreed, "but I am not sure that you really have a choice here."

Tyler once again felt anger building, "So it is threats then is it?" He barely contained his emotions when he said it.

"Threats my good Admiral?" Nayllen responded, "I won't need threats after you meet with my associates."

Tyler was confused, he had assumed that the associates had been the governor, but apparently there were others involved in this conspiracy.

"I see, and when will I meet these associates?" He asked racking his brain for some logical choice of who. A council member perhaps? Could be, the rumors indicated many were tiring of the war. He thought about Toosia's father and suddenly wondered if he were involved.

"In due time Admiral, they haven't arrived yet."

Tyler wasn't reassured, "Ok, then while we wait you can explain to me how the codes help you win the war?"

"Win the war?" Nayllen said in surprise, "who ever said anything about winning the war, I merely said stop it."

Nayllen's obfuscation was wearing on Tyler, and he held his anger barely in check.

You really shouldn't drink in these situations Tyler, you have far to much repressed anger within you.

Tyler ignored Adanni's commentary and stared at Nayllen, waiting for him to reveal more. At this point, Tyler didn't like how the proceedings were going. Nayllen was both obtuse and painting a picture that would sounded as though it would include the end of the Admiral.

As if reading his mind, Nayllen spoke up, "You are correct to be concerned about your situation Admiral—this may turn out badly for you regardless of whether you join us."

Tyler couldn't believe he was hearing that admission, "Then tell me why I should do it!" He demanded.

"Well, I am afraid the alternative would be far worse."

Again with the threats, "What do you need the command codes for?" Tyler demanded.

"To stop the fleet of course."

Tyler was amazed at how calm Nayllen remained when he said these things. How cold and calculating was this man? Tyler once again doubted the Admiral had been named for this person. At least he hoped he hadn't.

"Why of course, and that will stop the war because Krildon will be able to just walk in and declare victory." Tyler knew his voice held a strong edge of anger, but he didn't care at this point. Clearly these men were crazy, as well as dangerous.

Nayllen's emotions didn't change at all, "Admiral, I am surprised at you, you see everything from your narrow, military point of view. Very limiting."

Tyler snorted, "Yeah, I guess it is a hazard of my position."

Nayllen sat back and took a sip from his drink, "Admiral, I realize that this is difficult for you, but I must assure you that in the end, the war will be stopped and all of Poolto will benefit, even your family."

"Please leave my family out of it," Tyler said with an implied threat.

Nayllen smiled, "Yes, well I realize that your baby is on the way and that likely changes your attitude towards things greatly."

Tyler couldn't believe he had heard it, this man was something else. "You know about Toosia's pregnancy?" Tyler was incredulous.

Apparently the governor was likewise incredulous, the look of surprise on his face nearly matched Tyler's. "A baby Admiral? How wonderful!" The Governor said much too jovially under the circumstances.

Tyler ignored him, "How do you know she is pregnant?"

"Please Admiral," Nayllen said as though brushing it aside, "after everything I have shown you, I am surprised by your surprise."

Tyler had to admit, this man had revealed he had access to just about everything.

Except the command codes, Adanni reminded Tyler.

Perhaps that was a bargaining chip? Tyler thought, something he could use to help him out of the situation. But the danger of it being used was too hard to ignore.

Nayllen went on as though nothing were amiss, "Surely Admiral, you want your child to enter a world free from war?"

Tyler agreed that would be nice, but he wasn't sure it was something these men could deliver.

"I am still not seeing why stopping the fleet will help end the war?" Tyler pressed.

"No," Nayllen agreed, "I don't suppose you do."

Without saying more, Nayllen gave the governor a questioning glance as he looked at a clock on the table next to the governor. The governor followed Nayllen's gaze and shrugged. Apparently, whoever they were waiting for was late.

Tyler pressed further, "Then why don't you enlighten me?"

"I am reserving that for our guests." Nayllen said as though that were sufficient reason.

"Fine, where are they?" Tyler was losing his patience and his simmering anger was threatening to erupt.

"Fine question," Nayllen agreed, "Governor, why don't you see what their status is?"

The governor shook his head in acknowledgement and headed for his desk. He was nearly hidden behind the enormous desk, but Tyler could make out his face in the dim light of the viewer he was reading. Tyler remained quiet as did Nayllen. Both took turns sipping their drinks as they waited. The silence was awkward.

Who could they be waiting for, Tyler thought. He imagined someone from the Imperial Palace. Surely they had inside conspirators within the Palace?

I don't think so, Adanni said, *but I cannot offer an alternative.*

Tyler sipped more of his drink and noticed he had nearly finished it. He almost got up to refill it, but decided he was already drunker than was prudent in this situation. He put his head back into the seat and stared once again at the mural on the ceiling. His clouded mind drifted with random thoughts. He thought about Toosia and his unborn child. He felt a deep chill of fear.

To Tyler, the wait seemed like an eternity, but the Governor finally rejoined them. "Ah, sorry, a slight delay due to a security checkpoint. They've passed through fine and should be here shortly."

Security checkpoint? Why would that delay them? Tyler was confused.

Any thoughts Adanni? Tyler asked inwardly.

No, Adanni admitted.

Once again, they sat in silence, waiting. Tyler was still fuming and didn't feel socializing was appropriate. Nayllen looked as though he were prepared to wait for an eternity, his calm demeanor never changing. *Damn him!*

Finally, the Governor broke the silence, "Who would like me to freshen their drinks?" He asked.

Nayllen handed his glass to the Governor, as did Tyler. What the hell, it couldn't get any worse, and it felt good getting drunk. It gave him a renewed bravado despite the dangers. The governor returned with fresh glasses and Tyler drank a heavy portion in his first sip. Both Nayllen and the governor didn't appear the least bit concerned. At least Tyler had experience dealing with people when he was drunk.

I don't think the people you dealt with on earth were quite the same as these.

Tyler was tired of Adanni's comments and was ready to push him back away from his consciousness. He had second thoughts when he realized how valuable Adanni might be when the 'associates' arrived.

As though on cue, the opposite door to the room opened and two large guards entered, swept the room with their gaze before taking up positions on either side of the door. Tyler was absolutely stunned. The two guards were Krildon and the weapons they held looked serious. *That explains the security checkpoint.*

As they waited, another Krildon entered the room, but looked less like a guard and more like a bureaucrat. He waved at Nayllen and came down to the center of the room. As he approached, Tyler was taken by how large they were compared to the average person on Poolto.

The man stood at least seven feet tall and towered over Nayllen. His face was fierce, and the scaly skin and protruding fangs made him a truly daunting figure. At least Tyler thought he was. The voice however did not match his awesome appearance. Instead, it was smooth, gentle, and very high in timber. It surprised Tyler.

The man spoke gently, "Hello Nayllen, I am sorry we are late, we were almost detected by one of your checkpoints. Fortunately, your military codes worked." He held out his large hand and shook Nayllen's. He turned towards Tyler and smiled, if that was what you could call his contorted face. Tyler thought it looked more like a snarl.

"Admiral, what a privilege to meet you in person," he held out his hand to Tyler, "it is not everyday that a person is able to meet their greatest nemesis in the flesh."

Tyler stood up and shook his hand, he didn't like the way he had said 'flesh'. His hand was surprisingly soft despite the scaly appearance.

"And who do I have the privilege of meeting?" Tyler asked.

"Ahh," Nayllen said quickly, "I am sorry Admiral, let me introduce you to the Commander of the Third Fleet of the Krildon Republic Navy, Commandant Askgar Kulg."

Tyler nodded and found plenty of references to him within the Admiral's memories. The man was a remarkable tactician and had nearly defeated the Admiral more than once in great battles.

Tyler tried not to appear intimidated as he stared up at Kulg, "Indeed, I too am privileged to meet such a worthy adversary."

Tyler really didn't like where this was headed. The man was a military commander like the Admiral, and although he was fierce looking, his demeanor did not match his position. However, just meeting with him would be considered 'high treason' by any Poolto standard.

They sat back down and Tyler noticed that Commandant Kulg barely fit into his seat. It looked strange to see him sitting in such a tiny chair. Tyler thought it demeaned him. He may be an enemy, but he still earned respect.

The Governor turned towards Kulg, "A drink Commandant?"

"No thank you, I am fine," he replied in his lilting tone, "my guest should be here shortly."

Guest? Tyler thought, then this wasn't who they were waiting for? How could it get weirder than this? Tyler remained silent while Nayllen and the commandant talked about the trip to Siirneen.

Tyler was amazed that someone from Krildon could penetrate this far into Poolto space undetected. However, it wasn't hard to imagine how it could be done with Nayllen's assistance. Still, one look or scan should have been enough to see through any disguises they may have had. Tyler was once again impressed with the power Nayllen seemed to control.

He listened to the end of their conversation, "Yes," Kulg was saying, "your devices worked perfectly. However, without the diplomatic codes, they would have boarded us for certain. I know I would have." He concluded.

Tyler was about to ask about the devices when another Krildon entered the room. He looked more like an assistant than anyone they would be waiting for.

"Commandant, our guest is here." The person bowed towards them all and then stood to one side.

"Ah wonderful!" exclaimed Nayllen, and Tyler had to admit he saw a real look of happiness on Nayllen's face.

Everyone rose from their seats and waited. Tyler watched as a figure emerged from the darkness of the corridor beyond, walking slowly with a cane. It was the first time he had seen anyone use a cane on this world.

As the person entered the room, Tyler's jaw hung open in an expression of pure disbelief. The person they had been waiting on, the person who was an associate of Nayllen's and a conspirator was the Admiral's Father, Nattur Osloo.

Nayllen walked over to Nattur, his hand outstretched in welcome, while Tyler's head buzzed with confusion.

"But...but," Tyler stammered without control, "y-you are dead!"

Nattur looked over at Tyler, a small smile on his face, "Well my boy, I feel great nonetheless."

This was too much for Tyler. The combination of the drink, the news from Toosia, the implied threats from Nayllen, and his certain collusion in a conspiracy against the Empire was threatening to overcome Tyler. His head swam woozily as he sat back down and stared blankly at the floor.

Adanni's voice penetrated the fog that clouded Tyler's mind, *Warning Tyler, this is an unexpected turn of events and I sense real danger here.*

Talk about an understatement! Tyler felt fear begin to seize him. How could he deal with the Admiral's father? What if Nattur could recognize that Tyler was not his son?

It was a long time ago that the Admiral saw his father, I don't think that will be a problem, Adanni reassured. Problem was, Tyler didn't feel reassured.

Through his fog, he watched as they all took seats and stared blankly at him. Only the Admiral's father seemed to wear a slight look of concern.

"Nayllen," Nattur prompted, "are you feeling alright?"

Was he kidding? A part of the Admiral's memories reeled with the sight of his supposedly 'dead' father. These thoughts impacted Tyler as well. He had thought he had been prepared for anything, he even had handled the commandant pretty well.

But this...this was something that caught him off-guard and he did not know how to deal with it. A multitude of thoughts jammed his thinking, and he felt lost within his own mind. Only a loud voice cut through his reverie and brought him back to the present.

Answer him Tyler, we'll deal with it!

It was Adanni, obviously fearful of the awkward silence as Tyler was lost in confusion. Tyler quickly brought his attention back to the group and responded to Nattur's question, "I'm....I am sorry, I have no words to respond with father."

That much was true. He watched as the Admiral's father smiled slightly and turned a questioning glance to each of the others in the party.

"Indeed Nayllen, I imagine you don't!" His smile got broader and looked genuine to Tyler. "Don't worry son, it is me, despite what the Emperor wanted you to think. He knew I was alive, although I am certain he would never have told you."

Tyler was confused, the Emperor knew the Admiral's father was still alive?

"How could he," Tyler stammered, "I mean, how could the Emperor have known?"

Nayllen interjected, "I told him." Once again a flat statement and one that only reinforced this man's power and influence.

"Then why didn't you tell me?" Tyler said, a little too loudly.

"Easy son," Nattur interrupted, "I told him not to tell you."

The drink and the circumstance were more than Tyler could handle. He felt like everything was happening in slow motion. Why would the Admiral's father want the Admiral to think he was dead? It didn't make any sense. As though sensing his confusion, Nattur answered Tyler's question.

"I thought it would be better to have you think I was dead to ensure your fighting strategies were not compromised by my being captive."

"Then you are a prisoner?" Tyler asked, still confused.

Nattur smiled and looked over at the Commandant who 'snarled' back, "No, I was at first, but I have been a guest of the Krildon government for many years now. To them, I am still an ambassador to Poolto. I am safe to move about Krildon all I want, although that may be less safe these days. Especially after your last offensive."

Tyler listened, but it didn't seem to sink in. So he was still on good terms with the government on Krildon? That would explain why he was here, but not necessarily why he was conspiring with Nayllen and the Governor. Unless, they really were all traitors in league with Krildon to overthrow the Emperor. It was the only thing making sense at that point.

"Am I truly named after this man?" Tyler asked nodding his head towards Nayllen. Nattur followed his gaze and looked a little confused by the change in topic.

"Yes," Nattur responded gently, "didn't Nayllen tell you that he and I worked together on Krildon?"

Tyler didn't want to believe the answer, it meant the Admiral's father had really been a spy for the Emperor. A spy that had been denounced and left a prisoner on the enemy's world. Tyler didn't think Nattur looked like he would hold a grudge, but then again, the Admiral's memories were obviously naive about his own father.

"Yes," Tyler responded coldly, "he told me, I just didn't believe it."

Nattur's face changed slightly with the cold response Tyler had given him. Clearly he expected a much happier reunion with his son. *I am not your son, and I don't trust you*, Tyler thought.

A wise decision, Adanni agreed.

Once again, Tyler's anger began to rise. This time he welcomed it as it began to wear off the effects of the alcohol. He stared back defiantly at Nattur who was appraising him in a very calculated way.

"Hmmm…" Nattur began, obviously re-evaluating his son, or seeing him for the first time, "I see that my visit is not necessarily a welcome one."

He stated it as a fact rather than a question. Tyler had to concur with his deduction, but didn't say as much.

"Well father, I haven't seen you since the beginning of the war, you let me, and mother believe you were dead, you've been branded a traitor by the Emperor, and now you show up involved in a conspiracy with these gentlemen, who have all but threatened me and my family, and you are in the company of our enemy." Tyler let his anger loose as he said this. "Tell me father, why is it I should welcome you?"

No one reacted to his outburst, but Tyler was glad to have said it. He wasn't going to play the victim anymore. If they wanted him dead, then get it over with. At least they wouldn't get the Command Codes! He sat back and finished his drink, the buzz from before wearing off fast in his anger. *To hell with you all*, he thought.

Everyone looked at each other in turn, but nobody said anything. Perhaps he had finally shut them up.

Nattur sat back in his chair and stared across at Tyler, a neutral look on his face. Tyler returned his gaze unwavering.

"I understand I am to be a grandfather?" Nattur asked, obviously not wanting to deal with Tyler's outburst. "And here I thought Toosia was unable?"

"Well I guess life sometimes throws you a curve ball!" Tyler responded, not even realizing his 'earth' comment. He saw a look of puzzlement come over Nattur, and it was quickly replaced with the neutral composure.

"Yes," Nattur replied, "I suppose it does. Well for what it is worth, congratulations, I am very glad you are back together and will be a family."

Tyler thought he sounded sincere, but considering all of Nayllen's threats, he didn't think family life was in his future.

"Yes," Tyler responded, "I suppose we will be a family, although not if Nayllen has his way. He has already assured me that things will likely work out 'badly' for me, regardless of whether I help you or not. So please, excuse me if I don't get all teary eyed at your comments."

At that, Nattur looked over at Nayllen with a look of, was it anger? Who cared, it was obvious that the Admiral, and Tyler, were in too deep for anything good to come out of it.

Nattur turned back to Tyler, "I think Nayllen has over spoken his bounds, I am sure we can find a way for you to come out well in this."

Tyler noticed that Nayllen didn't respond to this rebuke in any way. He simply stared at Tyler, his usual calm cold face, measuring, and scheming. Perhaps this conspiracy was not as tightly bound as they would have Tyler believe. *Watch out Nattur, my namesake is far from trustworthy, his plans may not match your own.*

Tyler didn't put it past Nayllen to be conspiring against his own conspirators. Tyler could just imagine him turning them in to the Emperor if things didn't go as planned. Then he would maintain his own power, and raise his own status within the Imperial Palace.

Tyler spat back sarcastically, "Perhaps I can, after all, being a traitor is apparently not as deadly as one might believe." Tyler let the barb sink in.

He noticed the Commandant getting antsy at the exchange. Being in the middle of his enemy's territory was a big gamble for him. If it went poorly, he could easily be caught and tried as a spy. Tyler could only imagine what the Imperial Palace would have in store for the 'Commander of the Third Fleet of the Krildon Republic Navy'. Tyler doubted he would be treated as well as they had treated the Admiral's father.

Tyler turned to the commandant, "So tell me Commandant, do you share my father's belief that I will come through this well?"

Clearly the questioned bothered the Commandant, but his emotions were hard to read through his reptilian face.

He responded to Tyler in his high voice, but the force and command still came through, "I can assure you Admiral that this war is coming to an end. How and when will determine your fate."

Nattur shot another angry glance, this time at the Commandant, Tyler didn't miss the exchange. *Who is really in charge here Nattur?* Tyler began to think it wasn't the Admiral's father.

"I see," Tyler said, "then you must share Nayllen's assessment." Tyler turned back to the Admiral's father. "So tell me father, why then are you so optimistic about my future?"

Nattur regained his calm demeanor and smiled at Tyler, "Because you are my son, and I want only good things for you."

Fat chance, Tyler thought. What was his motivation? He had been branded a traitor, all of Poolto knew it and despised him. How could he hope to gain from this conspiracy? It was easy to imagine how the commandant and his world would gain, they appeared to be the ones who would come out 'good' in this plan.

"Right." Tyler said flatly.

"Ok Nayllen," Nattur said quickly, "I realize this is hard for you and I can see you do not trust me. I can understand. The war has obviously hardened you over the years, and I can see why you believe nothing but bad things will come from this." He paused, obviously trying to make due with the change in attitude. "Fine, I accept that. But my colleagues are right, this war will end and you can either be an active part of it or a victim from it. The choice is yours."

Tyler watched him closely, and felt he was finally being truthful.

"Perhaps I cannot guarantee you will survive this well, but I can guarantee that your family will."

That got Tyler's attention. So, they were going to use his family against him after all. Nayllen had already threatened it, but clearly Nattur was willing to put it on the table and get it done with. *Great,* Tyler thought, *happiness is once again in my grasp, but soon to be taken away.* Tyler sank back into his chair, a sense of defeat overcoming him. He knew he could be brave and fearless if he were involved, but he also knew he could do nothing that would threaten Toosia and their unborn child.

He looked back at Nattur who stared at him with a determined look, "Fine father, fine, you win, what is it you want from me and how will it end the war?"

He could see that his acquiescence had eased the tension that had been building. But why fight it anymore? They held everything and he held nothing, except the Command Codes. It wasn't a good bargaining chip, especially if they didn't actually need them to accomplish their goals. Nayllen had revealed as much.

Nattur sat back, his features easing, "Son, don't sound so fatalistic, it will be an end to a long and senseless war. Is that not worth something? A world where your child can travel the solar system, free from fear, free from killing? Free from anger?"

Tyler knew he was right, but he didn't believe it would all be paradise.

"Don't you also mean a world without a father?" Tyler knew it sounded petty, but he didn't care anymore. He could see that the comment stung the Admiral's father.

"It doesn't have to be that way son."

"Not according to your colleagues." Tyler responded.

"Son, listen," Nattur leaned forward in his chair, "what we need from you is dangerous, it is true there are risks, but you may yet prevail and come through this both alive and a hero."

Tyler shot back, "Didn't you know father? I already am a hero!"

"I know son, but a war hero. Wouldn't you rather be a hero of the peace?"

Tyler had to admit, the badge as a war hero had never sat well with him. He had never been a violent or aggressive man, which is probably why he had so many customers back on earth. No one ever felt threatened by him, unlike so many in the 'trade'. If he survived and became a hero of the peace, then he and Toosia could retire to their vineyard and live their lives out as a family. *If I survive!*

You are awfully quiet Adanni, have you no 'great' insight?

No, like you, I have no idea what any of their motivations are, but I still don't trust them. There is something here that I...

Adanni trailed off before finishing the thought. Damn Tyler thought, just when I actually need him. *What is it you sense or see Adanni, please share?*

Silence.

Tyler's anger began to rise when Adanni finally responded.

I sense something, but I believe I may be mistaken.

Nice, Tyler thought, it felt like he was dealing with Nayllen.

Thanks for your input, Tyler thought sarcastically. Only silence responded.

"Yes father," he turned his attention back to the Admiral's father, "I would love to be the hero of peace, I am just unsure you can provide that peace."

Nattur sat back again, his placid face staring around at his co-conspirators. Tyler couldn't tell what he was thinking but he just wanted the whole thing over.

"Alright Nayllen, fair enough." Nattur signaled to the governor for a drink, and the governor quickly went to the bar. At least Tyler could assume the governor was not in charge.

"Anyone else?" the governor called from the bar.

No one responded, so he returned quickly with Nattur's drink.

Nattur took a long drink before continuing, "As we all know, this war was started because of petty, corporate, territorial disputes that escalated into a political nightmare that we all currently live in. Philosophically, we can all agree on that, even the Emperor. However, over time, the effects of the killing and warfare have developed a 'grudge' or hatred for the other side. On Poolto, our own history has shown this to be true over and over again. Even Krildon has plenty of historical references that mirror this situation."

Nattur grabbed his drink again, and Tyler had to admit, he was telling the truth. Even he knew the same things happened on earth with many disputes. A minor dispute can escalate into a war, which can escalate into hatred, and which finally escalates into genocide. Tyler had to concede, both worlds were stuck in that cycle which nearly destroyed each.

Tyler interrupted, "Yes father, this is all academic, but what do you propose to do to break us out of the cycle?"

Nattur put his drink down, "By being the ones who step forward and say it must stop. By being the ones who have the power to make it stop."

Tyler thought about that, he could start seeing their plan forming in his mind. Take away the power of Poolto by disabling the fleet with the Command Codes, then, offer the end to the war. How else could Poolto, or the Emperor, respond? They would have to agree.

Tyler shot back, "And that will be it? Krildon will back down? Love, peace and harmony will prevail?" Tyler knew he was being overly sarcastic, but it still didn't jive with what he saw as the real outcome.

"Yes," Nattur agreed, "but not all at once, over time."

"And you Commandant," Tyler asked, "this is what you desire, an end to all hostilities? Forgive and forget?"

The Commandant was about to respond when Nattur interjected, "Son, Krildon is a democracy, not an authoritarian regime like Poolto. Their people desire peace more than they desire the end of us. Peace can prevail, but we must open the way for it to begin. The Emperor cannot be the one to offer this peace, his ego will not let him. He must be forced to accept it, and the only way is by taking away his power. You, and the military, are his power."

No denying that, Tyler thought, the Emperor himself didn't control the military, although his influence on it had recently been increased. No wonder the Imperial Palace was backing Teesen, they were slowly increasing their control of the military. Tyler knew that when push came to shove, Teesen would never go against the Emperor, and would likely even give him the Command Codes.

Tyler was beginning to see why he was in a 'no-win' situation. Once the military was under the total command of the Emperor, he could do anything he wanted, all in the guise of 'winning' the war. It was no wonder his propaganda machine worked hard to foment hatred against Krildon, he wanted nothing less than victory, no matter the cost to either world. The Admiral, and Tyler, had both been caught up in the same propaganda.

"Ok, what do you propose to do?" Tyler asked, suddenly a lot more receptive.

"We plan on bringing a treaty mission to Poolto to propose the end of the war. The Commandant here will bring nothing less than his own flag ship with a majority of the Krildon representatives on board to negotiate. The President himself will also be present."

Tyler watched as the Commandant shook his head in agreement.

"And I suppose that you need me to disable the fleet to ensure safe passage?" Tyler asked, although he knew that had to be it.

"Of course," Nattur agreed, "but also to ensure that the bargaining is heavily weighted on our side."

"Of course," Tyler agreed thinking that would be a perfect opportunity for an attack. "And why must I give the command codes to you? Can't I just disable them myself when the time comes?"

Nattur looked a little surprised by the question, "Well, I suppose that could be the case, but we need you with the Emperor at the time. Suppose something happens to you, especially if the

Emperor senses mutiny, his guards could easily overtake you before the fleet was disabled."

True enough, Tyler thought, but he still didn't trust them.

"Ok, I see your point. What will keep Krildon from attacking us when we are nearly defenseless?"

"Ahh, well you have the planet defense system don't you?" Nattur said lightly, "That should keep Poolto safe, even though I assure you they have no intentions of attacking."

"I see, well if it is on your word alone..." Tyler let his comment drip with sarcasm.

"Son, I realize that I may not deserve your trust, but this plan was conceived many years ago. Our only problem was how to get through to Poolto to deliver our message of peace. Fortunately, you finally gave us the opportunity we needed."

"Really?" Tyler said smartly, "So why do the Commandant and Nayllen believe you can still end the war without my help?"

Nattur glanced at both Nayllen and the commandant before turning back to Tyler.

"Well," he began, "if you don't help us, there is another way to end the war." Nattur paused, letting that sink in. He obviously hadn't wanted to divulge the information, but a shake from the head of the commandant seemed to give him the go ahead. "Krildon has developed a weapon that could destroy the Poolto fleet. In fact, if Vice Admiral Teesen's plan is put into place, it will be the last stand of a dying Navy."

Tyler saw a look a sadness come of Nattur as he said this. The end of the Poolto Navy? A new weapon, how? Then it came to Tyler in a flash, they had found a way to weaponize Scrilt!

"You've found a way to use Scrilt in weapons manufacturing and you think it will give you the edge in battle." Tyler said it as a fact.

Nattur raised his eyebrows, a look of pride on his face, "Very good Nayllen," he commended, "but it is much more than that."

"Really, how much more?" Tyler asked.

Nattur paused again, looking at Nayllen this time.

"Tell me son, your brilliant offensive plan, why didn't it succeed?" Nattur asked.

Tyler didn't know whether to respond, but figured Nayllen knew all of it anyway.

"Well, I am not exactly certain why, but I did suspect that we over-estimated how much of their fleet was actually around the home-world. I guess our intelligence was flawed." Tyler knew this was the official reason, but always had his own suspicions. He waited to see how Nattur reacted. He didn't react.

"I see," Nattur said, "what if I told you your intelligence was correct?"

Tyler was thrown by the question, "Then I suppose I do not know why we lost."

He thought about that admission, their intelligence was correct? But he remembered the conference and the fleet numbers they had come up against. Their intelligence had not been correct.

Nattur watched Tyler's confusion before continuing, "Yes son, your intelligence was correct, and yes, you are correct that much of the Krildon fleet had been around the home world."

"Then how do those two things mesh?" Tyler asked curious.

"Easily," Nattur stated calmly, "you were betrayed."

Tyler shot a glance at Nayllen, "Was it him?" he asked accusingly.

Nayllen stared back coldly, "Hardly Admiral," he responded indignantly, "I would not be so cold as to kill all those men."

"Then who?" Tyler asked, anger beginning to build. The part of him that was the Admiral began taking over and Tyler let his emotions out.

Nattur looked calmly at Tyler, "Why the Emperor did."

Tyler took the statement in, not wanting to believe it. How could the Emperor be the traitor? What would he get out of the destruction of half his fleet? It didn't make sense?

"The Emperor," Tyler said incredulous, "why would he betray his own military?"

"To get rid of you and to take over the military." Nayllen said.

Nayllen said it naturally as though it were obvious to a child. It wasn't obvious to Tyler. He knew the Emperor wanted him out of the way, but something that big, that seemed over the top even for the Emperor. Regent Sneerd on the other hand.

"Assuming that were true, why cripple your own military to take it over?"

"Your death and the destruction of half the fleet would ensure that whoever replaced you would be incensed enough to convince the military and the Supreme Council that Imperial control was necessary to deal the final blow to their enemies. They would have used your death to rally support that would back the Emperor and his ultimate goal, to win the war and conquer Krildon. He and Vice Admiral Teesen have been planning this for years."

Tyler had to admit, it did have a ring of truth and it did square with the events of the battle. Still, it was hard to believe they would spend life so casually to achieve such a goal. Then again, there were many examples where this had been done.

Nattur spoke up, "The problem was, you didn't die as they had planned, and that set them back tremendously. In fact, your own actions in the battle were better than they had thought, so the defeat was not so one-sided as they assumed. Over all, you did more to thwart their plans than you realize. After all, you came back a hero, and even they could not denounce you lest they admit the defeat."

That was true enough, the great lie rolled out to the people was based on the embarrassment that a defeat would cause. He remembered how it had been turned into a sneak attack by Krildon, once again a propaganda move by the Imperial Palace. It was all starting to make sense.

"I begin to see the possibility of truth in what you say, but what does the Scrilt have to do with this?" Tyler asked, wanting more information on what he obviously didn't know.

"Well," Commandant Kulg spoke, "I can answer that. Your brilliant plan and devilish battle tactics almost won that battle despite the fact we knew ahead of time, and despite our having overwhelming odds."

Tyler ignored the compliment.

The Commandant continued, "In fact, we only succeeded in thwarting your attack because of the Scrilt." He paused to let that sink in before he went on, "We have not only used Scrilt to enhance our weapons, but we have also developed a new polymer that when applied to our ships, yields them virtually invulnerable to your current weapons."

"You mean they can even withstand missile attacks?" Tyler asked.

The commandant appeared nervous at the question, "Well, no, they cannot withstand missile attacks anymore than they did before, but they can take a hit from any energy weapon and discharge the force harmlessly."

Tyler pressed, fascinated by what was being revealed, "Then our fleet could counter your fleet simply by using older technology?"

Again, Tyler noted the nervousness.

"Yes, you could," he started, and then added quickly, "but as you know, missile penetration through our defensive grids is usually only about fifteen percent effective, and you must also be at close range. That would put your fleet at a disadvantage from our new energy weapons."

"I see," Tyler said, "and what new power do these weapons have when Scrilt modified?"

This time, the commandant didn't want to answer. Instead, he looked at his fellow conspirators as though seeking advice. Nayllen jumped in to save him, "It's alright Askgar, he might as well know."

The commandant didn't look assured, but seemed to have made up his mind, "Fine, we have modified our energy weapons with Scrilt and have realized a thousand fold increase in energy output."

Tyler was stunned. A thousand fold increase—that was unbelievable. If it were true, he could see why they had confidence they could wipe out the Poolto fleet.

"But our scientists assured us that this substance was benign, surely you didn't get that much yield out of it?"

Nayllen leaned forward, "Remember who was in charge of those scientists Admiral. Krildon has been developing this technology for over thirty years."

"Then you knew about it?" Tyler accused.

Nayllen didn't flinch, "Yes, I knew about it, but I didn't know they had come so far with it. My partnership with Krildon didn't give me access to all their secrets."

Nattur spoke up, "That was where I came in. I convinced the Krildon legislature to hold off deploying the technology until we could use it as a bargaining chip in our negotiations."

"I see," Tyler said, "then you didn't use it when defending yourself in our offensive?"

The commandant answered plainly, "We did not have it fully deployed at that time, but we did have several squadrons that had been equipped with earlier prototypes. They made a significant difference, despite not having the full power at their command."

Tyler didn't like the smug look on the commandant's face, he almost could believe the commandant was ready to launch a full scale attack on Poolto.

"Why don't they just attack us then, they obviously have the upper hand?" Tyler gambled on a direct approach. The commandant looked a nervous, but Nattur was the one who responded.

"Don't think there aren't many who feel that way. Fortunately for Poolto, most of them are not in power. Cooler heads have prevailed and I have convinced them that a peaceful end to the conflict will be better than an all out victory."

Tyler had to concede, at least Nattur seemed to believe what he was saying. He wasn't so sure the commandant or Nayllen agreed.

Tyler wanted this to end, he'd had enough news for one day and it was clear their was nothing he could do to change the situation, "Fine, if I give you the codes, then Krildon will come to Poolto with an offering of peace under the threat of annihilation, or if I don't, you will carry through with your threat to annihilate us. Does that about sum it up?"

He could see that his cold statement of the facts didn't sit well with everyone, especially the governor. Tyler could imagine why he might feel uncomfortable—the colonies would be the target of the first wave of attacks.

Nattur looked at Tyler with a touch of concern in his eyes. *Too late for that pops*, Tyler thought.

"Nayllen," Nattur started, "son, it is the only way we can end this futile war. Is that not worth doing?"

Tyler had no choice, but he wasn't going down just yet. He was going to find a way to come out ahead in this. One way or another, he was going to have his family.

"Yes." Tyler said with little emotion.

Tyler sat deep in thought on the trip back to Poolto. After his meeting with the Admiral's father, everything had moved fast, too fast for Tyler's liking. His role in the conspiracy was going to unfold soon, and he had already turned over the command codes in preparation for the 'peace' mission from Krildon. Tyler only hoped peace was its true mission. He still held doubts.

It had been difficult to explain the situation to Toosia. Initially, he thought about hiding the truth from her, but ultimately decided that if he was to convince her to stay on Siirneen until this played out, he would have to come clean. When he had explained it to her, she took it with her usual calm demeanor; however, Tyler knew she was torn inside. It was not everyday that your husband tells you he is about to betray his world.

She had asked small, concise questions, but never about the Admiral's father. Tyler knew that had been a sore subject between them for years. Looking back through the Admiral's memories, Tyler saw that the Admiral's failure to support his father when the Emperor had brandished him a traitor had never sat well with Toosia. She came from a family where blood ties were stronger than civic duty or law. She had eventually accepted his lack of support, but had never agreed with it.

She had asked pointed questions about the entire plan and had good insight into potential flaws and pitfalls that Tyler had not considered. At first, Tyler thought she would blow the cover off the whole affair, but finally, she said she understood the situation and believed that if the conspirators were truthful, then they may really have a chance to end the war. Clearly, with a child on the way, she wanted that as much as anyone. Her last comment had resonated with Tyler's own fears about the situation. She had said that she probably could trust the Admiral's father, but that she couldn't trust Nayllen.

Tyler had agreed, but didn't voice the comment. It was enough that he would have to leave her on Siirneen while the conspiracy unfolded. At least she would be in the care of the Governor. Tyler believed that the Governor could be trusted. He didn't appear to hold much power within the conspiracy but was well placed to support the effort. The Governor had assured Tyler she would be taken care of like royalty—especially since she was with child. Tyler hoped he was right.

Tyler's own role in the conspiracy was not insignificant and he could see why survival was not assured. He figured he had the most dangerous part in the affair. When the time came for the 'peace' ship to enter Poolto space, it was critical that Tyler be in the company of the Emperor. This would signal the depth and breadth of the conspiracy to the Emperor. It would be dangerous since the Emperor could react irrationally and simply have Tyler shot on the spot for treason. Tyler had no illusions that the Palace guards would carry out that order, even if it was their 'National hero'.

The hard part would be gaining an audience with the Emperor at the right time. Nayllen had provided Tyler with a communication device that was impossible to detect, but capable of transmitting and receiving across long distances through interference and jamming. It was intended to prevent the Emperor from simply breaking off the negotiations once they started. Fortunately, because they possessed the command codes, the Emperor would not have any assets to attack at that point. Only the ground based missiles would be capable of reaching the peace ship, and those rarely hit their targets from so far away. Not even the planetary defense grid was capable of reaching the ship which would be just outside its operational perimeter.

Tyler had to admit, the plan seemed complete, but as the Admiral's last great battle had shown, nothing is totally within your control. Anything could go wrong, and often did. What if the command codes did not work? What if they only disabled a percentage of the fleet? Plenty could go wrong, and one or two ships that were not disabled could easily ruin their plan. Tyler didn't like the prospects of their plan failing. It would mean many people would die.

The powerful thought of settling down with Toosia at their Tooland Estate kept Tyler's optimism high. He thought back to Linda and the opportunity he had missed with her. He didn't want to miss that opportunity again, especially with a child on the way. He was so close to having a family, he had to make this work.

Unfortunately, even success could spell disaster for the Admiral. It would simple for the Emperor to make the Admiral a scapegoat. The Emperor would be within his rights to prosecute Tyler for treason even if peace were finally established. The anger the Emperor would feel towards Tyler would be hard to repress. History was complete with many tales of those who went against the Emperor. Some were executed directly, while many simply met with 'unfortunate' accidents. Tyler thought about the Regent and the mysterious disappearances since his rise to power.

What would prevent 'accidents' from happening to the Admiral or his family? Tyler hoped the Admiral's popularity would prevent that. Bringing peace to Poolto might endear him further with the public and establish his power further. However, he had to first survive the conspiracy.

The conference on Siirneen had been a success, and Tyler had been amazed at the readiness of the various command groups represented. Their primary concern had been supply routes and the new ships that were being pushed through inadequate field trials. Like the Admiral, the second in command did not relish the idea of going into battle with a ship that might simply fail in the midst of combat. They understood that most of the ships were newer, more advanced designs, but they also knew that could mean newer more deadly flaws.

Tyler did his best to assure them the ships would be ready for battle when delivered. If the message had come from anyone else, he doubted they would have believed it. Tyler didn't believe it either, but he knew it didn't matter since the battle would never be fought.

Through most of the conference, Tyler had let the essence of the Admiral control the proceedings. Tyler had withdrawn inside, battling his own thoughts about the upcoming crisis. Deep down, he knew the conspiracy could save millions of lives, but he couldn't shake the feeling that something hidden by the conspirators might yet cause loss of life. Tyler distrusted Nayllen and wasn't sure the many years of conflict between both worlds could easily be put aside by the Krildon public or its leadership.

With their fleet disabled, Poolto would be vulnerable, and Tyler thought it far too tempting a situation. Did they really want to end the war? Was Commandant Kulg really prepared to turn his swords into plowshares?

Tyler knew the Admiral's memories interfered with his ability to judge Krildon. The Admiral had spent a lot of time on Krildon, but he had been young and unable to fully evaluate its people or culture. The Admiral's memories overflowed with countless 'friends' of the family. Unfortunately, those childhood memories were inadequate to judge them.

As a historian, the Admiral had studied Krildon history nearly as much as he had study his own. But those studies had focused on military campaigns, tactics, and outcomes. These also didn't provide Tyler what he wanted to know. Krildon's history was as bloody and conflicted as Poolto's, or earth's for that matter. Did that tell Tyler anything? He didn't think so, it only confirmed that worlds start out barbaric and violent. Still, considering the length of the current war, could you say they had evolved past violence? Maybe not.

Tyler thought about Krildon's democratic government and believed it was one thing in their favor. Unlike Poolto, Krildon's leaders were elected on a regular basis. Since the war started, Krildon had elected ten presidents, each claiming to be committed to vanquishing their enemy. None had accomplished that goal, and the current president was on the verge of making peace. Tyler understood these battle cries were used to gather support for fighting a conflict. People grew weary of war, so governments had to continually rally support by 'villanizing' the enemy. Who wouldn't want to vanquish evil?

Poolto however, had only one Emperor since the beginning of the war. His power had been firmly established early on, especially after the missile attack that had nearly destroyed both worlds. His efforts and desire to destroy Krildon had been a powerful force, and people rallied behind his efforts. This was the reason betraying him was so dangerous. Tyler was going to make Poolto choose between their hero and their leader. Tyler wasn't certain the Admiral could win that contest.

To Tyler, a democratic Krildon sounded better than a world ruled by one Emperor. He had once been an American and had always believed in the democratic process, even if he had rarely participated in it. He just wasn't sure if that were enough to take such a gamble. Even democracies had moments when their own purposes went against their political ideals. The political ideologies of both worlds had never been a problem in the past, could it become one now? Would Krildon use this conspiracy to push their own agenda, an agenda that the Admiral's father and Nayllen were not aware of? Did they want democracy on Poolto?

Tyler thought it was possible, especially when they would have the upper hand. The conspirators did not appear cohesive during Tyler's meeting with them. He had sensed the Admiral's father was being used by Krildon to get the Admiral to play along. That hadn't exactly worked, so they had ultimately resorted to threats of using their now superior weapons technology. Tyler wasn't certain they had accomplished so much with the Scrilt, but if they had, the threat was genuine. This was where millions of lives could be saved.

In the long run, Tyler didn't really have a choice. He was committed and the only way he could stop it now was turn himself in and have them change the command codes. He couldn't risk his family and the lives of so many military personnel. He had to follow through and brace himself for the fate it would bring.

Despite these restless thoughts, Tyler had managed to drift off during the long flight back to Poolto. In his dreams, he found himself in a large white room with white furniture. It looked similar to what Tyler imagined heaven might be. He half expected to see Thosoland, but the room remained empty. After everything he'd been through, the white couch looked inviting. He sat down and relaxed into the soft cushions.

The whiteness of the room made it appear as if there were no walls, and the room simply expanded outward forever. It reminded

Tyler of his first encounter with the voices of the 'Universe'. Maybe they had changed their minds and didn't think letting him loose on the Universe was such a great idea. Tyler didn't care, the couch was very comfortable.

As Tyler leaned back into the couch, he stared down at his body. Surprisingly, it was the Admiral's body and not 'human'. It seemed strange, and yet somehow appropriate. Perhaps he was really becoming the Admiral? It seemed far better than the drug dealer he had been on earth. He thought about the Admiral's name, Nayllen. He almost liked it better than Tyler. Would he lose Tyler if he stayed the Admiral? Would he think of himself as Nayllen? He thought not as the 'other' Nayllen flashed through his mind.

Suddenly, a door appeared across the room. It wasn't really a door, but a black rectangular opening that just appeared in the wall. Finally, Tyler thought, he would find out why he was here. He thought he was dreaming, but wasn't certain.

Another person from Poolto walked in and moved across the room taking one of the comfy looking white chairs. Tyler didn't recognize the man, but smiled and said hello anyway.

The man smiled back and said hello, and Tyler instantly recognized the voice that came out. It was Adanni!

"Where have you been Adanni?" Tyler asked, realizing he was dreaming and that he had not heard from Adanni since joining the conspiracy. He'd been surprised Adanni had been so silent.

"I've been thinking." Adanni said quietly.

"Oh good," Tyler said a bit sarcastically, "I haven't been the only one!"

"No, you haven't."

Apparently the sarcasm was lost on Adanni. Tyler was frustrated, he had thought that they had an agreement not to interfere with his dreams.

Reading Tyler's thoughts, Adanni said, "Yes, that is true, we had an agreement, but I needed to talk with you...privately."

Tyler didn't like how he sounded, so introspective and non-aggressive.

"Well, you have me, what did you want to say? Did you want to tell me that I made a huge mistake joining this conspiracy? Or perhaps you want to tell me that we won't survive the ordeal?" Tyler let out much of his frustrations, but it had no effect on Adanni.

"No, no," Adanni responded, "you understand it as well as I do. This is about something…different."

Great, Tyler thought, *something else to worry about.*

"Fine, lay it on me." Tyler said flatly.

"You do not know much about me…or my kind, do you?"

Tyler thought about how little Thosoland had told him, "Not really." Tyler admitted.

"I can tell you we always seek out persons of power and we thrive in conflict and destruction."

Tyler could hardly believe he was hearing the admission. He had suspected there was an 'evil' component to Adanni, he just didn't know how 'evil'. Perhaps he would find out.

Adanni continued, "I myself have often participated in destructive acts on many worlds. My very being thrived on the mayhem my actions produced. The more convoluted the plots, dangerous the actions, and destructive the results, the bigger the thrills."

Tyler could hear excitement in his voice as he explained this. Tyler was certain now! If he ever gave control to Adanni, he would never get it back.

"Fine Adanni," Tyler said placidly, "you were a thrill junky, so what? Are you getting a good high off this latest adventure?"

Adanni paused as though considering the question. Tyler was instantly sorry he'd asked it.

"No," Adanni said emotionless, "but I think someone else is."

Tyler didn't understand what he was saying. Tyler wasn't getting thrills out of this, if anything, he was only getting gray hairs.

"Well if you mean me," Tyler responded, "just read my mind and you'll see I do not enjoy this."

"Not you," Adanni said it as to a child, "another being like myself—another Onyalum."

Another Onyalum? The thought chilled Tyler. Was there really another Onyalum behind these actions? An Onyalum that Tyler didn't control?

"How do you know?" Tyler asked calmly even as his insides churned.

"The pattern all fits. The betrayal of the Admiral's offensive, the attack on you, the current plans to attack again. These are all things I would...I would have done."

Tyler couldn't believe Adanni was being so candid. Didn't he realize Tyler would never let him have control after these admissions?

"Don't worry," Adanni commented, again reading Tyler's thoughts, "I have no intentions of taking over, or causing that kind of chaos again."

Tyler didn't believe him, despite sounding genuine

"Fine, we have another Onyalum, who do you suspect?" Tyler asked very curious, "Is it Nayllen? Or maybe Vice Admiral Teesen?" Both seemed like the perfect candidates to Tyler. Both held power, and both were involved in dangerous, chaotic events.

"Both fit the pattern," Adanni agreed, "but I honestly have no idea."

"So," Tyler's frustration was rising again, "you suspect an agent of chaos is causing many, if not all, of these events, and we, I mean I, may be playing right into their hands?"

Tyler's agitation and frustration finally had an impact on Adanni. Adanni stared back at Tyler with an expression of concern. Tyler was ready to explode again but waited patiently.

"Yes," Adanni admitted, "we may be playing right into their hands."

It was too much for Tyler, "Oh great!" he shouted, "maybe it was the governor and I just left Toosia and my unborn child with him!" Once out, Tyler's anger gained momentum. "Or maybe it is the Emperor, and we will be killed instantly when this thing starts."

He was wound up now and felt delirious with the release, "Oh, I know, it must Regent Sneerd, who else could cause such chaos and care so little for the people of Poolto!"

He let it pour out on Adanni but was amazed Adanni took it so calmly, like Nayllen. That comparison made Tyler even angrier, and his abusive language rose to a frenzied pitch. Finally, reaching a crescendo he stopped exhausted. He apparently had needed that release but was surprised how good it felt inside a dream. *What better place to lose it?*

Adanni let the silence linger, calmly staring at Tyler. When the silence began to get awkward, Adanni finally spoke.

"Your concerns and frustrations are well founded, the situation will not turn out well."

Tyler had nothing in him, so he stared back at Adanni, confused, sad, and angry. *Why me?*

Adanni chided him, "Self pity will accomplish nothing."

"Thanks, all better now!" Tyler tried to put force behind his words, but it just sounded petty.

Tyler tried desperately to free himself from despair. Surely there was something they could do to prevent or at least, minimize the damage.

"Is there nothing we can do to stop them?" He asked feebly.

Adanni appeared to think for a moment before responding, "Well, if we knew who it was, we might be able to do something. However, to be honest, I'm not sure how we would find out. I was very adept at making sure I was never discovered. You are doing a fine job as the Admiral—you've even fooled his wife."

Tyler hated to admit it, but he couldn't see how they would find them either. If they were like Tyler, they fooled everyone around them, even those who knew them well. Still...

"Assume for a moment we could determine who it was, what could we do?" Tyler added the Admiral's essence to solving this problem. He figured they might as well treat it no different than a military campaign or pending battle. They knew the enemy existed, now they just needed intelligence to discover where.

"Well," Adanni started, "I guess we could confront them, although that might also prove dangerous—or we could try to discredit them."

"Discredit them," Tyler was incredulous, "how would we discredit them?"

"We could convince people around them that they are an imposter. We could convince them the person was being controlled by an outside entity."

Tyler thought it sounded ridiculous, "Sure, we just say they are possessed…and after we are put in the nuthouse, how would we prove that?"

Adanni ignored the jibe, "We would have to build a case out of their actions compared to their actions before becoming Onyalum. Surely there will be differences."

Tyler doubted that would be a very strong case, "And what prevents them from doing the same thing to us? I haven't exactly been perfect since taking over."

Tyler thought back to the early days as the Admiral, he had made many mistakes and those around him had certainly shown concern over his odd behavior. Tyler was thankful most chalked it up to his injuries, but if he started accusing someone else of being 'possessed' that would certainly open the door for a similar accusation against them.

"I don't think that will do it Adanni, we may have to confront them."

Adanni stared back blankly, "Fine, but the point is moot, since we don't know who it is."

Tyler thought it sounded like Adanni was ready to throw in the towel. Maybe he was still a thrill junky and was ready to just wait for the ensuing chaos and destruction.

"There has got to be a way to figure this out." Tyler said hopeful.

In a flash of insight reminiscent of the Admiral, Tyler realized how they could discover the Onyalum. When Tyler took over the Admiral, he was near death. Assuming all Onyalum required the same condition, then they only had to find out if any of the suspects had been near death. Surely it was information they could track down. Generally, people didn't have brushes with death without a record of the incident.

Adanni had been listening to Tyler's thoughts, "You may have something, we could find out who has had close calls in the past. I suspect that if it has happened, it would have been recent, otherwise, the Onyalum would surely have caused the destruction of the person they inhabited by now."

Perhaps Adanni was going to help after all.

"Ok, who should we investigate first?" Tyler asked, hope starting to grow.

"All of them." Adanni said with assurance.

"Sure," Tyler agreed a little sarcastic, "we'll just tell our staff that we need them to investigate the personal health records of all these senior officials. Don't you think we'll raise a little suspicion?"

"Yes," Adanni agreed readily, "but if you tell the Marshall to handle it, it may get done discreetly."

Tyler had to admit, the Marshall was discreet. He just wasn't sure how to stop the Marshall's suspicions. The man would want to know why. Considering how much Tyler had lied to the man already, he wasn't certain how much the Marshall would take.

Loyalty was one thing, but betrayal was another. If the Marshall suspected the Admiral was involved in a plot to overthrow the government, or at least coerce it into peace, he wouldn't support the Admiral. They would have to walk a thin line with the Marshall, and Tyler had to think of a good reason to send him on this dangerous task.

As Tyler was about to ask another question, he was awakened by a flight attendant. They were ready to land, and Tyler couldn't believe he'd slept so long. Despite that, he felt rested and ready for battle. At least they had a chance, even if it was small.

According to the plan on Siirneen, Tyler was required to set a meeting with the Emperor in five to eight days upon his return. It was a difficult order to fill, but at least they had given him a three day window. Unfortunately, it didn't give Tyler much time to track down the 'Onyalum'. Even if Tyler tracked them down, he was not convinced he could do anything about it. Despite Adanni's suggestion, he didn't believe another Onyalum would give in to threats of exposure.

After returning to Yooso, Tyler had been busy with the commission. His leadership was desperately needed to evaluate and make recommendations for the next offensive. So far, everything they had employed to stall progress was working. Despite the delays, Admiral Teesen was taking it all in stride.

Clearly, the Emperor had cautioned patience while Tyler's plan played out. Regardless of motives and stalling, the commission was making progress. Troop readiness, supply chains, intelligence, and equipment availability were all shaping up for an offensive soon. Only Tyler knew the conflict would never get off the ground. Despite that knowledge, he welcomed the readiness—just in case.

Marshall Sliss had been eerily quiet about Tyler's trip to Siirneen. When mentioned at all, it usually revolved around the cover operations of the conference. Tyler was thankful the conference had been productive. Feedback from the field commanders was positive, therefore suspicions had been averted. Even so, Tyler knew his request for health information on several important people was taken begrudgingly, and with great suspicion.

The Marshall had taken the request calmly and only asked for what purpose the information would serve. Tyler had lied with an excuse that he was searching for ways to discredit individuals based on health reasons. The Marshall had appeared suspicious but accepted it nonetheless. When the Marshall noted the same charges could be leveled at him, Tyler had shrugged it off saying it wouldn't matter as his time in office was coming to an end. The admission hadn't surprised the Marshall, but considering how long both had been at it, he too may be ready to retire.

Whatever the Marshall thought, he had taken the request and promised quick and discreet action. Tyler suspected the cool interactions with the Marshall were an indication that his lies were slowly eroding the Marshall's trust. Tyler hoped what little trust remained would not be spent within the next eight days. After that, it probably wouldn't matter.

Tyler was operating on auto-pilot, letting much of the Admiral's essence run the commission. He participated only as much as needed, but the Admiral's persona was a fabulous administrator, so Tyler contributed little.

Toosia's cover story about taking care of 'family business' on Siirneen had held so far. Her family was suspicious, but daily calls to Siirneen alleviated them. Her calls to Tyler however, were not as 'normal'. She told him of the activities she saw on Siirneen, including a heightened state of security. This alarmed Tyler, the purpose of her staying was to keep her safe. He considered having her come back to Poolto and move into their Tooland Estate, but the Governor talked him out of it. It was becoming clear the conspirators were using her as a hostage to get Tyler to follow through. He didn't force the issue, but his concerns rose steadily.

The Admiral's staff had been performing flawlessly since announcing his step down. Their ability to get things done was not lost on the rest of the commission. In fact, the rest of the commission's staff looked practically incompetent in comparison. In particular, Officer Slaas was proving an incredible asset both on the trip to Siirneen and back on Poolto. She was even beginning to sound like the Marshall, and had both Officer Kooren and Vice Secretary Beelen doing her bidding. Tyler could see she would move up despite her boss stepping down. He made sure that glowing letters of recommendation made it into her file and that several duty options were available when she left.

Her latest coup had been the recognition of severe omissions in the planned 'shortened' field trials. She had stopped the trials even before consulting the commission, or Marshall Sliss. It had been a bold move and she had come out on top. She had found two glaring problems that everyone else had overlooked. Considering each proposed trial was several hundred pages in length, the catch had been a miracle.

The good news was it had proven a wonderful stalling technique that Admiral Teesen was fuming over. It had been his own staff that had missed the mistake when they created the proposals, so he couldn't exactly ignore the implications. They had lost face, while the Admiral had gained more ground.

There were downsides to the staffs' efficiency. The commission was making quick progress towards developing a readiness report with offensive recommendations. The current plan looked doable in several months time despite the stall in field trials. Tyler wasn't concerned, he knew it would soon mean nothing.

Fortunately, it gave him the opening he needed to meet with the Emperor. At their current pace, they would have recommendations in about six days. As the head of the commission, Tyler was responsible for personally delivering it to both the Emperor and Admiral Teesen while transferring the Supreme Military Command. That meant turning over the command codes, which Admiral Teesen would immediately change. Tyler couldn't let that happen. The good news was command turnover was a private affair, held in the Imperial Palace. It was a perfect way for Tyler to get his audience while giving the conspirators their chance to end the conflict.

So far, everything was moving forward. Despite this, Tyler felt certain his last days as the Admiral were drawing near. He tried to repress those thoughts and focus on what he would do if the Marshall found the information to track the Onyalum.

It was this thought that ran through his mind as he entered a conference room for a daily briefing. His wasn't in the mood for the meeting, but he had been the one to suggest having them, so he had to attend.

As he entered the room, most of the seats around the large table were already taken. The majority were occupied by the commissioners and their top aides, while the rest of the staff sat along the inside walls. Tyler took his usual seat at the far end of the table and noticed Marshall Sliss was unusually absent. Fortunately, one of the commissioners was missing, so Tyler didn't feel compelled to start.

While they waited, Tyler looked over the daily agenda on the viewer. Everything looked routine except a small entry at the bottom titled 'Intelligence Update'. Ordinarily, this wouldn't be unusual, but they'd just had an intelligence briefing the day before. It seemed unlikely pertinent intelligence would have suddenly become available. Tyler assumed they'd forgotten to remove it when updating the agenda. Still, a part of him felt unease.

Finally, the missing commissioner took his seat, removing Tyler's last excuse to delay. He hoped the Marshall would show up eventually.

"Good afternoon everyone," Tyler began, "shall we get started?"

Everyone settled and opened their viewers to follow along the agenda. Tyler turned the meeting over to Officer Slaas who had been appointed to run the meetings. She quickly reviewed the agenda before turning the proceedings over to the first speaker. Tyler noted she did not comment on the Intelligence Update at the bottom of the list. Perhaps it was only a typo.

Each speaker delivered their report in a crisp, military fashion, but Tyler's mind kept dwelling on the Marshall and his failure to attend. It was not like the Marshall and Tyler felt concerned. The Marshall's distance had steadily been increasing, and Tyler began to worry the Marshall's suspicions were deeply affecting their relationship.

Where could he be? Tyler thought.

Don't worry, Adanni answered, *he is too loyal to betray his beloved Admiral.*

Tyler didn't like the way Adanni had said it. He had great respect for the Marshall, regardless of what Adanni thought.

The man is a good man, Tyler retorted, *something you wouldn't know anything about!*

But you do, 'drug dealer'?

That stung. Tyler hated that Adanni had access to every one of his memories.

Adanni went on, *Did you give Mr. Barkowski the same respect?*

Tyler hadn't thought about that name in years. It hurt deep to have the wounds reopened. Mr. Barkowski had been a neighbor of Tyler's when Tyler had been attending the community college. Mr. Barkowski had stumbled upon Tyler's drug transactions, and although Tyler hadn't done anything about it, Raul had sent men over to intimidate the man.

Tyler thought about that incident with guilt and pain. The man had been a retired sergeant from the Army with a disability that affected his ability to walk properly. Tyler thought the man was a great neighbor, but he knew Mr. Barkowski wouldn't keep the incident to himself. Mr. Barkowski had been a 'good man' and he wanted people like Tyler out of the neighborhood.

Tyler had pleaded with Raul to back off, but Raul insisted a show of weakness would hurt business. Unfortunately, Mr. Barkowski was not easily intimidated, and practically threw Raul's goons out. Two days later, he had found his dog beheaded in the backyard. Tyler knew that would keep the man quiet but moved to another part of town anyway. The guilt had been hard to live with.

Tyler had suppressed the incident for years, but now Adanni dredged it up and threw it in his face. Adanni had a point—Tyler's past was filled with incidents where 'good' people were hurt. Tyler had no response.

That's what I thought, Adanni concluded.

Tyler was so lost in his memories, he had barely heard something about intelligence? He snapped out of it and focused on the new speaker. It wasn't a person he recognized.

"...and we believe that this area has been the proving grounds for new weapons. Until recently, we hadn't seen unusual testing at this facility. If our sources are correct in their analysis, Krildon recently conducted a test using a new particle weapon."

Tyler's heart skipped a beat.

"Although our sources did not see the test for themselves, reconnaissance photos afterwards revealed startling and disturbing facts."

The man paused while he fiddled with some of the controls on the table. Immediately, a three dimensional image of an asteroid appeared above the center of the table. By itself, it didn't seem 'startling' to Tyler, but the man continued to fiddle with the controls.

"Ahh, there we are." He said looking up from the controls.

Tyler looked at the new image and was disturbed by what he saw. One of the large craters from the first image was filled with red. It appeared like a large piece of a red asteroid had been jammed into it.

"The image you are seeing is the original image of this particular asteroid. The portion you see in red is the portion that is missing from our recent reconnaissance photos." The man paused while his audience took in the implications. "Let me give you additional details so that you understand the true nature of what we are seeing."

Once again he fiddled with the controls and the image changed. The image was quickly overlaid with various numbers and writing.

Tyler ignored that and stared at the blue portion that had been added to the red portion. It was not a large blue area, and in fact, was dwarfed by the red it sat within. Tyler feared the worst.

"As you can see here, this asteroid was nearly the size of one of our fleet refurbishing asteroids. As you know, those facilities are capable of servicing ships nearly as large as our flagship." Again, he paused while that sunk in.

Tyler already knew what they were seeing, and he dreaded what it might mean. He waited for the preliminary analysis.

The man started again, "The portion in blue represents how much of the asteroid would have been affected by a direct hit with our largest and most powerful missile. Yes, I said missile."

Tyler watched the effect on the crowd. Everyone was staring horror struck by what they were seeing. Not only was this suspected to be a particle weapon, it appeared to be capable of inflicting greater damage than their best weapon.

"As you can see, we believe the nominal yield of this new weapon is about one hundred times that of the yield of our largest missile. The part of the asteroid destroyed during this test was approximately thirty-one percent of the overall mass. Reconnaissance scans of the surrounding space confirm fragments in quantities nearly equal to the missing mass."

That was enough for one of the commissioners to react.

"Surely that was not a particle weapon," he said almost laughing, "they simply buried an atomic ordinance to create this effect."

Several others spoke out in agreement with the commissioner, but each looked nervous.

"Vice Secretary Hool," the man responded coolly, "Marshall Triin had the same assessment on first glance. However, if you look at the analysis of the debris field, you will notice the radioactive signature is nearly identical to that of a particle weapon, not an atomic one."

The commissioner kept pushing, "You said nearly, what was different?"

"That we don't understand," the man conceded, "but it is nearly identical to a particle weapon signature."

The commissioner seemed dubious, but Tyler didn't want to participate in the discussion. He knew what they had discovered.

A staff members against the wall sat up and spoke, "If that is the result of a particle weapon, then how big is the weapon? How does it get so much yield, and is it being deployed throughout their fleet?"

Again, the audience murmured in agreement with the questions.

"Well," the man hesitated, "we don't have sufficient intelligence to answer any of those questions…at this time."

The room exploded into an uproar as voices offered suggestions as to how to get the information, how to combat the new threat, or how to modify their own offensive plans. Tyler even thought he heard someone say they should abandon the offensive. Tyler knew all of it didn't matter, so he took control.

When Tyler stood up, everyone within the room sat down and turned their attention to him. He waited until everyone was quiet.

"Thank you Officer…" he started.

"Liiri sir," the man humbly finished for him.

"Yes, Liiri," Tyler was relieved for the reminder, "we thank you for this important bit of intelligence."

Tyler watched as everyone around the room waited for him to express his opinions and give them a direction to follow.

"I know Marshall Triin is analyzing this intelligence and will undoubtedly provide each member of the commission with a full report. After receiving that report, you should quickly provide your own analysis with an impact statement for your area. I assume Admiral Teesen has been briefed and that this information will eventually circulate throughout our field commands. Until then, we will wait patiently and hope additional intelligence can be ascertained to help answer the questions we all have."

Tyler quickly turned to Officer Slaas, "Anything else on the agenda?"

"No sir." She responded crisply.

"Very well, meeting adjourned."

With that, Tyler quickly left the room avoiding the questions his fellow commissioners were dying to ask. He knew they would wonder whether this intelligence would force them to abandon the offensive. Tyler knew the answer to those questions, but he wasn't about to share them with anyone.

He hurried down the corridor towards his office. He was concerned about the information coming to light. If they all believed it to be true, they would likely recommend an indefinite hold on the offensive until they could ascertain the real threat. Tyler thought about the Scrilt treated hulls of their enemy, and realized Poolto would not survive the offensive. Unfortunately, if the Emperor did not concede, they would learn too soon the truth behind this intelligence.

Tyler wondered how it had been gathered. It was just the kind of information that would make the current situation more dangerous and precarious. It was as if someone were constantly putting Tyler into a corner. Initially, he had wanted the offensive to be scrapped, but now, he needed it to attain his new goals, and this new information could prevent that. If the intelligence stalled the effort, Tyler wouldn't have a report to deliver. Therefore, his meeting with the Emperor would only be to transfer power to Admiral Teesen. If that occurred, it would be hard to synchronize the situation with the 'peace' ship.

Worse, Admiral Teesen could use this threat to demand that the power transfer happen immediately. Tyler could see the Emperor readily agreeing. That would be a disaster and could destroy the peace ship's efforts completely. In that case, Krildon would be forced to attack, and Poolto would likely be vanquished. Tyler's mood deepened.

Tyler finally caught up with the Marshall who excused his absence with the new intelligence report. He'd received it through his sources shortly before the commission and spent the rest of the time performing analysis and defining ramifications. As usual, his network worked diligently to provide the latest up to date intelligence. Unfortunately, Tyler suspected most of that intelligence was being fed to them by Nayllen, the Imperial Palace, or both. He didn't tell the Marshall about these suspicions.

For Tyler, the only thing that mattered was the timing of the peace ship. Now that information about new weapons had been confirmed, Poolto had no alternatives but to accept peace or face obliteration. The Imperial Palace pushed aside the new intelligence, claiming it was propaganda generated by the enemy to stall new offensives until their strength was increased.

Tyler was incredulous at the palace's reaction even though it fit neatly into a pattern of someone who wanted a disastrous conclusion. Till now, the Marshall hadn't delivered any information concerning 'near-death' experiences for their suspects. Tyler didn't push the matter since Marshall Sliss had become deeply suspicious.

Adanni had believed that the Marshall's loyalties were unfaltering, but Tyler no longer shared that belief. Tyler knew if the Marshall sniffed even a faint possibility of betrayal, he would do anything within his power to stop it. Tyler played it easy with the Marshall hoping their plan would unfurl without the further complications. Tyler found it difficult to be deceptive and felt enormous guilt because of it. The Marshall was a 'good' man and deserved better.

The final intelligence report still contained holes that fed opponents the necessary leverage to discredit it. Fortunately, this was the one time where Tyler was on the side of those opposing the intelligence. He recognized it was in his best interests to allow the rebuke and refused to take a position on either side. *Let the stalemate continue!*

The commission was evenly split between those who wanted to scrap the offensive and those who continued to support it. Tyler remained non-committal and kept re-emphasizing the commission's job was to ascertain Poolto's readiness rather than determine whether the offensive was warranted based on the latest intelligence. To support this position, he ordered the commissioners to shelve the debate and focus energies on the task at hand.

There were murmurs of dissent, but they begrudgingly agreed to set aside the issue and continue their original charter. Tyler was relieved to divert their attention, if only temporarily, but his actions had created even greater suspicions in the Marshall. The Marshall viewed the new intelligence as a perfect opportunity to stall the offensive, as they originally had planned. Many military personnel that supported the Admiral in the beginning now asked why he would not take a position on the issue. Support in the commission was faltering, and the Marshall was confused.

Tyler knew it soon wouldn't matter, so he tried his best to quell the Marshall's suspicions and calm the concerns of the commission. When pressed on the issue, Tyler let loose his most 'imperious' Admiral and refocused the staff on determining military readiness. Tyler even avoided meetings that didn't demand his presence. He knew he was walking a thin line, but time was running out and he had to keep them focused on the offensive. Only the palace and Admiral Teesen seemed thrilled with his non-committal approach. It disturbed Tyler making them happy, but he had his mission.

His desire to stay away from the inner workings of the commission forced him to accept a dinner invitation to his in-law's in Baneer. Their estate outside the capital was located within one of the rich suburbs of Yooso. He did not look forward to the questioning from his father-in-law on details of the commission, especially the reaction to the weapons intelligence. Tyler already knew the intelligence and the palace reaction were being met with skepticism on the Supreme Council, so he was prepared for lengthy discussions.

The distance to Baneer required Tyler to make the journey by air. Fortunately, he had access to military transports within the Supreme Military Command complex and easily secured a small four person transport to the outskirts of the city. Once in Baneer, it was a short ride by ground car to the councilor's estate.

As the car pulled into the estate, Tyler prepared himself for an interesting evening. He didn't like that Toosia could not accompany him, so he looked forward to an uncomfortable and awkward evening. He felt inadequately prepared to handle questions about Toosia. It was one thing to hide information from a distance, but in person became very difficult. He hoped their conversations with Toosia were enough to ease their suspicions. They were surely concerned for their daughter's safety, especially when she was pregnant with their grandchild.

One of the many attendants opened the door for Tyler, welcoming him to the Councilor's 'modest' home. Modest was not how Tyler would have described it. It was an extravagant mansion, but Tyler thanked him anyway. Like everything else in Yooso, the estate was very lavish. In the front courtyard, an enormous fountain of water danced amongst intricately carved statues. It flaunted their wealth by wasting one of the most precious resources on the planet. Tyler felt a little ill, but quickly remembered the Admiral was also one of the wealthiest people on the planet.

Tyler followed the attendant across the courtyard and into one of several entrances to the main building. If the Admiral's memories served, the entrance they entered was reserved for family and intimate friends. It was not the main entrance intended for 'formal' affairs. This one led to a small portion of the building that was more private and like a real home.

Tyler thanked the attendant and assured him he could find the rest of the way on his own. He headed down the corridor to where he knew they would be eating. Along the way, he passed the kitchen where the staff busily readied their dinner. He turned left down one more corridor before ending at an open archway. This led into a large, yet cozy room complete with dining table and living area.

The room was empty, but a fire burned gently in the hearth against the back wall. That told Tyler he'd found the right place. He walked over to the small bar next to the hearth and poured a large glass of brandy. He needed to steady himself if he was to make it through the evening, and what better way than alcohol.

He settled down with his drink in one of several comfortable chairs. As he waited, he surveyed the room comparing it with the Admiral's memories. The Admiral had not been in the room for many years, and Toosia's mother had clearly re-decorated since that previous visit.

The Admiral's memories painted a picture of a room much more elegant and formal. Now, the room was filled with brighter colors and a more modern style. The furniture was still comfortable, but the fabrics and styles blended with the new décor, giving the room a feeling of openness and space. Along the right wall, bookcases had been replaced with fine art depicting scenes from around Poolto. Around the rest of the room, paintings of plants and flowers hung on the wall lending a more natural feel.

Tyler approved even though it felt more feminine. Tyler figured it was where Toosia and her mother had spent most of their time together. Since drifting away from the Admiral, Toosia had spent more time with her mother than before.

"Ahh, there you are Nayllen," Toosia's mother came strolling into the room, "I hope your journey was well?"

"Yes," Tyler confirmed before getting up from his seat, "may I get you something to drink Tooriin?"

"Yes, thank you," she replied as she took a seat on the couch, "I'll take a glass of the white wine if you please." She smiled broadly at Tyler as he nodded and walked towards the bar.

"Hiirtee will join us soon," she finished.

Tyler didn't look forward to talking with the councilor, but at least Toosia's mother seemed in good spirits. He handed her the wine and took his seat.

"Have you spoken with Toosia recently?" Tyler asked to break the ice. Best to get this out of the way early.

Tooriin took a sip from her wine before responding, "Yes, in fact I just spoke with her."

Tyler was a surprised, but hopeful the conversation would quell any doubts or concerns they were having.

"Oh, well good, it has been a day since I last spoke with her," Tyler admitted, "is everything okay?"

"Oh yes," she said, "she is fine and looking forward to her return."

Tyler knew that she was scheduled to return in several days, but thought that it might be longer depending on how things played out. He hated having her so far away, but he believed she was safer on Siirneen than in the capital.

"Yes, I too look forward to her return." Tyler was sincere, but hoped he would still be alive when she returned.

Tooriin smiled tightly and agreed with a nod before taking another sip of her wine.

They sat in silence for the next few minutes, neither wanting to break it with small talk. Finally, Toosia's father came into the room, a broad smile on his face as he strode over to Tyler.

"Welcome Nayllen," the councilor greeted him, "we are so happy you cold join us despite your busy schedule."

"I am honored Councilor, thank you for inviting me." Nayllen bowed formally.

"Please Nayllen, call me Hiirtee," the councilor pleaded, "after all these years, I hope we can set aside the trappings of our positions while in the privacy of our homes."

With Hiirtee's light mood, Tyler thought the evening was shaping up to be ok.

"Sorry Hiirtee," Tyler replied graciously, "it is often difficult to step out of character…if even for an evening."

"Yes," the councilor said jovially, "I hope you don't insist on Toosia calling you Admiral?"

They laughed lightly, and Tyler began to relax, the brandy already taking effect. Tyler offered the councilor a drink, but Hiirtee declined as dinner was to commence. They took their seats around the small table, the councilor at the head and Tyler and Tooriin on either side.

They enjoyed course after course interspersed with light conversations about the Supreme Council, the local politics in Baneer, and the rising cost of property taxes outside the capital. Tyler was happy for the light conversation and wonderful food. The meal was a delicious assortment of fresh fruits, vegetables, and meats served with several bottles of fine wine. Despite his reservations, Tyler was enjoying himself. It was a great relief from the pressures he was currently under.

They finished the last of their meal, and the councilor instructed his staff to hold the desert until later. The staff accepted his orders and began clearing the table of dishes. Tyler was uncomfortably full and slightly drunk as he accepted another comfortable chair.

Tyler sat back with a fresh brandy and smiled broadly at his in-laws.

"A fabulous dinner Tooriin," Tyler said, "please thank your staff for me."

"Thank you Nayllen, I shall." She said quietly.

The last of the attendants finished clearing and walked out of the room, closing the recessed doors behind them.

As though waiting for the cue, the councilor spoke directly to Tyler, "Now that we are alone, we can discuss a matter of great importance that affects you and Toosia."

The statement caught Tyler off-guard and his earlier feelings of unease returned.

"I see," Tyler began, "is that why you invited me here?"

"Yes." The councilor's response was flat.

"Fine," Tyler prepared himself, "what is it?"

The councilor stole a quick glance at his wife before he began. Tyler could only speculate what it was about, but he assumed their concern for Toosia's safety while away was their number one issue.

"Well," the councilor began, "I am sure you are aware that we are concerned about Toosia and her safety, especially since she is pregnant?"

Tyler nodded in agreement, relieved that his assumption was correct.

"Well..." the councilor hesitated, "we have spoken with her at great length and she has tried to calm us by convincing us she is 'looking' after family interests."

Okay, Tyler thought, so far so good, yet it didn't seem like they were buying the cover story.

"We...well, we...I mean I, looked into this and discovered your family does not have any off-world interests to be looked after. The only off-world investments you own are stocks in companies that are supplied by several mining operations. That does not warrant a visit, let alone an extended stay."

The councilor paused and Tyler tried to hold down panic. They had looked into his investments? Their concern for their daughter was extreme and they were willing to do anything to protect her. Tyler remained calm, not wanting to respond until he had heard everything. The councilor paused as though waiting for a response, but continued when Tyler remained quiet.

"Of course we confronted Toosia with this information, and although she was angry at our prying, she finally confessed."

Tyler was very alert. What did he mean confess? What did Toosia tell them? She wouldn't have told them the truth, would she? Tyler wasn't sure—he had to admit he really didn't know her that well. He remained quiet.

The councilor took a drink and sat back into the couch.

"Nayllen," he began again, "I have to tell you that despite the pregnancy and the apparent change in you, we are still concerned about your relationship with Toosia."

The statement stung Tyler, but he couldn't blame them after the Admiral's years of abandonment. During that time, they had been certain the relationship was over, especially after they knew about the Admiral's affair. Apparently, even Toosia couldn't change their attitudes about the Admiral. Tyler wondered how he could.

"Nayllen," Tooriin broke in, "she has told us everything."

Everything? Tyler tried not to show his surprise or fear. He noticed that the councilor looked at his wife annoyed that she had cut to the chase.

"Yes," the councilor agreed, "she has told us…everything."

"Wh…what do you mean everything?" Tyler asked hoping that it was not truly 'everything'.

"She told us about you…your meeting with the governor," he stated calmly, "…your meeting with your father!" He emphasized that last statement, confirming Tyler's worst fears. She had told them everything, and now they felt they had the opportunity they needed to end the relationship they did not approve of. With one call, they could destroy the conspiracy and threaten the life of their daughter.

Tyler wasn't sure how to respond, "I see," he started, "and what do you intend on doing?" He feared the worst and was ready to warn them about Toosia being used as a pawn.

"We don't know, as yet, that is why we wanted to talk with you."

Tyler sensed the councilor was telling the truth, so he had to play his cards just right to survive this new crisis.

"Fair enough," Tyler responded, trying to keep the fear out of his voice, "but I must warn you, Toosia's safety will be determined by what you decide."

Tyler had to warn them. They had to know what they were up against. They both stole glances at the other, apparently trying to decide who should respond. Finally, Tooriin spoke up.

"We know that already Nayllen, she as much as told us that she was a 'guest' without her consent. However, we agreed with her that her place is here with her family, so we paid to have her 'rescued' and brought home."

"What?" Tyler was stunned. They had rescued her? A part of him was happy that she was out of their control, but he feared the repercussions of their meddling. What would Nayllen do when he found out? Would he send a message to the Admiral, perhaps a transport accident on her way home? Fear gripped him.

"Do you know who you are dealing with here?" Tyler demanded, the anger in his voice rising. "These people are capable of anything and know nearly everything that happens. I have seen it demonstrated. Nayllen Hooss is not a man to cross!"

Despite his outburst, both appeared calm. This only made Tyler angrier.

The councilor waited for Tyler to finish his tirade. Tyler finally stopped, having nothing else to say. He sat back down fuming. Toosia was definitely in danger now, especially if she came back to the capital.

"Don't worry Nayllen, she is safe." The councilor assured.

"Really," Tyler said bitterly, "you don't know Nayllen like I do—you don't know what he is capable of."

The councilor furrowed his brows in response, "Nonsense, I know Mr. Hooss…or people just like him. They want only one thing, power."

"Yes, so what makes you think he won't harm Toosia?"

The councilor's expression became flat, "Simple, he assured me he wouldn't."

"What," Tyler was outraged once again, "you spoke with him?"

"Yes, it was Hooss I paid to have Toosia released."

Tyler couldn't believe what he was hearing, they had paid Nayllen to release their daughter and guarantee her safety? It couldn't be. Why would Nayllen take money to release her? He was already rich beyond measure, why would money motivate him?

"Great," Tyler began, "and now you suppose paying him money is enough to secure her safety and yours? I doubt you have enough money to interest him."

"True enough," the councilor conceded, "but money is not all I have to offer." He paused while that sank in. "I offered him power, or rather what little I have in the Council."

Tyler couldn't believe what he was hearing—everything was being blown out of proportion. Now Toosia's father agreed to compromise his professional integrity, when all he had to do was wait? Tyler was certain everything was going to end badly, too much was unraveling, and soon it would be impossible to keep it all under wraps.

"So I suppose 'he' knows you know about the peace ship?" Tyler asked sounding more than exasperated.

"Of course," the councilor admitted, "at first I tried to play it off as though I didn't know everything…but he had a recording of my conversation with Toosia."

Tyler groaned inwardly, they were now all part of the conspiracy, and regardless of what happened, they were not likely to survive.

"So what did you promise him?" Tyler asked coldly.

"I promised that if their plan succeeded, I would support the new government and help win the Council over to their side…to embrace the new peace."

"And if it does not succeed? What then? My child spends the rest of their life without parents or grandparents?"

Tyler could see that last comment upset them, but he no longer cared.

The councilor looked straight at Tyler, a mean demeanor coming over his face, "Yes, Nayllen, that is what may happen if they do not succeed. But it is your traitorous behavior that may orphan your only child, so you better make sure their plan succeeds! At least then, our grandchild might have a family and a life in a peaceful world! You brought this upon us, so you better make sure we survive."

Tyler had never seen Toosia's father so angry, his own anger cooled from the display. He hadn't had a choice becoming a traitor, but he had been the one that had precipitated the events. If he would have just left everything alone, not been curious when he came across the listing flag ship, then maybe, the Admiral would have just died and none of this would have happened.

Adanni broke into his reverie uninvited. *Sure, and then the Admiral would not have given his wife the child she always wanted, the Emperor would not have any opposition to his destructive plans, and the planet would have been plunged into a final battle that would have spelled the end to this world!*

Shut up, no one asked you! Tyler let his anger vent at Adanni even though he knew he was right. It was as though fate had determined this world would be thrown into chaos, and only Tyler had the slimmest chance to thwart it.

"I didn't have any choice councilor." He said without any force, knowing it would come out lame.

"Maybe you did, maybe didn't. Either way, you have the power to make it come out right, even if it kills you. And I mean that literally, Nayllen. When the time comes, you better make the right choices and not sacrifice us to save your own skin. If that time comes, you better act the officer you've always been and meet your doom with integrity. It is the very least you owe your child!"

Tyler could tell what kind of ending they were hoping for. Even if he survived, his relationship with his in-laws was over. They would do their best to convince their daughter to end it as well. Considering what the Emperor was capable of doing, Tyler admitted his odds of surviving were not high.

"Why is Toosia coming here?" Tyler asked, once again worried for her safety.

"She is not," Toornii replied softly, "we are both meeting her at one of my family's properties in the Siirsee province."

"When are you leaving?" Tyler asked.

"Tonight," the councilor admitted, "after your return to the capital."

Tyler thought about that, at least they would be far from the capital. It might not matter if everything failed, but at least it was a temporary reprieve. Tyler felt sorry he would not be able to see her before it ended. He missed her and wanted to feel her touch once again. His love for her had grown strong, even as strong as his love for Linda, but he was not going to have another chance to show her that love. He would only be able to communicate it when they next spoke. If they spoke.

Tyler stood up, "I see, then I will let you get on with your travel arrangements."

He moved to leave, pressured by the deep concern for their safety. Travel accidents were not uncommon, and Tyler was certain Nayllen could easily organize one. He hoped the councilor's promise of support was enough to guarantee their safety. At least Toosia appeared safe, for the moment.

As he turned to leave, Tooriin stopped him, "Nayllen…" she paused as though what she had to say was difficult, "I know you will do the right thing for your family…and your world."

He smiled weakly at the vote of confidence—he didn't share her optimism. He glanced briefly at the councilor who stared back coldly, "Good luck sir, please take care of my wife and my child."

The councilor didn't respond, so Tyler nodded gently to Tooriin before heading towards the courtyard. As the ground car pulled away from the Slay estate, Tyler sat quietly thinking about the fate that awaited him.

When Tyler arrived back in the capital, two urgent messages waited for him. He hoped one would be from the Marshall with the information he needed to find the Onyalum. He felt utterly helpless and yearned for something he could pursue to improve his odds. Unfortunately, neither message was from the Marshall.

The first message carried the Imperial Seal of the office of Regent Sneerd. Tyler opened the message with dread. As he feared, the Palace had set the date and time for the turn over of the command codes. At this point, Tyler had no reason to delay, so he sent his acceptance. Now he needed to contact Nayllen and let them know the date and time.

As if by coincidence, the next message was from Nayllen, using the highest security encryption the military had. Tyler knew it wasn't coincidence. Nayllen had access to the nearly everything in the Imperial Palace, so finding out the date and time of the turn-over would have been easy.

Tyler opened the message:

> Date and time acceptable. Package arriving. Wear contents to meeting. Your family and planet are depending on you.
> NH

Short and sweet, just like Nayllen, efficient. Tyler groaned at the implied threat. He felt responsible for Toosia's parents joining the conspiracy and knew the pressure was on to ensure it went as planned.

Tyler needed to know who the Onyalum was prior to the turn-over. He still had a day before the meeting, so he hoped the Marshall would come through. His drive to find the Onyalum was so strong, he threw aside caution and called the Marshall directly to get an update. He knew it would raise more suspicions, but with only a day left, he had to risk it.

"Yes sir?" The Marshall answered crisp and remote.

"Sorry to bother you Marshall," Tyler tried to sound casual, "but I wanted an update on that background health information."

Tyler waited while the Marshall accessed information online.

"It is not complete, but should be enough to start with. I should have the rest of it by tomorrow evening."

Tyler did not like the sound in the Marshall's voice. Clearly he felt left out and used, but Tyler had no choice. He could not share anything with the Marshall for fear of failure. It was bad enough his in-laws found out. If his staff knew, they would have no choice but turn in their leader.

No one on the planet would understand, or believe the idea of an Onyalum. It would sound so foreign—it would only cast suspicion on himself. He had to continue lying and hope the Marshall's loyalty outweighed his suspicions.

"Thank you Marshall, please send me what you have and I'll expect the rest tomorrow."

"Yes sir." His response was cold and distant.

Tyler couldn't even say goodnight before the Marshall disconnected. That was truly out of character, and it worried Tyler. Nonetheless, the information he promised began streaming into Tyler's personal system.

Tyler left the office and moved into his living quarters to view the information from the comfort of a couch. He poured himself a tall glass of wine and settled in to read the data. He switched on the main viewer on the wall and downloaded the information sent by the Marshall. As usual, the information was neatly organized and easily queried.

Tyler took a large sip of the wine and began analyzing the information. According to the categories provided, the Marshall had retrieved only the information on Admiral Teesen, Nayllen, and Regent Sneerd. Apparently, the information on the Emperor was forthcoming. No matter, Tyler was more interested in these three anyway.

He took another drink and opened the files on Admiral Teesen. He read through the medical and biographical information on the Admiral and immediately discounted him. According to his records, the man had almost never been sick in his life. The only injury he had sustained was during a Twiiling sport match in college. He had collided with an opposing player and both were knocked unconscious for a brief period. Tyler noted the game was similar to Lacrosse on earth.

Temporary unconsciousness would not have provided an opportunity for Onyalum possession, so that ruled out Teesen. Adanni confirmed as much as Tyler moved on to Nayllen.

Before he opened Nayllen's file, a pop-up message informed Tyler the information had been sealed by the Imperial Palace and opening it constituted a breach of imperial security punishable by imprisonment or death. It was a standard Imperial Seal, but what concerned Tyler was why Nayllen's records had been sealed by the palace? Tyler ignored the warning and opened the file. He was already a traitor—one more charge meant nothing.

By the time he finished looking over Nayllen's records, he had finished his glass of wine. He quickly refilled it and dug deeper into Nayllen's childhood. It appeared Nayllen had been a very sick child, including an incurable, at the time, childhood disease that affected normal muscle development. He'd been bedridden for most of his childhood, and was once brought back from near death when his chest muscles failed and he stopped breathing.

Tyler was astounded, not only had he stopped breathing, but twice his heart had stopped on two different occasions. It was a miracle that he had survived to adulthood. According to current records, a cure was found and new treatments had all but changed Nayllen into a normal, healthy adult.

It was enough for suspicions, but being so long ago almost ruled out Nayllen. What Onyalum would have chosen a bedridden child near death? He came from a rather obscure family of modest means, so little back then would have indicated the child would become a significant power. Current records indicated no health issues. Not even a single surgery.

Tyler was frustrated. Nayllen could have been possessed when he was a child, but Adanni agreed it was highly unlikely. Unfortunately, Tyler had to conclude it was probably not Nayllen. Tyler had hoped it would have been. It explained so much for Nayllen to be the evil spirit hell-bent on destruction. Now however, Tyler had to believe Nayllen was nothing more than bad seed seeking power and influence. Perhaps his childhood illness was reason for his adult callousness.

Tyler drank heavy from his wine and felt numb from the effects of his healthy nightcaps. He didn't care, it felt wonderful. Numb, that was what he needed to get through this crisis. He took another drink and opened the file on Regent Sneerd.

Surprisingly, his records weren't sealed. They were filled with intricate details that seemed extraordinary in official records. For instance, Tyler found references to behavioral problems when Sneerd had been a small child, including handwritten accounts from his mother. Apparently Regent Sneerd had been a trouble child. *That fits!*

Tyler ran through the records astounded at what he was seeing. Sneerd had been in and out of multiple institutions for troubled youth, and even a brief stint in a penal institution. He had swarms of doctors who constantly tried to determine the cause of his behavior, and his parents spent millions trying to rehabilitate him.

Tyler was amazed a man with such a checkered past had reached such powerful heights. But then, the Emperor was known to hire such thugs. Who else would do the work no Emperor would himself do? So much about Regent Sneerd began to make sense. He was devious and dangerous, and as far as Tyler was concerned, the number one suspect. Who better to attract an Onyalum than a person who was already destructive?

The only thing missing was a near-death experience. Tyler read past his college records and into his first career. Not surprising, he had been recruited by the Imperial Palace into the intelligence community for 'unspecified' posts. Tyler thought he knew what that meant—assassination.

He had served in 'unspecified' posts for over seven years before being promoted into the Emperor's personal staff. From there, he moved rapidly up through the ranks as he befriended the Emperor and influenced the political arena. At the early age of thirty-five, he was appointed to his current position of Regent. It was the highest post within the Imperial Palace.

Nice, the Emperor had an assassin as his highest advisor and chief of staff. It spoke volumes about the Emperor and his government. It was easy for Tyler to understand why traitors wanted to overthrow the Emperor and start a democratic government. Tyler couldn't understand why it hadn't happened before.

However, no one on Poolto really complained about the current government. Sure, there were some who had their own agendas, agendas that differed from the palace. But Tyler assumed they were minorities that were quickly 'dealt' with. *By Sneerd no doubt!*

Most of the common people enjoyed a prosperous life and rarely complained about the government. Why would they want it changed? He thought he began to see a potential flaw in the conspiracy. Even the National hero may not be enough to convince the average person of Poolto that a democratic government was necessary.

With democracy, the average person would have to become involved with their government in a more intimate way. They would have to pay attention to its inner workings and make sure those in power were held accountable. Tyler doubted most wanted that responsibility. He thought back to many Americans who were not involved in the government and didn't vote. It would likely be the same on Poolto. That's when you had to watch out for 'who' was in power. Tyler thought about Nayllen.

He finished his second glass of wine and refocused on Sneerd's records. There had to be something to cast suspicion on him besides his obviously evil nature. However, Tyler wasn't finding anything. Sure, he had been sick and he had injuries, especially during the fighting when he was younger.

Unfortunately, his records when he was 'unspecified' were virtually non-existent. Obviously, those records were sealed and totally inaccessible. Anything could have happened during those seven years. It was dangerous work and you were bound to be in positions where injury and death were commonplace. But Tyler could find nothing.

He had a new thought and switched his search tactics. Nearly everyone received physicals when appointed to high positions. If anything serious had happened to Sneerd during those seven years, it might show up in a physical later on. He found the date when Sneerd had been appointed Regent and accessed the Imperial health records. He found it, a full physical examination upon acceptance of the post!

Tyler scanned the document, ignoring most of the information he didn't understand. He finally found a complete body scan that had revealed every single scar, burn, bruise, and contusion he had ever had. There were many, but nothing that would have been severe enough to place him near death.

Damn!

This was obviously going to be harder than Tyler had first thought—even with such prolific records. He refilled his glass while he pondered the problem. He began scanning all current medical records for anything unusual. Nothing appeared lethal or cause for alarm.

He had wanted Nayllen to be the one who was possessed, but failing that, he had always assumed it would be the Regent. Now however, he didn't know what to think. Perhaps it was none of them. Maybe they were just greedy, evil men.

He had scanned through the Regent's mission entries and was ready to give up when something caught his eye. It was a simple file that had a special security lock on it. There were many of those files, but this one was named 'Treerdeen'. The Admiral's memories stirred at the name, and Tyler searched them to find out why.

His search yielded only a small reference to the asteroid in an old battle report. According to the battle report, the asteroid had been lost. That didn't seem to warrant any special interest, but he was willing to search anywhere at this point.

Turning on another viewer, he called up information on the asteroid called Treerdeen. Unfortunately, he was not getting any hits. He changed his search parameters and tried searching for asteroids lost in the war. Finally, he got a single hit, but it didn't have any information. It was a simple list of asteroids lost during the first five years of the war.

At first, it appeared that the list was simply names in three columns. Treerdeen was near the bottom with one other name to the right of it. The other name was Kaagan, but Tyler assumed that was just another asteroid that had been lost during the war. It took him a moment before he realized all the names to the right of those in the first column were Krildon names.

He saw the pattern. The first column contained the names of Poolto asteroids lost during the first five years of the war. The second column contained the new name for the asteroid after it was captured by Krildon. The third column, which Tyler noted had few names, contained the names of asteroids that had been re-captured by Poolto. It all made sense, the new name for Treerdeen was Kaagan, and was likely still a possession of Krildon.

He opened another search query and entered Kaagan. According to the search results, Kaagan was both an industrial park on Krildon and an asteroid captured during the war. He looked through the information but only got general descriptions of

Kaagan and its economic feasibility. Apparently, the asteroid had little in the way of resources, but did provide a tactical advantage.

He was getting frustrated since there was nothing to connect the Regent with this asteroid other than the locked file. He made several attempts to unlock the file himself, but nothing worked. All his military command codes failed.

The drink and the searches were taking their toll, and Tyler was ready to call it a night. He was about to shut down the viewers when he thought about searching the military records for Kaagan. Surely if it was lost in the war, there would be some records within the military, especially if it had tactical value.

He queried several databases and got only marginal hits. Finally, while searching the procurement records, he found a report labeled 'Battle Losses – Asteroids'. The dates coincided with the first five years of the war. He opened it and found an entry for Treerdeen. According to the records, Treerdeen had been a small military outpost built as a refurbishing station near the frontlines. It was still under construction when Krildon attacked the facility.

Tyler scanned through various lists of equipment and ordinance that had been on the asteroid at the time of the battle. From an overall war standpoint, Treerdeen had been an insignificant loss other than its location. Tyler was ready to give up when he saw a personnel manifest list scroll by. He stopped and moved back to the manifest. The list contained names and identification numbers, no rank or military affiliation. Tyler couldn't even tell who was civilian or who was military. However, he noted that near the top of the list was the name, A. Sneerd.

Tyler thought it couldn't be coincidence—Sneerd had been on that asteroid. In fact, he had been on the asteroid when it had been attacked and captured. If that were true, then Sneerd had been captured. Tyler easily confirmed this when he found a prisoner exchange comment. Apparently, all captured personnel had been eventually returned in exchange for Krildon prisoners.

It was starting to make sense why this file was locked. If the public found out Regent Sneerd had been a prisoner of Krildon, then suspicion would have been cast on him and the Imperial Palace. No returned prisoners were ever fully trusted again. It was military policy to discharge all prisoners returned by the enemy. They were not treated poorly—they were simply removed from positions of authority. Many were given pensions for their 'honored service' and put out to pasture.

This is what made Sneerd's capture so problematic. He was then, and still is the highest ranking person on the Imperial Staff. Despite his capture and six month detainment, the palace had kept him in his position. Why would the Emperor ignore the general policy? Did Sneerd have information on the Emperor that would persuade him to bury this? Tyler didn't think he could find out without opening the file. He wondered what Sneerd had been doing on such an insignificant asteroid to begin with, especially one so close to the front.

He had to see the contents of that file even if it didn't confirm his suspicions of Onyalum possession. He called up Officer Slaas and woke her. He hadn't realized how late it was, but then, he only had a day to work this out.

"Officer Slaas," he began, "I have a sealed file from the Imperial Palace that I need access to. Unfortunately, the contents are…delicate and cannot be seen by anyone other than myself. Is there any way to break the seal myself?"

She looked tired, but was giving it thoughtful deliberation before answering.

"I think there might be sir, but I'll need to contact someone I know from the academy." She paused and looked concerned. "Sir, should I be concerned for my career if I help you with this?"

Tyler was surprised at her bluntness, but she had a right to know. "It might look bad if something came of it, but for the moment, it is between you and I."

"I understand sir," she said calmly, "I don't think I'll need the file, but can you send me a brief description of its security seal?"

Tyler agreed and forwarded the description. Officer Slaas promised him news as soon as possible. Tyler instructed her to keep all information in verbal communications to prevent any 'trail' from being formed. She agreed and said she would call immediately when she had something.

Tyler was curious, what did the file contain and how could that information be used against Sneerd? Would it be enough to convince the Emperor to accept peace? Tyler doubted it but was willing to use anything at that point—even if it was thin.

He ran down the next day's schedule before turning into bed. If he was lucky, he could still get a few hours sleep before his first meeting. It was with Marshall Sliss, and he dreaded the possible questions he would face concerning the medical information. He needed to stall the Marshall but was too tired to think of anything. Perhaps in the morning he would have fresh ideas? At least he'd likely be sober.

The final day proceeded fast. Tyler woke early with a pounding headache from a hangover. Fortunately, after eating breakfast, he felt significantly better by the time he met the Marshall.

Despite his earlier dread, the meeting was brief, professional, and somewhat cold. Even though Tyler had expected the Marshall to question him about the medical information, the Marshall uncharacteristically remained quiet and on-task. Since Tyler felt woozy from the night before, he was happy to avoid the conversation. He even held back from asking for the missing medical information on the Emperor.

As the day wore on, meeting after meeting became a blur in which Tyler barely participated. He could not take his mind off of the upcoming events. He played out the scenario over and over in his mind, but was never satisfied with how he handled it. He had to admit, he was unskilled as a traitor, and everything he believed in did not necessarily match those of his co-conspirators. It made it difficult for Tyler to support the cause with 'real' conviction.

Around lunchtime, he received a message from Officer Slaas urging him to contact her. When he was released for lunch, he made his way back to his office and contacted her. It was a brief call as she wanted to see him in person.

When she arrived, she was all business. Despite the implied threat to her own career, she had tracked down an illegal method to crack the sealed file. Tyler wanted her to simply tell him how, but she insisted doing it herself to save time. Tyler didn't ask how she found out, but let her do the work while he sat back watching. Only once did he see a look of curiosity on her face. The look came as she noted the file name, but was quickly replaced with professional focus as she worked to break the seal.

It took ten minutes before the contents of the file began to scrolling across the screen. As if wanting to protect herself from further implication, Officer Slaas immediately turned away from the open file and asked if there were anything else she could assist him with. Tyler told her no, thanked her, and released her to her duties.

He spent the rest of lunch reading the contents of the entire file. It had been created by the Intelligence branch of the Imperial Palace, and Tyler was surprised it had been with the rest of Sneerd's personal files. Nonetheless, it was a summary report on the incident at Treerdeen. The report had been requested personally by the Emperor. Apparently, the Emperor had originally wanted to maintain the policy of relieving the prisoner of war from his post, but a report had been requested to see if they could avoid it.

According to what Tyler read, Sneerd had been on Treerdeen at the request of the Emperor himself. Unfortunately, the report did not stipulate why. Tyler assumed the report was not classified at the same level as the mission Sneerd had been on.

The report listed various meetings between Sneerd and a variety of people, both civilian and military. It read rather normal until the part where the attack began. At that point, Sneerd had been in a meeting at a non-military facility far from the military depot. It had probably saved his life as most of the military personnel and facilities were destroyed during the attack.

When the people he'd met felt the bombardment, they had immediately moved to an escape vehicle built into the facility. Although the vehicle could not adequately fit all the people at the facility, they loaded it up anyway. The overloaded ship had just been capable of launching as the Krildon destroyed their facility. As the escape vehicle made its way back towards Poolto controlled space, it was hit by a missile intended to disable the ship.

Unfortunately, the overcrowding caused the missile to create greater damage than simply disabling the ship. Instead, the ship decompressed, and by the time it was captured, nearly everyone was either unconscious or dead. Among the dead was one A. Sneerd. Remarkably, he'd been brought back from death by the surgeons on the enemy ship. Seven other dead were also brought back to life.

Tyler thought the story had too many similarities to his own. At that point, he had to assume Sneerd was the most likely candidate. It was both logical and now practical. Even after being a prisoner for six months, Sneerd had been placed in isolation for nearly a year undergoing extensive psychological evaluation. Remarkably, he had been the one who had requested the treatment and evaluation. All of it was carried out by the Intelligence branch at a secret facility located somewhere within the Imperial Palace.

The rest of the report listed the results of various testing they'd done, with a final page outlining the overall results of the incident with a recommendation to re-instate Sneerd to his post as Imperial Regent. Apparently, the Emperor had been satisfied with the results or he would have removed Sneerd from office.

Tyler didn't know what type of testing Sneerd had been through, but some of the Admiral's memories suggested it was something akin to torture. Tyler had a new respect for the man's toughness. It was no wonder he was such a dangerous individual. Tyler knew he would have to play his cards carefully—Sneerd was not a man to trifle with.

All of this left Tyler feeling greater anxiety about the upcoming command code turn-over. If Sneerd were possessed, then he might also suspect the Admiral. Tyler was no match for a man who had gone through so much coupled with intelligence experience. He felt a chill of fear as he returned to rest of the meeting.

Everything was beginning to feel like a dream, and Tyler went through the afternoon schedule in a trance-like state. In his mind, various worst-case scenarios played out over and over again. Even the Admiral's most powerful tactics were unable to devise a suitable response. Tyler was alone against very formidable powers. Even Adanni remained unusually quiet.

This feeling of loneliness continued to haunt Tyler as he made his way back to his quarters. His agenda complete, only a night of 'sleep' stood between Tyler and his fate. He had no illusions about sleep. Although he needed the rest to fortify his resolve, he also knew the import of tomorrow's events would deny him that basic necessity. Instead, he retired to the couch and opened another bottle of wine. Perhaps inebriation would bring sleep—if only a less restful one.

In the morning, Tyler drifted through his normal routine: breakfast, the latest news, daily briefings. Tyler ignored most of it. Instead, he wrestled with the fear and anxiety of the meeting to come. He was to report to the Palace later that morning in the transport provided. It seemed odd they ordered transport since Tyler could easily walk the distance. His anxiety barely in check, he dressed in his formal attire, as appropriate for the palace.

Before catching the transport, Tyler met briefly with his staff. The Marshall was notably absent, and no one could explain why. Despite that, Officer Slaas took charge and quickly ran down the list of items on the agenda. The only message Tyler had from the Marshall was a private note indicating the information he requested was delayed another day.

Tyler read the message with little concern. He was certain the person to fear was Regent Sneerd and he still didn't have a plan to deal with it. The staff meeting ended abruptly while Tyler was lost in thought. He noticed puzzled looks and quickly took charge to release the staff. He knew they expected a response, but he delayed the questions until returning from the palace. *Assuming I return.*

Although the Admiral had been to the palace many times, the memories of it didn't ease Tyler's anxiety. He desperately wanted a drink but was glad he was sober for the meeting. Dutifully, he wore the small device Nayllen had provided. He had almost left it behind, but had remembered it at the last moment. Nayllen had failed to tell him what it was for, but he wore it anyway. He only hoped it passed the security screening.

It, and he, both passed through security. The Admiral held no memories of security checks so invasive for someone of his position. Tyler assumed they were new precautions due to the secrecy surrounding the new offensive. Regardless, he was extremely nervous when placed in the scanner.

The scanner had only detected his personal communication device and not the device Nayllen had provided. *Chalk one up for Nayllen!*

As Tyler was escorted by three palace guards, he noticed that not much had changed in that part of the palace. It was still elegantly decorated and adorned with some of the finest art of Poolto. Tyler admired many of the pieces, especially one scenic painting that looked like the Tooland Estate Winery. It made Tyler think about Toosia and settling down. If he survived this, they would move to Tooland and raise a family. *If I survive.*

Adanni had remained eerily quiet leading up to this. He hadn't even visited Tyler's dreams. Tyler assumed his lack of real sleep didn't provide the opportunity. Still, he had tried to engage Adanni several times, but was quickly put off. The last thing Adanni had said was 'If I am needed, I will speak up'. Tyler wasn't certain but he almost sensed fear.

They moved out of the public areas and down several levels to more private floors. Tyler had two guards leading with one following behind. It made Tyler feel like a condemned man on the way to the gallows. He hoped his nerves weren't as visible as they felt.

Finally, they came to the end of a long corridor barren of décor. The two guards stopped and stood at either side of the simple door. The Admiral had no memories of this area, and it fed into Tyler's fears. One of the guards opened the door and stood nodding for Tyler to enter. Tyler braced himself before entering the room.

Despite the bland corridor, the room was large and grand in design. Tyler noted a large dais with what could only be called a throne to his left. To his right was a series of tiered seating that looked similar to jury seats in a courtroom. Dominating the center of the back wall was a very large view screen that dwarfed everything else. Tyler figured it was at least thirty feet tall and just as wide.

The ceiling soared a hundred feet up, ornately decorated in gold trim and intricately carved figures. Tyler didn't recognize the various scenes they depicted, though it made him think of the governor's office on Siirneen. However, this room was square and twice the size. He half expected to see the Emperor on the throne, but it was empty.

In fact, Tyler was the only person in the room. He was a little surprised but took one of the comfortable seats facing the viewer in the middle of the room. His anxiety still churned, and being alone in the room made it grow dramatically. The Admiral's memories of taking over the command codes did not match the situation Tyler found himself in. *Calm down! Things change over so many years.* He did not re-assure himself.

Tyler nearly jumped at the sound of a door opening to his right. Several attendants entered followed closely by Admiral Teesen. Tyler rose from his seat and nodded to Teesen. He noted Teesen looked somber despite getting what he'd always desired. Admiral Teesen moved to a chair near Tyler and remained standing. Tyler followed suit as the attendants placed small devices next to each of their chairs. Tyler recognized them as the command code transfer devices.

After placing a device near the empty seat across from Tyler, the attendants stood behind each chair waiting. Finally, a new attendant entered the room to announce the Emperor.

"Supreme Commander of Poolto Forces and Admiral Osloo, please honor our beloved and great leader, Emperor Hallen Yooso IV." With that he bowed deeply as the Emperor made his way into the room.

The Emperor wasted no time taking his seat across from Tyler. Tyler and Admiral Teesen took theirs in turn, Tyler waiting last as demanded by rank.

The Emperor began. "Perhaps before we get started, we should transfer the codes." He signaled the devices next to each of their seats.

Tyler was confused. Before they get started? He had thought the entire reason for the meeting was the transfer. Did they expect him to report on the commission's progress? He was not prepared to do that. The commission hadn't even finished the report.

Tyler leaned forward, "I'm sorry sir, did you say before we get started?"

"Indeed," the Emperor stated cryptically, "just take the device next you and we can begin."

Tyler saw Admiral Teesen and the Emperor pick up their devices. What was he to do? He had assumed a more elaborate ceremony before handing the codes over. In the past, each member had taken pledges and verified their identity before beginning the transfer. How could they bypass that process? Tyler was confused and felt a little fear. He'd not been prepared to act so quickly into the meeting. Nayllen had said he would receive a signal that would indicate the peace ship's readiness. He hadn't said what the signal would be.

He had no choice, he had to divert suspicions and follow along. At least Regent Sneerd was not present. He picked up his device and waited.

"Good," the Emperor said as he fiddled with some controls on his device, "I believe we each stick a finger into the hole on the left side of the device and then press the large button on the top. That will verify our identities so we can proceed."

They each placed their fingers into the small holes and pressed the button. Tyler felt something warm against the tip of his finger followed by a tiny prick. It was not painful, just unexpected. Instantly after the prick, Tyler felt a cooling sensation sweep over his entire finger. Suddenly, a blue light lit next to the button. It took only a few moments before each of them had blue lights displayed. Tyler was relieved to see his light matched theirs.

"Excellent, we are who we believe we are. Now, we each will be given a statement on the small viewer on the backside of the device. Please read the statement's carefully before pressing the large button again to confirm your acceptance."

Again, Tyler followed suit as each of them flipped their device over to read the displayed text. Although the screen was small, Tyler could easily make out the text. The statements displayed matched the pledges of the Admiral's memories. Apparently the process had been automated to make it more efficient. Just what Tyler didn't need, efficiency.

Tyler quickly read the statements before turning over the device
and pressing the large button. Like before, the device displayed a
blue light.

Damn! Tyler thought, they were nearly to the transfer. There
was still no signal from the peace ship. Once he turned over the
codes, Teesen would quickly change them or use them to re-enable
the fleet after they were disabled. Tyler was running out of time
and he didn't know how to stall.

"Fine," the Emperor's light glowed blue, "Admiral Osloo please
enter your codes into the device using the viewer on the backside.
I'll enter the Imperial transfer codes, and at that point, Admiral
Teesen will receive the command codes on his device. He will then
memorize these codes before ending this part of the meeting."

There it was again, a reference to there being more to the
meeting than the transfer. Tyler had no choice but to comply.
Nothing he could do at that point would stall the proceedings
without raising suspicions. He hoped the peace ship, or Nayllen,
was watching. Otherwise, the codes would soon be Admiral
Teesen's. Protocol dictated he had to immediately change them,
although that would take time to propagate them to the fleet.

Tyler flipped over his device and began entering the command
codes. He entered them as slowly as he could, thinking that
something would happen to stall it at any moment. Nothing
happened. The Emperor had already entered his own codes and sat
waiting, a blue light displayed on his device.

Tyler could no longer stall and so he completed the long
sequence before flipping the device over and pressing the button.
It took only a moment before his device displayed a blue light.
Just as quickly, a blue light lit on Admiral Teesen's device. On that
signal, Admiral Teesen flipped his device and began memorizing
the codes. If the Admiral's memory held true, Admiral Teesen
had about three minutes to memorize the codes before they were
erased. So far, it had all followed the Admiral's memories except in
the past they had used one device.

Finally, the blue lights went out on all three devices as the
process completed. The peace ship was too late. Tyler still held
the device, fear paralyzing him. How would he proceed? The

device vibrated gently in his hands as the self-destruct mechanism destroyed the circuitry inside. He placed the device back on the table as despair swept through his body. He'd let down his family, and now they might pay the ultimate price.

How could he have known it would happen so fast? What could he have done? Surely Nayllen knew what had been happening, how could they blame him for the failure? Where were they? Where was the signal?

Admiral Teesen got up from his chair and moved to the console beneath the large viewer. Tyler knew Teesen was preparing to change the codes, and there was nothing he could do about it.

The Emperor, looking satisfied, put down his device and signaled to an attendant. At his signal, the attendant walked over to the door on the right and opened it. Tyler watched several people enter through the door and take seats in the tiers. It looked like a jury returning from recess.

At the same time, the main entrance opened behind Tyler and he watched as a line of guards took up positions along the interior wall, blocking the entrance and looking menacing. Tyler was extremely nervous. This wasn't part of the ceremony. What was going on?

He looked to the Emperor who ignored him. He looked at Admiral Teesen, but he also ignored the changes as he changed the command codes. Tyler's anxiety was rising, though he tried to look normal.

He stared back at the rows of people filling the tiered seats but didn't recognize one of them. Since none of them wore rank or uniforms, he assumed they were civilians or part of the Imperial staff. Was this a new part of the ceremony? He didn't think so.

Admiral Teesen finished changing the codes and returned to his seat. As if in a parade, signals to waiting people were sent through the door. Tyler watched in horror as each person entered the room and took seats behind the Emperor's.

First in line was Regent Sneerd who did not take a seat but signaled to those behind him to take one. Behind the Regent was Marshall Sliss, followed closely by Eyleeria. Neither made eye contact with Tyler, and he immediately knew nothing good was about to happen.

The last person to enter was none other than Nayllen Hooss, looking smug and content as usual. He took his seat and the Emperor stared coldly into Tyler's eyes.

"Admiral," he began, "you are probably wondering what is going on and why I have ordered these people to appear before us."

Tyler merely nodded.

The Emperor, satisfied with the gesture, continued.

"Very well, I will tell you. We have grave concerns over your behavior recently. In fact, we believe you to be involved in a vast conspiracy to overthrow this very government. In essence, to betray this planet to our enemy."

Tyler was stunned. He'd never expected this, and he had no idea how to react.

He remained emotionless, "I see, and what proof do you have of this charge?"

"A great deal actually. Today, we are here to understand the charges against you and to analyze the evidence before you are formally charged. The people over in the stands consist of civilians randomly chosen to evaluate the evidence against you and to determine if charges are appropriate." The Emperor swept his hands toward the waiting jury.

Tyler followed the Emperors hand and surveyed the jury again. Some held looks of disbelief while others stared back menacing. The Admiral was a National hero, and those that were shocked must have been disturbed by what they were hearing. At least his reputation held some sway on the proceedings. He tried desperately to think of what evidence they could have to charge him, but he couldn't think of anything directly. Still, with Nayllen sitting there, anything was possible. Had everything fallen apart and Nayllen was betraying him to save himself?

"And these people to my left?" Tyler asked waving a hand at Nayllen, the Marshall, and Eyleeria.

The Emperor gazed at them before responding. "These are your accusers here to give evidence."

Great. He could understand why Eyleeria was there, she obviously wanted revenge because he had rejected her. But the Marshall and Nayllen? Nayllen was part of the conspiracy, how could he give evidence? Tyler thought about his family and Nayllen's hold on them. Maybe that was it, they would be hostages to prevent Tyler from implicating Nayllen. Perfect, he was all alone.

He looked at the Marshall who still wouldn't meet his eyes. The Marshall knew about Nayllen, so how could he now sit with him now as an accuser? It didn't make sense. What evidence were they going to present? How could Tyler defend it?

As if reading his mind, the Emperor spoke to Tyler. "You will not be able to defend against anything you hear today, you may only listen until charges are brought against you and you have your day in court."

So, that was it, he was defenseless against his accusers. The Emperor signaled to an official 'looking' attendant who stepped forward, standing in front of the jury.

"Ladies and gentlemen, we are here to bear witness to accusations and evidence against Admiral Osloo to determine if the heinous charges against him are warranted. I realize this may be upsetting, especially in light of his position as our National hero. It is both unfortunate and yet prophetic that his father also betrayed our world."

That stung Tyler and he began to realize how this had all been set up—perhaps long ago. He waited to hear the testimony. He was curious to see what evidence they had to determine how he had been betrayed.

Eyleeria was the first to be questioned. Tyler had no idea how she could have evidence that would constitute treason. She answered basic questions about how long she had worked for Admiral Osloo and what their relationship had been. Tyler hated the looks on the faces of the jury when she revealed she'd had a romantic relationship with the Admiral for many years. So much for his moral reputation.

The next question caught Tyler off-guard. Perhaps he hadn't heard right? The interrogator had asked how long she'd been employed by the Imperial Intelligence branch. Tyler couldn't believe it. She answered calmly that she'd been recruited while attending the military academy.

She was a spy! The thought cut deep into Tyler. Admiral Osloo had been under surveillance for most of his career. Not only that, it had been from his lover. Tyler felt totally doomed.

She recounted the accident that had placed Tyler into the coma. She also mentioned how he had significantly changed after regaining consciousness. He had spurned her advances, gone back with his wife, and regularly made religious comments. Tyler moaned as he thought about to his small indiscretion. He'd hoped it would not come back to haunt him, but now it was used to cast greater doubt and suspicion.

Still, she had said nothing that constituted treason. He waited as the interrogator asked new questions.

"So Miss Snillen, what evidence do you have to as proof of the Admiral's treason?"

She nodded to an attendant who went to the console underneath the main viewer. The viewer came alive and after some fiddling, a picture filled with static began to take shape. Tyler watched in horror as the viewer displayed him with the governor, the Admiral's father and Commandant Kulg. The picture was fuzzy and inaudible, but it was easy to make out everyone in the room. Tyler noted that Nayllen's picture had somehow been conveniently removed from the scene. The seat where Nayllen had sat was vacant.

Eyleeria looked extremely proud of herself. "This was taken on a recent trip to Siirneen for meetings with field commanders. At that time, I had reasonable doubts about the trip and therefore placed a device on the Admiral to collect additional intelligence. The device was cleared through the proper Intelligence channels of course."

Of course, Tyler thought, probably at the Emperor or Sneerd's request. The Admiral and Tyler had been so naïve, how had the Admiral lasted so long?

Easy, he hadn't been a threat before.

Adanni's impromptu comment was cold comfort.

"As you can see, the Admiral and Governor Niis met with the Commander of the Third Fleet of the Krildon Republic Navy, Commandant Kulg. Even more shocking, the Admiral's own father, a branded traitor of Poolto, was alive and present." She cast Tyler a malevolent look as she said this. "Although we were unable to capture the audio portion of this meeting, we can only assume meeting a known traitor and one of the highest ranking military officials of our enemy was not a social visit."

The jury stared at the viewer incredulous. As far as they knew, the Admiral's father had been dead. The fact that he was not fed their worst fears. Some cast furtive glances at Tyler, but none looked sympathetic. He began to understand why they'd believed he would not survive the conspiracy.

But what had happened to the conspiracy? Where was the peace ship? Had everything failed? Was the peace ship a ruse? Was everything designed to discredit him and brand him a traitor like the Admiral's father? Why? He had turned over the codes, relinquished command, what more could they want? Did the disgrace and fall of the National hero really serve their purposes? How would the war effort continue without a rallying figure? He could not see the pattern, and sat lonely and confused.

He began to realize no peace ship was on its way, and no signal would be sent. Like Tyler, Nayllen had probably betrayed them all to gain political clout. Perhaps it had been one big charade, designed by Nayllen to promote himself and his goals. Tyler didn't know what those were, but considering evidence had been tampered with, Nayllen clearly had the backing of the Emperor.

Power, was that what all this was about? Tyler thought about Toosia and her parents, would they survive? If they did, would they survive the disgrace? It was certain Toosia's father would be removed from the council. He might also be implicated, especially if he had really trusted Nayllen. Or maybe that was it! Perhaps he had brokered a deal with Nayllen to protect he and his family when this all unraveled. Tyler no longer knew who he could trust.

He even began imagining Toosia was part of the betrayal. She and the Admiral had been disillusioned for so long. Maybe she had fallen out of love with him during all those years. The Admiral's affair would have been enough for her to throw aside spousal loyalty. Did he really believe that making love to her twice and getting her pregnant was enough to overcome the years of abuse and humiliation she had suffered? Perhaps she too longed for this day—revenge at last!

He'd been betrayed by everyone he'd known. It was fitting, the betrayer betrayed. Tyler had known deep down that he had been out of his league from the outset. Only now did he see how naive and unprepared he truly was. He didn't have the experience and inherent distrust to recognize the webs that had been woven around him. His own arrogance had been his downfall. He should have listened to Adanni a long time ago and stopped playing with the big boys.

He thought about Adanni and his unusual silence. If ever he needed him, now was time.

And what would you have me say? Adanni asked coldly, *I told you this would happen.*

That's it? Tyler exclaimed incredulous, *Just an 'I told you so'?*

Yes, was all he got back.

Adanni's lack of participation made Tyler angry. His anger grew to embrace everything that had happened to him since that fateful accident in the park so long ago and so far away. This was the fabulous life he was to experience? This was his destiny? To screw up everything and destroy all he had tried to save?

He swore at Thosolan, at Adanni, and at the Universe that had let him live. He'd been doomed from the moment he took over as the Admiral.

The sound of Marshall Sliss brought Tyler back to the proceedings. The Marshall, with clear pain in his voice, recounted the strange events and behaviors since the Admiral had come out of his coma. It was plain to see the Marshall had been alienated by the 'new' Admiral, and had finally taken action against him. Tyler had known the Marshall would be the hardest one to fool. Apparently, he had not.

Tyler was touched by the fact that the Marshall was cushioning everything he said with an implied excuse that the Admiral's actions were a direct result of his injuries. His contention, despite

the interrogators admonishments, was that the Admiral had
suffered extraordinary battle fatigue and could no longer make
sound decisions. He recounted battle after battle, painting a
sympathetic picture of a great man who had finally succumb to his
own wartime successes.

Tyler could see some in the jury looked sympathetic, others
looked doubtful. Finally, the interrogator pushed to the part that
was likely responsible for the Marshall's cave in, the health record
information Tyler had requested. According to the interrogator, the
query for such information had been intercepted immediately and a
full investigation started. Once it had been traced to the Marshall,
he had been confronted and confessed.

Tyler didn't blame the Marshall. Tyler had never confided
in him and had let his suspicions run wild. It had been only a
matter of time, and maybe a part of the Marshall wanted to get
caught. Maybe he had wanted to be confronted so that he could
tell someone about his beloved Admiral who had flipped his wig.
Tyler felt sorry for the Marshall. He only hoped he would be spared
similar charges for his testimony. He deserved to retire with honor.

When asked why the Admiral had wanted the health records,
the Marshall responded with what he knew. He told the jury the
Admiral had wanted to use the records against those persons, but
the Marshall admitted he didn't know how. The interrogator seized
on that to suggest that the Admiral was looking for susceptibilities
that could have been exploited for assassination.

The Marshall was shocked by the suggestion, but Tyler noted
several jury members shot questioning and unsympathetic looks
his way. Considering everything they had heard, it made logical
sense to jump to that conclusion. If you believed the individual
was plotting to overthrow the government, then assassination was
a well known tool to reach that goal. Tyler could hear another nail
pounding into his coffin.

The Marshall fought valiantly against the accusations, but
finally, he conceded such a conclusion was in the realm of
possibility. With that final admission, the Marshall looked beaten
and old. No longer the crisp, efficient military manager, he now
was a shell of a man years beyond his former glory.

The unfairness fed Tyler's anger. This man had been loyal and faithful to his planet, serving in untold campaigns alongside many great leaders other than the Admiral. He was a legend in his own right, and more decorated than most of the current active personnel. Only the Admiral held more honors.

The Marshall deserved more than this, but Tyler had let him down. It was Tyler's fault this man had been shamed, and forced to betray his commander. Tyler had caused the admission to collusion in a scheme that was tantamount to treason.

Tyler directed his anger inward. He had betrayed the one man who had served the Admiral faithfully. He now feared for Officer Slaas, a capable officer who might now be caught in the web of treason, another victim of Tyler's ineptitude. She would be forced to resign, or worse, charged with treason, or at least unknowingly aiding a traitor. Either way, Tyler feared she would be implicated. If they had caught the Marshall, she didn't have a chance.

All the Admiral's staff were at risk. It didn't matter if they knew directly or not, no one would trust them again. They would be forced out or given assignments that placed them in peril. The vast sweep of the consequences boggled Tyler's mind. How had he caused so much damage in so little time?

Even the Admiral's family, if they survived Nayllen, were in danger of treason. It stood to reason that if Toosia's newfound marriage with her husband just happened to coincide with his betrayal, then she could be just as culpable. She'd even traveled to Siirneen where he'd met his co-conspirators. If she hadn't wanted revenge, she would now.

What I fool I was! I even helped them trap me.

Tyler watched Marshall Sliss make his way back from the stand. He was a fallen man and didn't glance once at Tyler. Tyler could see the deep despair on the man's face. Tyler was seized by guilt.

"I call to question Mr. Nayllen Hoos." The interrogator announced loudly.

Tyler watched Nayllen take the stand but caught the Marshall sending an evil look at Nayllen. Obviously the Marshall knew Nayllen was involved but was unable to say anything about it. It wouldn't save Tyler, but it certainly would have brought a level of fairness to the proceedings. Tyler listened to Nayllen's testimony intently.

Nayllen recounted his meeting with the Admiral at The Grand Anoor Casino, but his version of the meeting was skewed and inaccurate. According to his testimony, the Admiral had approached 'him' to recruit him in the conspiracy. His well known connections with the palace would have fit perfectly into the conspirator's plans.

Tyler fumed as the lies poured from the man's mouth. How could Tyler have thought he was anything but a double-faced back-stabber? Would it have changed things? Nayllen had held all the cards from the beginning. Shuffling, dealing, and playing a game that Tyler didn't even know. Nayllen had warned Tyler at the outset that he was outgunned and would suffer. It was true, Tyler would suffer.

As a concerned citizen, Nayllen had naturally turned over the treacherous information to the palace and worked diligently to 'assist' in the investigation. Tyler wanted to hit the man—beat him to a pulp. Tyler had been set up good and hadn't seen it coming. But why? Nayllen's motivations still remained mysterious.

Tyler listened calmly to lie after lie. Based on his testimony, he sounded like a National hero. If Tyler had any chance before, it was gone. The jury would have no choice but to rule the charges were warranted. After that, it became a public trial. Tyler didn't relish the prospects of a trial. The Admiral's reputation—gone. The lives of his family and friends—gone. Everything destroyed by Tyler's innocence.

His body yearned for a drink, something to take away the pain of guilt and submerge him in a self loathing numbness that turned into a dream.

That's it, the chilling thought came to him, *I can end it all... kill myself and save everyone the embarrassment of a public trial.*

Sure, and then they'd go after everyone else with vigor. He had no illusions this would be used for propaganda, a way to garner support for the palace's agenda, whatever that was. Tyler thought about the Regent and looked over at him. How much of this was due to him? Was it due to an Onyalum that possessed him? Tyler tried to peer through his cold exterior to find the alien within. He saw nothing to indicate possession.

Nayllen finished his testimony and returned to his seat, a slight smile on his face. The interrogator was releasing the jury to deliberate their decision, a decision Tyler already knew, guilty.

The jury filed from the room as the Emperor sent Tyler a cold and penetrating stare. Even Admiral Teesen appeared disconcerted by the accusations leveled at his former commander. Tyler remained emotionless and unmoving. At least he wouldn't give them the satisfaction of watching him cower and hide from the truth. He'd stand tall and defend the honor of the Admiral as best he could.

Hah! Adanni scoffed, *you've done a fine job of it so far!*

Tyler ignored the jibe. The Emperor rose and released the Marshall and Eyleeria. He even signaled Teesen out, although Teesen appeared shocked to be excluded. Regardless, Teesen followed everyone else out of the room. After they'd gone, the Emperor signaled his guards to exit out the main entrance. Finally, the Emperor turned back to Tyler as Nayllen and Regent Sneerd watched curious.

"Well Admiral," he said slowly in a condescending tone, "it looks like you've put yourself in a fine position." He stole quick glances at Sneerd and Nayllen. "The infamous military tactician, outmaneuvered by a civilian." He sat back down folding his hands together. He looked far too smug, an unusual show of emotion. "You are free to defend yourself now, we are not on record. What do you say—traitor?" He spat the last word at Tyler.

Tyler wasn't sure how to respond, he hadn't expected any of this, least of all a private conversation with the Emperor. He glanced at Sneerd and Nayllen, well almost private. He figured they would hear the accusations, reach the inevitable decision, and place him in custody. What could he say? Not-guilty? That was a joke—clearly Nayllen had the upper hand.

He looked at each in turn. They stared back cold, only Nayllen had a slight smile on his face. Tyler pictured his face bloodied and disfigured, but it didn't help. What did he want to say in his defense? Accuse Nayllen? Plead insanity? Nothing sounded plausible, so he said the only thing that came to mind.

"I believe your Regent is possessed by an alien entity."

Tyler regretted it the moment he said it. Both the Regent and Nayllen looked dumbfounded. Only the Emperor remained passive, an upraised eyebrow the only indication he'd heard Tyler.

The Regent, looking confused, glanced back and forth between Tyler and the Emperor, not certain how to respond or whether he should. Tyler didn't see fear on the Regent's face, but there was definitely confusion. Tyler didn't know how to take that. Maybe he wasn't possessed? Then again, if the Onyalum had been inside for years, his reactions would be well rehearsed and second nature. There was no way Tyler could tell.

The Emperor, staying cool, signaled Nayllen to leave. Nayllen appeared shocked, but quickly left. Tyler was certain he could rule out Nayllen as the Onyalum, but the Regent? Tyler had played his one card, but wasn't sure how to finish the hand. How could he prove it? He couldn't.

As Nayllen left, the Regent moved into the seat where Teesen had sat. His look turned cold again, a blank slate upon which Tyler could read nothing. He and the Emperor stole glances with each other, until finally the Emperor stood up and walked back to the console under the large viewer.

"I had my suspicions about you Admiral from the very day I first met with you after your 'failed' offensive." Tyler didn't like the way he emphasized the word 'failed'. "I sensed you had changed, perhaps for the better, but then, perhaps for the worse."

The Emperor played with some of the controls while he continued. "We have never been allies, you and I, but neither were we adversaries. I kept an eye on you, and you, through the Marshall, tried to keep an eye on me."

Tyler wasn't sure where this was heading. It seemed an odd response to the accusation he had just leveled at the Regent. Tyler glanced at the Regent, but he was staring at the Emperor, waiting.

"I never suspected this treachery, and even when it had been brought to my attention, I was confused by the lack of motive? Your distrust of the palace could not have been sufficient to warrant treason. A decorated officer, the Supreme Commander, a man whose feats are only equaled by his integrity. Why would this man choose to abandon his ethics, and his world?"

The large viewer lit up, and the Emperor grabbed a remote before returning to his seat.

"I knew your father wasn't really a traitor, but at the time, it served my purposes. I suppose in some way you posed a threat in the beginning, so I made sure you understood no one was above 'my' law."

Tyler was amazed he was hearing admissions from the Emperor. He had no reason to share such things, why now?

The Emperor continued reminiscing, "I felt secure, and you went on to be a great leader of warriors. You served my purpose well. I did not always agree with your battle decisions, but I was bright enough to understand when your tactical prowess was greater than my own, so I let you have free reign—within reason." He paused in thought. "It had always been a fine arrangement, until the last offensive. Shortly after your recovery, you seemed eager to turn against me, eager to carry out your own agenda, regardless of what the palace wanted…of what I wanted."

Tyler could sense a deep anger in the Emperor. He wondered where it was heading. Perhaps the Emperor would kill him now and bypass the lengthy trial and public incrimination. That suited Tyler fine, he no longer cared about himself, only those who had served the Admiral.

The Emperor pushed a button on the remote before tossing it to Tyler. "There, this is what you were seeking, have a look."

Tyler watched as the display listed a series of files that Tyler recognized as the Emperor's medical records. He wasn't sure what to do. What was the Emperor angling at? Did he understand what Tyler had wanted to know? It seemed unlikely. Then again, Tyler had nothing to loose, so he took the remote and began scanning the medical records.

"You see, when you requested the medical records, I was puzzled at first. Why would you want those, surely they could not provide you with anything valuable? Oh, yes, the interrogator seized on it with accusations of assassination. A cheap and paltry trick simply designed to slander your character. We knew it was not the case. You are neither capable of, nor experienced in the art of assassination. We know since we are practiced in that art."

Tyler assumed he was referring to the Regent when he said 'we'. He kept scanning the records, looking for something during the Emperor's childhood. What if he found it? Then what? Accuse the Emperor too? That didn't seem plausible. But what if he could rule him out? Maybe then he could turn the Emperor on the Regent, but again, he had no proof.

Careful Tyler, something is wrong. I do not believe it is as it seems.

Tyler ignored Adanni's warning, it didn't matter anymore. There! He found something, a record of a hospitalization when the Emperor was only eight. He opened the file and began reading through it. The Emperor talked in the background.

"...only then did it dawn on me that you were not as you seemed. The pieces fell into place and the pattern revealed itself. We felt almost stupid when we realized what was going on. How could we have been so blind..."

Tyler had it...the Emperor had been hospitalized for poison. He'd suffered an assassination attempt at the age of eight. His own sister had done it, but she'd been dealt with silently by his father, the Emperor at that time. Apparently blood was not thick in this family.

He read more details, and found what he'd feared most, the Emperor had died from the poisoning, but had 'miraculously' recovered though not from any medical assistance. The poison was known to be one hundred percent fatal. That meant...

"...and so we came to the only logical conclusion Admiral, you are the one possessed by an alien entity."

Had Tyler heard him right? They were accusing him of possession? How...wait a moment it was beginning to make some sense.

"You are both Onyalum!" Tyler exclaimed, certain he was right. How else could they suspect him? How else could they know why he wanted the medical records? Unless of course, they wcre both possessed!

The Emperor and the Regent exchanged brief smiles before staring back at Tyler.

"Very good Admiral, or should I call you something else?" The Emperor sat back in his chair, leveling an inquisitive look at Tyler, "My real name is Creedan, but please, continue to call me the Emperor." A malicious smile formed on the Emperor's face.

The Regent spoke as well, "I am Goyar, but please call me Regent Sneerd—I truly prefer that name."

Tyler was stunned, two Onyalum on the same planet, both in the highest ranking positions, and working together. Thosolan had told him they were isolated loners who took their own pleasures. He never realized they might work together.

It is not unheard of, Adanni confirmed.

"My name is Tyler." He said flatly.

"Tyler," the Emperor pondered the name, "it does not sound like an Onyalum name, is it from some previous being you have possessed?"

Tyler was cautious, he wasn't certain what they were capable of.

"No, it is my name." At least that was the truth.

The Emperor looked as though he didn't believe him, but seemed willing to let it pass.

"Very well 'Tyler', we will refer to you as the Admiral." The Emperor looked satisfied. "What shall the three Onyalum do?"

Tyler didn't think he had any leverage, even being Onyalum, yet he was willing to try.

"Share the power?" he suggested.

"Hmmm," the Emperor considered, "I think not Admiral, your treason has made me far too wary. Understand, it is not anything I myself would not have done, but being Onyalum, I know not to trust them."

"Yet you trust Goyar?" he accused, "I mean 'Regent Sneerd'." He quickly corrected.

The Emperor exchanged a quick smile with the Regent, "Yes, we have been together for millennia," he said quietly, "we are like…brothers."

Perfect, that was all Tyler needed, two Onyalum that were like brothers.

"I don't care about myself, do as you will, but my wife and my child, please let them live." Tyler pleaded, hoping he could at least save them.

"Your wife and child?" The Emperor sounded amazed, "They are of no concern to me. Nayllen however..."

Nayllen was dangerous, and the Emperor obviously had his own doubts about the man..

"I suppose that Nayllen does not know your true identities?"

"Of course not." The Emperor conceded.

"Surely, you are able to control him?" Tyler tried again to help his family.

"Well," the Emperor began, "we can control him a little. He is very powerful and has more resources at his command than even we do."

The admission confirmed what Tyler had seen Nayllen demonstrate. He thought back to that early meeting with Nayllen and wondered how much power he really held. What was his game? Tyler still couldn't see it. He had power and control over much of the current government. He profited handsomely from the war, so what was missing that he needed to possess?

"Then you must know his complicity in the conspiracy with my father?" Tyler put it out there with nothing left to lose. He noticed both of them showed a look of surprise.

The Emperor immediately responded, "Nayllen Hooss has been involved in the conspiracy?"

"Yes," Tyler confirmed, "he was the one who recruited me, despite the testimony he gave today."

The Emperor absorbed his words and glanced questioningly at the Regent. Tyler couldn't believe it, they too had been victims of Nayllen. Then what was real? What game were they all unknowingly players in?

As if in answer to that question, alarms suddenly rang throughout the room. Tyler looked at the viewer as it changed from the Emperors health records to a series of defense system screens. Using the Admiral's memories of the system, Tyler could see they had detected an enemy intrusion in Poolto controlled space. The display showed twenty five Krildon ships, shown in red, traveling in battle formation. Was this the peace ship? It looked more like an invasion.

"What treachery is this?" The Emperor exclaimed as he leveled an accusatory look at Tyler.

"I don't know." Tyler lied. But then, he wasn't sure he was lying. This had not been part of the plan.

"Regent," the Emperor commanded, "get Teesen on the phone and mobilize our fleet." Tyler noted a real sound of concern in the Emperor's voice. Over the concern a layer of anger rose to the surface.

The Regent moved to the console, but stopped short as the viewer changed in response to the grim reality of the situation. All of the 'green' ships, the Poolto fleet, turned yellow. It was a clear sign they were being systematically disabled. Somehow, the command codes Tyler had given Kulg were working. The invasion fleet was disabling the Poolto fleet. Hadn't Teesen changed the codes? How could they still work?

The Emperor was howling, "How can this be? What has Teesen done?"

"Perhaps you should ask Nayllen." Tyler suggested calmly.

The Emperor glared at him, then signaled to the Regent. The Regent quickly pushed buttons and a part of the viewer changed to Nayllen's face. From the scene behind him, Tyler thought he appeared already in space.

"Yes Emperor," Nayllen asked casually, "what may I help you with?"

"Is this your doing Nayllen, have you been plotting with Krildon to overthrow me?" The Emperor's voice was tightly controlled and simmering.

"Whatever do you mean Emperor? You know I am loyal to you and you alone. Is this some feeble attempt by the Admiral to clear his name? What has brought this on?" He sounded genuinely surprised, but Tyler knew it was a lie.

Tyler hated to admit it, but he was good. He sounded very convincing, and even the Emperor was beginning to have his doubts.

"Well Admiral," he said between gritted teeth, "tell him what has happened."

"Yes, Admiral, do tell." Nayllen agreed.

Tyler looked at both of them and didn't know how to respond. What was Nayllen playing at, where did his loyalties really lay?

"We are under attack Nayllen, and the Poolto fleet has been disabled using the command codes I gave you and my father." Tyler said it with little emotion. It would be easy enough for Nayllen to simply dismiss the charge out of hand.

"I see," Nayllen said softly, "and I suppose you believe this trash?" He looked down at the Emperor from the viewer.

The Emperor looked from Nayllen to Tyler, not knowing who to believe. "I believe none of it," the Emperor said coldly, "and I no longer believe you Nayllen."

Nayllen gave an exemplary look of surprise to this revelation, but he quickly recovered and simply stated, "Suit yourself Emperor, you're in charge." With that he disconnected the transmission. The viewer returned to its previous display.

"Why was he off-world Emperor?" The Regent asked, also confused by the exchange. "Where would he be going? Why now? Is it a coincidence?"

"Good question Regent, but I don't like the possible answers."

Tyler could see neither of them trusted Nayllen anymore. Tyler knew their suspicions were well founded and was happy to have one small victory over Nayllen. Unfortunately, the enemy fleet still moved closer. By now, all the green lights on the viewer had turned yellow. The Poolto fleet was completely helpless.

"Regent," the Emperor returned to their immediate problem, "bring up our planetary defense network, I want to see if it has been tampered with or disabled."

The Regent complied and the viewer changed to the defense grid surrounding the planet. As far as Tyler could see, the defense grid was intact and operational.

The Emperor signaled to the Regent, "Good, back to the fleet display, and get Teesen in here."

The Regent switched the viewer back before making a quick call to track down Teesen. Luckily, the Admiral had still been in the palace and came through the door within minutes of the call.

"What is going on?" He demanded as he walked into the room surveying the viewer.

"We are under attack Admiral." The Emperor replied with little emotion.

The Admiral looked confused, but tried to take charge of the situation, "Well, let's deploy our fleet and counter-attack."

Tyler could see he realized his own mistake before he'd finished. The yellow lights sprinkled throughout the display yelled clearly they were sitting ducks.

"Nice Admiral," the Emperor chided, "why didn't we think of that?" The Emperor's tone was mocking and condescending. "Try your command codes, see if you can enable our fleet!"

Teesen hesitated and then moved to the console. Tyler watched as he desperately entered his command codes. Tyler hoped they would work, the thought of an invasion was chilling. Teesen looked confused and tried again. Nothing.

"Sir," Teesen turned to the Emperor, a look of concern and dread on his face, "the codes I have do not match the codes of the fleet. I...I don't understand, I changed them immediately!" He gave Tyler an accusatory stare.

"Fool," the Emperor admonished him, "the update to the fleet never occurred. Now of course, you cannot use the old codes since the systems in the palace do not match those of the fleet. We have been outsmarted by our own security!"

Tyler thought about the device Nayllen had him bring to the meeting. Was that what caused the external update to fail? *Clever!*

Teesen shut up looking rejected and confused. The Emperor ignored him and turned to Tyler, "Well Admiral Osloo, our National hero, what do we do now?"

Tyler thought about it, there really was no choice, "Surrender Emperor."

The Emperor stared blankly at him while Admiral Teesen looked like he was going to keel over from shock.

"To whom I wonder?" The Emperor asked in response.

The large viewer suddenly filled with an immense picture of Nattur Osloo, the Admiral's father.

"Ahh, Hallen," Nattur smiled broadly, "and I see you have your new Admiral with you."

The Emperor frowned at the viewer before casting a dangerous glance at Tyler.

"So Nattur, I see that branding you a traitor so long ago was well founded. The prodigal son returns to decimate his home world, is that it?" The Emperor was mocking, yet Tyler could hear fear, or was it frustration?

"Yes, that about sums it up Hallen." Nattur was neither smug nor mocking, his tone very professional. "I will, of course, ask you to surrender first, but then I know you won't, so we will have to demonstrate our resolve and lose innocent lives."

The Emperor regained his calm, apparently analyzing the situation from every angle. Tyler knew he was hoping to find some way he would survive the crisis. Tyler knew Creedan would be desperate to retain his power. Tyler began to see why the conflict started and spread—the Onyalum had wanted war and chaos. Perhaps to Onyalum war was one big chess match. Either way, they wouldn't lose, only the people of Poolto.

The Emperor sat down and casually looked up at Nattur, "These innocent lives you speak of, are they military or civilian? After all, I have a right to know whose lives I will be spending, or rather, whose lives you will be murdering."

The Admiral's father accepted the comment without emotion. Tyler wondered if the man had changed after so many years captive. To all appearances, the Krildon were vicious, barbaric creatures, but based on their culture and government, they actually seemed more passive of the two species. Tyler wanted to believe they were going to do the right thing, that they truly wanted peace, but seeing the Admiral's father so coldly talk about spending innocent lives, he had his doubts. Maybe the Krildon were cold blooded killers, out for revenge, out to dominate the solar system. Tyler couldn't tell.

"I see that once again Hallen, you play at the game as though you have nothing to lose. I assure you, you have everything to lose."

The Emperor pondered his statement. Only he, the Regent and Tyler knew he didn't have anything to lose. Tyler was afraid the Emperor would call his bluff, make him kill and destroy for the one last pleasure before being defeated. Tyler didn't want that to happen. Too many lives were in the balance, and Tyler had to act.

"It is over Emperor," he said quickly trying to defuse the tension that had been growing, "why waste so many for no reason?"

Tyler was desperate to make the Onyalum inside either expose itself, in which case he might have a chance at taking over, or at least convince it that there were other worlds besides this one. Maybe it would decide to leave peacefully, go find somewhere else to play its dangerous chess match.

"Why indeed," the Emperor said casually, "perhaps a question we should be asking your father?" He stood back up and glanced quickly at the Regent and Admiral Teesen. Teesen was shocked enough to stay out of the conversation. "Tell us Nattur," he asked quietly, "how many patriots must die to try and save 'your' world?"

Tyler didn't like the direction it was heading, the Emperor was calling Nattur's bluff, forcing him to demonstrate resolve. People were going to die and Tyler didn't have any way to stop it. Tyler's mind raced and drew nothing but blanks. The Emperor continued.

"A million? Two million? A billion? Please Nattur, how many will you spend to displace me as Emperor? That is the ultimate goal isn't it, to replace Poolto's rightful ruler with someone else? Someone like you perhaps?"

Tyler could see anger and frustration coming over Nattur's face. Tyler knew he would have to react, show his resolve. Before discovering the Emperor was Onyalum, the peace mission seemed plausible. It had seemed capable of forcing the Emperor into peace, but now, only destruction seemed likely.

Tyler glanced at Teesen who was looking back between Nattur and the Emperor, trying to decide where the crisis was going and how it might end.

"Admiral Teesen," Tyler tried to engage him, "doesn't peace sound better than destruction? You have pledged your life to protect Poolto, what is the right move to make here? What is the right 'tactical' move?" Tyler was pleading with him to take a stand, but he only looked at the Emperor confused.

"Please, Admiral Osloo," the Emperor scolded, "unlike you, Teesen is loyal to the rightful ruler of Poolto. Unlike you, he knows that surrendering would be worse than death!"

The Emperor spat on the ground, "You come for peace Nattur, is that it? And I suppose Krildon also yearns for peace instead of revenge and domination? Who better to trust than Krildon!"

Nattur was unmoved by the Emperor's theatrics. "That's right Hallen, they want peace, not domination. I have the elected President of Krildon here to negotiate a peace deal to end the war and maintain the current government on Poolto. You could remain Emperor, but you would have to live with peace."

The Emperor practically laughed at Nattur, "Oh yes, I am sure they want me in power when this is resolved. Why we'll be best of buddies in no time." He turned to Admiral Teesen, "Is that what you believe Admiral? That your enemy has disabled your fleet, come with a fleet of its own, and with newer and more powerful weapons, just to ask for peace?"

Admiral Teesen didn't know how to respond and stood staring at Nattur. Finally he spoke, "Why did you bring so much force if all you want is peace?" He asked boldly, a resolve coming over his face.

Tyler groaned inwardly, he had lost the Admiral as a possible ally.

Nattur responded quickly, "Would your 'Emperor' have just welcomed a single peace ship with open arms? Would anything but a show of force persuade your 'Emperor' to abandon the war effort?"

Tyler thought Nattur looked desperate to stall the show down, but the Admiral showed no signs of backing down.

"I see," the Admiral said calmly, "then the way to peace is through a show of force, is that it?"

The Emperor looked pleased at Teesen, an evil smile filled his face.

Nattur looked resigned to the course he had to take.

379

"As I said before, your 'Emperor' will refuse and then we will show our resolve. Innocent lives will be lost Admiral, both military and civilian. Is that what you want when you have an opportunity to end it all here, without bloodshed?"

Teesen pumped himself up and looked over at the Emperor, "The Poolto military is not afraid to die defending the freedom of its homeland. We are at war, and during war sacrifices must be made."

The Emperor jumped in looking smug, "Well Nattur, I guess we have spoken, please enjoy the blood that will stain your hands for eternity. This planet and its people will never surrender to the enemy your traitorous soul has aligned with!"

He signaled to the Regent who cut the power to the large viewer, and Nattur's face, looking sad faded from the screen.

The Emperor turned to Tyler, "Well Admiral Osloo, I guess the end of Poolto may be near. Anything you wish to do to help save it, considering your treachery is to blame?"

Tyler didn't know how to respond, it was clear that the Onyalum was bent on fighting to the end. Tyler could only imagine the number of lives that would be lost.

Tyler made one last desperate gamble, "Is there nothing that would convince you and the Admiral that they really want peace? A gesture, an act, anything?"

The Emperor laughed, but the Admiral looked deep in thought. When the Emperor noticed Teesen's hesitation, he quickly spoke to defend his position, "Please Admiral, don't listen to this traitor, he is just like his father!"

"Am I Admiral?" Tyler asked quietly, "I know we have not always seen eye to eye, but have I ever done anything that wasn't for the good of the war effort? Anything that wasn't good for Poolto? I am, and always will be, a defender of my planet. I am asking, no pleading with you, please listen to me."

The Admiral remained deep in thought, staring at Tyler as thought trying to read his mind, "Emperor, perhaps we should at least hear him out, maybe they really do want peace? What can it hurt to delay them while we prepare a defense strategy? We can lead them on as though we are interested. What would it hurt?"

Tyler felt a rush of hope, perhaps they could avert this disaster. He looked at the Emperor who remained as cold and remote as ever.

"Admiral Teesen, you are the most mindless moron I have ever met in the military." He walked up to the console and turned back to face them all. "True, it was one of the reasons why I selected you, but now that decision appears to be a liability." He touched the console and the planetary defense grid displayed. "You would listen to this liar, a known traitor? Do you really believe they are here for peace?"

He signaled to the Regent who smiled and brought up a tiny screen, Nattur's face came into focus.

"Nattur," the Emperor said peremptorily, "my fine set of advisors think I should test you and see if peace is all you really want. Apparently, in desperate times, loyalty to their Emperor is not required."

Tyler didn't like the sound edging in his voice—it sounded calculating. Nattur appeared unsure of how to respond. The Emperor continued.

"I suppose I will have to appease them, show them the hard truth about Krildon and traitors." He touched several switches on the console and another portion of the viewer changed to a code entry prompt. The Admiral's memories recognized it at once! It was the defense grid shutdown command. Only the Imperial Palace had the capacity to turn off the grid.

"You see," the Emperor explained as though to children, "if I shutdown the defense grid, we would be entirely defenseless. If you were only interested in peace, then you would do nothing to take advantage of that situation." He entered the codes into the prompt and engaged the shutdown. Immediately, the grid lights on the viewer began changing as each individual satellite began its shutdown sequence. "Of course," he continued, "if you wanted to conquer us, then you would take advantage of this rare opportunity to strike at the heart of our planet!"

Tyler knew the defense grid could be restarted, but the entire sequence took at least an hour from start to finish. Unfortunately, only the Imperial Palace could restart it, and he had no illusions that anyone within the palace would go against the Emperor. They were utterly defenseless.

Tyler watched Nattur as someone from behind him confirmed the defense grid was shutting down.

"Fine Hallen," Nattur spoke quickly, "we'll meet your challenge."

The Emperor touched more controls on the console and the fleet operations screen once again filled most of the viewer. Tyler could see the red lights of the Krildon fleet suddenly moving at a rapid pace towards Poolto. As if Nattur noticed the same thing, he turned from the viewer and yelled out to those on the Krildon ship.

"Wha…what are your doing?" He demanded.

Tyler watched as Commandant Kulg stepped into view and pushed the Admiral's father aside.

Before switching off the viewer, Commandant Kulg said only one thing, "Goodbye Emperor."

The screen went blank as the red lights on the larger part of the viewer began to spread out, some heading towards the yellow lights of the disabled fleet but most heading towards the Poolto.

The Emperor was laughing an empty and dark laugh, "You see 'Admirals', you can never trust an enemy or a traitor."

Tyler looked at Teesen who stared in shock as the Krildon ships bared down on the planet. He turned towards Tyler, fear gripping his face, "I thought you said they wanted peace!"

Tyler had thought so too, but apparently, like Nayllen, the Krildon had their own plans. He knew when he met Commandant Kulg that he was not a man who would simply follow someone like Nattur, or Nayllen for that matter. He had his own agenda and Tyler knew that meant nothing less than complete victory. When all was said and done, he was a military commander and would not pass up an opportunity to defeat his enemy. Assuming they did want peace, they could now achieve it without loss of any Krildon lives. Only Poolto would suffer.

Tyler stared back at Admiral Teesen blankly, "I thought they did too."

They all fell silent as the Krildon ships took up positions around their planet. Already, a display showed they were systematically taking out all the defense grid satellites—just in case the Emperor changed his mind. Tyler didn't think he would. He had a look of disgust on his face but was obviously resigned to his fate.

Alarms sounded throughout the room as red lines streaked from the Krildon ships. The lines slowly descended to the planet below. Tyler knew what they were—they were particle weapons or missile signatures. The Krildon ships were firing on Poolto. Nothing could stop them now. Millions, maybe billions would die.

The Emperor watched gleeful as he changed the viewer to an aerial view of the capital city. Apparently, a satellite was still operational above the capital. He fiddled with the controls and the viewer switched to a higher vantage. They watched in horror as the powerful blast headed their way. The bright light descended towards the city.

"You see, my friends," the Emperor spoke his last words, "trust no one!"

Tyler felt nothing but saw a bright flash of light that turned everything white for a long time. He heard and felt nothing, only the silent white light. After what seemed an eternity, the bright white disappeared and Tyler found himself floating above what was left of Yooso.

The destruction was total. Nothing remained of the city except large craters and burning piles of debris. Tyler's mind reeled with the revelation. The city had been home to over twenty million people—all gone in an instant.

He thought back to the final moments, and remembered seeing multiple lines descending from the multiple Krildon ships. How many cities had been lost? How many lives? The number boggled the mind. Smoke and flame rose from the ground beneath him, but it didn't obscure the devastation. The Emperor, the Military, and the Council were all gone.

Tyler could imagine the Poolto fleet, disabled and helpless in space. Krildon ships would have shot them like fish in a barrel. How many more lives lost? Whatever remained of Poolto would have to surrender.

It felt strange to be back in his ethereal form. He had been the Admiral for so long, he had grown accustomed to feeling and hearing. Now, only silence filled his mind. Once again, he was alone in the Universe. He could 'feel' the millions of pieces that were his essence drifting apart as though ready to leave the destruction below him. He pulled them together and surveyed the horizon.

Nearby, he saw what looked like smoke forming a dark cloud. It took a minute, but he quickly recognized it was another Onyalum coalescing. He quickly asked Adanni, *Can Onyalum speak with one another in this form?*

Adanni sounded bitter when he answered, *Yes.*

Tyler watched another cloud forming next to the first one. Both hovered darkly above the burning chaos below. In response to his question, another voice spoke into the silence.

So you are not an Onyalum, although one lives inside you. What are you then 'Tyler'?

Tyler couldn't tell which one had spoken, the voice didn't sound like either the Emperor's or the Regent's. He guessed they wouldn't once the bodies had been destroyed.

And which Onyalum do I have the privilege of talking with? Tyler asked, desperate for some reference.

In response, the dark cloud to the left swirled slightly as the voice responded, *You are speaking with Creedan.*

Tyler had figured as much, he seemed to be the one in charge of the two, *I am from a planet called earth, far from here…I know not where.* He didn't think there was any harm in telling the truth.

The dark cloud swirled again, *Then you were a being of matter?*

Yes, Tyler answered.

The cloud stopped swirling as Tyler imagined it thought about his comments. *Then how is it you have an Onyalum inside you? Is not your form now that of an Onyalum?*

Tyler didn't want to relive the specifics of the accident that brought him here. He was still unsure how it had happened. *Yes, I am now in the form of an Onyalum, and yes, an Onyalum lives within me.*

Tyler's patience was wearing thin as the devastation and loss Poolto had suffered began to sink in. He thought about Toosia and her family, wondering if they had survived. Would Nayllen survive? Probably, he was a person who was always needed, even if it was by the enemy. They may never trust him, but they would certainly use him. Perhaps he was even on one of their ships during the attack.

What is the name of the Onyalum inside you? Creedan asked.

Adanni answered before Tyler could, *I am called Adanni, and I do not wish to associate with you...or your 'brother'.*

Tyler was a surprised by Adanni's reaction, surely he would feel more comfortable with his own kind than with Tyler.

The two clouds swirled slightly and a sound that may have been laughter rang inside Tyler's consciousness.

Very well Adanni and Tyler, thank you for your assistance, this world had become boring anyway, time to find another one to rule.

Tyler thought it was Creedan who had said it, but wasn't sure. He wanted to respond, but both dark clouds blinked out of existence leaving Tyler and Adanni alone, hovering above the burning embers of a shattered world.

Purgatory

After the destruction of Yooso, Tyler had no idea what to do. He fell into a deep despair, haunted by the bitter loss of a chance at a normal life. He had missed the opportunity with Linda and now he had lost it with Toosia and their child. He'd found the Universe to be cruel and unfair, and he hated them for the retribution they'd bestowed upon him.

Anger and anguish fueled his hatred towards everyone and everything. He wanted to destroy the Onyalum that had helped bring on the devastation, but they were gone, lost in the Universe forever. He vowed if he ever ran into them again, he would have his revenge for the pain and suffering they had caused.

He thought about Nayllen and the Admiral's father, as culpable as the Onyalum. All had been pawns of the other, but neither had suffered. Tyler was certain Nayllen felt no remorse for the way things turned out. He stood to gain power and prestige in the wake of the destruction.

Tyler could only guess at Nattur. Like Tyler, he'd been used by his 'allies' to achieve what they had longed for, peace, but under their conditions. Perhaps he was as innocent as Tyler, or perhaps he was like Nayllen and also wanted to achieve his goals no matter the cost. Either way, both reaped the rewards of their treachery.

With no one left in the Imperial Palace, there was no one to uncover the conspiracy. In fact, no one person on Poolto even knew what had happened, except Nayllen and Nattur. Sure, the military had been disabled by the command codes, but no one knew how.

It was inconceivable to think the Admiral, their National hero, had anything to do with it.

Everything had worked out perfectly for the conspirators. Nayllen and the Admiral's father were able to spin their own propaganda, and they started by laying the blame on the Emperor and the Imperial Palace.

Tyler uncovered this as he lingered around the remnants of Poolto. He observed and watched various viewers as they spun the details of the awful tragedy. Like some bitter ghost refusing to let go, Tyler floated in silence, searching for answers, and searching for Toosia.

He was often tempted to take another body, to become a member of their world once more, but every time he thought about it, he realized he would never be able to see his child, or be a part of its life. The pain fed his anger, so he watched their world pass by, detached and silent.

From his travels around Poolto, he caught many broadcasts that spun the lies Nayllen and Krildon had constructed. Evidence was fabricated, and Tyler knew who'd done the fabrication, Nayllen. All of it painted a picture of an insane Emperor out of control.

According to the propaganda, Krildon had been on a real 'peace' mission when the Emperor had gone mad. His ravings and irrational behavior could not be stopped. Somehow, he had decrypted the command codes and disabled the fleet. Krildon, on a peace mission, had stood on the sidelines in horror as the Emperor wrought destruction on his own world. Even valiant efforts top aides and staff could not prevent the horrible destruction that rained down on Poolto. The Emperor had used the Imperial codes to turn the defense grid on his own planet. The blasts rained down on an unsuspecting planet.

Krildon had watched in horror as the Emperor destroyed his own planet rather than discuss peace. It was a horrific lie, but no one remained to counter it. Nayllen's knowledge and control of the military and government ensured no one would find a shred of evidence, other than the evidence he wanted them to find.

Tyler had to admit the plan was brilliant and had worked perfectly. This only increased the rage that grew within him.

Krildon, the true murderers, were now portrayed as the 'kindly' and 'helpful' neighbor who wanted nothing more than to assist Poolto in rebuilding their tattered world. It made Tyler sick to see the lies they spread, blindfolding the public to the truth.

Everything they had wanted came to pass. There was peace between the worlds, and the way they had achieved it ensured no animosity between the two species. Instead, a new distrust for anything 'royal' or 'imperial' spread through the remaining populace. They were ready to embrace democracy.

Unfortunately, Tyler had been a part of that lie. In fact, this lie was no different than the one they had fabricated after the Admiral's failed offensive. Tyler had been a willing participant in all of it, and he realized he was as much to blame as anyone. It didn't matter he'd been used by the others in the conspiracy, he'd put his own selfish needs above that of the planet, and now millions of lives had paid the price.

As he watched the broadcasts, he saw the Admiral's father return to his shattered world, the father of their hero, now their savior. He promised to rebuild the broken pieces, bring Poolto into a new age of peace and prosperity. He was named interim president with promises to hold 'free' elections after rebuilding the cities and the economy. He promised a 'free' Poolto, one without a dictator that fed his own greed.

Remnants of the royal family and the ruling governors were put on notice that their days were numbered. Through crafty negotiations, each agreed to uphold their offices throughout the rebuilding until free elections put new governors in their place. It was all done perfect, everyone bought the ruse that offered neat and clean excuses. It promised a brighter future and created the perfect villain. Unfortunately, now the 'real' villains were in charge.

Tyler knew the 'new' Poolto government would be a puppet government of Krildon for a long time. With Krildon's good 'graces' and infinite assistance, they had ensured a place at the table of Poolto's future decisions. Everyone was happy, except those who had lost so much.

The numbers kept coming in, month after month, year after year. The final tally, assuming such a thing could be found, was seven hundred and thirty nine million killed in the Emperor's 'mad' attack. It was staggering, and everyone readily agreed to dismantle the military and the defense grid that had caused the tragedy. With Krildon as your helpful neighbor, why would you need a military?

Not surprisingly, Krildon decided not to abandon their fleet, at least not yet. In fact, reports indicated Krildon was maintaining a peace keeping fleet above Poolto—to protect from renegade imperial members bent on regaining the power they'd lost.

Tyler knew it was a farce. Krildon had succeeded in conquering their enemy, and the irony was, they had used Poolto's own National hero to do it. It was more than Tyler could bear. He was responsible for the hundreds of millions killed. Whole families had been lost with the destruction of so many major cities.

Tyler had been certain Toosia and their child was lost. He had no idea where she and her family had been hiding. Even if he knew, he had no idea of how to find it. Poolto was a large planet, and even an Onyalum had difficulty tracking down a few individuals across an entire world.

He had been ready to give up when he'd caught a broadcast about the Admiral's father. President Nattur Osloo had finally been reunited with his grandson, Nayllen Osloo II. Tyler could not believe it, his son was alive. He watched as Toosia and little Nayllen were paraded on stage with the Admiral's father. The son of the National hero would now become a hero himself. They would use him as a tool for Poolto to rally behind, to support the new movement, and embrace the free government.

A sea of emotions ran through Tyler. He was happy, angry, and sad at the news his son was alive. It may have been the Admiral's body, but Tyler thought of the child as his and his alone. In the silence he now lived in, he screamed in anguish at the unfairness that held him back from the joy he'd wanted.

The outburst had even scared Adanni, who had taken a willing back seat to Tyler's ravings. Even though it had been years since the devastation, the rebuilding moved quickly. Tyler watched his son, now a small child, play a prominent role in the rebuilding of the world his father helped destroy. Tyler took some comfort in the fact the Admiral remained a National hero. He knew Toosia and her family knew the truth, but she would never reveal it for fear of her only child. The only thing left from her marriage.

It had taken time for Tyler to track down Toosia's location, but once he had, he never left their side. Like a guardian angel, he watched their lives as they picked up the pieces and rebuilt Poolto. Tyler cried as he saw the pain and the joy on Toosia's face as she nurtured and raised their son.

Tyler was happy she never re-married, despite her parents attempts. She was happy with little Nayllen, it was enough to fulfill her life and bring closure to the previous life she was glad to leave behind. Her father, now sitting on the President's council for rebuilding Poolto, was more prominent than before. He and a handful of other Councilor's had escaped the bombardment. The rest had perished with Yooso. Yooso, now being rebuilt, was renamed Osloo City in honor of their beloved Admiral.

As the years passed by, the pain, guilt, and anger ate at Tyler, twisting him inside, turning him feral in his ravings. The few times Adanni had tried to reason with him, Tyler had lashed out with all the control he possessed. Before he realized it, Tyler had forced Adanni into a deep exile, back in the furthest part of his subconscious. Like a distant memory, Adanni existed far from the Universe he had once been an integral part of.

Tyler didn't care, he blamed Adanni for all the sins of the Onyalum, for making Tyler what he was, and for making him feel the pain and loneliness of his stark existence. He gladly exiled Adanni, even felt a thrill of excitement at the sheer force of his new and cruel will. He vowed to make the Universe pay for his pain—he would make everyone pay for it!

Nayllen Osloo II was a young man, and as always, Tyler remained by his side. His mind was twisted, and his anger continually fed his demented spirit. He took little joy in watching his son's life, but he was unable to tear himself away and return to wandering the Universe.

Tyler barely paid attention as Nayllen II readied for school. Nayllen had become the top of his class and was said to be following in the footsteps of his father. Tyler took no pleasure from his son's accomplishments. He selfishly stayed, watching his son, living vicariously through him. Tyler was bitter and the anger that consumed him prevented him from finding pleasure.

He watched morosely as Nayllen II kissed his mother and left for the University. Tyler followed as usual. Nayllen II insisted on driving himself to school, and Tyler hovered inside the vehicle, absently making the appropriate transitions to keep up. It all became second nature, and Tyler did it without thought. With Adanni in exile, Tyler was truly alone, watching his son like a never ending movie filled with pain.

As the vehicle made a right turn, Tyler made the appropriate transition but suddenly felt a pulling sensation. It felt like something he distantly remembered. His anger obscured those memories, but the power of an Onyalum broke through his haze and demanded his attention. He realized the feeling was that of being pulled inside another body.

Tyler was certain nothing had been near him when he had made the last transition, so what was happening? Had he accidentally made a wrong transition? He wasn't sure if that were possible.

All the thoughts ran through him in an instant before he 'felt' a world and a body around him once again. Slowly, a light steadily increased until Tyler found himself inside a booth at Dale's Diner in L.A. Sitting across from him was Uncle Sal, a big smile on his face. It took Tyler a moment to realize what was happening. He didn't want this, he didn't want to leave his son, but try as he might, he was trapped inside the 'body', unable to transition back to Poolto.

He looked down at the body and was repulsed by human form. After being on Poolto for so long, he felt more like the Admiral than the cheap drug dealer he'd been in L.A. Being with uncle Sal brought back painful memories of the world he'd lost and the life he'd never have. Anger threatened to consume him.

"Let me go!" he screamed at uncle Sal, "I do not want this world and I do not want your help!"

As if he had not heard Tyler, uncle Sal smiled at him as the waitress brought over two blue plate burger specials.

"Here you go honey," she said playfully, "two blue plate burgers and two beers."

Tyler glared at uncle Sal as he thanked the waitress and began preparing his burger.

"Are you deaf?" Tyler demanded, "I told you I don't want to be here!"

"But the food is so good," uncle Sal said gently, "at least stay for lunch."

Tyler wanted to hit him even if it was uncle Sal. He was ready to strike when he remembered who uncle Sal really was, Thosolan. What would a god do if Tyler struck him? The thought suddenly scared Tyler so he sat stewing in silence.

Uncle Sal dug into his burger, enjoying it way too much. Ketchup and mustard ran down his chin, and he wiped at it lightly, thoroughly engrossed in the experience. Tyler looked down at his own plate, but felt sick with the thought of it.

He looked at the cold beer in front of him and decided that was acceptable. He drank it down in one gulp, the fresh crisp taste like music to Tyler's mouth. He called for two more and promptly drank Thosolan's. Thosolan didn't seem to care and nodded approval to the waitress who looked concerned with Tyler's display.

"Well good," uncle Sal said quietly, "your thirsty. At least I won't be eating alone." He took another bite of his burger and smiled at Tyler who stared blankly.

Apparently his new body wasn't used to the effects of alcohol, and Tyler quickly felt the numbing he desired. The waitress brought two more, and Tyler drank both without a care. The waitress stared in disbelief until uncle Sal interjected, "He has just lost a loved one…it's ok."

Her shock was quickly replaced with a look of pity and she whispered quietly that she would 'bring' a couple more.

Tyler watched uncle Sal through the haze of alcohol and he laughed hysterically at the caricature of the man he'd once watched as a child. His anger had been replaced with a feeling of reckless abandon. He relished the feeling and went on the offensive.

"Nice place you got here, uncle Saaal!" He said the name with sarcasm and disgust.

"Thank you, but I can't take the credit." Uncle Sal confided, "Your memories are so rich with the details of your old world, I was able to create this quite easily."

Tyler snorted in return. "My old world," he mocked gesturing grandly, "Poolto is my old world...the world that I destroyed!"

Uncle Sal stopped eating and gave Tyler a sad look, "I think you had help destroying that world."

"Yeah, but I was the one who betrayed it...I was the one who let it fall into the hands of those treacherous backstabbers!" The anger rose to the surface once again, and Tyler noted several people, including a policeman, turned at his outburst. He didn't care, let them stare. They weren't real anyway—just shams constructed by uncle Sal for his own enjoyment.

Uncle Sal stared back calmly, ignoring the people around them. "Remember Tyler, it was I who created Poolto—it was my world, not yours."

That caused Tyler to pause, but only for a moment. Damn this god if he wasn't going to let him grieve in guilt. "I don't care, it was my world."

He knew he sounded petulant, but the alcohol and anger brought out the worst. He wanted to lash out at everything, to cause the pain he himself felt. He wanted to reach out and smash the faces of those smug people who stared at him from around the diner. Damn them and damn Thosolan!

Uncle Sal took it calmly, but a serious look was replacing the smile he had before. He wiped his mouth carefully before pushing his blue plate burger aside. Tyler sat back, challenging him with his stare.

Uncle Sal folded his hands together and leaned forward, "Is that not what you wanted? To live in another world and experience another life?" He gave Tyler a challenging stare back.

The alcohol began dulling Tyler's speech, but he tried to come back with something witty, "Yee...es, but I...I didn't expect to blow up the planet!" A hiccup interrupted his flow, but he plowed on, "I didn't es…spect to lose my family, my life, my so…" he hiccupped again, "…my son!"

Uncle Sal looked concerned, "Didn't you learn anything from our last meeting? Life is not perfect, it is messy, and often involves pain and suffering." He paused and looked around at the people who stared. "But it also contains wonder, and joy, and…new life." He emphasized that last part, and Tyler understood his point.

"What good is creating new life if you are not there to enjoy it!" His drunken yelling got the policeman looking again, and he was conferring with the waitress. Tyler ignored them.

Uncle Sal considered his response, "I understand Tyler, I too have created many worlds and then left them to grow on their own. They have grown into wonderful worlds, worlds that embrace all the Universe has to offer. Why can't you embrace it?"

"I don't want to embrace the Universe," he spat angry, "my problem is the Universe!" He stood up from the booth and yelled down at the shocked Uncle Sal, "The Universe is what created me, and made my life a living hell! I didn't want this," he gestured wildly at himself, "I don't want this! Why can't you understand that?" He accused Uncle Sal, as he wobbled on his feet.

He slammed his hand down on the table just as the policeman came over to their table.

"Ok buddy, let's calm down, I am sure we don't need to upset all the patrons…" Tyler watched as the policeman moved slowly his hands outstretched, "can't we just go outside and talk about this in private?"

Tyler stood up straight and nearly fell down from the alcohol, "Calm down you say…you're not even real!" He turned around wildly, barely able to stand, "None of you are real. Your just this man's imagination!" He pointed at uncle Sal who now looked sad, but said nothing.

"Ok," the policeman said calmly, "we are all not real…but why don't we go outside anyway?" Hands held out, he inched closer to Tyler who rocked back and forth, dizziness beginning to threaten.

Tyler reached for the back of the booth he was next to, the occupant moved as far away as possible, frightened by Tyler's outbursts. *Yeah*, he thought, *beware the crazy man*! I am the possessor of bodies, the demon in the night, the destroyer of worlds! He liked the sound of those titles—that's what he had become, a demon!

He felt his strength waver in his legs and he began to fall. The policeman took the opportunity to move in and grab Tyler. Tyler tried to fight him off, but his strength waned through his haze. The policeman tried to wrestle Tyler to the floor, but Tyler used his last ounce of strength for a move the Admiral had learned when a young officer. It flipped the Policeman onto his back, and in one swift movement, Tyler had removed his revolver.

Like a madman, he held out the gun towards the stunned policeman now laying still on the floor, a look of disbelief and fear covering his face. Tyler backed to the rear of the diner, patrons moving out of his way. He loved the feel of the power he held, the power to hurt, and cause pain.

That's right, he thought, *back off from the crazy demon-man, I am the one who causes great pain!*

He backed against the counter, everyone's attention riveted on him. He looked around smiling an evil smile. He briefly locked gazes with uncle Sal, but uncle Sal only stared with pity. This made Tyler's anger erupt.

He pointed the gun into the air and let out a blood-curdling scream containing all the anguish he'd held inside. With tears pouring down his face, he placed the gun to the side of his head and pulled the trigger. Instantly, he felt the familiar rush as his spirit exited the body.

He was sober again and plunged into silence. In an instant, Tyler transitioned to a galaxy far from Thosolan, and far from Poolto. It was a place he knew nothing about, but it came unbidden to his tortured mind. In a blink, the diner and its stunned patrons disappeared, replaced by the silent blackness of space. Once again, Tyler was alone, adrift in the Universe.

About the Author

After working many years in the high tech industry, NB VanYoos currently teaches high school mathematics. Following his passions to teach, he now applies that same passion to his writing. This is the first book published by NB VanYoos, and stands as the first in a multi-book series. The author currently resides in Colorado with his wife, daughter, and their two dogs.

Printed in the United States
36299LVS00004B/40-255

9 781420 868562